when
silence
Sings

Books by Sarah Loudin Thomas

When Silence Sings
The Sound of Rain
A Tapestry of Secrets
Until the Harvest
Miracle in a Dry Season

when silence Sings

A NOVEL

sarah loudin thomas

BETHANYHOUSE
a division of Baker Publishing Group
Minneapolis, Minnesota

© 2019 by Sarah Loudin Thomas

Published by Bethany House Publishers
11400 Hampshire Avenue South
Bloomington, Minnesota 55438
www.bethanyhouse.com

Bethany House Publishers is a division of
Baker Publishing Group, Grand Rapids, Michigan

Printed in the United States of America

Library of Congress Cataloging-in-Publication Data
Names: Thomas, Sarah Loudin, author.
Title: When silence sings : a novel / Sarah Loudin Thomas.
Description: Minneapolis, Minnesota : Bethany House, [2019]
Identifiers: LCCN 2019019804 | ISBN 9780764234002 (trade paper) | ISBN 9780764234842 (cloth) | ISBN 9781493420230 (ebook)
Subjects: | GSAFD: Christian fiction.
Classification: LCC PS3620.H64226 W48 2019 | DDC 813/.6—dc23
LC record available at https://lccn.loc.gov/2019019804

Scripture quotations are from the King James Version of the Bible.

This is a work of fiction. Names, characters, incidents, and dialogues are products of the author's imagination and are not to be construed as real. Any resemblance to actual events or persons, living or dead, is entirely coincidental.

Cover design by Kathleen Lynch/Black Kat Design
Cover imagery by Nikki Smith/Arcangel

Author is represented by Books & Such Literary Agency.

19 20 21 22 23 24 25   7 6 5 4 3 2 1

For Dave Long

With thanks for being the sort of editor
who pushes me to dig deeper.

You have heard of the California gold rush
Way back in forty-nine,
But Thurmond, on New River,
Will beat it every time.
There's people here from everywhere,
The colored and the white,
Some mother's son bites the dust
Almost every night.

Captain H. W. Doolittle, conductor
for C&O Railroad

chapter
one

Colman walked along the last car of the coal train, tapping each wheel with his long-handled hammer, listening intently to the *clang clang clang*. He cocked his head to the left and closed his right eye so he could hear better. The tone was just about perfect. Good—no cracks.

He moved on to the final wheel, pushing his free hand deep in his coat pocket. Signs of spring were all around, but here in the shade of the train it was plenty cold yet. He hoped he wouldn't hear the flat ping of a cracked wheel on this his last task before calling it a day. He'd been told not everyone could detect the often slight difference in tone between a solid and a damaged wheel, but he'd been gifted with the ability. Although there were days when he wasn't sure his keen hearing was such a gift.

He tap-tap-tapped the last wheel, held the back of his cold hand to the axle box to check for overheating. Satisfied, Colman straightened to roll his shoulders and stretch his spine.

That was when he saw Sam, one of the chief clerks, hurrying toward him, head down and steps tight like he might break into a run. Colman tensed. Sam wouldn't rush unless it was important. In a yard as large as this one, it never paid to be in a hurry among the rails.

"Caleb's been shot." Sam raised his head and cast Colman a worried look. "Word's spreading through town fast. I know you and him grew up together. Thought I'd best come tell you, so you can prepare yourself." He jerked a thumb toward a string of businesses located farther up the track. "There's a mess of your kinfolk at the Lafayette Hotel, and they're talking revenge. Thought you might be able to talk 'em down."

"Is Caleb alright? How bad's he hurt?"

Colman forgot about his plans to go home and work on his latest sermon. His cousin Caleb had been like a brother when they were boys growing up among all the Harpe young'uns in Thurmond. It was once they were old enough to take an interest in the Harpe-McLean feud that they'd drifted apart. Colman's mother insisted her family have nothing to do with feuding, which put Colman on the outs with most of his kin. Then, after she died, he'd gotten a steady job with the railroad as wheel tapper and took up preaching whenever someone would let him. Nobody expected a preacher to go around feuding. Caleb, on the other hand, preferred to work odd jobs for ready money and then devote himself to gambling and drinking—maybe other things, too.

"All I heard is, he was shot while playing cards over at the Bearskin Inn last night."

Colman stiffened. "Who shot him?"

Sam blew out a heavy breath. "Jake McLean."

Colman ripped his cap off and flung it as hard as he could. If he weren't trying to be a preacher, he'd cuss sure enough. "I shoulda known it would be one of those sorry, no-account . . ." He caught himself and grimaced. "Sorry. Old habits die hard."

"I thought you didn't much buy into that old feud." Sam trotted along as Colman strode toward the station, hammer swinging in his hand.

"I don't. But that doesn't mean I'm not going to get mad when a McLean shoots a Harpe."

Sam pulled ahead so he could look Colman in the eyes. "I heard it all started when that Holy Spirit preacher come and stirred up the town back in 1832."

Colman shot him a sharp glance. "That's the story, but I don't pay it any mind."

"Is it true the Harpes have—" he paused and lowered his voice—"a special way about 'em? Like you with your hearing?" He flapped a hand beside his ear.

Colman stopped short and glared at his friend. "You been listening to the old women talk? I thought you knew better than that."

Sam shrugged. "Can't help what I overhear. Some say the Spirit got ahold of the Harpe clan that day and their people have been touched ever since. Some say the McLeans refused to believe and their lack of faith has cursed their line right on down to the current batch."

"Touched. Cursed." Colman snorted. "I've been hearing those stories all my life. Probably the feud started over a horse or a parcel of land. Who knows? If what you say is true, then how come Serepta McLean owns half the land and most of the coal around here? Does that sound like she's cursed?" Colman started moving again.

Sam hurried to keep up. "You can be rich and still be cursed," he replied. "Besides, she married in."

Colman stowed his hammer and headed along the tracks. Sam was right. Curses and blessings didn't always look the way you might think. And while some called his own ability to hear things no one else could a gift, he knew it all depended on what it was you heard and what you were expected to do about it. Sometimes a gift turned out to be a weighty thing to carry around.

Several men Colman recognized were tromping up the stairs to the lobby of the hotel located mere yards from the railroad tracks. It didn't take any special gift to feel the roiling energy spilling out of the room and onto the tracks. He drew closer, his nerves singing like wires in a storm. A deep foreboding swept over him, and he had to stop and catch his breath against the vibration that started in his gut and made his head swirl. Like a cracked wheel that could derail a train, Colman had the feeling something was about to knock him off track.

⁂

Colman eased into the room like he thought he might step on a snake. Just about everyone present was either a Harpe or married to one. And they were all mad. He stepped over beside his cousin Don. He'd married into the family five years earlier and didn't hesitate to take up the family's prejudice toward anyone associated with the McLeans. Being a newcomer, he was also more accepting of Colman.

Don gripped his elbow hard. "You heard?"

Colman nodded. "Jake shot Caleb. He at the hospital? How's he doing?"

Don squeezed harder. "Caleb's not just shot, Colman.

He's dead. Died this morning. That coyote Jake shot him in the back and left him for dead, but he was still alive when Irene went hunting him and found him barely hanging on outside the Bearskin Inn over in Glen Jean." He spoke the curse that was in Colman's heart. "Caleb must've suffered something awful. Made Irene promise she'd see him avenged and then he died right there in her arms."

Colman wished for something to hold on to. He'd felt called to preach for a while now and wanted to be a peaceful man who turned the other cheek, but this was too much. Surely God wouldn't let those blasted McLeans get away with something like this. And while he knew vengeance was God's, he also knew God could use men to carry out His plans. He closed his eyes and forced a prayer for guidance into his head, if not his heart.

"Colman, we're getting up a bunch to go after Jake. About time you pitched in, ain't it?" A distant cousin loomed in front of him.

Colman swallowed hard. Some of his own kin called him a coward or worse, but he'd stuck by his mother's wish that he steer clear of feuding. If he could just get a church, maybe they'd leave him alone. He had his eye on that new Thurmond Union Church perched on the side of the mountain with a view of the river and valley. Don cocked an eyebrow at him, and he heard the unspoken challenge.

"Romans twelve, nineteen," he said. "'For it is written, vengeance is mine; I will repay, saith the Lord.'"

"You said it, brother." Don slapped him on the back and sneered. "And this right here"—he waved his hand to encompass the room throbbing with men—"is the hand of God."

As the evening wore on, darkness and thoughts of the area's rough terrain persuaded the men to wait to hunt Jake down. Plus, word got around that Jake had hightailed it out of the county, if not the state.

"Coward done run off, and a good thing too. Eye for an eye." Caleb's father, Colman's Uncle Webb, looked him up and down. "That's in your Bible, too. We'll get Jake next time he comes around. My boy will be avenged."

Colman thought to say something about New Testament grace, though he doubted anyone would listen, and sad and angry as he was, he didn't much feel like suggesting a low-down murderer like Jake McLean deserved any kind of grace. He was still hoping God might go ahead and do some smiting of His own and save them all the trouble.

He dragged on home tired, hungry, and sad. While Caleb might have gone astray here and there, he didn't deserve to be shot down over a game of cards. And his sometimes girl, Irene, sure didn't deserve to find his bloody body only to watch the last of his life ebb from it. Colman wanted nothing more than to fall into bed and sleep, but he knew he'd be expected at the wake that night if he didn't want to be a total outcast. Goodness knew Dad wouldn't go. He rarely left his house clinging to the side of the mountain. Colman washed his face, put on a clean shirt, and made his way to Uncle Webb's place.

The women had washed and dressed Caleb in his best suit. Colman arrived just in time to see his cousin Miriam remove a towel soaked in soda water from the dead man's face. He flinched to see the pale skin and eyes weighted with coins. As many times as he'd sat up with a dead body, he never got used to it. Caleb didn't look like himself anymore—some part of him was long gone.

They'd taken down a door to use as the cooling board, which was balanced across two chairs. Family members drank coffee and ate molasses cake, talking in low voices. Caleb's mother sat in the kitchen, crying softly. Sometimes at a wake there'd be whiskey and folks would get to telling stories, but this night the air was somber and heavy. Colman got some coffee and settled in to keep watch.

The funeral was late the following day. Colman debated staying away but knew failing to appear would be seen as breaking faith with the Harpe clan, and too many already shunned him. He'd have to lose a leg or worse if he wanted to miss this event.

It was every bit as bad as Colman expected. He was just grateful no one asked him to deliver the service. The preacher from the church the Harpe family founded when they broke with the McLeans knew his audience well. He sang Caleb's praises while presenting Jake as a demon doing the devil's bidding. Though Colman didn't disagree, he wasn't sure it was the right tone to strike on such a sad day.

The coffin stood open in front of the pulpit, Caleb looking foreign with his hair combed neatly and his hands folded over a Bible on his chest. Colman doubted he'd held a Bible since he was a boy. Folks had slipped a few things into the coffin with him—a hunting knife, a rock gleaming with mica, and the ace of spades. The playing card peeked out of Caleb's left coat sleeve. Colman thought it was disrespectful but decided to let well enough alone.

As the service wrapped up, Uncle Webb made his way to the pulpit. He leaned there heavily, bracing his hands on either side, head hung low. About the time the silence began to feel uncomfortable he turned red-rimmed, bleary eyes on those gathered before him.

"Word has reached my ears that Serepta McLean has sent a message."

Colman stiffened. Serepta was the matriarch of the McLean clan and Jake's mother. When her husband died, everyone quickly learned that she had long been the power behind that throne. In a place where women were expected to keep house and raise children, she'd managed to carve out a veritable kingdom. And anyone who expected her to be a pliant female quickly learned otherwise.

"Serepta has this to say . . ." There was an uneasy pause as Webb's weighty gaze rested on first one and then another of those gathered in the room. "She says the world's a better place with one less Harpe in it."

Even though Colman knew the sound came from human throats, the roar seemed to emanate from the very walls, floors, and ceiling. It surrounded him and echoed in his chest until his heart started beating rough and ragged. He breathed slow and steady, as though he could calm the room and his own racing pulse at the same time. That message was just the sort of thing Serepta would say. Cold and hard as the woman herself.

Webb raised one hand, lifting it high until all the voices stilled. "I vow that Jake McLean will die by my hand. God and each one of you are my witnesses. This abomination will not go unpunished."

This time the roar was one of approval. Colman, sitting in a pew near the back of the church, slipped outside. They had more men to carry the coffin than they needed. He'd wait for them to come out and lay Caleb to rest in the cemetery, where even now he could see purple-and-white crocuses pushing up through the soil. Death. Life. And then death again.

He tried to see Jake from God's perspective but failed. All he could see was a bad man who had taken the life of a . . . well, not a good man exactly. Maybe the life of a man with the potential to be good. Jake, on the other hand, murder just might be crossing a line too far to ever find your way back to good.

He joined the stream of people following the coffin from the church. He saw his father leaning against a fence post, watching the procession. He nodded, and Dad nodded back. Irene leaned into some other women, sobbing and wailing. Webb preceded the coffin to the grave Colman had helped dig that morning. It had taken them more than half the day, working with shovels in the heavy clay-thick soil. Colman got there first and cut the greening sod carefully, setting it to the side so it could be laid on top again. He knew he'd take more care than anyone else, and it seemed important to him to be able to cover over the dark scar in the earth. As if it were possible to heal this wound—to forget it, even if none of them were ever able to forgive it.

Because, God forgive him, he wanted revenge, too.

Colman stood to the side as they lowered Caleb's coffin into the cold earth. The grave was close to a cedar tree that had been growing in the cemetery for decades. When they dug the two-and-a-half by eight-foot grave six feet down, they'd had to cut off roots sticking out from the sides. The sharp scent of cedar filled the small space. Colman closed his eyes and remembered his grandmother's cedar chest where she stored quilts, fine linens, and sentimental bits and pieces. Cedar preserved things—kept the moths away. Colman felt anger tighten his belly. Nothing would preserve

Caleb now. He told himself that vengeance wouldn't ease this pain, but the need to do something—to take action— was strong. It was going to require long hours on his knees to let this anger go. That is, if he decided he really wanted to release it.

chapter
two

Hinton, West Virginia

Serepta didn't have time for this nonsense. Didn't have time
for Jake's nonsense. She knew her eldest son had made some
poor choices before, but killing a member of the Harpe clan
over a game of cards? It was a complication she did not need.

While a slow, simmering feud could be good for business
and keep the competition off-balance, outright war would
make it harder to do business, whether that was selling coal
or moving bootleg liquor. Those paired commodities were
two legs on the three-legged stool of her empire, with the
final leg being her own iron will and reputation. And now
Jake was putting the family's reputation at risk. It was hard
to convince the world that the Harpe clan deserved whatever
trouble came to them if her own son, a McLean, was the
one breaking the unwritten rules of the feud by shooting an
unarmed man in the back. That was why she'd taken such
a hard line in sending a message to Webb Harpe. He and
the rest of his kin had to know she stood by her offspring
no matter what.

Mack, her younger son, slipped into the room. "Maybe now you'll see that Jake doesn't have the constitution to follow in your footsteps."

Serepta glanced at the son who favored her with his dark skin and wide blue eyes the color of the sky on a too-hot day. "Your brother is the eldest, and I've been grooming him for too long to simply set him aside because of one mistake."

"One?" Mack shook his head. "You know there's been more than one. It's just that this one can't easily be swept under the rug. You sent me to school to learn about business. Let me show you what I know."

She moved to the wide window of her office at Walnutta. Rich draperies framed the view overlooking a manicured garden that would soon burst into bloom. She might have come from nothing, but anyone visiting her home now would see that she had impeccable taste as well as the means to satisfy it. Was she risking her legacy by entrusting everything to Jake?

"You've already told me what you think makes the most *business* sense, and you're wrong. Disposing of liquor sales—even at a profit—would be foolish."

Mack joined her at the window. His expression was calm, but frustration emanated from him in palpable waves. "With sufficient capital you could rule not only the coal industry but also natural gas. And you wouldn't have to deal with the likes of crooked lawmen like Harrison Ash. Growth is coming, and we could be in the perfect position to capitalize on the many innovations that will require fuel—and not only from coal."

Serepta frowned and let him see it. She'd thought giving him training in business would benefit her. If she'd known it would give him such foolish ideas and aspirations, she would have saved her money. "My answer remains no. Now, if you can't be a help, at least try not to be a hindrance."

Mack's lips tightened and thinned much the way she knew her own did when she was angry. He clenched his fists but did not speak. Instead, he nodded once and left the room, shutting the door a little too firmly behind him.

Serepta watched a bird building its nest in a rosebush. She'd tell Charlie to remove the messy pile of twigs. If only her sons were so easily dealt with. She wouldn't be around forever and feared the world she'd so carefully constructed would crumble before she was cold in the grave if both sons persisted in their foolishness. At times she even wondered if they were intentionally trying to undermine her.

Turning to her desk, she straightened her blouse and smoothed her hair back into its tight chignon. Immediate action was required if she wanted to strengthen her position in southern West Virginia until at least one of her sons came to his senses. A public appearance was in order, and she knew just where she would make it.

Ill will and schemes for revenge stewed all week among members of the Harpe family. Colman managed to steer clear of much of the talk by keeping his head down and focusing on his work at the rail yard. He was also making notes for a series of sermons centered around Revelation and end times. There was going to be a tent meeting in nearby Glen Jean, and he felt sure he'd be asked to fill the pulpit a night or two. There were rumors the revival was a trial run for whoever was going to be asked to serve at the Thurmond Union Church. This could be the opportunity he needed to get his foot in the door.

But Friday rolled around and no one asked him to speak. Instead, it seemed a preacher from North Carolina had been brought in, a fellow with a reputation for preaching love and forgiveness. Which were fine things to preach, but Colman didn't think a peaceful message like that would bring the crowds in. Not the way a little fire and brimstone would. He told himself he wouldn't go to the revival that started Sunday evening. But when the weekend came, he decided it wouldn't hurt to go and see the competition.

The first night of the revival drew a decent crowd. When Colman arrived, he found Sam leaning against a tree just outside the tent.

"Hey there, Sam. Didn't expect to see you here."

"Aw, word got around that this feller is worth listening to. Plus, I thought a McLean or two might show up and stir the pot."

"They'd better not."

"No. I guess they'd better not. Still, I didn't have anything else going on this evening."

Colman watched the crowd—at least two-thirds women and children—filter into the tent and settle. A cluster of elders from the Thurmond Church sat off to the right. Allen Spatchcock nodded at him, face solemn. Allen knew Colman wanted to fill the pulpit—they'd talked about it twice. Colman forced a smile and nodded back. He eased under the edge of the canvas and perched on a folding chair, angling his body so that his feet were pointed toward the trees. He'd listen for a while, but he didn't see any reason to stay all night. If that bunch didn't want him, he had better things to do.

While they'd been having a streak of warm days, it was still cool of an evening. He saw women tucking shawls and sweaters around their shoulders and bullying children into jackets. He snugged his own coat across his chest and settled in to pass judgment on this out-of-town pulpit pounder.

When Preacher Hickman stepped up onto a plywood riser at the front of the tent, Colman didn't find him much to look at. Tall and lanky, his Adam's apple was too big and his suit coat too long. Not to mention the ridiculous curl of hair that tumbled across his forehead. Colman didn't hold out much hope he'd be any good. Which might have given him a measure of satisfaction if he let it. But he figured if he was going to sin by carrying anger against the McLeans around with him, he'd best ease up in the area of passing judgment on this wayside preacher.

The young reverend invited them all to bow their heads in prayer as he asked the Lord's blessing on the words he planned to share that night. As he worked his way toward amen, Colman sensed a stir in the crowd. It began down near the front and rippled toward him like a wave from a pebble dropped into a pond. He lifted his head as soon as it was proper and saw people shifting and angling for a better look. He did the same.

The pebble dropped among them was none other than Serepta McLean. She'd settled in a chair in the middle of the front row as they prayed. Colman could see her glossy dark hair, shot through with silvery threads. Rumor had it she was a Melungeon. She'd been a Mullins before she wed, and that was surely a swarthy bunch prone to keeping apart from the rest of the world.

It was as though a copperhead had slithered down the aisle and curled in front of the pulpit. How dare she? He noticed two of her hired men standing just outside the tent, eyes roving the crowd gathered there. On the lookout for trouble. The covey of elders glared, but none moved toward her. Colman halfway hoped they'd be foolish enough to give the hired men what they were looking for.

Serepta turned in her seat, slow and regal, to scan the crowd. There were quite a few Harpes in attendance, anger rolling off them like early morning fog rising from the valleys. He wouldn't have thought someone who condoned murder would bother to come hear a preacher, but maybe that wasn't her intent. Maybe it was like Sam said—she was stirring the pot.

He watched the unlikely leader of the McLean clan peruse those near him until her gaze finally rested on him. Her eyes were like the flash of a bluebird's wing against her dusky skin, like a speck of unexpected color on a winter day. Her hair was pulled starkly back from a broad forehead, and her pale lips formed a straight line. Her eyes narrowed as she watched him. He thought he saw an almost imperceptible nod as though she were approving something. Certainly not him. Then she turned to the front again as Preacher Hickman launched into his sermon.

Colman was so distracted by Serepta that he had a difficult time following what the preacher was saying. He kept forcing his attention back to the animated words pouring forth from the lanky young man up front. His voice boomed, and in spite of the stir Serepta was causing, Colman could tell the people around him were captivated by the words this man was sharing. But he couldn't seem to pin them down, couldn't get them to stick in his mind.

Until a phrase nearly poleaxed him.

". . . evil has come up before God. He has eyes to see the darkness dwelling in each person's heart. And yet He is slow to anger, gracious and merciful."

Colman shook his head. The words struck a chord that

seemed to vibrate through his very soul. *Eyes to see . . .* He had the feeling Serepta's eyes saw more than he knew. Had seen more than he wanted to know. He felt a ripple of compassion pass through him. It was like hearing a cracked wheel—foreign and strange. He shook it off and refocused his attention.

". . . preach against wickedness. Do not turn away from God's love."

Again the sensation that was almost a pain, as though opposing forces inside him were doing battle. And then a conviction washed over him, not so much in audible words as in an idea. A deeply compelling idea. *Tell the world about Me.*

Oh yes. That he would do. Just as soon as that gaggle of elders gave him the chance.

But there was more. *Tell the McLeans about Me.*

Colman froze. He knew that voice and wasn't sure which scared him more—obeying it or ignoring it.

Serepta sat statue-straight in her chair right in front of the preacher. She paid him little mind, preferring to dig deep into her own thoughts. She'd seen the stir her entrance into the tent caused and was torn between pleasure that she had such power and frustration that she'd been forced to wield it here.

She hadn't set foot inside a church of any kind since her father forced her to go with her mother as a child. The only daughter of a man who valued sons, he thought women should keep house, attend church, and serve any man who asked, silently and speedily.

The noisy preacher thumped the pulpit in front of him. She

23

fixed her gaze somewhere around the middle of his forehead, so it would appear she was listening. She didn't suppose anyone would be fooled into thinking her particularly pious, but it would certainly give them something to talk about, heads together in little clusters of gossip. Though she supposed she was a sinner, likely the only difference between her sin and the woman's sitting two chairs down with her ankles crossed and her hands folded in her lap was the degree.

Of course, this evening it wasn't her transgression but Jake's that had driven her to the tent meeting. While there were reasons to kill a man, losing at cards wasn't one of them. Jake seemed to have inherited all of her fire and none of her ability to bank it.

In some deep recess of her mind, she knew what Jake had done was inexcusable. And yet it was up to her to show the community that she stood by her boy, even approved of his actions. To do otherwise would be to show weakness. And she hadn't shown weakness since she'd learned to stand up to her father's whippings when she was eight.

According to Mack, Jake lit out of town about five minutes after he fired the fatal shot. Which was just as well. Serepta was too angry with him to see his handsome face right now. He had his father's good looks—blond hair and fair skin in contrast to her own dark features. If only a woman would tame him like she'd done his father.

The preacher finally came to the end of his sermon. She hadn't heard a word. But she'd been seen and knew there were more than a few Harpes under the tent. She'd spotted Colman Harpe, who fancied himself a preacher. A wry smile twisted her lips. If he really thought of himself as a man of God, how would he be at turning the other cheek? She stood and tugged her jacket down over her trousers. In the mountains it was still a scandal for a woman to be seen in pants, and so she wore them all the time.

Exiting the tent, Serepta scanned the crowd once more. She didn't see Colman anymore. Maybe he'd turned his cheek so far that it had taken him right out of her sight. Fine. So long as he told the others that she'd been there. So long as they all knew she had nothing to be ashamed of. Nothing to fear.

Colman watched Serepta sail off toward her waiting car, a thug on each side of her but two steps behind like some sort of human train. Silence and stares gave way to murmurs and darting eyes at her passing. The Harpe clan would be chewing on this for a while.

The group of elders—Allen chief among them—stood with Preacher Hickman, who was watching Serepta go with a look like she'd taken his best hunting dog with her. He shook his head and tucked his Bible under his arm. He clasped Allen's hand, gave it a firm shake, then turned and made his way to his own car, which looked like it might break down—or rust out—at any moment.

Colman eased closer and listened.

". . . still think he could do a fine job. This feud nonsense will die down. It always does." That was Percy Harpe, second cousin to Colman.

Allen sighed and chewed on a thumbnail. "He was right clear about not wanting to play referee for this feud. Even a month ago I would've said it wasn't a problem, but with Jake shooting Caleb and then Serepta showing up here . . ." He shook his head. "Add to that all the doings over at the Dunglen Hotel and, as he said, he's not sure he's the right *fit* for our church."

Percy grunted. "Well then, who in tarnation is a good fit? If a young go-getter like that one don't want it . . ."

Allen's eye caught Colman's, and Colman held it. Allen squinted at him, then jerked his head in a *come here* gesture. Colman sauntered over.

"Guess you might've heard what we're talking about, you having such sharp ears and all."

Colman suppressed a grin. "Can't help it if God blessed me with ears to hear."

"Hunh." Allen darted a look at the other elders, and Colman could almost hear what they were thinking. "Seems Preacher Hickman won't be joining us over at the new church."

"Shame," said Colman.

"Right. Thing is, we need a preacher who's proved he can do the job. Preached more than two or three times and demonstrated that he's got the calling and not just the hankering."

Colman felt cautious hope rise in him and tried not to look overeager.

Percy stuck his face in front of Colman's. "How many heathens have you won to the Lord?"

Colman jerked his head back like a turtle taken by surprise. "What do you mean?"

"How many souls have you ushered to the gates of Glory?" Percy poked him in the chest with a finger.

"I, well, I couldn't say for certain." He tried to salvage his answer. "Guess that's between them and God in the end."

Percy rolled his eyes and shook his head. "I told you he's too green."

Allen patted the air like he was smoothing Percy's temper. "I know. I know." He turned to Colman. "Maybe if we could see some evidence of your effectiveness as a shepherd for our flock, we'd be more inclined to give you a try." He squinted one eye and raised the opposite brow. "Now Reverend Hickman was afraid of a little old feud. I hear you've stayed out of it over the years. Seems like if you could pour some oil on that sea of troubled waters it'd be a pretty good indication that you're the man for us."

"I'm not sure I follow you," Colman said.

"Either win that godforsaken woman to the Lord or run her out of the country," Percy blurted. "Show her the error of her ways. Convince her to fly right or peddle her poison somewhere else."

Allen held up his hand. "Show us that you can tell the McLeans about God," he said. "That's all we're asking. It's up to God to set their hearts right—Serepta's included. You do that, and I think we'll have a pulpit for you."

Colman swallowed hard. This was the second time he'd heard those words, and there was no more pretending it was only his imagination.

chapter
three

Colman did not sleep well that night in his rooms on the third floor of the National Bank of Thurmond. Normally, the sound of trains passing served as a lullaby, but on this night the whistle and chug rattled his brain. He finally rose from bed and opened a window to the cold night air still sharp with the scent of coal from the last steam engine. He breathed it in, the hint of spring tangible just under the familiar smell.

He'd heard directly from God a time or two in his life. First when he was just a boy and swore he could hear heaven's music in the wind and the gurgle of a stream. His father told him not to talk nonsense, but his mother would take him into the woods with her and ask him to describe what he heard. She said he'd been given a gift for hearing more than the rest of the world—called it his legacy as a member of the Harpe clan. He guessed he'd developed an affection for words then as he tried to find just the right description to please his mother.

After she died when he was thirteen, he'd stopped listening for a while. And then, when he wanted to listen again, it was as though the sound had dimmed, become more distant. That was when he heard from God again. It was a call to tune his heart to the Lord and share the gospel from the pulpit. He'd gladly followed that leading even though most of the Harpe men scorned it, saying a preacher wasn't much good to them when it came to feuding. The way Colman saw it, being a preacher didn't have to interfere with his scorn for the McLeans—it just meant he wouldn't join in the rougher aspects of the ongoing conflict. He figured the McLeans were like the Canaanites. God sent Joshua and his crew into the Promised Land to rout them out. Not everyone would make it into the kingdom.

Tonight, though, words escaped him. Well, except for the words seared on his heart under that tent and then when they fell again from Allen's lips. *Tell the McLeans about God.*

He knew it was a command but couldn't think why God would send him on such a fool's errand. Especially one that would put him at odds with his own family. While Allen might like to see Serepta and her clan following God, he suspected Percy and most of the others just wanted her to stop causing trouble for them.

The McLeans mostly lived over in Hinton and on toward Lewisburg, although one of them owned the Dunglen Hotel across the river from downtown Thurmond. The hotel— once the site of a fourteen-year-long poker match—was being managed by Alden Butterfield, a McLean flunky in from Pittsburgh. There were bawdy girls, drinking, gambling, and who knew what other evils going on over there. Especially in Ballyhack, the rough area nearby where many of those who serviced the hotel lived.

The McLeans came and went a fair amount but mostly stayed on the far side of the river. Which made it all the more astonishing that Serepta had slithered out from under her rock to make the journey to Glen Jean for a tent meeting—sitting under the nose of Preacher Hickman as his voice echoed through the tent. If God had a message for her, He'd missed His opportunity right there.

Of course, she was just one woman accompanied by two ruffians. There was a whole pile of other McLeans who didn't hear that preacher's message. Colman chuckled. Shoot, he didn't much hear it himself, and he could hear better than most everyone.

He sobered. No, what he heard was more than any preacher had told him. Squinting into the night, Colman saw the first light of false dawn illuminating the horizon. He could see the trees silhouetted against the sky and heard a mourning dove coo—fooled by the early light. Well, he was no fool, and this command or request or whatever it was just didn't make sense. Nope, he wasn't going to let anyone trick him into entering enemy territory. Not even with the promise of a pulpit. God and the church elders would just have to get someone else to do their dirty work.

He slapped his hands together and climbed back into bed to burrow under the warm covers. He closed his eyes and yet, somehow, sleep eluded him.

⁓

Just like he did every Monday evening, Colman trudged up the steep road above the river to visit his father. Walter Harpe receded into himself the day his wife died and had been of little use to anyone—including himself—since. He'd worked the rail yard like a machine, there but not there, until one day he'd lost all but the ring and pinkie fingers on his right hand in an accident. He was "retired" then and received a small pension that allowed him to continue existing in the little house on the side of the gorge above Thurmond. Colman visited him every week, even though it didn't offer him much pleasure beyond the knowledge that he was fulfilling his duty as a son.

He swung onto the porch of the teetering house, a packet of hoop cheese and crackers under his arm. His father sat in a sagging, woven-bottom chair, staring off into the valley. His right hand was tucked in his pocket even though there was no one but Colman to see the curled stump.

"Hey there, Dad. Brought you some cheese and crackers."

His father's eyes flicked toward him and then back to the sky, where a pair of turkey buzzards turned in lazy circles.

"Something dead down there along the river." He watched the birds some more. "Them birds have the patience of Job. Been circling the past hour it seems." He coughed. "Maybe whatever it is ain't quite dead yet."

Colman didn't have much to say to that. "Want me to fry some potatoes and onions to go with this cheese?"

"Alright."

As Colman stepped toward the door, he saw movement on the path and watched to see who else was coming to see his father. He'd been sure he was the only one to bother anymore. As the man approached, he realized it was Uncle Webb. His belly tightened. Webb hadn't been to see his baby brother in years as far as Colman knew. What could he want now?

Dad turned bland eyes on Webb. "You're just in time for supper. Sit and eat with us."

Webb stepped up to the porch and braced one booted foot against the edge, leaning on his knee. "I'm not here to eat, Walter."

Dad nodded as though it didn't matter to him one way or the other. Colman guessed it didn't.

Webb squinted at Colman. "Thought I'd find you here. Figured it'd be a good chance to talk to two Harpe men at the same time."

Colman squared himself in the doorway, crossing his arms over his chest. Webb saw him as little more than an oddity to be tolerated since he had decided to put preaching ahead of feuding.

"Jake McLean's been seen over around Hinton. We're getting a bunch together to see can't we run him to ground. Thought you'uns would want to come with us."

Colman's father pulled his right hand out of his pocket and looked at it as though he were seeing it for the first time. He turned the blunted stub one way and then the other. "You know I give up feuding when I married Annie. Even if I wanted to come, I cain't shoot. Cain't even hardly hold on to ride a horse. Guess I'm not much use to anybody."

Webb grunted and shifted his attention to Colman. "You're able enough."

Colman seethed. His father had long been a disappointment to him, but he was still a man, and Webb had no cause to dismiss his own brother as if he were a hound dog that couldn't hunt anymore.

"Able enough to know when a battle's not worth fighting." He spit the words out before he could think them through.

Webb lowered his foot and straightened his shoulders. "You sayin' Caleb's death isn't worth avenging?"

Colman grimaced. "Caleb and me grew up like brothers." He paused, took the breath he should have taken the first time. "I'm saying two wrongs don't make a right."

Webb snorted. "And I'm saying an eye for an eye. Guess I

knew what to expect when I headed up this hill. Just wanted to give you one last chance to act like a Harpe." He spit a stream of tobacco juice onto the porch step where it splattered and ran down the side. "Heard you might even be planning to take the Word of God into the enemy's camp."

Colman stiffened. "So what if I did? Seems like everyone ought to hear the Good News. Even the McLeans."

Webb narrowed his eyes. "Might be I'd take umbrage with a Harpe being the one to tell it to them." He tilted his head to the side. "And I reckon there are plenty of other Harpes who'd feel the same way. Guess it might not be worth the trouble—even if you did get a job out of the deal." He turned, took two steps, then looked back. "Standing behind a pulpit won't do you much good if folks refuse to sit in the pews." And with that he strode away.

Colman and his father watched him go. Then Dad turned his eyes back to the empty sky. "Them buzzards must have found what they was after," he said. "You gonna fry some taters?"

Colman sighed and went inside.

Serepta pulled her tailored jacket tighter around her as she stood between imposing columns outside the massive Greenbrier Hotel. Jake sent word he'd meet her there where she kept a suite to host clients for her bootleg business. She and Jake both knew the Harpes wouldn't dare try anything at a ritzy place like this, miles away from their home turf.

Even so, she wasn't sure she wanted to see her son.

The breeze made her wide-legged trousers flap at her ankles, and more than one society matron looked askance at her standing there with legs planted wide, back straight, head held high. She'd never been accused of being beauti-ful, but she knew she cut an imposing figure with her stylish menswear clothing and simple pearls. The necklace with its perfect, graduated gems was the first thing she purchased once she'd asserted control over her husband's estate. It rep-resented her freedom and her worth.

There was good money in bootlegging, even though Pro-hibition had ended more than five years earlier. Plenty of places still restricted the sale of alcohol, and the McLean clan was well known for supplying the commodity. Serepta may have come from humble beginnings, but she made sure no one could tell it by looking at her.

A hand touched her elbow from behind, sending warmth up her arm. She turned to see Charlie Hornbeck standing there. Her cook, handyman, and more, Charlie was every-thing her husband had not been. Smart, quiet, gentle, and dark. With his rich black skin, he was the only person she knew darker than she was. He had worked for her father-in-law, who had more or less given her Charlie as a gift. If he'd only known what a gift. Charlie was worth more than six nor-mal men and was the only person whose advice she trusted. He was also absolutely devoted to her, and she—well, what she felt for Charlie came as close to devotion as she supposed she was capable. His eyes stayed serious behind spectacles.

"Jake's inside."

She bit the inside of her cheek and nodded. "I'll be right there." She took a deep breath and went to face her eldest son.

⁓

"It was an accident, Ma."

She raised one eyebrow.

"Well, it was. Mack was there. Ask him."

Mack—that was an interesting tidbit. Serepta stowed it away for later and refocused on Jake standing sullen before her. "So?" She let the single word hang between them.

"So, you can't hold me accountable for something I never meant to do."

"Oh, but I can. And I do. As does the Harpe family. You're just fortunate no one wants to involve the law."

He kicked at the leg of the writing desk in the hotel suite where she'd chosen to meet him. "Chief Ash wouldn't dare cross you anyway. I don't know what you've got on him, but he practically goes belly up when he sees you coming."

She kept her voice cool and quiet. "Are you suggesting that you have no real remorse for shooting a man in the back? Over a game of cards?"

"Aw, it's not like I'm glad I did it." He spread his hands wide. "But what can I do now? Can't take it back."

"No. That you cannot do."

He shrugged. "So then what do you want from me?"

She sighed. What she wanted was a son with the judgment and cleverness required to lead their family. At fifty-one, she was getting tired. She needed someone who could handle bootlegging, mining, and keep lawmen like the rawboned Harrison Ash in hand. He might be on her payroll, but that didn't mean he always did precisely what she wished.

Jake was her firstborn. He arrived five years after she married Eli McLean—a natural leader with no inclination to do it. Eli's father, Silas, the patriarch for years, feared the McLean clan would splinter under his eldest son's easy hand. Then Serepta entered the picture. Silas was one of the few who understood—and accepted—Serepta's control over her husband.

It had taken a great deal of planning and care to avoid having a child those first years of marriage. And she only relented when her father-in-law made it clear she was expected to produce an heir. Two more sons followed soon after Jake's arrival with the last a difficult birth that resulted in a sickly child who died when he was nine months old. That was the end of her interest in bearing children.

"If only you'd been a daughter."

"What's that?" Jake stopped pacing and leaned closer.

"I said I want you to go to Pittsburgh and talk to some suppliers there. Keep out of the way until the sting of loss has eased for the Harpe family."

"You want me to run?"

She leveled her cool blue gaze at him. "You already did. Keep going."

He cursed and stomped from the room, but she knew he would do what she said. She'd instilled a deep respect in her boys from the day each one was born. Some might have called her tactics cruel, but from the moment she held Jake she knew her heart was more at risk than ever before. So she hardened it.

And hard it remained.

chapter
four

Colman couldn't say why, but he felt an urge to visit his father again even though it wasn't Monday yet. Maybe it had something to do with the way Uncle Webb was stirring folks up. Or maybe it was because he had yet to decide if he was going to preach to the McLeans. There were strong arguments on either side of the idea. Dad had never been one for dispensing advice, but maybe that was because Colman never asked.

Webb and a bunch of Harpe cousins had laid off work to ride out earlier that week hunting Jake. As they gathered near the rail yard, Colman kept his head down and didn't make eye contact with any of them. Even so, he could hear their muttering without trying. They turned back up late that evening, tired and frustrated. Colman watched them from the window of his room overlooking the tracks and decided he'd stay inside. But by Thursday the flame had died down, at least temporarily, and something in his gut whispered that he should go talk to his father.

He climbed the hill and was surprised to find that Dad wasn't sitting on the porch as he usually did when the weather was fine. Stepping up onto the wooden planks, he called, "Halloo, Dad, you home?"

It was a funny question. He was pretty sure Dad hadn't gone much farther than the general store on the ground floor of the Lafayette Hotel, which was where he went for his scant provisions since he'd stopped working.

Colman heard a sound like the splash of water on a rock and pushed open the creaking screen door. The house still smelled faintly of the onions he'd fried on Monday. He'd made enough for Dad to have leftovers—maybe he'd warmed them this evening.

"You in here?"

"I'm here."

Colman walked through the small front room to the kitchen at the rear. His father sat at the table, a bottle and water glass in front of him. The clear bottle with a diamond pattern etched into it was more than half empty, and brown liquid glistened in the glass. The sharp scent of alcohol bit the air. Colman couldn't remember seeing his father drink anything other than water or coffee. "That bottle looks familiar," he said.

"Ought to. Serepta McLean has good taste. Even in the style of bottles she uses for her illegal hooch."

Colman tried to school his expression but knew his eyebrows were climbing his forehead. "Where'd you come by McLean whiskey?"

"Webb brung it to me." He raised the glass to the light, seemed to take pleasure in the honeyed glow of the liquor, and swallowed some. "I was bad to drink after your ma died. Give it up when . . ." He held up his right hand and wiggled the two remaining fingers.

Colman couldn't have been any more shocked than if his

father had announced he was leaving for Timbuktu in the morning. He'd never known him to be drunk. He glanced at the bottle, noting again how much was gone. "That full when you started?"

His father's eyes rested on the bottle with a vague look of surprise. "Guess it was."

Even now he didn't seem drunk, wasn't slurring his words or acting funny. Well, except for voicing thoughts more interesting than what was for dinner. Colman wondered if that was a sign he really could ask his father the kind of questions that gnawed at a man.

"Why'd Webb bring you whiskey? I thought he was put out with you and me."

"That's why." Dad smirked and took a long swallow. He set the glass down. "Want some?"

Colman shook his head. "What do you mean 'that's why'?"

Dad hooked the two remaining fingers of his right hand around the neck of the bottle and tipped more whiskey into his glass with admirable precision. "You can hear things nobody else can."

Colman grabbed the back of a chair to steady himself and then eased into it. His father had never acknowledged the notion that any of the Harpes—much less his own son—had a special gift.

"Webb can do something particular, too." He raised his glass to the light. "He knows right where to jab a man so as to hurt him the worst." He lowered the glass without drinking. "And here I sit, letting him do it."

Colman felt as though someone had changed the basic rules of nature. As though night was suddenly day, and up was down.

"You don't have to drink it just because Webb wants you to."

"That I do not." Dad tipped the glass to his lips once more. "Son, did I ever tell you about the crew I worked with before . . ." He held his mangled hand up again.

Colman couldn't remember the last time he'd really looked at his father's scarred hand. Usually he kept it tucked away, but tonight he didn't seem to care. If it weren't for that—and the way he was suddenly willing to talk—Colman would have sworn he was drinking iced tea.

"I know some of 'em are still there at the rail yard. Johnny and Elam worked with you, didn't they?"

"They're the ones. We're all come down from the four Harpe brothers who were there the night the Holy Spirit descended on this valley. Reckon we worked together as good as we did 'cause we all carried the same blessing. Or burden."

Colman felt the hairs on the back of his neck stand up. He'd surely never heard his father talk like this before. While everyone around had heard the story about the church split between the Harpes and McLeans and how some of the Harpes had special gifts, it wasn't something his father had ever talked about. He schooled his expression, afraid that if he spoke he might break whatever spell Dad was under.

"Summer of 1832 it was. Your great-great-grandfather Philip Harpe and his three brothers teamed up with some of the McLeans to start a church. They brought in a Holy Spirit preacher, and word was he could preach so hard it'd set your hair on fire." He turned the whiskey glass with his left hand, watching the light play across the viscous liquid. This much, Colman knew.

"My grandpa—he died when you were still a squirt—said something happened one night. Folks told stories about tongues of fire descending. Next day, first one and then another claimed they had 'gifts.' Funny thing was, only the

Harpes made that claim. The McLeans got all het up. Said the Harpes were playacting for attention." He swallowed some more whiskey, his Adam's apple bobbing. "Guess it drove a wedge between the families. Split the church, sure enough." He turned eyes devoid of emotion on Colman. "Guess some folks are still holding on to all that mess. Webb sure is."

Colman cleared his throat and swallowed. "You believe that stuff about gifts?"

Dad looked back into his glass and swirled the liquid. "Don't you?"

<hr />

Serepta stood in deep shade at the station in Ronceverte, watching clouds build on the horizon. They were great tumbling columns of gray that might fill her with wonder if she let them. Although she'd been confident Jake would board the passenger train and make his way to Cincinnati, she'd learned it never hurt to be certain. She watched him lean over the back of a bench, flirting with a poor country girl. Toying with her, more like. Serepta was tempted to make her presence known, if only to save the girl the trouble of her trifling son. But doing such a kindness was not in her nature. Let the girl learn the hard way, like she had.

Jake boarded the passenger train, and she watched until she saw him settle in a forward-facing seat at a window. She could tell he'd put his boots up on the seat opposite. Of course he had. She longed to slap his feet down and give him a stern look, except it was best he not realize she was watching nearby.

The train pulled out of the station even as a distant whistle let everyone know another train was approaching. She snugged her jacket around her waist and ran fingers over her pearls to ground herself and push away any doubts. Jake was on his way and that was all that mattered. Now she could focus on relieving Mack of his ridiculous ideas about how to conduct *business.*

A sudden screeching of wheels, a grinding of metal, and then a horrific crash echoed through the town. Everyone, including Serepta, turned toward the sound as a few people began running. Charlie was at her side in an instant. He curled an arm around her waist, then remembered himself and took a step back. He didn't speak, didn't urge her to do anything, but instead stood there waiting to see what she would do. He was always and ever at her disposal should a need arise. Emotion welled within her for this man, but she quickly tamped it down.

"Let's investigate," she said.

He nodded and followed her, two paces behind, toward the source of the sound. While the crash had been brief, there remained the throbbing of an engine and now the cries of people clearly in distress. The sharp bite of coal smoke stung the air. Serepta wasn't thinking of helping; she was simply feeling the need to know what was happening.

A man with his arm around a sobbing woman hurried toward them. "Don't go over there," he said. "It's awful. Nobody should see such as that, much less a lady."

Serepta kept right on walking. She'd never claimed to be a lady.

Men from the train scrambled to the ground. One lost his lunch in the weeds along the tracks. What might have been a truck smoked and steamed, a mangled mass of twisted metal. Serepta realized the people who had been in the truck—maybe riding in the bed—were scattered on the ground. Bloody. Battered. Dead.

To call the scene horrific was hardly sufficient, and yet she felt removed from it. As though someone were describing it to her after the fact. She'd learned this trick when her father had been cruel to her. Or worse, ignored her. She'd been able to step away and view whatever was happening as if it were a set of images she could analyze and learn from.

Today she was learning that the bodies on the ground appeared to form a family. There was a man still pinned behind the steering wheel of the truck who didn't seem to fit with them. An uncle? A friend? But on the ground, she could see what she decided were a mother, a father, and four children. Such a waste.

Others gathered around the bodies. Someone laid his coat over the woman. A bystander sobbed while one of the men from the train wept into his hands where he'd dropped to his knees beside the tracks.

"She's alive!"

The shout ushered in a moment of silence, followed by chaos as those gathered rushed to the side of a man in overalls kneeling beside the smallest child.

"Where's the doctor?"

Another man carrying a black bag stopped his examination of the form still inside the truck and hurried over, waving everyone back.

Serepta watched as he checked the child—who couldn't have been more than three or four—inch by inch.

"She's unconscious, and I'm pretty sure this arm is broken, but otherwise I think she might be alright."

"I seen it," the first man said. "Her daddy flung her into the air right afore the train hit. The engineer was braking as hard as he could, but Bart Jenson—he's the driver—must've stalled out." He blinked and looked to the sky as though seeing the event replayed there. "I thought it was a sack of something at first, but then I seen it was a child."

The little girl appeared to be unconscious, which was likely a blessing. The doctor gave instructions for her to be taken to his office while he finished confirming what they all knew. No one else had survived.

Without putting a great deal of thought into it, Serepta followed the man cradling the child against his chest. It was almost as though a rope tugged her along. She would see what happened to this child.

chapter
five

At lunchtime the next day, Colman went looking for Johnny and Elam. He found them where they'd crossed the tracks from the engine house to sit on steps cut into the steep hillside. They nodded in welcome, and the three ate in silence for a few minutes.

"Guess you two worked with Dad back in the day," Colman said.

"Yup." Johnny swiped at a sheaf of dirty blond hair falling across his forehead.

"And how exactly is it that we're kin?" Colman asked.

Johnny swallowed his last bite of jelly biscuit and brushed his hands against his pant legs. "Our great-granddaddies were brothers."

Colman nodded and bit into a hard-boiled egg. How was he going to steer this conversation the way he wanted it to go?

"You been talking to your pa?" Elam leaned his elbows on the step behind him. A head shorter than Johnny, he wore his dark hair slicked back behind ears that stuck out further than usual on a human being.

"I have." Colman tried to laugh. "He's been more talk-ative of late."

Johnny nodded. "Heard Webb brung him liquor." He shook his head. "Ain't that just like Webb? He knows once Walter starts he can't stop." He looked at Colman with sad eyes. "The day your momma died I thought if the liquor didn't kill him he'd surely drown, he drank so much. And you wouldn't have known he'd touched a drop if it weren't for the empty bottles and the smell. Guess he was trying to kill hisself, but he caught sight of you and asked me to hide the rest of the liquor from him."

Elam unscrewed the cap on his thermos, and the aroma of coffee filled the air. "Only other time he drank like that was the anniversary of her death a few years later." He chuckled. "Except he was the sort of feller who didn't miss a day of work unless he was dead. And since he weren't quite dead yet, he come on in and, well, that's the day he lost most of his hand. I thought he'd give it up for good after that, but ole Webb . . . well, sometimes the ones who are closest to you cause the most trouble."

Johnny folded the paper sack his lunch had been in. The paper was worn to the softness of fabric from many uses. "So, what'd your daddy tell you? That story about tongues of fire descending on the Harpes back in 1832?"

Elam snorted. "Reckon the Holy Spirit descended on the McLeans, too. Cain't help if they weren't willing."

Johnny shot his cousin an inscrutable look, then turned back to Colman. "What you want to ask us? Spit it out. I can see it's gnawing at your innards."

Colman picked up a twig and snapped it in two. Johnny was right, he just needed to get this out. "I've been wonder-ing what sorts of 'gifts' the Harpes are supposed to have. I mean, we all know I can hear real good, but is it more than that?"

Johnny squinted into the sun-bright sky, his hair falling back over his eyes. "You want to answer that one, Elam?"

Elam shrugged. "I've got the second sight."

Colman saw Johnny roll his eyes. "Just 'cause you guess things right sometimes." He jerked a thumb at his companion. "Elam calls it second sight. Others call it luck. I call it coincidence."

"Aw, now, Johnny. The boy's sincere. And you know his daddy has a way about him, too. And then there's Webb, who can spot a weakness at a hundred yards. Just 'cause you ain't figured out your gift don't mean the rest of us are whistling Dixie."

Elam turned to Colman and leaned forward. "Not every Harpe has a gift. I think you have to be open to the Spirit's leading." He shot an intent look at Johnny. "Some are more open than others." He turned back to Colman and laid a callused hand on his arm. "You can hear more than most. Question is, are you listening?"

Johnny slung the last bit of coffee from his thermos into the grass. "Maybe I know what my gift is, I just don't much care to use it. Ever think about that?"

"Most every day," Elam said with a chuckle. "I figure the Spirit blessed you with a knack for aggravating folks. Too bad we can't unleash you on the McLeans."

The men laughed and stood to return to work.

As they started away, Colman called out, "What's Dad's gift?"

"Sobriety," Elam said and picked his way across the tracks.

Blessedly, the child remained unconscious until after the doctor set and splinted her arm. He fashioned a sling and then looked to Serepta. The man in overalls who carried the child in had sidled away while the doctor was focused on his work. Only Serepta remained, with Charlie waiting outside.

"I don't suppose those folks were part of your family?" the doctor asked.

"Not to my knowledge."

"Do you know if anyone around here is related? Someone needs to take charge of this child."

"I'll take her." Her own words surprised Serepta. "Until her family can be found," she added.

"I should ask you by what authority, but I know who you are, and I suppose you operate under an authority all your own." The doctor began putting away his supplies. "I've given her something to help her sleep. And these"—he jiggled a small bottle of pills—"can be given for pain, although it would be best to just keep her comfortable and hope the pain isn't too bad. It was a clean break, so I'm hopeful she'll do alright."

Serepta nodded. What had she just done? She'd spent a lifetime making well-thought-out decisions with clear benefits. Being frustrated with her sons and wishing for a daughter were not good reasons to take in an orphaned child. "How old is she?"

The doctor eyed the little girl and bobbled his head. "I'd say three, but I'm just guessing. Hopefully when she wakes up she can tell you."

Serepta nodded again. She wasn't sure why it mattered. Except that her earliest memory was from when she was four, and maybe she hoped this little one would not recall the day her family was violently torn from her. Serepta had seen—and even caused—plenty of violence in her life, yet she found herself wishing this child might be spared that.

"I don't suppose you know her name."

"The fella who carried her in here said it's Emmaline."

The ghost of a smile crossed Serepta's lips. It was a good name. It fit the dark curls and the tiny turned-up nose. "Shall I take her now?"

"I've done all I can. Are you going to carry her yourself?"

Serepta answered him by scooping the girl into her arms. She might be petite, but she was ox-strong and proud of it. Besides, Charlie was just outside if she needed help.

"Watch that arm." The doctor made sure it was snug against the child's chest. Serepta felt the girl shift and turn against her bosom, snuggling tight. She wrapped her arms tighter and felt a lump form deep in her throat. She swallowed it down and moved toward the door.

"I'll let you know if any family turns up," the doctor said to her back.

Serepta paused but didn't turn around. "You do that. I'll be at home—I'm taking her to Walnutta with me."

Colman wasn't sure what to expect when he went to his father's house the following Monday. He'd been pondering all he'd heard and still wasn't sure what it meant to him. And then there was the call to tell the McLeans about God, a notion that weighed heavier by the day. As if he needed to pick up where that Holy Spirit preacher had left off a hundred years before.

This time, Dad was in his usual spot on the porch. He stood as Colman approached.

"Tonight I'm cooking," he said.

Colman tripped on the bottom step, righted himself, and followed Dad into the house. If that didn't beat all. Dad hadn't cooked for him since the first year after Mom died. As soon as Colman showed the least inclination to take on kitchen duties, Dad let him.

"Johnny brung me a mess of ramps."

Colman didn't need to be told. The air was filled with the aroma of the pungent, garlicky greens. His father dished some boiled ramps into a bowl and set it on the table next to a bottle of vinegar. A cake of corn bread had been turned out onto a plate, and ham sizzled and popped in a skillet. Once all the food was on the table, they sat, said grace, and dug in.

As he ate his fill, Colman supposed he'd regret it tomorrow when his very pores would give off the sharp aroma of the ramps, but they were so good he couldn't stop eating. His father ate as he usually did, as though it were a job to get done. There was little conversation.

Finally, as Colman was topping the meal off with another wedge of corn bread slathered in apple butter, his father cleared his throat.

"I may have said some things the other night that took you by surprise."

Colman swallowed his last bite and rubbed his fingers on his pant legs. "You were some wordier than usual."

Dad nodded. "I've not had much to do with the feuding between the Harpes and the McLeans. I was mixed up in all that before I married your mother." He smiled. "You might say she distracted me." The smile faded. "And you know how she felt about feuding. Then after she was gone I didn't much care about anything. Although I always did care about you, even when I didn't act like it."

Colman could hear dogs barking from across the river.

Like someone was coon hunting in the dusk of May. Just this once he wished he couldn't hear anything beyond the words his father was laying out in the air between them.

"Your ma would be awful proud of you—a preacher and all. And I expect she'd be glad you're not out there feuding." His throat convulsed. "Although I think, maybe, you don't have much love for the McLeans."

"Why would I? They lie, cheat, and steal. And now one of theirs has murdered one of ours."

"But you didn't go with Webb to hunt Jake."

Though it was a statement, Colman heard it as a question. "I don't like the McLeans, but I guess God will deal with them in His own time. If I aim to be a full-time preacher, I'd best steer clear of that sort of thing."

A smile bloomed on his father's face. "Your ma liked to talk about God's timing. She said it was perfect. Said it even when she was eat up with the cancer and knew she wouldn't be here much longer." He picked up their plates and slid them into a pan of soapy water in the sink. "Son, you need more family than I can give you. I've got this notion it's time for you to know some of your kin better. When Johnny brung those ramps, he said him and Elam were hitching a ride this weekend to do some trout fishing over near White Sulphur Springs. You oughta go with them."

Colman hesitated. Was this a new command from God, to draw closer to his family? Surely his own kin was more important than a bunch of McLeans, who weren't going to be convinced by him anyway. Shoot, they'd as soon cut him as hear him preach. It was a fool's errand to enter enemy territory and expect to change anything.

"Sounds like a fine idea," he said at last. "Guess I don't have anything better to do." And with those words he felt a rush of relief partnered with a feeling akin to being caught snitching a biscuit from the dinner table before saying grace.

His father nodded, and just like that Colman had the sense Dad had used up whatever words were in him. The openness, the sense of connection and sharing, guttered and went out. Colman helped clean up the kitchen, and the two men didn't speak another five words between them before Colman left for home.

* * *

Serepta cursed and flung her pencil to the desktop in the bright office. Another shipment of whiskey on its way to Pittsburgh had been intercepted, and she was pretty sure she knew who had done it.

Webb Harpe. Since he couldn't find Jake to avenge his son's death, he was exacting payment another way. It wasn't so much the loss of profit—although that surely stung—it was the fact that every time one of her shipments went missing, a measure of respect went with it. If she couldn't keep her liquor secure, what other weaknesses might people suspect her of having? She needed to have words with that worthless Police Chief Harrison Ash. She expected more from him than simply looking the other way.

The thought that even now Harpe family members were drinking her whiskey and laughing at her was almost more than she could bear. She gazed out the picture window at the rolling land surrounding the two-story Queen Anne Victorian. Walnutta had been built and designed by Ellen Lively in 1906 with the help of a female architect—highly unusual in those days. Since she'd learned the story at fifteen, Serepta had coveted the graceful home with its sweeping porches and bright rooms. When Eli died she didn't waste any time procuring the property, regardless of the cost. Now the thought that the Harpes might undermine all she'd fought for tarnished the satisfaction she normally took in the lovely home.

Emmaline stirred where she'd been sleeping on a pallet near Serepta's desk, as if troubled by the emotion sweeping through the room. She blinked huge wet eyes and began to cry. It had been two days since Serepta carried the little girl home, much to the obvious surprise of her staff. Charlie was the only human being who could even come close to sassing her. When she'd loaded the child into the back of the car so he could drive them home, he'd looked at her with lips pressed tightly together, as though holding words in.

"Do you have something to share with me?" Serepta asked him.

"No, ma'am. I surely don't."

That, of course, spoke volumes. Charlie knew better than anyone that she didn't have the patience for an injured child traumatized by the loss of her family. And knowing his opinion made her all the more determined to prove him—and maybe herself—wrong.

Now she closed her eyes and took a calming breath. She needed to offer some sort of comfort, even though her own spirit was disturbed. Crouching down beside the child, she peered into brown eyes so dark they were nearly black. They stared at each other a moment, and the child stopped crying, as if assessing Serepta had required her full concentration. Finally, she held out her good arm, a silent plea.

Serepta wet her lips. She'd carried her own children, so why should this be any different? She scooped the child up and carried her to a sofa, settling there. One wiry little arm tightened around her neck as the child buried her face against her blouse.

"Want Momma."

It wasn't a plaintive cry but more a statement of fact.

"I imagine you do," Serepta said.

Emmaline lifted her head and examined Serepta once more. "Get Momma?"

Serepta released a long, slow breath. "I cannot."

The little face scrunched. "Get Momma."

"Entering into a lengthy explanation of why that's not possible would be a waste of time." The girl sighed and leaned against Serepta. "But there is something I *can* do." She stroked the curls without thinking. "Remember this, Emmaline. When you're faced with something impossible, consider what is possible and do that instead."

Did she feel the small head nodding? She glanced down. Nodding off, more like.

"Charlie," she called.

He appeared so quickly that she figured he'd been standing outside the room, likely watching her.

"Bring the car around. We're going to Ivy's."

Charlie brightened and hurried off to do her bidding. He approved. And although she told herself his approval didn't matter one whit, Serepta felt something like satisfaction stir inside her.

chapter
six

On Thursday morning, Colman stood in the passenger depot examining schedules. If it weren't for his father suggesting a fishing trip, he could easily be heading for Hinton Saturday morning, trying to turn up a church or wayside pulpit where they'd give him the chance to preach to a McLean or two. Of course, he'd probably get shot first. Still, the notion that it was what he was *supposed* to do gnawed at him.

"Howdy, Colman. Your dad invite you to come fishing with us?" Elam swung through the door and nodded to the man working the counter. "Hey there, Fenton. You got us down to ride along with those empties headed for White Sulphur Springs tomorrow?"

"Sure thing. And you can catch a passenger train back Sunday afternoon. Wish I was going with you. Haven't camped out along a good trout stream in way too long."

Colman wrestled with his conscience. Was he really going to ignore what felt like a command straight from God? Especially since it might win him a church to pastor? He shook his head. While the temptation to earn a pulpit was strong, the thought of preaching to McLeans was like drinking milk after the cow had been in the spring onions. And if he actually did such a distasteful thing and wasn't killed by a McLean, Webb would likely shoot him as soon as he got back home.

Elam stood, looking at him expectantly. The poor fella might have unfortunate ears, but he also had a friendly face, and Colman suddenly realized how much work it was being on the outside of the feud and the family. It would be such a relief to just be one of the fellows off for a weekend of fishing. He hadn't done such as that since his mother passed. And he was tired of trying to live up to the idea of being a man of God.

"Looking forward to it, Elam. What do I need to bring?" Committing to the trip filled him with equal parts guilt and delight. He cocked his ear toward the delight and found he could hear the burble of a creek, the singing of birds, and the soft whir of a line releasing from its reel. Not to mention the laughter of companions.

Elam slapped him on the back. "Shouldn't need more than a fishing rod and some dry socks. Meet us down here with your gear midmorning. We'll have our lines wet before lunch."

Colman's current work schedule meant he didn't need to be back on the line until Tuesday morning. He grinned. Yes indeedy, he'd use this time to learn everything Johnny and Elam knew about the long-standing feud. Maybe he could find some other way to put it to rest and win the Thurmond Union Church pulpit without ever saying howdy-do to even one McLean. Or earning the wrath of his uncle. He headed on home to find his rod and reel, whistling as he went.

Friday dawned bright and lovely. Robins flocked on the holly trees, and Colman had the feeling the season's cold was finally behind them once and for all, although he supposed there'd be a round of blackberry winter yet. He tried to focus on the beauty of the mountain morning, but still a thread of uneasiness ran through him. He settled his pack on his shoulder and decided that was one thread he wouldn't tug on.

He arrived at the station early to catch a ride with Johnny and Elam on one of the coal trains delivering a run of empty cars to White Sulphur Springs. The steam engine sat puffing and throbbing on the tracks. He tried not to think about how they'd pass right through the heart of McLean territory along the way. Johnny slapped him on the back, surprising him. How had he failed to hear the man's approaching steps?

"Elam's gonna act as fireman on this run, and I'm gonna ride in the engine with him and Mike—he's the engineer. You might want to hop the caboose—more room there. Ron's the brakeman, but he don't usually have much to say. You ready for a quiet ride?"

Colman smiled. "A quiet ride sounds like just the thing. I haven't been sleeping so good lately."

Johnny nodded and headed for the engine while Colman swung onto the caboose as the cars began to ease out of the yard. The smell of burning coal filled the air. Colman felt a sense of freedom wash over him. It was good to be heading out, fishing tackle in hand, with all the trouble over Caleb's murder and this pesky notion he was supposed to preach to the McLeans somewhere behind him.

Ron, a nondescript fellow with a beard, nodded. "Can you fill in as flagman if we need it before we get to White Sulphur Springs?"

"Sure thing." It was easy enough to carry flags back a ways

to signal any other trains if they stopped. Especially since he didn't expect them to stop on the two hour or so trip.

Satisfied, Ron climbed into the cupola so he could see the length of the train as it wound through the mountains. He'd be keeping an eye out for signs of trouble along the cars, although since they were hauling empties, he'd more likely take a catnap. Which suited Colman just fine. He was content to sit here and watch the world go by. Hopefully he wouldn't spot any McLeans out the window.

The rocking of the train and the lack of conversation conspired to leave Colman jerking his head up off his chest. The conductor's cot was made up neatly against the wall. Colman glanced at the brakeman, who was also nodding, and decided it wouldn't hurt a thing if he stretched out for a minute. He hadn't slept well in more than a week, and a deep weariness tugged at him. Lying down, he was asleep in moments.

"Wake up, man! How in tarnation are you sleeping through this?"

Colman jerked upright as Ron tugged at his arm. He swung his feet to the floor and shook his head. He couldn't remember ever sleeping so hard. "Where are we? What's the matter?"

The wild-eyed brakeman jerked his head toward the window, which was a swirl of white. Colman blinked and rubbed his eyes. It was dusky dim inside the caboose and cold. He reached out to touch the window and realized it was snowing outside. Not just snowing, it was a blizzard.

"When did this kick up?" he asked.

"Started after we passed through the Big Bend Tunnel. Sunshine when we went in, and that"—he waved at the window—"when we come out."

Colman considered where that put them. "Are we much past the tunnel?"

"Not much. Snow's piling up so the train has to push through it, and we're slowing down. We've got to be burning coal faster than we can spare it."

"Not a whole lot between Hinton and Alderson," Colman said.

"Don't I know it. This ain't natural."

With a lurch and deep grinding sound, the train came to a halt, throwing Colman and the brakeman onto the floor in a heap. They stared at each other.

"Guess we'd better see if we can get to the engine," Colman said.

"I ain't even got a coat." His new friend looked scared.

"I'll go. Give me that blanket off the bed."

Wrapping himself like an old woman in an oversize shawl, Colman pushed the door open against a northerly wind that felt like it was trying to peel the skin off his face. Thankfully the train wasn't long, and he was able to stagger to the engine where any puffs of steam were lost in the swirling maelstrom. He fell inside the tight confines. Johnny and Elam looked almost as scared as the brakeman.

"Thirty-odd years on these rails and I've never seen anything like this." Mike, the engineer, kept adjusting his hat.

"Can we push through it?" Colman peered out the front into blinding whiteness.

"Don't see how. Might have to wait it out."

Colman shook out his blanket and laid it over the engineer's seat. "It's warm enough."

They each settled into postures of waiting. They tried some conversation, but that soon petered out. After an hour or so, the door burst open again and Ron tumbled inside.

"I thought you all might be dead or worse."

Colman wasn't sure what could be worse but didn't ask.

"How're we gonna get outta this fix?" Ron asked.

Mike adjusted his hat once more. "Wait."

"Well, the storm sure ain't easing up any. If anything, it's worse."

No one had anything to say to that. They lapsed into silence again, the only sound being the howling, pelting wind and the settling of coal in the firebox. They dozed and waited until a blast of wind shook the weighty iron engine.

"This ain't no natural storm!" The outburst came from Elam, who'd barely spoken until now. "This here coal won't last forever. If we keep burning it to stay warm, we won't have enough to get us to Alderson, much less White Sulphur Springs. And there ain't much but deep valleys and high mountains between here and there."

"Surely another train will come along," Colman said.

Elam stared pointedly at the window.

Colman chewed on his lower lip. "Well? What do you suggest we do?"

Elam's ears started turning red. He looked sideways at Johnny. "You fellers know I've got the second sight."

"Aw, here we go," Johnny said, throwing his hands up in the air.

"Hear me out," Elam said. "This here storm is God's wrath. And someone on this train has brought it down on us all."

Ron looked like he would run if there were a direction open to him. Colman shifted and crossed his arms tight across his chest.

Elam pointed a shaking finger at him. "That's the sign. I saw a vision of a man with his arms crossed just like that. Saw it dancing in the flames last time I checked the firebox."

The other three men, including Johnny even, turned terrified gazes on Colman.

He shook his head. "Hold on now. That's pure foolishness."

"What have you done?" Mike had a quaver in his voice.

Colman swallowed past a lump in his throat. Was it possible? Had his refusal to do what God wanted brought this storm down on them all? But that was ridiculous. God didn't work like that.

"I . . . nothing." With a jolt, Colman realized he'd just spoken the absolute truth. He'd done nothing when God wanted him to do something. He pressed his palm against the cold glass of the train window. He thought he could feel bits of ice battering the other side. What if he were somehow to blame for their predicament? "This might be my fault." He said the words low, almost to himself.

"That's what I'm saying," Elam chimed in.

"So, what do we do about it?" Mike finally removed his hat and punched his fist into it. "Toss him out into the snow?"

All four men looked at Colman.

"You don't have to toss me. I'll go."

"That's pure crazy," Johnny said, hair falling into his eyes. "Are you saying you'll just wander off into this storm to die?"

"No. I'm saying I'll hike on ahead to Alderson and send for help."

"I reckon Hinton's closer, but either way that's pure crazy," Ron said. "It's miles either direction and rough going for a man on foot, even in good weather. You'll fall or freeze before you make it there."

Colman closed his eyes to listen to the storm. The keening was constant, without any sign of a break.

"Tell you fellers what we're going to do." Mike put his hat

back on. "It's on past lunchtime, so we're going to make a meal out of the pound cake my wife gave me for her sister over in White Sulphur Springs. Then we're going to bank that fire and bed down right here in the engine to wait it out. Come morning, I'm willing to bet this storm will have blown over and then we can decide what to do." He nodded as though pleased with his solution. "Might be able to dig out enough to get a good start and plow on through."

Colman couldn't deny the plan sounded a whole lot better than heading out into the storm. Still, having recognized his failing, he wanted to set things right. "I don't know . . ."

Mike pulled out a tin with the cake in it, cut off a hunk, and handed it to Colman. "Eat up. My wife's cake is so good it's practically manna from heaven. I don't guess God would begrudge you a last meal."

Grumbling a bit, the other men settled down to eat and get as comfortable as the tight quarters allowed. The maelstrom outside dimmed the light and muffled any sound. It was like being inside a cocoon, and soon everyone was snoring but Colman. He stared into the swirling white that had narrowed their world to this small space inside the engine of a train. He told himself the storm might not have come from God. It might just be a freak of nature. But his gut told him otherwise. And if that was true, then his stubbornness had put these men in danger.

Colman waited until he was sure the others were hard asleep. He didn't know how he was going to find his way with the storm reducing visibility to a few feet, but he felt certain there was no other choice. The other men slept on as Colman stood and buttoned his shirt to his neck, then stuffed his pants down inside his boots and retied them snug. He used a pocketknife to cut a hole in the middle of the blanket he'd wrapped himself in earlier, turning it into a sort of cape that hung down all around him. As an afterthought, he grabbed one of the signal lanterns and a box of matches. He could use it to signal for help if need be. Tugging his wool cap firmly down over his ears, he took a deep breath, opened the door, and plunged into the storm.

chapter
seven

Charlie parked the burgundy Ford Model A where the road petered out into little more than a dirt track. He opened the door for Serepta, his hand lingering at her waist as she helped the child out behind her. They would walk the last half mile or so while Charlie remained behind to ensure no one trifled with the car. It was a cold day for walking, which wasn't that unusual in the spring when the weather could turn suddenly. Serepta looked to the east, where an ominous wall of clouds sent gusts hinting of winter toward them every now and again. She hesitated, but the worst of the weather didn't seem to be moving their direction, or at all for that matter, so she kept going.

Emmaline appeared to be a good walker, only occasionally stopping to pounce on a pretty rock or poke at a clump of greening grass. And once she was mesmerized by a squirrel that froze on a low-hanging limb and flicked his tail at them. At that point, Emmaline turned toward Serepta with such a look of wonder and amazement that she couldn't help but smile. Oh, to be so easily amazed.

They entered a wood and saw a cottage nestled along the

edge of the trees beyond a creek. Serepta helped Emmaline, hopping from stone to stone to keep their feet dry as they crossed the burbling water. As they stepped onto dry ground, Serepta realized she could hear singing. She let Emmaline poke at the water with a stick while she stood and listened.

When was the last time she was this still and peaceful? she wondered. The water, the child, and the sound of a hymn being lifted to the sky all conspired to soothe her ruffled spirit. She inhaled the cool spring air and . . . but no. She would not let her guard down. Not even here. Not even with Ivy Gordon.

"Come along, Emmaline."

She took the child's hand and tugged her toward the cottage. Emmaline came willingly enough, carrying her stick like a sword in the hand that wasn't confined by a sling.

"There are no dragons to slay here," Serepta said. "If there were, I would not bring you."

Emmaline looked at her with huge trusting eyes, and Serepta felt her heart catch. Thank goodness no one could see her traitorous heart.

The singing grew louder as a slender woman with a long silvery braid trailing over her shoulder rounded the cottage. She wore a wide hat, and every inch of skin was covered, even her hands with cotton gloves.

"Why, Serepta, this is a treat."

Serepta caught herself before she snorted. Trust Ivy to be the only person in the world who would honestly consider her visit a treat. She was also just about the only person in the world Serepta never suspected of having an ulterior motive. As best she could tell, Ivy was as guileless as she seemed. Not to mention powerless the way the locals gave her a wide berth.

"Who do you have with you?" Ivy crouched down and looked Emmaline in the eye.

The child tilted her head. "I'm Emmaline. I'm four. My arm is broked."

Well, Serepta thought, *that answered at least one question.* "She's an . . ." Serepta glanced at the girl still wielding her stick. She wouldn't know what the word *orphan* meant, would she? "She's in my care for the time being."

Ivy nodded and reached out to take Emmaline's hand. "Perhaps she'd like to see my garden. Bits of green are pushing up through the soil now."

They walked to the side of the cottage, where a low rock wall enclosed a kitchen garden. Ivy knew the uses of just about every plant native to their mountains. She cultivated herbs along with her flowers and vegetables, and was happy to offer up various cures to anyone who needed them. She'd learned from her mother, Olivia, who had tended Serepta after her last child was born. Ivy came along soon after that, even though Olivia had never married. Rumors abounded about who the child's father was, but Serepta steered clear of such nonsense. There was also talk about how Ivy had been "marked" by her mother's indiscretion. Maybe that was part of what drew Serepta to the younger woman. Olivia died a few years back, and now Ivy lived with her grandfather and earned their keep with her simples and cures.

Ivy turned over a spade of soil and showed Emmaline the earthworms wiggling there. Once the child was sufficiently enthralled with watching the worms, Ivy came and stood beside Serepta.

"I heard about the train hitting that poor family." She paused, and the moment felt pregnant with unexpected reverence. "It was good of you to take in the child."

"Was it?" Serepta glanced at Ivy. "You know I have a reason for everything I do."

"That's the way with most people. Good reasons, bad reasons, God uses it all."

This time Serepta did snort. "From where I stand, God is a meddlesome tyrant who enjoys watching His creation writhe the way Emmaline watches those worms."

Ivy smiled and shook her head. "God gives us all gifts and blessings—even you. It's up to us to find the good even in the hard things."

Serepta flipped her hand in the air. "Sometimes God steps aside and lets men have their way. I saw enough of that in my life to know that if I wanted to succeed in this world, I'd have to take the reins. And so I have." She crossed her arms tightly across her chest. "You can wait for difficulties, or you can hand them out. I prefer to take a more active role in my destiny."

Ivy laughed, but it wasn't the sort of laugh that made Serepta feel as though she were being mocked. Rather it suggested that while Ivy didn't agree, she cared about Serepta just the same. The fact that the younger woman gave her that feeling made her the one woman in the world Serepta would trust with the task at hand.

"You have an interesting way of looking at the world, but I haven't given up on you yet," Ivy said.

"I don't know what you mean by that and I don't care. I didn't come here to discuss theology, but to enlist your help with Emmaline."

Ivy frowned. "What do you mean? People don't usually want me around their children." Her hand strayed to her cheek.

"I have a great deal of business to tend to, and she needs more watching than I can offer. I thought she could come to you after breakfast and stay until I fetch her home for supper." *Home.* The word tripped off her tongue so naturally. Was she providing this orphaned child with a home? She liked the shape of that idea, and yet something held her back from embracing it fully.

A shadow passed over Ivy's cerulean eyes. "Are you sure? I've always enjoyed children, but some folks think—"

"Nonsense. You know the opinions of others are of no concern to me."

Emmaline ran to them, a worm clutched in her grubby hand. She held it up to Ivy, who crouched for a closer look, and then to Serepta, who looked at it without the least bit of interest.

"Worm," said Emmaline.

"So it is," said Serepta. "The first of many you will encounter in this world, and likely the least harmless. Now put it back where you found it, so we can go." She tugged her sweater tight around her shoulders and wished she'd brought a wrap for the child. The clouds had shifted their direction, and the wind was becoming more insistent. It was storming somewhere not far away, and they would be cold by the time they got back to the phaeton.

Emmaline returned to the slice of soil marring Ivy's otherwise immaculate garden and dropped the worm. Serepta watched her, thinking that while dealing with the human equivalent of worms was inevitable, she was going to do everything in her power to ensure that none of them ever damaged Emmaline the way they had damaged her.

～～～

Colman felt as though the wind had stolen the breath from his lips. He clutched the blanket around him, trying to keep it tight enough to hold in what heat he had left. Of course, slogging through the snow was helping to generate heat. He'd been afraid the railmen would try to keep him from attempting to walk out if he roused them. Now he wondered if that might not have been better. No. He steeled his resolve. If God meant for him to die in a blizzard, so be it.

He slipped and righted himself. He'd heard that freezing to death wasn't too bad, that basically he'd go to sleep and not wake up. He wondered if he should have made his way back toward the tunnel. It was more than a mile long and would have offered some protection. And maybe it was still sunny on the far side toward Hinton. But he choked on the idea of retreating to the McLean stronghold, so he trudged on.

He tried to shake the snow from his eyelashes, where it was melting and refreezing. His toes were already stinging, and his fingers felt like sticks of wood. He plunged ahead, trying to follow the rails, which were little more than indentations beneath a foot of snow.

After walking for what felt like an hour, he staggered and fell to one knee. He looked back and could no longer see the train. The thought that he could have avoided all this if he'd simply done what God asked crossed his mind. Was it too late?

As if in answer, the howl of the wind eased from an angry roar to an almost caressing swirl of air. He would keep going. Those men back there were counting on him. He pushed ahead, moving uphill now, which was somewhat easier with the mountain rising to meet him. The day grew brighter, even though the snow continued to drift around him.

As Colman topped a rise, the wind suddenly stopped, as if someone had flipped the switch on an electric fan. He looked around, squinting against the brilliance of a million shards of light. There was no sign of the train behind him, nor any sign of the tracks up ahead. He whirled around. He ought to be able to see the river. He plunged to the right and then the left, searched for steel beneath the heavy snow. Failing to find it, he wondered how he could have strayed from the tracks. The joy beginning to blossom in his chest gave way to a stunning realization that he was lost in a wilderness of white.

From the setting sun, Colman calculated it wouldn't be long until darkness overtook him. He'd continued on, focusing on keeping the rays of the sun behind him in hopes that would point him in the right direction. Then, like magic, the slant of the rays caught against a layered rock face with an opening beneath. He staggered toward it, as exhausted as he'd ever been, hardly trusting his eyes.

Colman stepped past the opening, tumbling to the rock-strewn ground as soon as he was free of the nearly knee-deep snow. He felt surprise when he realized he still clutched the signal lantern in his left hand. He set it aside and sat still a moment, basking in the warmth reflecting off the stone around him. Already he could see water dripping from above as the snow began to melt, adding to a stream tumbling down inside the cave. Maybe the weather would warm again as quickly as it had turned to ice.

Noting the stream of icy water, he found that in addition to a bone-deep weariness, he was desperately thirsty. He crawled to the stream, cupped a hand in the clear water, and lifted it to his lips. Even cold as it was, it felt wonderful going down. He saw that the cave went deeper into the mountain, a dark tunnel leading away from him. Although curious, he was too tired to investigate. Instead, he made his way back to a spot of fading sunshine and removed his hat to take in the meager warmth. The blizzard had given way to spring in a matter of hours. If he'd stayed with the train, they'd likely all be fine right now. But no. He couldn't shake the notion that the storm was God's way of reminding him who was in charge. Maybe he'd do well to listen better in the future, but for now Colman guessed the worst was over.

Colman thought he'd fallen in the snow and was sitting on death's doorstep. He leapt to his feet and stumbled over stones on the rough ground. He wasn't trapped in the snow—he was inside the cave he'd found late in the day. Tired, warmer, and no longer thirsty, he'd fallen into a troubled sleep until the chill of darkness had finally wakened him. Or was it the chill itself? There was something else niggling at him . . .

A long, echoing whistle blasted through the gloaming. Colman jerked his head around and bolted up a rise above the cave. In a far valley he saw the faint snaking outline of a train chugging along its tracks, a lantern swinging from the caboose as it disappeared around a bend. His train—it had to be. They'd left him. And while he supposed it would have been foolish for them to wait, he felt bereft . . . abandoned. Maybe not just by the men on the train but by God himself. Had he run right out of his Father's will?

A shiver rolled through his body, and he realized the blanket he still wore draped over his body was damp where the sun hadn't had time to dry it. Walking out into the darkness now would be a fool's errand. He thought to light his lantern to see if he could find enough wood to build a fire, but first he stepped out into what had become inky darkness and looked all around, praying he would see a light somewhere in the distance.

Nothing.

No light.

No hope.

Turning back to the cave opening, wondering if building a fire was worth the bother or if he should just give up now, he heard a sound. It vibrated deep in his chest. A growl. The throaty rumble drew closer until his chest throbbed with the noise and with the flailing of his own heart.

It occurred to him that maybe he didn't want to die after all.

Whatever it was came silently toward him, and he backed up toward the cave praying he wasn't about to be cornered in an animal's lair. The sound wasn't right for a bear, and all he could think of was the story his grandmother told him about a mountain lion stalking a neighbor walking home late one night. Hardly anyone saw the big cats anymore, but if one still prowled these mountains, this seemed a likely spot.

As he stepped back inside, he tripped over the lantern. He quickly snatched it up. With a shaking hand, he fumbled in his pocket for the box of matches. He planned to use the brief illumination of a match to get his bearings and hopefully light the lantern. His heart throbbed in his chest as he struck the match. But instead of focusing on the lantern, all he saw was a pair of glowing eyes moving back and forth not more than twenty feet away. Colman would have screamed if he'd been able to summon enough air to make a sound. Instead, he dropped the match. It landed in a patch of spilled kerosene and flared. The cat or whatever it was darted away, and Colman plunged into the depths of the cave.

To avoid falling, he dropped to his hands and knees, lantern handle clenched between his teeth. The blanket straggled behind him. He scrambled over rough ground until he fell into a crevice in the floor. He curled his knees to his chest and covered his head. His breath rasped. He waited, listening.

At first he couldn't hear anything but the thrumming of his own heart. He released the lantern, swallowed, breathed deeply, and slowly uncurled, willing himself to slow his breathing and calm down. He tuned his ears to the air around him.

He heard the faint drip-drip of water. Perhaps a rustle of wings or of tiny rodent feet. And that was all. He didn't hear growling or heavy animal breathing. He didn't hear movement. The energy that accompanies any living thing—especially a large mammal—was absent. If the cat had followed him, it was stiller than he was.

Colman let out a breath that felt as though it carried a measure of fear with it. He felt for his matches, managed to get one out without dropping the box, and struck it. The rasping grit of the match and sizzle of fire sounded like a cannon to his desperate ears. He saw that the lantern had survived his flight. It took a second match to finally light the wick. Colman looked around. He was in an even larger space than the original opening had led him to believe possible. It could even be called a cavern. He slid down a slope to try to see just how large the space was. He saw more water, so he scooped up another drink. This time, rather than cool and clean tasting, the water was tepid and had a sulphur taste. He spit it out and considered whether or not it was safe to drink.

There were plenty of sulphur waters around this part of the state. Even a big fancy hotel over in White Sulphur Springs that was owned by the Chesapeake & Ohio Railroad. He'd hoped that working for the railroad might mean he'd get to see it sometime. Although right then he'd be glad just to see the sky, much less a hotel for rich people.

He considered that if people traveled all up and down the coast to "take the waters" at the Greenbrier Hotel, then sulphur water must be safe to drink. He held his nose and gulped some of it down. The liquid hitting his empty belly reminded him that he was hungry, too. But since there was nothing to be done for it, he ignored the rumble in his gut.

He smiled to himself. If his stomach had growled like that when the cat was behind him, he might have frightened it away. And if it was possible for him to see humor in his situation at this point, maybe it wasn't quite as hopeless as he imagined. He'd make his way back to the mouth of the cave, gather wood, and build a fire between himself and whatever might be outside. Then he'd rest and wait for the dawn. If the weather really had turned back to spring as quickly as it seemed when he fell asleep, he would continue walking out in the morning. And with no blizzard to blind him, the way should be much easier. Sure, he'd be mighty hungry by the time he finally found some food, but he'd been hungry before.

Resolved to make the best of the situation, Colman splashed water on his face, then stood and started back toward the opening. But wait—he glanced around. It would be a shame not to explore at least a little. And the cat or whatever it was might still be outside. He drew a deep breath and let his shoulder relax. Why not check out this cavern a bit? It would make for a good tale to tell, and he might even find a treasure here. Colman laughed at himself. Surviving a blizzard and whatever it was that had been after him was making him bold. Perhaps it was time to see his predicament as an adventure and get what he could out of it.

Twenty minutes later, having failed to find treasure while realizing that he'd banged his left knee up pretty good, Colman headed back for the entrance. He scrambled over rocks until he thought he saw stars through the opening up ahead. He lifted the lantern high to make sure he was still alone—no mountain lions or other critters.

And he was.

Only he wasn't at the mouth of the cave. Furrowing his brow, he looked around. Had he gone the wrong way? He backtracked, paying close attention to the passage itself this time. There weren't any side passages, so he hadn't turned wrong. Back in the cavern, he looked all around and realized there were several passages leading away. But he was certain this was the one he'd passed through in his flight from the cat. Maybe he hadn't gone far enough. He went through again.

An hour or more passed before Colman stood back inside the cavern, his heart like a chunk of ice in his chest. He'd tried two other passages with the same result. As impossible as it seemed, he was alone inside a mountain and did not know the way out. He sat on an outcropping and examined every inch of the space around him in the flickering light of his lantern. Nothing looked right. Nothing looked familiar.

He'd been frightened when he thought a mountain lion was after him, but that fear was joy compared to the sensation bubbling in his gut at this moment. He was lost deep inside a mountain, and no one knew where he was. Burying his head in his hands, Colman tried to stay calm, to think through his predicament, to decide on a course of action.

And then his lantern went out.

chapter
eight

Emmaline was inconsolable. Serepta had grown accustomed to people obeying her commands—catering to her wishes. But this morning, when she told Emmaline to get up and eat breakfast so she could go to Ivy's, she'd refused. A four-year-old had bested her.

She'd sent Charlie for Ivy what seemed like an hour ago.

When Ivy stepped up onto the front porch, Serepta fought the impulse to simply hand the child over for disposal. She greeted the younger woman with steel in her voice. "This child is impossible. Hopefully you'll be able to quiet her. If not, other arrangements will have to be made."

Ivy didn't flinch. Serepta had been dealing with the herbalist long enough to know she was tougher than she looked. And she'd never shown fear in Serepta's presence, although she'd surely heard enough stories to frighten most young women. Ivy simply firmed her jaw and marched into the bedroom where Emmaline curled crying in the middle of a too-big bed, having refused to budge since Serepta wakened her.

Serepta let her shoulders fall as she listened to Ivy croon to the child. She stole a look and watched the woman rock

Emmaline until her cries subsided to gasps and then hiccups. She felt moisture rise to her own eyes as the child's anguish abated, but as soon as it did, she whirled away to tackle the day's work.

She managed to put all thoughts of the little girl aside for a few hours as she dug into the communications and planning required to distribute illegal alcohol throughout the state of West Virginia and into Kentucky and Ohio. Prohibition may have been repealed, but there were still plenty of dry counties populated with folks thirsty for a taste of something stronger than lemonade. She wrote a note to Harrison Ash, requesting that he visit within the week. Thurmond's chief of police was happy to accept her money, but she was concerned he was getting lax in his duties.

As midmorning approached, she rubbed her dry eyes and set down her pen. Perhaps it was time to see how Emmaline and Ivy were faring. They'd been so quiet all morning that she'd almost forgotten about them.

Then a wail pierced the air, and Serepta let her shoulders sag. Apparently whatever reprieve Ivy won had been short-lived. She started from the room when she realized there were more sounds than the child's cry. Sounds of men and horses.

Running now, Serepta met Charlie in the front hall. He held up a hand, and she froze. He lifted the muzzle of his rifle and pointed it toward the front door.

"What is it?" Serepta hissed.

"Bunch of them Harpes just rode up the drive."

"Why did Emmaline scream?"

"She and Ivy were picking posies out front. Scared 'em good."

"Where are they now?" Serepta retrieved a pistol from the storage bench in the base of the hall tree.

"Ivy done scooted the child round back."

Serepta nodded and moved toward the front door.

"Where you goin'?" asked Charlie.

"To see what our guests want."

She tucked the pistol into the waistband of her trousers where it could easily be seen and then pulled on a jacket. She stepped out onto the wide wraparound porch and felt as much as saw Charlie ease out behind her, rifle cradled in his arms. It felt good to have him at her back. She stood at the top of the steps and waited.

Several men led by Webb Harpe rode horses up to the steps. One circled the house as if to see who might be hiding in the dairy, the smokehouse, or the corncrib. Serepta stared her enemy down.

"We're looking for my nephew," Webb said.

"And you thought he'd be here?" Serepta braced her hands on her hips, pushing her jacket back a notch as she did so.

Webb's eyes flicked to her pistol and then back to her face. He might doubt any other woman's willingness to shoot him, but not hers.

"Colman was on his way to White Sulphur Springs by train when he went missing not so far from here. Seemed like a good place to check."

"Ah, the one who fancies himself a preacher." She sneered. "Did you think he'd come and try to save my soul?"

"Some things aren't worth saving."

Serepta wanted to laugh. As if such shallow words could wound her. Instead, she leveled her cool gaze on Webb and waited. Sometimes silence was the most meaningful response.

"You got Jake in there with you?"

Ah-ha. Now Webb had revealed his true intent. "What business is that of yours?"

"He killed my boy."

"That he did."

Webb spit and narrowed his eyes. "Can't let him get away with something like that."

Serepta kept her peace.

"I'm betting if it'd been the other way around and your boy was the one dead, you'd be hunting his killer."

Serepta slowly lifted her chin and looked down her nose at Webb. "My boy would have had the sense not to get killed."

Webb's jaw clenched, and she could see a vein popping out on his forehead. Good. Angry men made mistakes.

The horse he was riding sidestepped, and Webb got a gleam in his eye. "Had any liquor go missing lately? Guess somebody didn't have the sense to keep that from happening."

Now it was Serepta's turn to grit her teeth. But she wouldn't let this buffoon push her into doing anything foolish. "Liquor's a lot easier to replace than a son. Maybe you'd better start looking to replace that wife of yours with one young enough to make you another heir." She heard Charlie grunt but didn't acknowledge the sound. It was too far, she knew it, but she would not let this man best her, even when it came to cruel words.

Webb's face paled, then flushed scarlet. He reined his horse around. "Come on, fellers. We've got a man to hunt and kill."

It was as though the words they'd spoken still hung there in the chill spring air. And they left Serepta cold—her words almost as much as Webb's.

After several hours—or had it been days?—the darkness began to feel like something brushing across Colman's skin.

He stopped his crawling to reach up and run a hand over his face. It was an odd sort of relief to feel the shape of his nose, the scruff of his beard, his dry and chapped lips. He closed his eyes so they would stop trying to find light in the blackness engulfing him. Except that closing his eyes made him hope there would be light when he opened them again.

And there was nothing.

He'd slept for a time. Or maybe several times. He remembered leaving the cavern after sleeping. Then he'd slept again at some point. He supposed wandering through this maze of a mountain might not be the wisest decision, but it was better than simply waiting in one spot to die. While the men from the train might send someone looking for him, if the snow melted there wouldn't be any tracks or other evidence to tell them where he'd gone.

Colman had never felt more alone in his life.

He still had two matches in his pocket but hated to use them. He'd lit three other matches to check his location as he moved around. Each time he found himself in a slightly different passage that came from nowhere and continued into the same. He'd hoped to find some wood or something else he could burn, but short of setting fire to his own clothing or the blanket that offered a measure of warmth, there was nothing. He'd stumbled across some water earlier, although he was thirsty again, so it must have been a while now.

He rested on his haunches, hand against the wall to his left. He decided somewhere along the line to keep following his left hand. If he never let it leave this side of the passage, it seemed like at least he would not end up doubling back on himself. Each time he had to lift his hand to negotiate rocks or give his knees some relief, he felt a moment of panic. What if he somehow put his hand back in a different spot and missed . . . what? He didn't even know anymore.

Colman bit back the panic that had become a constant companion. Each time it swept through him he felt as though it sank a little deeper, as though he were getting closer and closer to a terror that would consume him. Kill him.

If only it would kill him all at once, he might welcome it. He wished he'd gone ahead and faced the mountain lion or whatever it had been. A terror he could see, smell, and feel would be preferable to this slow agony.

He stopped to quiet his breathing. He wasn't sure if he was panting from the exertion of pulling himself through the rough cave or from fear. As his breathing slowed he thought he heard something. The sound reminded him of stew bubbling in a pot. Was he so desperately hungry that he was imagining things? He inhaled deeply as if to smell the richness of his mother's beef stew, but instead he smelled sulphur. The aroma had come to him off and on all through the cave. Now the smell combined with the bubbling sound filled his mind with images of a fiery cauldron in hell. The panic was about to overtake him again.

He pulled out a match and lit it.

His eyes shied away from even this small light, but he forced them open and looked around hungrily, taking in the rocky floor, the rough walls, the . . . dead end. No. He would have to turn back. Then he saw a dark puddle that was indeed bubbling. Before he could make heads or tails of it, the match burned his fingers. He dropped the blazing stub and reared back when the very air seemed to burst into flame, then extinguished in a sulphur-scented puff. The image of the light remained burned in his mind's eye, then even that faded away. He couldn't think what had just happened, but the burst of light made the darkness seem even thicker. He felt a heaviness in his mind and his limbs that begged him to stop his striving. He turned and began crawling back the way he'd come, trying to focus his mind but failing. Finally, he curled on his side, wrapped his hands around his head, and cried out to God.

***

Colman woke, blinking to clear the darkness until he remembered it was permanent. Or as good as. The skin of his face felt tight where tears had dried when he'd finally slipped into oblivion for as long as God granted him sleep. His head felt like he was coming off a three-day drunk. His stomach rolled, and he dry-heaved, his belly too empty to produce anything. Maybe that water hadn't been good to drink. He lay on his side and wondered if this was the end. Colman realized he was finally willing to resign himself to the fact that he was being punished—and rightfully so—for his disobedience.

Tell the McLeans about Me.

He could almost hear the words echoing through the cave. It wasn't a complicated message. Carrying it out, though, that was trickier.

Colman rolled to his raw knees and clasped his hands, sweat prickling his skin even in the cool of the cavern. It was his childhood pose for prayer. He remembered his mother kneeling beside him to hear his prayers each night. He'd peeked at her more than once, but she never moved, never cracked an eyelid, simply waited for him to speak to God. He tried to remember when it stopped, when he got too old and imagined himself too grown to kneel beside his mother. In that moment he missed her more intensely than ever before.

Shoulders bent, eyes shut tight, sick in body and soul, he

bared his heart to God. He prayed for a long time before finally coming to the end of himself. He took a breath and found a few more words buried in his spirit.

Father, I suppose I'll die here in the dark. I'm sorry for my disobedience. I'm sorry for the pain I've inflicted and the blessings I've withheld. Please forgive me. If I ever see another person—especially a McLean—I promise I will declare that salvation comes from you. My joy is in my salvation.

Colman stayed there, his knees throbbing against the stone floor. Then he blew out a shuddering breath and opened his eyes to find . . . darkness. He blinked and rubbed his itching, burning, useless eyes. Had he really been expecting to see light just because he'd poured his heart out to God?

He patted his pocket. Did he dare light his final match? He was beginning to think this was the spot where he would lie down to die, and seeing the space, however briefly, felt like a comfort. He fumbled for the matchbox, his fingers thick and clumsy. His hand cramped and he dropped the box, the sound of the lone wooden match rattling inside and then the rattle stopped, and he knew he'd just heard a tiny stick of wood hit the floor of the cave.

Colman froze. Then slowly, gingerly, he began to pat the stones and debris around him. Once, he could have sworn he bumped into a wooden crate but knew it was just him wishing. His searching grew more and more frantic until at last he groaned and lay down, a condemned man. So . . . this was how it would end. He thought he'd feel worse about it, but in a way it was a relief. He'd failed God and supposed he deserved to die here, deep inside a mountain. Maybe he could go to sleep and not wake up.

Serepta drove Emmaline to Ivy's by herself the next morning. Charlie hated it when she took the car without someone to drive her, but she did it anyway. Driving made her feel freer than almost anything. She wasn't going to let Webb Harpe and his men change the way she lived her life. Of course, the fact that she was going out alone with a child was a pretty big change. Still, she told herself it was her choice and had nothing to do with the Harpe clan.

The day before, Ivy had suggested that Emmaline's crying fit might have come because she didn't want to leave Walnutta and Serepta. With so many changes already, the little girl was likely clinging to anything that seemed even remotely familiar. So this morning Serepta had simply fed the child breakfast and loaded her in the car. As they neared Ivy's cottage, she began talking to Emmaline.

"Today you will stay with Ivy."

Emmaline gave her a suspicious look but didn't say anything. The child could speak well enough, although her words were few and far between. Most of her communication related to having her own needs met. "Hungry," "tired," and "Mommy" were among her favorites, not to mention "no." If Serepta had been told she was about to have someone in her life who told her no all day long, she would have laughed. She didn't much tolerate being refused anything. But the girl's sheer obstinance impressed her. Sometimes she would even refuse something she wanted, as though trying to exert control over some aspect of her life.

Serepta could understand that need. And so when Emmaline said no, Serepta let whatever it was go if possible. Charlie clucked and shook his head, yet Serepta knew in her bones it was the right thing to do.

Which is why she didn't ask Emmaline if she wanted to go

to Ivy's this morning. She had to take her even if she refused to go. And worse, Serepta thought there was a fair chance the girl would prefer being with Ivy over her. If that was so, she'd rather not know it.

The car bumped over the ruts leading to the cottage where Ivy lived with her grandfather. She parked the car and laid a hand on Emmaline's curls. "Sometimes being an orphan is better," she said, mostly to herself.

They got out and walked through the woods to the cottage. Ivy stepped outside, staying in the shade as much as possible. She wore a smile beneath the shadow of her ever-present hat. Serepta felt her own lips curling in response before she caught herself. Ivy wasn't a friend, she was an employee—a supplier of herbs and salves. She'd do well to remember this was nothing more than a business arrangement.

"Good morning," Ivy sang out, and Emmaline made for her like a bumblebee to a newly opened morning glory.

"Morning," Serepta said. "I thought I'd leave her with you until late afternoon. I didn't bring anything today, but Charlie can send her lunch tomorrow."

"Oh, that won't be necessary." Ivy crouched down, and Emmaline leaned into her. "We'll feast on fresh air and bird-song, and if that doesn't hold us, I might could rustle up some biscuits."

Emmaline giggled and smiled, making Serepta have second thoughts about leaving her with Ivy. What if the child became so attached to Ivy that she refused to come home? Truth was, the girl didn't really have a home. Serepta had learned that her family had been in the process of moving to Hinton so the father could work for the railroad. No other family had turned up since the accident, and there was literally nothing and nowhere for the child to return to.

"You send word if you have any trouble," Serepta said. "I'll see you this afternoon."

"Yes, ma'am."

Serepta started back toward the car, then returned and knelt in front of Emmaline, who gazed at her with serious eyes.

"Home is with me," she said. "I know it doesn't feel like it right now, but you'll see. I'll be back for you."

Emmaline nodded and glanced at Ivy, who smiled and smoothed her curls.

Serepta stood and headed down the path again. Before she lost sight of the house, she looked back to see Emmaline laughing as Ivy tucked herbs and early flowers into her sling. A stab of something like regret pierced her heart, though she couldn't say why.

chapter
nine

An angel was singing, piercing the silence. Colman guessed he'd made it to heaven in spite of his shortcomings. Maybe he wouldn't get many jewels in his crown, but he thought that wouldn't matter so long as he was free from the dark of the cave. He wondered if he would see his mother.

He couldn't make out the words at first, just the melody. Then it came to him—"Sweet By and By." He grunted and sat up. Funny, he thought his aches and pains were meant to be gone now, and shouldn't there be heavenly light? Fear crept back into his consciousness, but the pure melody continued, and surely that was a good sign. He felt the blanket from the train still wrapped around him, the floor of the cave still beneath him, and darkness still hemming him in.

Well then. Not dead. So where was the singing coming from?

He got to his hands and knees, wobbling from side to side, and crawled in the direction of the angel's song. There was a slight incline with loose stones and dirt. He started up it, being careful not to hit his head or anything else. As he moved, he dislodged a large stone, and dirt gave way beneath him. He rolled to the side and lay on his back, panting. Was this some sort of cave-in? Was he making things worse? He grunted. Things couldn't get much worse.

Rolling back onto his hands and knees, Colman stilled. The sudden movement had made stars burst behind his eyes. The dizziness was almost worth the sensation of light, even if it was imaginary. He breathed deep and waited. But some of the specks didn't go away. He sat back on his heels, blinking and rubbing his eyes.

Was that light? And was the singing louder? Now the melody he heard was "Softly and Tenderly." His mother used to sing that one. He lunged for one of the specks of light—imaginary or not—and began clawing at the earth.

When the fall of dirt and rocks finally gave way to freedom, Colman couldn't stand to look at the light. He gulped fresh air, longing to soak in the sight of the trees, the sky, the sun . . . but it hurt too much. Eyes squeezed tight, he crawled to level ground and knelt there, hands pressed to his eyes. He just needed a moment to adjust. A moment for the world to stop spinning.

The singing stopped, and as he heard footsteps approaching, Colman tried to look and see who or what it was. Fear gripped his belly, sending it into spasms once more. He squinted and blinked against the oppressive brightness that sent bolts of pain into his skull.

"Keep them closed."

The voice was soft, almost musical. The unexpected sweetness of a human voice brought tears to his throbbing eyes.

A gentle hand touched his forehead. "You look like you've had a rough go of it. Were you lost in the caves?"

"Who are you?" His voice sounded rough and raspy, barely intelligible even to him.

"My name is Ivy. I live near here."

"Where's . . . here?"

"Near Hinton—my grandfather and I live outside the town proper."

Colman shuddered, tried to open his eyes again. He staggered to his feet, but then stopped. As if he could run away. Hinton was where Serepta McLean lived, where God wanted him to go and share His message of love and grace. How far had he traveled beneath the earth? How was it possible that he'd ended up right where God wanted him?

That same soft touch brushed his arm. "If you'll let me, I'll walk you to our cottage. You look—" there was a long pause—"like you could use a good meal and maybe a bath."

Colman realized he was shaking. How long had it been since he'd eaten? Water inside the cave was all he'd had since eating cake on the train Friday. And based on the way his insides felt, the water hadn't helped matters.

"What day is it?"

"Monday."

Colman tried to take a step and felt the woman beside him catch him under the arm and prop him up. No wonder he'd lost track of time. He suddenly felt too weak to stand and sank back to the earth.

"Wait here," the sweet voice whispered in his ear. "I'll be right back."

Colman didn't know what else to do, so he stayed, the coolness of the dirt beneath him seeping into his pants. But at the same time he was acutely aware of the warmth of the sun on his face, the sound of birds in the trees, and the music of water running over stones nearby. A soft breeze stirred the hair on his forehead, and he turned his face into it, breathing the mingled perfume of nature. He squinted against the light, but his eyes hurt and everything was blurry. Had he somehow damaged his eyes inside the cave?

This time when he heard footsteps, he felt certain it was the woman returning, and he was glad rather than frightened.

"It's Ivy," she said. "And my grandfather is coming, too. We'll help you back to the cottage so we can see to your needs."

"Howdy." This voice was rougher, deeper, but still beautiful to Colman's ears. "Take a swig of this."

What felt like a jar was pressed into Colman's hand. He lifted it to his mouth and took a sip—it was cool with a refreshing flavor. What were they giving him?

"Water with some mint in it is all," the woman said. "It'll be easy on your stomach if you haven't eaten in a while. Just take a little—you don't want to overdo it."

Colman obediently took another swallow and found it surprisingly rejuvenating before it suddenly came back up without warning. A feeling of being at the mercy of strangers washed over him. But what choice did he have? Somehow his plans to go fishing in White Sulphur Springs had resulted in his being spewed out of a mountain in the very place God told him to go. He guessed he would just have to trust that something bigger than him was at work here.

"Think you can walk with our help?" the man asked.

"I can," Colman replied. And this time his voice sounded more like his own.

Colman held the warm cup in both hands, sipping beefy broth a little at a time, hoping it would stay down. The heat, aroma, and taste were all exquisite to his deprived senses. He could even feel the steam curling against his face and imagined that it soothed his sore eyes. He could see a little, but the world remained hazy. Ivy and her grandfather were little more than shapes moving about.

"More?"

He sighed. If she were half as pretty as she sounded, she'd be the most beautiful woman in the world. He squinted, trying to see her better, but it was no use. He could tell she was small and had light hair, but little beyond that. He resigned himself to being treated as a half-blind invalid for now.

"Ivy, someone's coming."

Colman turned toward the grandfather's voice. He'd said his name was Hoyt.

"I'll go see," she said. "It's about time for Emmaline to go home."

Colman heard a voice outside and shrank back into the corner where he sat propped on some sort of cot, hoping he was out of sight. Though he couldn't say why, the thought of someone else seeing him while he was incapacitated disturbed him. And who was Emmaline?

He wondered if his father knew he was missing yet. Surely he'd be missed when he didn't show up for dinner this evening. What had Johnny and Elam told everyone? Did they think he was dead?

"You expecting company?" he asked, hoping the shape near the crackling fire was Hoyt.

The older man touched his arm and settled near him. "Folks come and go. Ivy's herbs are in demand, and locals stop by now and again. And these days she's been helping . . . a friend care for a child."

Emmaline must be the child. "People come for herbs?"

"She knows all about plants and roots and berries. Makes teas and poultices with 'em—all kinds of cures and helps for folks. I seen her mixing something up for your eyes and your belly a little while ago. I expect she'll have you right as rain in no time." He chuckled. "Must've drunk some of that bad water comes up around here. Let's hope it don't send you to the outhouse."

Colman didn't like the sound of that, but since he was feeling better, he relaxed and took another sip of broth. Hopefully whoever was outside would move on. He perked his ears at the sound of voices. There was Ivy's sweet tone and then another woman with a deeper tenor to her words. She spoke with an almost flat cadence that seemed familiar, yet Colman couldn't place it. Probably just reminded him of someone else. While the words didn't hold much interest for him, he liked the smooth, easy rhythm of their talking that told him the women were comfortable with each other.

Even so, he thought he felt a measure of tension flowing from Hoyt.

"Everything alright?" he asked.

"Sure, sure. She's a regular. Been bringing that child round for a few days now."

The voices came closer, and Colman felt the presence of more people in the cottage. It must be a small room, as tight as it felt with the warmth and presence of bodies inside. The sense that someone was examining him intently washed over him. Maybe the child was studying him, although wouldn't she have already seen him by now?

"You have a guest." It was the second woman. Although her tone was flat, Colman had the notion she wasn't happy about his being there.

Colman felt multiple eyes on him, although he couldn't make out faces. How did he factor into this conversation?

The second woman spoke—low and throaty. "I wouldn't want her to be exposed to . . . just anyone."

If it were possible to feel someone's eyes reading his very soul, that was what Colman felt at that moment.

A childish giggle came to Colman's ears, and he couldn't help but smile. Such a sweet, innocent sound. It complemented Ivy's singsongy voice. He had a vision of a home with a wife and child, not so different from the one he'd grown up in.

"No, wait . . ."

The other woman's cry preceded the pressure of a wee hand on Colman's leg. He reached out and laid his own hand over the warmth of the fingers pressing against his knee.

"It's alright," he said. "I expect she's curious." He dabbed at his watering eyes with a sweet-smelling handkerchief Ivy had given him. He could just make out a mass of dark hair and maybe a cherub grin.

"Of course." The voice was stiff, hard, as if the woman didn't approve of him. But how could that be? She'd just now seen him. He didn't much know anyone in Hinton, since the Harpes and McLeans didn't mix any more than they had to. Maybe she was just uneasy because of how unkempt he was.

"Don't fret about me," he said. "I'm a wandering preacher, and these folks have been kind enough to see to me after I had . . . a spot of trouble."

"Indeed. Are you . . . what's your name?"

"Colman Harpe. And you are?" He held his hand out in the direction of her outline.

"No one of consequence."

No touch met his, so he lowered his hand and accidentally

bumped the tangle of soft curls. The child giggled again, and he let his hand rest there on her head for a moment, a soft smile touching his lips.

"Get on back to your momma, you little scamp," he said.

He heard a soft gasp but couldn't tell where it came from. Then the room emptied, and he was left alone again. He tried to puzzle through the day—escaping the mountain, being found, trusting strangers he couldn't see, the child and her mother . . .

"Hey now, you'd best rest your head before you fall over."

It was Ivy again, easing him down on the bed piled with quilts or blankets. She helped him recline and tucked the covers around him as if he were just a boy in need of a nap. He let himself relax, thinking that maybe that's exactly what he was.

Serepta panted softly in the back seat of the car being driven by Mack. He'd stayed in the automobile while she fetched Emmaline. Which was just as well since Colman Harpe had been sitting inside the little cottage where the herbalist plied her trade. Preacher indeed.

She'd wanted desperately to ask what he was doing there all dirty and wild, as though he'd been rolling in filth. And he didn't seem to recognize her or to even see her for that matter. He'd dabbed at his eyes as if there were something wrong with them. Perhaps Webb hadn't been telling a tale when he said his nephew had gone missing. Was Colman hunting Jake? Had he been injured in some way? What was the "spot of trouble" he mentioned?

And then . . . he'd thought she was Emmaline's mother. Up until that moment she'd been plotting, calculating, considering what the presence of her enemy so close to her home might mean. But when he told Emmaline to get back to her momma, it was as though a prophet had spoken the secret hidden in her heart. And her heart had been so long under lock and key that hearing its hope voiced was like seeing the sun rise in the middle of the night. If there had been a chair handy, she would have sunk into it.

What cruel trick would allow her enemy—her damaged enemy—to see so clearly what she hardly dared put words to herself?

She would not bring Emmaline again so long as Colman was in the house. Ivy said she understood, but she'd looked disappointed. Serepta refused to acknowledge the sorrow in the other woman's eyes as she marched Emmaline back to the car. Now she looked down at the child whose head bobbed as she tried to stay awake in the swaying car. Sliding over, she tucked Emmaline close to her side and saw that within seconds she slept. A fierceness rose in her unlike any she'd felt for her own sons. Yes, Ivy might provide practical care, but Serepta would be this little girl's rock in the storm. Her safe place, her refuge and defense against all enemies. She would provide the one thing she'd never had in all her years growing up with a tyrant of a father and then being married to a big talker who left her to raise their boys alone.

Security.

chapter
ten

Colman woke to the aroma of bread baking and the sound of soft voices in hushed conversation. For a moment he lay still, luxuriating in the comfort that enveloped him. Finally, he stirred and stretched. A hand brushed his shoulder.

"Think you can handle some supper?" Ivy asked.

He sat up, blinking, thinking maybe he could see a little better. "What time is it?"

"Evening—the sun's just setting."

"Sunset? I'd like to see that." He rubbed his eyes, but Ivy stilled his hands.

"Best not rub at them. I have some ointment I think might help." She tilted his head and dabbed something cool in the corners of his eyes. He blinked rapidly and found the paste soothing to his itchy, irritated eyes.

"Will this help me see better?"

"I hope so. Now let me get ready and I'll take you out to see the setting of the sun."

She led him out into the cool evening, where he could feel the fading warmth of the day's last light on his face and could hear birds chattering about going to bed. He continued to blink and resisted the urge to rub his eyes. The rest and the ointment seemed to have eased the worst of the blurriness. While the world remained soft around the edges, he could make out larger details with the colors of spring taking on an unexpected richness.

He saw the trees leafing out, the grass beginning to green, and in the distance mountain upon mountain rolling away to a glory of orange and red as the sun dimmed and dropped below the horizon. He breathed in and felt as though the air reached all the way to his toes, invigorating and strengthening him.

Those days inside the mountain, he'd despaired of ever seeing the sun again, much less a sunset such as this. It was almost worth the agony of the cave to be reminded of the beauty of the world around him.

"Have you ever seen . . ." Words failed him as he turned to look at the profile of the woman beside him. At first he thought he was seeing a ghost. The pale slip of a woman in the broad hat squinting at the view looked ethereal. Her face was so white he thought she might be cut from chalk. Her hair wasn't much darker, almost silvery. She firmed her chin as though bracing herself for something and turned to face him. Even her eyes were pale, although they at least were a washed-out blue.

"I've seen many sunsets from this very spot," she said. "But this evening I think I can see it through your fresh eyes, and no, I've never seen anything so lovely."

Colman couldn't tear his gaze from the woman beside him, and she seemed to steel herself under his close attention. He looked away, trying to refocus on the dying light as the sun dipped lower behind the mountains.

He heard Hoyt clear his throat behind him and glanced at

the older man with his full white beard and serious gray-blue eyes. Unlike Ivy, his flesh looked ruddy. "How about we get you cleaned up afore supper."

Colman looked down at himself for the first time. He was filthy. Dirt ground into the knees of his pants, dust layered over his shirt. Thankfully, he'd let them take the remains of the blanket he'd dragged through the mountain with him. Probably they'd set fire to it. He reached up and felt his face, a shadow of beard and who knew what else. He guessed he didn't have much room to judge Ivy's looks.

"I'm a sight," he said.

Ivy laughed quietly. "And now you can see what a sight. Go on with Grandpa and tidy yourself. We'll be having ham and that bread I baked for supper."

Colman swallowed, hoping he could stomach something that good. The soup he'd had earlier stayed down so far, and he longed for a proper meal. He hobbled after Hoyt, who showed him a wash station on the back porch. After brushing his clothes, combing his hair, and washing the skin that showed, he felt like a new man—if one in need of a shave. Looking around at the darkening evening, the stars beginning to show, and the flicker of lantern light inside the cottage, he supposed in a way he was a new man in a new place with a new task. And with God's help he'd do it this time around.

After removing cotton gloves to dish up the simple meal, Ivy took a seat to Colman's left, and he wondered if it was on purpose so that he wouldn't be gazing at her across the table. "You mentioned you're a preacher earlier. Is that true?"

"Not full time—I preach when I get the chance. Hope to have my own church one day. Mostly I'm a wheel tapper for the C&O Railroad. But I guess when I don't show up for work tomorrow I may not be that much longer."

She darted a look at her grandfather, who nodded in reply. "You also said your name is Harpe. Are you one of the Harpes from over in Thurmond?"

"I am. Didn't realize our fame had spread this far."

Hoyt chuckled. "There's famous and then there's *infamous*."

Colman swallowed and wiped his mouth. "I guess you might be referring to our ongoing . . . disagreement with the McLean family."

"Feud is what it is," Hoyt said. He laid his fork down and looked Colman in the eye. "We're hoping since you're a preacher, it might be you don't have any truck with all the wrangling back and forth."

The warm food in Colman's belly felt like it was hardening. "I've never shot anyone, if that's what you mean."

Ivy watched him intently, and he forced himself not to examine her as closely. "But you don't like the McLeans," she said.

It was a statement, not a question. Colman pushed his plate back and leaned heavily on the table. "I'll tell you the honest truth. I don't like them. But I'm here to preach to them just the same."

Hoyt's bushy eyebrows shot into his hairline. "Why would you do that?"

Colman's laugh came out shaky. He ran a hand through hair still damp from rinsing it with wash water. "God's not giving me much choice. Can't say as I'm excited about carrying the gospel to a bunch of outlaws like the McLeans, but back there in the mountain I got the sense it was preach to 'em or else."

"Or else what?" Ivy asked.

Colman picked up a piece of bread and took a tentative

99

bite, hoping it would settle the uneasiness in his belly. He chewed and swallowed. "Or else make my bed in the roots of the mountain."

Hoyt chuckled and stroked his beard. "God has a way of making His position clear to a man, don't He?"

Colman grinned. "Guess maybe I'm more scared of Him than I am any McLean."

"You'll do," Hoyt said, and for the first time since boarding the train to White Sulphur Springs, Colman thought maybe this crazy plan wouldn't be the death of him after all. Then he ran outside and lost his dinner.

⁓

The next morning, Colman woke to hot coffee and warm oatmeal with fresh cream. He ate a few bites, and since the food stayed down, he decided he'd quit while he was ahead. He passed on the coffee, even though the smell of it was enough to give a dead man hope.

Ivy handed him more ointment for his eyes. When he'd examined them in the small glass over the washbasin on the porch, they looked red and felt full of grit. And his vision wasn't back to normal yet.

"Are your eyes still bothering you?" Ivy asked.

Colman stretched his lids open and blinked a few times. "Guess they are some. I thought a good night's sleep would've fixed them up."

"Did you use that chamomile wash I gave you?"

"Last night before bed."

She cleared the dishes, then came back, tilted his head into the light, and peered into his eyes more closely. He squinted, trying to take advantage of this opportunity to examine her face. Her skin looked translucent. Even with his sore eyes, he could see the blue of veins beneath her flesh. What was she?

"Does the light bother you?"

"It does. I figure I'm not all the way adjusted to being out of the dark yet."

Ivy made a humming sound. "The light troubles my eyes, too." She grimaced. "Although there's no cure for me. I wish I had some fresh eyebright, but it won't be blooming again until late summer. Rinse your eyes with the chamomile every few hours and then apply the ointment. I'll check them again when I get back."

She moved away, leaving Colman blinking. "Where are you going?"

"To tend to the child brought here yesterday. Her . . . caretaker has her hands full with other matters."

"So that wasn't her mother?"

"She's an orphan. Her family was killed when a train hit the truck they were traveling in."

Colman felt a stab of sorrow for the child. It had been hard enough to lose his mother when he was thirteen, but at least he could remember her.

"Can I come with you?"

Ivy, who had begun packing a basket, froze. "Why would you want to do that? You should spend the day resting—recovering. You still haven't eaten enough to keep a sparrow alive."

"I . . . I need to be a help if I can. It's good of this woman to take in the child. She should have all the help folks can give her. Maybe I can start sharing the gospel with her. Shoot, she might even be kin to the McLeans."

Ivy planted her hands on her hips and looked him up and down. "Oh, she's kin alright."

Colman gave her a puzzled look.

"The child's been taken in by Serepta McLean." She jutted her chin in the air, almost daring him to make his next move.

"The head of the McLeans? She took in an orphaned child?" Colman couldn't have been more shocked if she'd told him a mountain lion had taken to suckling a lamb.

"That's right."

"And she came to you?" He felt a mixture of confusion and disgust. Why would someone as kind and gentle as Ivy have anything to do with a viper like Serepta McLean?

"I've been caring for anyone who would let me since my mother taught me the healing power of plants. When I'm tempted to pick and choose, I just remember that God loves everyone—no matter how wrong we might think they are."

Colman let that settle over him. She was right, but doggone if he wanted to admit it.

She came closer and laid a gentle hand on his shoulder. "Stay here today. Talk to Grandpa, enjoy the sunshine, bathe your eyes, and try to eat some more. If you want to help this child, there will be time."

He nodded. "Guess maybe I am still a bit peaked."

She smiled, and it was almost as good as when he saw that spot of light inside the cave. "I'll see you late this afternoon." And then she gathered her things and was gone.

Colman felt an odd sort of emptiness descend in her wake.

~~~~~

Serepta was not pleased when Jake turned up at the house shortly after Ivy came to watch over Emmaline. First, there was no need for him to put himself in the way of the Harpe men while their anger was still so fresh. And second, he was

102

supposed to be seeing to the receiving end of liquor deliveries in Cincinnati.

"Aw, Ma, you've got men to handle all that boring business stuff. Me, I'm more of a front man. Let me work the sales. You could set me up with a dance hall, and I'll sell hooch on the side."

Clenching her jaw, it was all Serepta could do not to slap her son's smug face. He was too much like his father, but with an ornery streak that felt like it must have come from his grandfather. He had the same selfishness that had made her childhood such a misery, although he was lacking his grandfather's outright cruelty. Seeing part of her father's vile temperament in her son made her wonder if she had somehow passed it on to him. If she'd known that was possible, she never would have borne a child.

"That's a ridiculous idea and you know it. You'd drink more than you sold, and you'd get in trouble with the girls within a week." She ignored the storm in her son's eyes. "But I will let you handle some *sales*, as you put it."

"Oh yeah?" He looked eager now.

"I need someone I can trust to round up a few more partners who can arrange for crates of liquor to be transported in coal cars."

Jake stretched his neck and looked thoughtful. "You mean railroad men?"

Serepta schooled her expression. Was this a mistake? Was her son too dunderheaded to do even this simple task?

"Yes, men who have access to the cars and can bury crates in the coal. Deep enough not to be seen, but not so deep they get broken. We need men who can help with the loading and unloading both."

"Guess I might could find a few men like that."

Serepta exhaled on a hiss. She might regret it, but it was time for Jake to step up and be more active in the family business. And if she couldn't keep him out of Webb's way, at least she could keep him too busy to go looking for additional trouble.

"Go talk to Charlie. He'll give you the particulars about payment and movement of the goods."

"Ma, I don't know why you let that . . ."

Serepta glared at her son, daring him to speak slightingly.

". . . colored man get so wrapped up in your business."

"I won't defend him to you, but if you ever find someone half as smart, loyal, and ready to do what's needed, you'd be wise to keep him close."

She spun on her heel and left Jake lounging on a settee. Once in her office, she paused and examined herself in the glass over the mantel. When she married him, Eli had loved to lay his pale flesh alongside hers, so he could marvel at the sharp contrast of her olive complexion. At first, she'd been grateful for a kind touch, but eventually she'd come to resent the implication that she was different.

And she was. Her father had been from a tight-knit group labeled Melungeons by their neighbors. Serepta didn't know if there was any truth to it or what it meant exactly. Or rather, she did know what it meant—that they were lower-class citizens with their swarthy skin, dark hair, and icy blue eyes. One rumor held that the first Melungeons were the result of an illicit union between the devil and a Cherokee woman.

She shuddered and turned away. Knowing her father, she'd believe the part about the devil. But she'd also had aunts, uncles, and cousins who didn't fit that mold. They were good people, she supposed, just not brave. If they'd been brave, they would have stopped the cruelty she suffered at the hands of her own father.

But no. She would not remember. There was trouble enough in her life now. She didn't need to go digging into the past to dredge up pain. The clock on the mantel struck the hour. Time for Ivy to leave for the day. She needed to pay her and take over Emmaline's care. She pulled some cash from a box in the right-hand drawer of her desk and stepped out into the hall.

Emmaline rushed her, a bright blue feather clutched in her grubby hand. "Look," she crowed.

Serepta did look. But it wasn't the feather she noticed. It was the way her son had his arm braced against the wall, blocking Ivy's path. He was talking to her close and low. Serepta couldn't hear his words, but she understood his body language all too well.

"Jake!" she barked.

He jerked and stiffened.

"I'll thank you to allow Miss Gordon to proceed down the hall."

Jake lowered his arm and turned lazily. "Miss Gordon and I were having a conversation." He winked at Ivy. "A most pleasant conversation."

Ivy's expression told Serepta that she found Jake's words anything but pleasant. And Serepta knew her son well enough to recognize that he would never seriously consider wooing a woman thought to be the illegitimate descendant of a semi-mythical race of people from North Carolina. As the story went, the moon-eyed people were run out of the state by local Indians who feared them. The pale people with large blue eyes were said to have taken refuge in West Virginia. Local superstitions held that they had magical powers and only came out at night to avoid the glare of the sun. The notion that Ivy had been fathered by one of them was just as farfetched as her own ancestor being the devil. Still, Jake would never take such a woman seriously—although she was pretty enough in her pale way for him to trifle with.

"I've typically found that in order to have a conversation, both parties must be willing participants. Now, Miss Gordon has more important things to tend to."

Jake sneered. "Like watch a throwaway kid?"

Serepta felt anger expand her chest and push at the back of her throat. But she knew better than to vent words she hadn't measured carefully. Ivy slipped past Jake, the flush on her cheeks a stark contrast to her white skin. Serepta drew her into the office.

"I'll thank you to tend the duties you've been assigned," she said to Jake, dismissing him with a nod. She took Emmaline by the hand and turned her back on her son.

chapter
eleven

Colman hated the idea of someone as kind and gentle as Ivy spending her days with Serepta McLean. He was willing to preach to the woman, but God-fearing folks like the Gordons should be shielded from the kind of poison that was the head of the McLeans. Especially Ivy, who was already afflicted in her own way.

"Thought I'd come with you while you watch the child tomorrow." Colman spoke the words in a way he hoped would let Ivy know he wasn't going to back down.

Ivy sighed. "That won't be necessary. After Jake turned up, Serepta agreed that Emmaline will come here again. It's not far. Her man Charlie will bring her over each morning."

Colman tried to hide his relief. He had a message of grace he'd vowed to share with the McLeans, except he wasn't sure yet how to go about it. He needed more time to sort out what he was going to do. He also needed to get a message to the rail yard and to his father before they gave him up for dead.

He rubbed his eyes. They felt better, while his innards weren't faring as well. He'd spent a fair amount of the day in the privy, and while he'd managed to get some more bread and broth into his belly, he knew it wasn't enough to help him get his strength back. All the things he needed to do weighed heavily on his mind.

Ivy clucked her tongue and smoothed a cool hand over Colman's forehead. "You're still peaked. What have you eaten today?"

Hoyt volunteered the information for him. "Bread and broth. Not enough to keep a gnat alive."

Ivy bustled into the kitchen and began rummaging and stirring. She soon returned with a bowl of something creamy and a slice of bread she'd toasted over the open fire. She dolloped the cream onto the bread and handed it to him. "Small bites."

Not knowing what he was biting into made it easier to follow her suggestion. But regardless of that, he wasn't about to turn down anything this dear woman offered him.

Colman nibbled on the bread, which had a nice crunch to it and just a hint of smokiness. The topping felt smooth on his tongue, tangy and sweet and rich all at once. He took a bigger bite, finding that it sat well in his tender stomach. "This is good."

"You sound surprised," Ivy said.

"Well, I figured if it's supposed to be medicine, I might not like it much."

"It's just clabber milk and honey. It'll build up your strength, and the sour milk will help stave off whatever's working in your belly."

Her mention of something sour in his belly almost set Colman off. But he took a deep breath and finished the meal despite that. Soon he felt better for getting the bread and cream inside him. Ivy beamed like he'd just won a blue ribbon in clabber eating.

Colman grinned and nodded at her. "I'm thinking I might go outside now and walk a bit."

"If you feel up to it, it'll do you good," she agreed. "Why don't I come with you? Grandpa, would you like to come with us?"

Hoyt took the last bite of his own simple meal. "Don't reckon I will. These old bones are better suited to putting up by the fire and working on my carvings."

Colman thought he caught a twinkle in the old man's eye. Regardless, he didn't mind walking out with Ivy on his own—she was pleasant company. He stood and felt the world sway left, then right, then settle on the straight and narrow. Maybe they wouldn't walk far.

Ivy donned her hat and gloves even though the day was waning and hooked her arm through his. He hoped it was because she wanted to and not because she was afraid he might fall over. Although he'd take her gentle touch either way. They set out into the cool spring evening, and for just a moment Colman almost forgot about his time in the cave, the hard task before him, and the feud that was likely to escalate once word got out that Jake was back in town.

They strolled down to a creek and sat awhile on a rock with the last rays of the sun on their backs, the light glinting off the rushing water. Colman felt certain there was some good trout fishing here, and he wouldn't mind wetting a line sometime.

"You said you want to preach to the McLeans," Ivy said. "How will you do that?"

Colman scratched his bristly chin. He was going to have to shave soon. "I'm not sure. I just know it's what I'm sup-posed to do."

Ivy nodded slowly. "Well, if you're supposed to be preach-ing to your enemy, how'd you end up lost in a cave?"

"I thought I was going fishing," Colman answered. He shook his head and chuckled. "But really I was running away from God, and He saw fit to throw me into a hole in the ground to stop my running."

"He does work in the strangest ways." Ivy peeked at him from beneath the brim of her hat and smiled.

A wave of emotion rose up in Colman, but he didn't dare name it. He wanted to ask about her pale skin and the way she covered up when she went outside, but he didn't know how to do so without offending her. Instead, he sat there quietly and watched a pair of squirrels playing round and round a tree. He'd never been much for courting ladies and was surprised at the direction of his thoughts even now. He scrambled for something to say.

"What about you? Other than rescuing strangers and caring for orphans, what do you do with your days?" he asked.

Ivy laughed, low and sweet. "That's the most of it. Although caring for orphans isn't something I'm usually . . . allowed to do. As I said, I'm known as something of a healer around here, putting to use what my mother taught me about how to use plants and such." She ducked her head so that he couldn't see her face. "There are . . . rumors about me, what with my pale skin and the way I can't stand the sun." She tilted her head so she could peer at him. "I can see you want to ask about it."

Colman felt his face flush. "I don't guess it's any of my business."

This time her laugh was harsh. "Nor anyone else's. And yet folks hold the color of my skin against me. As if I can do anything about it." She stood abruptly and took a few steps away, her back to Colman. "I've had my heart set on being a midwife ever since Mother let me help her with a birth when I was nine. There's nothing more wonderful, more miraculous than the birth of a child." She let her chin drop. "When that babe I helped with died nine months later for no reason anyone could see, people said it was because of me." She turned toward him, her blue eyes looking even larger with their nearly invisible lashes. "So, while folks are happy to come for my poultices and tonics, they won't let me near a child. They say—" she stopped suddenly—"well, it doesn't matter what they say. I just wanted you to know about me before someone else decides to tell you."

Colman stared at his shoes. "I've been on the outside of things most of my life. My mother made my father give up feuding, and then when she died, Dad, well, he dried up I guess. So, folks, even my family, have never had much to do with us." He risked a look at her and saw that she was hanging on his words. "Guess what I'm saying is, I know about being shut out. You don't have to look different to be treated different." He gave her a lopsided grin. "And anyhow, you don't look that different. As a matter of fact, I'd say you're right . . . pretty."

She bit her lip and smiled. "Your eyes are still sore, aren't they?"

They laughed together, and the air seemed to grow softer around them as the moon rose behind her shoulder. She removed her hat, and moonlight turned her hair into a fall of water.

"I can see better in this light, even if you can't," she said. "My eyes don't care for the sun."

Colman tried not to stare at those eyes, which were like clear quartz catching what little light remained. She was more than pretty, now that he thought about it. He gave himself a mental shake. Maybe she was bewitching him. If so, he sure didn't mind. He moved toward her, not entirely sure what he planned to do, when a sound drew him up short. Horses approaching. He moved between Ivy and the coming riders. He was too weak to do much more than that, but no one else need know it.

He recognized the handsome silver sorrel even before the riders were close enough to call a greeting.

"We thought either you was dead or the McLeans got you." Uncle Webb reined in his mount and looked Colman up and down. "Johnny and Elam figured they let you go off and die in that freak snowstorm. Elam talked like it was his fault, but he's always been off in the head."

"Had an unexpected detour," Colman said.

"You want to fetch on home with us? Trouble's brewing round here."

Colman widened his stance as much to steady himself as to look confident. "Guess I'll hang here awhile."

Webb considered Ivy, and Colman didn't care for the look in his eye. Finally, he nodded. "Well, we might could use someone on our side round these parts. 'Course you might be at some risk. You well enough to handle it? You look puny."

"I've come here to preach. You let Sam down at the station know I might be awhile. I'd appreciate it if you'd let Dad know, too." Colman puffed his chest out, even though he felt like sinking to the ground.

Webb laughed so hard, Colman thought he might fall off his horse. "Preach? What you gonna preach? Hellfire and damnation? 'Cause these McLeans sure are riding hard for the devil."

"Guess I'll leave their salvation up to the Lord. Even so, I have a calling I'm bound to follow."

Webb leaned forward over his horse's neck. "Son, your

great-granddaddy would roll over in his grave if he knew you were consorting with the enemy." He sat back up. "And unless you give me some hint you've got an ace up your sleeve, I might take issue myself."

Colman wanted to sit down more than he'd wanted anything in his life. Webb was a hard man, but he'd never given Colman trouble. This evening, though, he felt like he was tiptoeing through a field of rattlesnakes.

"I guess everyone needs a chance to hear the gospel news."

"Hunh." Webb tugged his horse around and tilted his head toward the group of men with him—some Colman knew, while others were strangers. "I'll ride on over the hill with these fellers. But we're planning to be back before long. Hope you ain't here." He heeled his horse into a trot. "Unless you're a mite clearer on where your loyalties lie."

The group of men rode slowly away, trickling over the crest of a hill. When the last rider disappeared from sight, Colman sagged to the ground.

Ivy was there immediately, an arm around his shoulders. "Are you alright?"

Colman's laugh shuddered out of him. "I don't expect to die, but I guess I've had better days."

Ivy kneaded his shoulder, silent for a moment. "And worse ones, too?"

With her help, he struggled back to standing again. "Yes, ma'am. That's the God's-honest truth right there."

Charlie slipped into Serepta's office, where she was working late, and stood waiting near the door until she acknowledged him.

"What is it, Charlie?"

"You've always let me speak the truth even when it wasn't something you wanted to hear."

Serepta stiffened. "That's so."

"I got a feeling you're putting too much stock in Jake."

Serepta rose from her chair and leaned with her fists on the desktop. "He's my son."

Charlie nodded. "Too much like his daddy in some ways."

Serepta flinched at hearing Charlie speak what she had thought more than once. Charlie was with her now because Eli had let him do his thinking for him. Her husband had known he could steal a black man's thoughts and ideas and no one would ever notice, much less question it. Eli's callous treatment of Charlie was how she'd first come to realize how much she valued and respected this man who was so much more to her than an employee. "Do you have evidence to support your opinion?"

Charlie shifted from foot to foot. "There's been talk—"

Slashing the air with her hand, Serepta cut him off. "You know how I feel about idle talk."

This time, Charlie's eyes turned sharp. "Seems like you've gotten some mighty useful information from idle talk in the past."

"Not about my son." She sat in her chair again and picked up a pencil, leaning over the ledgers spread out before her. She knew there was a pattern to the missing whiskey, if only she could discover it.

Charlie understood that their conversation was over.

Once he was gone, Serepta dropped her pencil and leaned back in the chair, watching dusk close over sprays of forsythia outside without really taking in the beauty. Had she hurt Charlie's feelings? Should she let him speak? She certainly trusted him more than Jake. But hearing him out might be the end of any hope she had of seeing Jake surprise her by meeting expectations. It wasn't as if she'd given him a job that was critical to her success. Finding more men to help transport liquor was helpful but not urgent. No, she decided, this was a risk she would take. And Charlie would tell her if the situation became truly dire, whether she wanted to hear it or not. That, she knew, was one thing she could count on.

chapter
twelve

Colman eased into the wooden tub of odorous water. There were plenty of ritzy resorts around—the Salt Sulphur Springs, Red Sulphur Springs, and of course White Sulphur Springs, but this shed was Ivy's own invention. Hoyt had knocked together a simple structure around a wooden tub sunk into the ground with sulphurous spring water running into it. He figured this would have to help since it smelled so bad. Hoyt sat on a chair nearby, whittling away at what looked like a bear.

"You ever get in here?" Colman asked.

"I have. Helps my rheumatism."

"Do you stink for a week afterwards?"

Hoyt laughed. "Only two or three days."

Colman eased his head back against the rough edge of the tub and tried to focus on the feeling of weightlessness and peace brought on by being submerged in warm water. If he didn't breathe through his nose, it was pleasant. The cramping tightness in his gut loosened and he fully relaxed—maybe for the first time since he got out of that godforsaken cave. And he felt clean. Hoyt had even brought a razor and some scissors, so Colman could get shut of his scraggle of a beard after he'd "taken the waters," according to Ivy's prescription.

He might have been dozing when sharp thumping on the rickety door jerked him upright. Hoyt was already on his feet, peering out the window. "Looks like we've got company."

Colman started to rise. "Let me get my britches on."

Hoyt waved him back down. "I'd sit tight if'n I was you. They're coming in whether we ask 'em or not."

The door flew open, slamming against the wall, and three men stalked into the tight space. Colman tried not to look as foolish and exposed as he felt. He recognized Mack McLean, and the other two looked enough like the first to be family—almost certainly they were all McLeans or close kin.

Mack carried a rifle, loosely cradled in his arms. The other two men were armed, as well.

"You fellers after some spring gobblers?" Hoyt asked. He'd settled back on his chair and resumed carving.

"Oh, we're after a turkey alright," Mack said.

Colman felt gooseflesh raise over every bit of exposed skin. Was he to be tested so soon? He hadn't preached a word yet.

Mack stepped closer. "Are you Colman Harpe?"

"I am."

"Are you here to hunt Jake for killing your cousin?"

"Nope." Colman thought maybe he ought to say more, but no words came to him.

"Why didn't you go on home with Webb then?"

Colman shifted and braced his arms on the sides of the tub. "I came here to preach the gospel. I won't pretend I'm not upset about Caleb, but vengeance is the Lord's, not mine." He swallowed hard. Did he really believe that?

"Hunh. I've never trusted a Harpe before. Not sure why I should start now."

Colman shrugged, the movement making the water slosh. "Can't think of any way to persuade you."

Mack laughed. "You puny as you look? I hear Ivy's been doctoring you."

Colman looked down at his chest and saw that his ribs were indeed more prominent than they'd once been. He guessed maybe he didn't look like much right then. "That's why I'm here now. Doctor's orders." He stood and wrapped toweling around himself—he couldn't tolerate sitting there vulnerable another minute. "I appreciate your concern," he added with a half smile.

"Oh, trust me, your health is very important to me." Mack balanced the rifle across his shoulder. "But shooting a sick man in a barrel of water doesn't seem sporting. You go on and preach or whatever it is you do, but know that we're watching you closer than you realize." The men behind him shifted their guns, too. "And if we think you're spying or trying to harm a McLean or our family in any way . . ." He let the sentence trail off as he swung the rifle around, pausing briefly with it pointed at Colman's chest. Then he nodded once and turned on his heel.

As the men disappeared out the door, Colman sagged against the side of the tub. Hoyt hurried to support him.

"I don't guess that's the kind of cure Ivy was hoping for when she sent you over here."

Colman laughed and ran a shaky hand over his chin. He still needed to shave. "Even so, I think it might have worked. Leastways my gut's bothering me a whole lot less now that I know my hide's at risk."

Hoyt chuckled. "A matter of perspective."

Colman collapsed onto a bench beside Ivy's fire. Spring was steady coming on, though he still felt chilled. He supposed it took a man a little while to warm up after standing in front of a bunch of armed men in the altogether. He chuckled as Ivy walked in with Emmaline.

"What's tickling you this afternoon?"

Colman flushed to the roots of his hair. "Oh, nothing worth sharing."

"Hmmm." Ivy eyed him up and down. "That almost certainly means it is, but I won't press you. Would you keep an eye on Emmaline while I start supper?" She started toward the stove, then turned back. "You look nice without your beard."

Colman ducked his head and rubbed his chin. "Be glad to watch the child. Between Hoyt and me, we oughta be able to keep up with a four-year-old."

Hoyt laughed. "Don't go talkin' too big now. I've run acrost more than one young'un who could wear me down. Once they stand upright, peace is a long time coming again. And this one's done got her sling off, which means she'll be twice as ornery."

Emmaline stood near Colman. The arm that had been broken looked pale and puny now that it was free from the sling. She seemed to be favoring the arm, so he tried to think of a way to distract her from it. He leaned closer to the girl. "You like songs?"

Her already-big eyes widened and she nodded.

"Well then, scoot on up here beside me and I'll see can't I remember one."

She eased forward like she was afraid she might knock something over and slid up onto the bench, leaving a fair gap between them. Hoyt settled deeper into his own chair and laced his hands across his belly as though ready for a show.

Colman made a to-do about scratching his chin, then scratching his head. "Now, I know I have some songs stuck up here somewhere." He tilted his head and thumped it with the heel of his hand until Emmaline giggled. "Boy howdy, I think I just knocked one loose."

The little girl sidled closer.

Colman glanced at Hoyt. "You know 'Leaning on the Everlasting Arms'?"

Hoyt grinned. "Yes sir, but you're on your own with this one."

Colman mock-frowned and cleared his throat more than he needed to. Once he saw Emmaline was leaning toward him with eyes wide and mouth open, he began.

"What a fellowship, what a joy divine,
Leaning on the everlasting arms."

He took a breath and realized another voice had joined in with his.

"What a blessedness, what a peace is mine,
Leaning on the everlasting arms."

It was Ivy, and her voice was like a burst of birdsong after the passing of a storm. It was all he could do to keep on singing when he wanted to just stop and listen to her alone.

"Leaning, leaning, safe and secure from all alarms,
Leaning, leaning, leaning on the everlasting arms."

Ivy moved toward them, her pure soprano blending with his baritone like they'd sung together a hundred times. Emmaline clapped her hands, hopped off the bench, and began dancing.

"What have I to dread, what have I to fear,
Leaning on the everlasting arms;

I have blessed peace with my Lord so near,
Leaning on the everlasting arms."

After another rousing chorus that even Hoyt joined with a tolerable bass, they all clapped and laughed together. In spite of his lingering illness, Colman couldn't remember the last time he'd felt this fine. For a moment, he had the notion that passing through the mountain and coming out on the other side might have been an odd sort of rebirth for him.

Emmaline spun until her little skirt flew around her and flung herself into his legs, wrapping her arms around his calves and looking up with luminous brown eyes, her curls going every whichaway. She didn't speak, but her expression told him all he needed to know. And seeing the delight in this child's eyes made everything he'd been through feel as if it had been worth it just to get here.

Then he looked up and saw Serepta McLean watching them like a hawk watches a mouse. His gut tightened, and the feeling of peace fled.

She'd arrived in time to see the child dancing while the adults sang that ridiculous song. She'd heard those words in the church her mother dragged her to. Safe and secure indeed. No one in that blasted church had kept her safe or secure. Least of all her own mother.

Colman Harpe looked up and met her eyes. She expected to see something like anger or maybe even fear, but in that moment he looked mostly pleased. Happy even. Like singing a silly song about everlasting arms with a child was all the satisfaction he needed.

But then his expression changed. What had been open and transparent grew shuttered and cold. The thought that his expression was like looking into a mirror flitted through her mind, but she chased it away.

"Emmaline. Time to go home," she said.

The child danced toward her, curls bouncing. She grasped Serepta's hand and tugged. "Sing!"

Serepta gaped at her. Of course she wouldn't sing. Oh, but to be asked. Her mind jumped back to a time when she was first married and so glad to be free from her father that she had, indeed, sung. She'd been hanging Eli's britches on the line after washing them with her own two hands. She couldn't remember what she'd been singing—not a hymn surely—only that she'd felt freer than ever before in her life.

"My little warbler," Eli said, suddenly appearing on the far side of the clothesline.

She'd startled and stopped singing, but the look in his eyes had been so gentle—admiring even. She wasn't little and yet she thought maybe her voice was bird-sweet. Not a lilting soprano but rather a husky alto that must have lit a fire in her husband. He'd claimed her, and for once she simply let him.

"I don't sing," she said to the child, whose eyes quickly dimmed.

She bent low, pulled Emmaline's dark hair back from her seashell ear, and whispered, "At least not for just anyone."

Emmaline giggled and clapped her hands, and although she tried not to, Serepta smiled. She recovered quickly, however, and cast a baleful look at the adults in the room. She finally settled her gaze on Hoyt. "I hear Mack and his men came to see you."

Hoyt looked back at her, expression blank.

"Or did I hear amiss?"

"Oh, I seen him," Hoyt said. "But he didn't have much of use to say."

"Oh?" She raised her brows, inviting Hoyt to continue.

"You can 'oh' me all you want, missus, but if you've got a question, you'll need to ask it outright."

"Grandpa, Mrs. McLean is our guest." Ivy's voice was gentle but firm.

"I don't have a question exactly. I just want to be clear where your loyalties lie if Emmaline is going to continue visiting here."

"I thought Ivy was doing you the favor with that one," Hoyt said.

Serepta snorted. She almost admired the old man. And in a way, it was refreshing to be sassed.

"There aren't many who would leave a child with her." She ignored the look of pain that flashed across Ivy's face. It was no more than the truth, and they all knew it. "I see no reason not to speak plainly."

Hoyt crossed his arms and looked thunder at her. Emmaline crowded closer, seeming to sense the tension.

"You have a Harpe staying under your roof." She looked Colman in the eye while Ivy laid a hand on his shoulder. "If you plan to support his family in avenging themselves upon my son, I'll have to take countermeasures."

Hoyt slapped his hands on the arms of his chair and stood. "If you've come here to insult and threaten—"

"Grandpa." Ivy's voice rang loud and clear. "If you'll allow me to speak?"

The old man nodded and slowly sank back into his chair. Colman looked like he was sinking lower in his own chair, his complexion gone gray and greasy. Maybe he was sicker than she realized.

"Serepta, if you fear my grandfather and I are planning to take sides in whatever disagreement is current between your kin and the Harpe family, I can tell you exactly whose side we're on." She paused. "Mercy."

Serepta blinked and let her fingers tangle in Emmaline's soft hair as she puzzled over what Ivy meant.

Ivy sighed and took a step closer, reaching out to brush Serepta's sleeve—the gentlest whisper of a touch. "What I mean is we intend to care for anyone and everyone who needs our help. Whether that's a man with the gripe"—she glanced at Colman—"a child in need of care and consolation"—she smiled at Emmaline—"or anyone else in need of understanding."

Serepta felt as though the hot air building inside her chest had cooled and escaped. She felt empty and strangely alone, even here in the presence of others.

"Excellent," she snapped. "I wanted to make sure we understood each other." Then she took Emmaline's hand and returned to her car, grateful she was driving since Ivy's answer had left her feeling more out of control than she had in a long, long time.

chapter
thirteen

"That woman didn't understand your meaning one bit," Hoyt said. "And Colman here is about to fall out of his chair."

Colman did think he might slide on down to the floor. It seemed like the world would be steadier and firmer there.

"Oh my stars!" exclaimed Ivy. "You'd best lie down."

Colman nodded and let her help him to his pallet. He'd wanted to take Serepta McLean down a peg or two more than anything, but every time he'd thought to open his mouth, the notion that he'd lose his lunch if he did stopped him.

He closed his eyes and tried not to focus on the cramping pain in his gut. Ivy smoothed his hair back from his forehead, and he was thrust back in time to his mother's cool hand on his fevered brow.

"Why haven't I recovered?" he asked, almost afraid she might tell him.

Ivy's hand left his head, and he felt bereft. But she returned quickly with a chipped teacup.

"I made this yesterday, in case you should need it." She held his head, which helped him to swallow the liquid in the cup. Its bitterness was masked by the addition of sweet honey.

"What is it? Will it end this misery?"

"A tea from hollyhock root. It helps with . . . bowel issues." She pinked, but Colman couldn't even summon the strength to feel embarrassed.

The roiling in his guts eased, and he breathed long and deep. When would he be fully restored? He'd thought the worst of his problems at an end once he escaped the cavern and determined to do what God wanted. Yet this lingering illness wore him down and stole his determination.

"You didn't mention seeing Mack McLean." Ivy turned from Colman to her grandfather. "Either of you."

"Didn't want to worry you," Colman muttered. "Nothing much happened anyhow."

Hoyt barked with laughter. "It was a sight, but not one for your tender eyes."

Colman felt a wave of heat wash his cheeks.

"This young feller stood his ground like a true man of faith," Hoyt said.

Ivy looked at him as though taking his measure, her pale face serious. He realized he wanted to meet her expectation, whatever it was.

"I'm not happy about my cousin dying," he said, propping up on one elbow so he didn't feel quite so much like an invalid. "But I'm supposed to turn the other cheek, and I mean to do it if I can." His speech made him feel even better than the bitter tea Ivy had given him.

"I reckon he means it, too," said Hoyt. "Leastways he stood up to 'em like a man of integrity would. Although he might have chosen a different outfit given the chance."

Colman cast a baleful look at Hoyt, who began to snicker. The humor of the situation didn't escape Colman, and he soon found himself chuckling along with him.

Ivy looked mystified, then finally broke into a radiant smile of her own. "I don't quite understand what you two are laughing about, but I'm glad being braced by a member of the McLean family can tickle your funny bone."

"It sure does," said Hoyt. "Especially when a man finds himself exposed for all the world to see."

After several days of rest and a steady diet of Ivy's tonics, Colman thought he might be able to venture into town and get the lay of the land. If he was going to preach to these people, he would need a time and a place to do it.

After breakfast he set out for Hinton but hadn't gone even a mile on foot when he realized there was a steady flow of traffic turning onto a lane up ahead. And since sweat was beading his brow and his feet felt like lead in spite of the comfortable spring weather, he decided he might ought to see what the hubbub was about rather than walking all the way to town.

As he approached a plain house, he saw a laughing group of women circled up underneath dogwood trees fluttering with pink and white blossoms. He approached the cluster of women, forcing what he hoped was a confident smile. Some of the ladies were mending clothes while others sifted through a basket of jars with what looked like dried twigs and leaves inside them. He thought he recognized the basket from Ivy's cottage.

"Good day, ladies. I hope I'm not intruding."

An older woman with gray hair twisted behind her head stood and considered him. "You that feller from over Thurmond way what got lost in the caves?"

Colman felt his smile slip. "That would be me. I'm a

preacher. I aim to share the Good News with folks wherever I can."

The woman grunted. "A preacher and a Harpe too, the way I heard it."

"Yes, ma'am."

She eyed him from the crown of his head to the toe of his boot. "You look too puny to cause trouble, and I ain't never heard nothing bad about you in particular. I guess if Hoyt hasn't sent you packing, you must be alright. Come sit a spell if'n you ain't too proud to mingle with womenfolk. I'm Lena McLean."

He ambled over and sat down on a chunk of wood destined to be chopped into pieces for the stove. "Ladies," he greeted.

They nodded and smiled. They ranged in age from young mothers to grannies.

"Preacher, is it?" Lena settled in a ladder-back chair, a gleam in her eye. "Well now, my girl Nell was just pondering a question you might could help us with."

Colman felt his pulse quicken. So they wanted to test his Bible knowledge. Well, he'd read the Good Book enough times, he hoped he could satisfy them.

Nell, a pretty young woman with golden hair, blushed and focused on the child's shirt she was mending. "I've just been wondering where Cain got his wife."

Colman brightened. He could answer this one, although not everyone liked the answer. "Well, after Cain murdered his brother, Abel, God made him a fugitive and a vagabond, and he ran off to the land of Nod to the east." He leaned forward, bracing his elbows on his knees. "Now, the Bible doesn't name every child Adam and Eve brought into the world. It just says that Adam 'begat sons and daughters.'

And it tells us those sons and daughters begat children of their own. So, Cain's wife had to be one of them—likely a niece or a cousin."

Lena snorted. "Or a sister for that matter."

Colman grinned. "Or a sister. That notion doesn't always sit so well."

"Hunh. Guess they weren't as particular back then," she said.

"Nor did they have as many suitors to choose from," added Nell. "Not that there's a pile of 'em around here."

"Nonetheless, if you read Genesis, you'll find there was plenty of begetting going on," said another gray-haired lady, sparking a wave of blushes that might have even washed over Colman's cheeks.

From there, the conversation turned to pending nuptials in their own part of the world, much to Colman's relief. He sat back, leaning against the trunk of a tree and letting the easy conversation of the women wash over him. From weddings, their conversation moved to children, and then to the herbs and roots in the basket that had, indeed, come from Ivy.

"Why isn't she here?" Colman asked. Heads snapped his direction. He wondered if they'd forgotten about him.

Nell rushed to answer. "She just sends her herbs and such for us to pick through. We leave our payment in the basket and send it back."

Colman furrowed his brow. That was no answer.

Lena grimaced and folded her knitting into a sack. "I know you can see she ain't like other women. You being a preacher and all, surely you know it's best not to mix the races. That's what got Israel in trouble over in the land of Canaan. Ivy's a good girl and a dab-hand at cures, but it's best she not mix with folks overmuch." She looked around the group and lowered her voice as the women leaned in of one accord. "Word is her daddy was one of them moon-eyed people. That's why she can't stand the light."

Colman forced his eyebrows back down. He'd heard stories about a race of small, pale people with big blue eyes who'd been run out of western North Carolina and fled all the way to West Virginia, but he'd never seen one. He was torn between calling the story about Ivy utter nonsense and wondering if there might not be some truth in it. She surely was different from anyone he'd met before. Still, he felt the urge to defend her.

"Be that as it may, I suppose the thing to do is to love your neighbor no matter what she looks like."

Nell piped up. "Oh, we love her fine. She's sweet as she can be." She lowered her voice. "We just can't risk her around the children, being as she's marked and all."

Lena nodded. "That's right. Children are too tender and innocent to defend themselves. Especially wee babes. Ivy may be alright, but it's not worth the risk."

While Colman felt uncomfortable with the conversation, he didn't want to upset the apple cart with this being his first time talking to these folks. He'd ponder what to say and save it up for the next time. Best not to speak in haste and repent at leisure.

"Dogwood tea," a woman said, leaping to her feet and touching a flowery branch. She spoke to the woman to her right. "Ivy says it's good for easing sore muscles if you use it externally. But taken by mouth, it can break a fever. I just remembered. Try that for Avery next time he takes a fever." She snapped off a flower and resumed her seat, examining the creamy petals.

"Can I see that?" Colman asked, seeing a way out of the conversation about Ivy.

She nodded and handed him the flower. He looked at it closely, remembering what his grandmother told him when he was a boy. "I guess you all know the legend of the dogwood?"

All eyes turned to him with expectant looks. He supposed at least some of them knew the legend but didn't want to get in the way of hearing a good story. He smiled.

"Dogwood trees used to grow big as oaks," he began. "As a matter of fact, they were so big and strong and had such good wood, the Romans used one to make the cross they crucified Jesus on." The ladies were still now, almost reverent in their attention. "But after His resurrection, Jesus took pity on the tree and said that never again would it be used for such a purpose. From that day to this, dogwoods don't get much bigger than this one here." He stood and patted the trunk he could easily circle with both hands. "And this"—he held up the flower—"is shaped like a cross with two short petals and two long. And at the tip of each petal is a nail scar." He showed them the crimped pink-stained petals. "While in the center rests a crown of thorns. I guess, if we take the time to look around, reminders of God's gifts and graces are all around us, just waiting for someone to notice them."

A gentle breeze wafted through the trees and set the branches of the dogwood to stirring as if in approval. Colman looked around the group and saw smiles softening faces that likely saw more than their share of grief as the women struggled to raise families and support their husbands in this hardscrabble mountain land.

Nell dimpled at him. "That's the nicest sermon I've heard from a preacher in a long time."

Colman felt a surge of pride and noticed Nell had soft brown eyes to go with her golden hair. He looked through the branches of the tree to the cloud-dotted sky beyond and thought maybe it was the nicest sermon he'd preached ever.

Harrison Ash was late. Serepta drummed her fingers, caught herself, and moved to touch her ever-present pearls instead. Thurmond's police chief was supposed to have arrived twenty minutes earlier, and she was eager to get this meeting over with. She started to open the drawer holding her cashbox but stopped. She knew perfectly well the money was there. No need to fuss about.

She blamed Colman Harpe for her agitation. He was still hanging around with the Gordons, and word had it he'd begun to preach. She guessed that wasn't the worst thing he could do, but she didn't like it all the same. Made it seem like he was settling in, getting comfortable. It was one thing to let a tired, toothless bear pass through her territory. It was quite another to let him stick around and grow new teeth. She would have to do some investigating to see if Colman was on the mend—to see if he might prove a threat after all.

Charlie appeared in the doorway of her office. "He's here."

"Alright. Sit him down in the entry for five minutes before you bring him in."

Charlie winked. "He's already been sitting there ten."

She wanted to frown at the liberty Charlie was taking. Instead, she decided to keep her expression blank. "You're awfully sure of yourself."

He smiled and eased back down the hall. Moments later, Harrison stomped into her office like a grizzly bear wearing a Stetson hat. She thought the hat—not to mention his notched pistol—unnecessary embellishments, but the large man enjoyed his cowboy swagger. At well over six feet and built like a bull, he dwarfed Serepta. And yet they both knew she held the power in their relationship.

"How's Mrs. Ash?" Serepta asked.

His forward momentum came to a stop, and he narrowed his eyes. "The same," he growled.

"I suppose you haven't changed your mind about taking her to task."

"Is that why you sent for me? To remind me you know I was the one she was trying to shoot that night?"

Serepta let her lips curve. "Perhaps if you had wed a woman closer to your own age, she would be easier to manage."

Harrison took his hat off and slapped it against his thigh. "State your business, woman."

"Several shipments of liquor have been taken. If I can't trust you to protect my merchandise, what am I paying you for?"

Harrison dropped his bulk into a chair. "Where'd they go missing?"

"On the way to Cincinnati. I know perfectly well that Webb Harpe intercepted one shipment, but there have been two others since." She opened a desk drawer. "I need you to do more than look the other way. I need you to help me learn who is stealing from me."

Harrison ran a hand through his thick, dark hair and let one side of his mouth lift. "Whoever it is must be a fool to trifle with you. I might have notches in my pistol"—he ran a thumb over the butt of his gun—"but you . . . you'll do worse than kill a man." He stood and jammed his hat back on. "I'll see what I can find out."

Serepta withdrew several bills from her cashbox. She slid them across the desk. "That would be most appreciated." She gave a catlike smile. "Tell Mary I send my best."

Harrison grunted. "You can be sure I will. I may not be the sharpest stick in the forest, but I know she didn't decide not to take another shot at me on her own."

"Isn't it fortunate you're more valuable to me alive?"

Harrison barked a laugh, tipped his hat, and left the room. Even as she heard the front door close, Charlie stepped back inside her office and set a lunch tray on the corner of her desk. She leaned back and sighed. "There are too many unknowns in my world at the moment."

Charlie stood waiting for her to continue.

"Between merchandise being taken and Colman Harpe setting up camp in my territory, I feel uneasy."

"Might be time to give up either the bootlegging or the feuding," Charlie said. "Maybe both."

This time she didn't hold back, but frowned at him. "That's a little more sass than I expect, even from you."

Charlie let out a sigh. "I just hate to see you all eat up worrying about this."

"The world is filled with worry, and I prefer to choose my share." She picked up half of an egg salad sandwich and nibbled a corner. "When you take Emmaline to Ivy's, do you see much of Colman Harpe?"

Charlie scratched his chin. "He's often about the place."

"Does he look well?"

"He looks better than he did. But I'd say he's still puny."

"I hear he's been preaching to folks even so."

Charlie's face cracked into what might be called a smile, which was a rarity for him. "Not preaching exactly. I guess what he's doing is storytelling. Gets up the Bible stories like they're mountain yarns. Makes Noah sound as though he lives the next holler over. And the way he tells it, ole Goliath is a corn-fed mountain man what stands two feet taller than anyone else around." He chuckled, dry and rusty. "Even Jonah's tale turns into a fishing story gone sideways."

Serepta pressed her lips together, even though she knew it made them look thinner and harder. Or maybe because she knew that. She'd given up caring if others thought her pretty a long time ago, and Charlie . . . well, he saw her in a way no one else did.

"Where is he telling these *stories*?" She injected as much disdain into the word as she could summon.

"Mostly in Lena McLean's garden. You know how the women gather there sometimes with their mending."

"It's just the women and children, then?"

"Seems like." Charlie pushed her tray closer, probably worried that she hadn't been eating enough lately.

Serepta took another bite of her sandwich to appease him. "I suppose that's alright for now. So long as he's not stirring folks up."

Charlie looked almost pleased. He reached out and touched her wrist, a light caress, then turned and left the room. Serepta laid the sandwich back down. The few bites she'd taken felt like lead in her stomach. What with her worries over Jake, the threats from Webb Harpe, missing liquor, and now wondering what Colman was up to, her appetite had faded.

She'd always considered herself a shrewd woman of business, so this state of affairs was doubly frustrating. And she really didn't have anyone she could discuss it with. Charlie was the only man she trusted, and his solution was for her to play it safe. She should be able to take one of her sons into her confidence, but Jake was a hotheaded fool, and Mack—

well, if he knew money was getting short, he'd push even harder to sell out the liquor business.

No, she would have to solve this problem on her own. She sipped from the glass of tea Charlie had included on her tray. It was thin and watery with the bits of ice chipped into it long melted.

She looked to the door as she heard a car pull up, followed by a door slamming and the patter of little feet across the wide front porch. She tucked two cookies from her tray into her pocket and went to meet Emmaline, welcoming the interruption.

chapter
fourteen

Colman exited the shed after yet another soak in water that smelled of rotten eggs. He hardly noticed the smell anymore, which worried him. What if he smelled that bad when he got back to Ivy's place? Of course, she was the one who "prescribed" his taking the waters every other day, so she could hardly complain that he stunk as a result.

He still had sick spells, although he told himself they weren't happening as often and weren't as bad. Even so, when he looked in a mirror he thought his face was leaner than it had been, and he longed to look hale and hearty again. He walked the short distance back to the Gordon cottage at a brisk pace, hoping the exercise would improve his health. By the time he drew near, he was panting and well aware that he was still a long way from fit. He paused to catch his breath, not wanting Ivy to see him struggling.

As he waited for his heart to slow and his breathing to steady, he realized there was an aroma much nicer than sulphur in the air. He closed his eyes and inhaled, drawing the sweetness in. Looking around, he spotted a white lilac bush, its blossoms nodding in the breeze. He whipped out his pocketknife and cut a bouquet of them.

The look on Ivy's face as he stepped into the cottage and presented her with the flowers pinched his heart. He wondered if a man had ever carried her flowers before. He supposed her otherworldliness might keep suitors away. Fools.

"Thought they might cover up any sulphur smell I carried back with me," he said with a half smile.

Ivy buried her nose in the blooms, inhaling the pleasant aroma. The paleness of the petals brought out a hint of color in her cheeks—or perhaps it was emotion as she turned those eyes like the sky toward him.

"And white at that." A slow smile spread across her face. She gave him a gentle hug and kissed his clean-shaven jaw, making his heart flip.

"The ladies sent word for you," Ivy said as she arranged the flowers in a crock.

Colman settled in a rocking chair and stretched his tired legs out in front of him. "About what?"

"Your preaching."

Colman laughed. "I haven't started it yet and I'm thinking I'd better get to it soon before God decides I need more spurring on."

"But your stories—that's the preaching they mean."

"Stories? Those are just Bible tales told with a little local color. I wouldn't call that preaching."

Ivy began preparing the evening meal of trout that Colman and Hoyt had caught early that morning. "I'd call it the best kind," she said. "The ladies have enjoyed it so much that they want to get up a brush arbor and bring their men around of an evening."

Colman sat up straighter. "I can't sit around telling stories to a bunch of people expecting a sermon."

"But what if they were expecting stories?" She rolled the

trout in cornmeal and set an iron skillet with a spoonful of bacon fat in it to heating on the wood stove.

"I'd say that was an odd thing to expect from a preacher."

"And I'd say it's a fine way to share God's own Good News without boring people to tears."

Colman's mouth watered as the trout hit the hot grease and sent up a nutty aroma. "Are you saying my preaching is boring?"

"Not your preaching." She cast him a coy glance over her shoulder. "Your preaching sounds an awful lot like tall tales told around the fire of an evening."

Colman laughed. "You're telling me those ladies want me to tell their husbands tales?"

"I am." She deftly flipped the fish in the skillet, then moved to toss some gathered herbs and greens with vinegar and a little fat for a kilt salad.

"I might could give it a try then."

"Wonderful," she said, and the joy on her face made him certain he was doing the right thing. "Now, go see if you can run Grandpa to ground, and we'll eat up this good fish you caught."

The crowd gathering under the brush arbor thrown up by Hoyt and some other men took Colman by surprise. It was midafternoon on the fifth of June. They'd chosen a spot in a stand of saplings that meant they could use some of the trees where they stood to support crosspieces for the makeshift roof. Colman closed his eyes and inhaled the sharp, bright scent of pine from the boughs laid across the top of the arbor. Opening his eyes, he noticed the way sunlight filtered through the dense branches, casting a green-gold light on the people clustered beneath it—most of them McLeans or kin to them. This should be an enemy camp for someone named Harpe.

Colman knew full well that folks expected brush arbor meetings to last for days, if not weeks. He wondered if he had the stamina—or the words—to give them what they wanted. Especially considering that what he wanted was to blame them for the death of his cousin, as well as the suffering of his family. He'd spent the morning sitting outside the cottage with a pencil and paper, trying to think what God expected him to say. Even now he clutched the smudged paper in his hand. He read over it with dismay. Nothing seemed worth speaking aloud to these people.

Ivy materialized at his elbow, wearing gloves and her hat—gauzy fabric draped over the brim to further shade her neck and shoulder. "Are you nervous?"

Colman swallowed what felt like a frog in his throat. "Maybe some." He hated to admit his weakness but couldn't bring himself to lie to her. She'd seen him plenty weak.

"Tell them a story," she said. "The Spirit will lead you from there." Then she walked away from the crowd and stood in deeper shade beneath an oak tree. Colman realized folks were watching her with looks that ranged from curiosity to suspicion. He didn't like it but guessed now wasn't the time to say anything.

Colman crumpled the paper in his hand and shoved it in a pocket. Tell a story. He licked his dry lips and stepped up to a post with a split log laid across it for a pulpit.

"How's about we get started with a prayer and some singing?" he said to the gathering.

Heads nodded here and there, with a few eager faces looking at him with expectation and others with suspicion. He bowed his head and prayed a simple, short prayer asking God to bless them and to guide his words. It was the most heartfelt prayer he'd sent up since he begged God for his life in the cavern.

"Alright then, who wants to lead us off with a song?"

Colman figured if no one volunteered, he'd jump in with "Shall We Gather at the River." Then with hardly a glance at the crowd, Ivy stepped forward, opened her mouth, and began singing in her soft, lilting soprano.

"O they tell me of a home far beyond the skies,
O they tell me of a home far away;
O they tell me of a home where no storm clouds rise,
O they tell me of an unclouded day."

Colman felt tears rise behind his eyes and blinked hard to fight them back. The people gathered in the shade of the arbor seemed spellbound, listening, until Hoyt joined in on the chorus.

"O the land of cloudless day,
O the land of an unclouded sky;
O they tell me of a home where no storm clouds rise,
O they tell me of an unclouded day."

By the time they'd finished the chorus, dozens of voices had joined in and were singing in harmony. Colman added his own, though he wanted nothing more than to listen to the music of the words pouring out of the mouths of people he still thought of as his enemies.

They finished the song and then sang two more. By the time they were done, Colman had a story in mind to share with everyone.

"Over in White Sulphur Springs, there was a farmer who had twelve strapping sons. Ten were by his first wife and the last two by his second wife, who was the prettiest, sweetest thing you ever saw. And maybe because of that, the farmer loved those two least boys more than the first batch—especially the next to youngest, who was named Joe.

"Well, as you can imagine, boys being the way they are"—a chuckle ran through the crowd—"the older ones got jealous and decided they'd teach Joe a lesson. But things got out of hand, and they ended up talking some gypsies into taking their little brother away with them as little more than a slave. . . ."

And so he told them the story of Joseph and his wayward brothers as if they lived in Fayette County. He told about Joe rotting in jail until he earned the jailer's trust, how he eventually made his way to the mayor's house, and how the mayor's wife tried to seduce him. He told about Joe getting to be deputy mayor in spite of all those troubles and how his brothers showed up one day needing help.

"Then Joe had 'em right where he wanted 'em," Colman said.

He could see folks leaning forward, some of the younger ones with their mouths hanging open. These people liked a good story, and Joseph's tale was one of the best.

"And you know what he did?" Colman leaned over the pulpit as though he had a secret to tell. "After he toyed with them awhile, he . . . forgave them."

Those who knew the story smiled like they were in on a joke, and the ones who didn't know it looked like he'd just tricked them.

"I know what some of you are thinking," Colman went on. "Why didn't that boy get his revenge? Why didn't he make his brothers suffer like he'd suffered? That'd be fair. But here's what ole Joe had to say: 'But as for you, ye thought evil against me; but God meant it unto good.'" He let that sink in for a minute. "Basically, Joe said his brothers had failed when they tried to do something bad to him because God's plan was bigger and better than theirs. God took the bad that was in their hearts and turned it into something better than even Joe himself could have dreamed."

Colman settled back on his heels. He was tired. He'd been storytelling for a long time now. His throat felt dry and his legs shaky. Worst of all, his gut was telling him he might need to excuse himself before long. But he wasn't quite done. He looked to Ivy, whose expression was one of utter delight. He took a deep breath.

"You see, we can do all kinds of things to try and make our situations better or someone else's worse, but in the end, God's got us beat. Whatever His plan is, that's what's going to happen." He gripped the side of his makeshift pulpit. "Do you folks want to be at peace?"

Heads nodded, and a sprinkling of people voiced an amen.

"Do you want to feel joy?"

This time the amens were louder.

"Then stop fighting God," Colman said. He bowed his head, then raised it again. "It's like a fly trying to move an elephant. You might think you're making headway, but if you are, it's only because you and the elephant were already headed the same direction."

Colman wanted to sit down. A sick feeling rose to the back of his throat, but he swallowed it down. Ivy's expression changed, and he suspected she could see his discomfort. Hoyt moved to his side as if she'd sent him.

"Close with a song," he said.

"How's about we sing 'Have Thine Own Way'?" Colman said.

Ivy led off the singing as Colman eased to the side of the arbor and found a stump to rest his weary body upon.

"Have thine own way, Lord,
Have thine own way.
Thou art the potter I am the clay.
Mold me and make me after thy will
While I am waiting yielded and still."

As the song ended and Ivy began another, Colman watched in wonder. How had he come to be here? Was he like Joseph—carried along by bad choices and circumstances beyond his control to finally be in the spot God had intended all along? He shook his head. He'd do well to practice what he preached.

"What do you mean 'everyone's at the camp meeting'?" Serepta felt like her blood had gone hot all through her body. "What camp meeting?"

Charlie flinched. "Colman Harpe has been preaching since Wednesday afternoon. They threw up a brush arbor over there near the Gordons' place, and he's been drawing a bigger crowd every evening."

Serepta moved behind her broad desk and pressed her hands flat against the cool surface as though pressing down her anger. "So the rabble has gotten over their fear of Ivy Gordon, then? Send Jake in to me."

"Yes'm." Charlie ducked out like he was glad to go.

Serepta stared a hole in the ledger centered on her blotter, considering her options. Jake wandered in and slouched into a leather chair across from her. He didn't speak, but just looked at her the way he had when he'd been a boy and she deprived him of something he wanted.

"Who have you found to stow our shipments on the trains?"

Jake rolled his eyes. "Don't you think I've found anybody?"

"I'm assuming you have. Now I want to know *who*."

"Might be better if you didn't know. No one can make you tell what you don't know." He grinned, lazy and sly.

She stared until he shifted and straightened up. "Do you suppose anyone can make me tell something I don't want to share?"

"Could happen," he said, eyes downcast.

"Tell me who you've enlisted."

"Aw, it's some brakeman comes through here every other day. Willis, I think." He looked up and to the right. "No. Ellis. His name's Ellis."

Serepta counted to ten. "I don't suppose you know his last name. Or where he lives. Or if his allegiances might be split."

"Whatever that means," Jake said.

"Give this *Ellis's* information to Charlie. I have another job for you."

Jake came to attention. "I've been dealing with Ellis, and I guess I can keep it up just fine. There's no call to get your house . . . man involved."

Serepta wondered if keeping her rage bottled up might eventually do her harm. She longed to cut loose and rain her wrath down upon her eldest son. But not right now. Glancing down, she noticed that she'd balled her hands into fists until her knuckles turned white. She sat, flexed both hands, and folded them in front of her on the desk. "I need you to go to the camp meeting Colman Harpe is running over at Hoyt Gordon's place."

The change in conversation seemed to confuse Jake. "Camp meeting?"

"Yes, son. I realize you're not one for church, but I need to know what's happening over there."

"Ma, it's not like I'm scared or anything, but aren't those

Harpe men still hunting me? You sending me to a shootout at a camp meeting?"

Serepta longed to lay her head in her hands, except she wasn't about to let Jake see her exasperation. "Colman is the only member of the Harpe family there, and he seems to be under some mistaken impression that he's going to bring holy enlightenment to the McLeans. He told Mack he's here to preach, and now it would seem he's doing just that."

"So? What harm is there in sermonizing?"

Serepta shrugged. "Perhaps none. Then again, he wouldn't be the first preacher to wrap his personal agenda in pretty words from the Bible. I need you to go over there and tell me what he's up to. Take Mack if you want."

Jake rose to his feet as though it took a mighty effort. "And when did you think I'd find time to chase after this preacher?"

"This evening. I expect you to go this evening."

Jake gave her a disgusted look, but she knew he'd go regardless. He was lazy, insolent, and headstrong. But she'd also been teaching him to fear and obey her ever since he was a small child. Oh yes, he would do what she asked. Whether he would do it well . . . that was another matter.

chapter
fifteen

Colman wasn't sure he could keep this up much longer. He didn't know how he'd already done it for three days. More and more people kept coming. After telling Joseph's story, he'd told them about David and Goliath, Moses being found by Pharaoh's daughter, Joshua fighting the battle of Jericho, and Daniel in the lions' den. He hadn't even touched on the New Testament yet. He just got up in front of the crowd and told the stories he knew so well. And somehow they all ended up being a lesson on listening to and obeying God.

Ivy handed him a napkin with fried chicken and a cold biscuit on it. He'd talked all afternoon, but he supposed the people gathered here even now eating the dinners they'd carried from home expected him to keep going.

"I don't know what I've got left to tell them," he said to Ivy. "Maybe it's time the people went on home."

Ivy sat next to him. "Let's bless this food and then we can talk," she said. Bowing her head, she took his hand, the texture of her glove an unexpected softness. "Father, thank you for sending Colman to share your Word in a way that seems friendly and familiar to all these people. Please continue to use him to accomplish your good work here on earth until we join you in heaven. In Jesus' name, amen.'"

Colman tried to pay attention to the prayer rather than the bone-deep weariness dragging him down. She released his hand and removed a glove so she could eat. He followed suit, finding the crunch of the chicken and rich, buttered biscuit comforting.

"Do you really want me to send everyone home?" she asked.

Colman let his shoulders sag. "It's not that I want them to go, it's just I don't think there's any reason for them to stay."

"They're staying to hear the Word of God."

Colman set down his spoon. "They're here for entertainment. I talk about the Bible like it's a bunch of tall tales. I'm probably doing those people a disservice. It's a wonder God hasn't struck me down."

Ivy laughed. It was like someone tapping a spoon against a crystal goblet—pure and clear. When her face lit up that way, her eerie otherworldliness fled.

"Why's that funny?" he asked.

Ivy turned those still-water eyes on him. "Because you have no idea what a gift you're giving to hungry people." She wiped her fingers on a napkin. "No, starving people. All the McLeans have known of the Harpes for generations is hatred. You've brought them truth from an unexpected source. I imagine it's like it was for you when you first saw the light after being in the cave so long." She laid a gentle hand on his arm. "At first it was overwhelming—too bright, too vivid. But when your eyes were ready, you could see things about the light that weren't obvious before. You noticed the beauty and the wonder because you'd been deprived of it."

She picked up her chicken again. "These people have been

robbed of love and peace and God's own joy thanks to a feud hardly anyone understands. You've reminded them that there's more to their world than hating the Harpes."

Colman could hardly breathe. "How'd you know what it was like when I came out of the cave?"

She shrugged and smiled. "I could hear it in your voice. I could feel it in your touch." She looked deep into his eyes, and he shuddered. "I've lived without certain things now and again and supposed it must be the same for you robbed of light, of human contact."

Colman vowed he would not cry. Not here, not in front of this remarkable woman who seemed to hear his heart the way he could hear a flaw in the wheel of a train when he tapped it.

"But I didn't even want to come." His voice was hoarse, rough with emotion.

"Sometimes God does His best work with unwilling tools. I think He does it to prove it's Him and not us."

Colman nodded. "Alright then." Maybe he could find something to say after all.

———

Colman stepped up to the pulpit one more time. He was weary all the way to his bones. But then he spotted Ivy sitting in the front row. She'd come out of the shadows to sit among the people. Rubbing a hand across his face, he felt the way his cheekbones had sharpened, his face all jagged planes since he'd taken ill. He guessed these folks weren't coming because of his good looks.

"Let's pray," he began.

As he lifted words up to God, he felt something like power flowing into him, and every sound of nature rang as distinct—from the rushing of a creek in the distance, to dogs barking up the holler, to spring peepers blending their voices with the sigh of the evening breeze. God's chorus of creation.

"Amen," he said. "Ivy, will you lead us in a song?" He hoped to set an example for these folks by continuing to include her.

She smiled, and it was as though she knew just what he needed as she began singing "Revive Us Again." Colman fought tears as the people sang the second verse.

"We praise thee, O God, for the Son of thy love,
For Jesus who died and is now gone above."

He lifted his face to the sky so the people wouldn't see the emotion washing over him.

"Hallelujah thine the glory, Hallelujah amen.
Hallelujah thine the glory, Revive us again."

During previous meetings, they'd sung three or four songs before getting started, but tonight, as the last notes of the song rose to heaven, Ivy sat down and shifted her attention to him.

Colman inhaled long and slow. He had no idea what he was about to say; he just started speaking.

"Once upon a time there was a man who lived in the prettiest place you can think of. He had all he wanted to eat, good work to do that wasn't too hard, and lots of friendly animals to keep him company." He smiled and looked around at the people gathered before him. "But as perfect as everything was, there was just one thing missing. He was lonesome. A hound dog can be real good company, but he doesn't usually have much to say. And a good horse can be a big help around the farm, but he's not much for sitting close beside you near the fire of an evening."

A few folks smiled and looked tickled.

"So God looked down at that man and said, 'It's not good

for a feller to be alone. I'll make a helpmeet for him.' He put the man to sleep and did a little operation, taking out just one rib." Colman held up one finger. "And from that one rib he made a woman, which just goes to show God's a whole lot smarter than the rest of us put together."

The audience chuckled, and Colman saw a few men wrap arms around the women sitting close beside them.

"When that feller woke up, he had about the best surprise of his life. And he called that woman 'bone of my bones and flesh of my flesh.'" Colman paused. "I wish I could tell you they lived happily ever after, but I think most of you know what happened next." Faces turned sad, and Colman figured he had them right where he wanted them.

"But I'll tell you this. Even after Adam and Eve got kicked out of the most perfect place ever created, they still had each other. If I remember right, Adam lived more than nine hundred years. I imagine having a wife by his side all that time was a comfort." He looked from face to face, feeling a catch in his chest when his gaze fell on Ivy, still apart from the rest. "I guess what I'm telling you is that life is hard, and being sinners, we're bound to mess it up. But when you have each other—whether a husband, a wife, children, or good friends—you don't have to fight the battle alone. Seems to me God did a fine thing giving us people to love. Might be we need to do more of that."

As though the breeze carried words, Scripture verses came to Colman. "'A new commandment I give unto you, that ye love one another; as I have loved you, that ye also love one another. By this shall all men know that ye are my disciples, if ye have love one to another.'"

He bowed his head and felt the exhaustion return, as if it had been waiting until he finished speaking. He wanted to sink to the ground right there and then, but first he had to extricate himself from this meeting.

Ivy began singing like she knew he needed rescuing. The entire congregation came to its feet and sang along. Colman didn't even notice what the hymn was, but instead eased to the side of the arbor where Hoyt stood, shoulder ready for him to lean on. As he slipped away, he looked back and saw that not everyone was standing and singing. There, in the back row, sat Jake McLean, legs stretched out and feet crossed like he was relaxing at home. He watched Colman the way a fox might watch a chicken. A shiver ran up Colman's spine, but he shook it off. He lifted two fingers to his forehead and saluted Jake, who nodded in return.

"He's got 'em eating out of his hand," Jake said. "Although he looks like a worn-out scarecrow. Seems like the last time I seen him, he was fit as a fiddle. But these days you might cut your hand if you slapped him, his face is so bony-sharp."

Serepta wanted to pace the room, but she refused to let her nervous energy show. "Sit up straight," she snapped at her son, who lounged in the leather chair facing her desk.

Jake obeyed, likely without thinking about it. If he'd thought about it, he would have refused just to be contrary.

"How many are coming to these meetings?"

Jake scratched his chin. "Looked to me like a hundred or so. Talked to some folks who'd been there before, and they said it's more every night."

"And how many are McLeans?"

Jake shrugged. "Most of 'em, I guess. Either McLeans or kin to us."

Serepta circled the desk, unable to remain still another second. She stood over Jake, who shifted as if trying to put some distance between them. "Would you say he's preaching *peace*?" She enunciated that last word with great care.

"Peace? He yammered on about Adam and Eve—although I didn't get that's who he meant right off. Then there was a bunch of mumbo jumbo about people loving each other." Jake got a gleam in his eye. "'Course, that Ivy Gordon makes me think we could all use a little more loving. She might look spooky, but the shape of her—"

Serepta struck him. The sound of her palm against his cheek echoed through the room and left a terrible stillness in its wake.

Jake didn't move for several beats. Then he stood as though it required much thought. He looked down at Serepta, the mark of her hand on his face. "Ma, I ain't no child to be smacked. I think it'd be best if you didn't do that again."

Serepta felt shaken. She'd whipped Jake when he was a misbehaving boy, but it had been years since she'd laid a finger on him. She walked back behind her desk and sat before her quivering legs gave her away. An apology rose to her lips, but looking at Jake's stony face told her he would take advantage if she showed her soft underbelly.

"Colman Harpe must be stopped," she said.

Jake glared at her.

"I've left him alone up until now because he's been in Ivy Gordon's care, and she's never been part of the feud."

The hardness around Jake's eyes began to lessen. Serepta wished the angry outline of her hand would fade with it.

"I need Ivy to help with Emmaline," she continued, "and yet we can't let Colman continue preaching peace, love, and forgiveness. The rest of the Harpe clan will see our allowing it as weakness." She stretched her shoulders, trying to ease the tension in her neck where she fastened the clasp of her pearls each morning. "They may even have sent him to infiltrate and effectively neuter our cause."

Her word choice had Jake's attention now. His manly pride ran deep, and he wouldn't like her hint that he might be made to appear less of a man.

She tilted her head to one side. "Spread the word but do it with care—quietly. Let it be known that I want Colman's preaching to stop. And I'll be more than happy to handsomely reward the man who sees to it."

Now Jake looked downright pleased. "What if I was that man?"

"I won't say it shouldn't be you, but you already have a bull's-eye on your chest as far as Webb Harpe is concerned, so I'd advise you to look out for your own skin before you go chasing after someone else's."

He narrowed his eyes and nodded. "I'll get the word out, Ma, don't you worry."

"Excellent. I know you'll do a fine job." Her legs had stopped shaking, and the mark of her hand on her son's face had faded to a soft pink. "Just remember, Ivy Gordon must not know."

Jake nodded again, grinned, and left the room. Serepta watched him go, wondering if she'd trusted him with more than he could handle.

chapter
sixteen

"You might as well tear that brush arbor down." Colman lay on his pallet, shivering. "I've used up all the words I've got."

Ivy knelt beside him and bathed his face with water that smelled of flowers. "You have a fever."

"Well I'm freezing."

He knew he sounded testy, but he was tired of being sick. Tired of people expecting him to get up in front of them under that arbor. Tired of trying to do whatever it was God had sent him here to accomplish.

Ivy ran the scented rag over his face again. He closed his eyes and leaned into her hand. "Why do you keep taking care of me? I should have left a long time ago."

"You need care and I'm able to do it. I think it's my job—my calling maybe. I've been taking care of people for as long as I can remember." She dropped the cloth into a basin and sat back on her heels. "I took care of my mother when she was dying."

Colman opened his eyes and considered her sweet face. "That must have been hard."

"You'd think so, wouldn't you?" She gathered her supplies

and stood, moving to the table where she was making some sort of poultice. "It was the greatest blessing of my life. I was able to ease her final days." She returned, pushed him gently onto his back, and tucked the poultice inside his shirt. "And I got to be with her when she died."

Colman inhaled deeply. The poultice seemed to be un-knotting his insides in a way that let him relax in spite of his shivering. "You call that a blessing?"

"It was. She'd been so sick, so weak, but just at the end she opened her eyes and looked right at me. 'Do you see them, Ivy?' she asked. I looked all around but didn't see anything. Then she said she'd be waiting, and she was gone."

Colman didn't know what to say to that.

"The look in her eyes . . . well, whatever she was seeing, it was better than anything this world can offer. Although I was sorry to lose her, I was glad for her at the same time. And one day I'll see her again."

"How old were you?" Colman asked.

"Eleven."

"My mother's gone, too." Now, why had he told her that?

"What was she like?"

Colman shifted, the warmth of the poultice like having a kitten sleeping on his chest. "She was like a chorus of song-birds on the first day of spring."

Ivy laughed. "Well, she must have been wonderful then. Did she want you to be a preacher?"

"She did." Colman fell silent, and Ivy waited. "But I didn't move that direction until after she was gone. I've been aim-ing for a church of my own. I think that's what she would have wanted for me."

"I imagine she knows all about you. Do you think she'd be proud of your brush-arbor preaching?"

Colman smiled and relaxed deeper against his pillow. "You know how to persuade a fellow, don't you?"

Ivy laughed again, the prettiest sound Colman had heard since his own mother had laughed. "I just go where the Spirit leads me."

"Hunh. Guess maybe I'm not completely done preaching yet." He sighed. "But I think I might need a day or two off before we pick up again."

Hoyt entered the room in time to hear Colman's last statement. "You need a break? I reckon that can be arranged. I'll let folks know they need to come back next Friday evening, and you can preach at 'em all weekend. They ought to tend to their jobs and farms anyhow."

Colman wormed his shoulders deeper into his blankets and gave thanks for the reprieve. He only hoped he'd be feeling some better when Friday rolled around.

Emmaline had been fractious lately. She hadn't asked about her mother in over a week, and Serepta thought she was past the worst of her grief. But today the child was crying after her entire family. It was as though she'd finally come to the realization they were beyond her reach and she was powerless to do anything about it. Serepta could understand the frustration, but telling a four-year-old there was nothing to be done was useless.

"Don't want it," the child said, pushing her cup of milk away. "Want Papa."

Her abrupt movement spilled some of the milk on Serepta's freshly pressed slacks, and she had to force herself not to react. If it had been Jake or Mack doing that as a child, she would have whipped them, but she knew Emmaline was lashing out at something she couldn't see or touch.

"Milk will make you grow strong," she said, dabbing at the spill with a handkerchief.

"I am strong," Emmaline said, spreading her legs and squaring her shoulders in a bullish stance.

A smile quirked Serepta's lips. "So you are. But don't you want to be even stronger?"

"Why?"

Serepta stilled. Why indeed? "So that no one will take advantage of you. No one will make you do anything you would rather not. The stronger you are, the more control you will have."

Emmaline tilted her head. "Why?"

Serepta sighed. "Trust me." She lifted the silver cup and drank some of the milk. Emmaline crept closer and reached out a chubby hand. Serepta pressed the cup into it, and the child, with a last suspicious look, drank the contents down.

"There now. Don't you feel stronger?"

Emmaline squinted her eyes and leaned against Serepta's legs. The contact was weighty but in a pleasant way. It struck Serepta that this child trusted her when hardly anyone else did.

"No."

"Well, drinking all your milk is the first step toward stronger. Now, let's get ready for bed, because the second step is a good night's sleep."

Emmaline sighed as though resigning herself to the inevitable and dragged down the hall toward the room that had been outfitted for her. Serepta followed, pondering the truth of her own words. Good food and rest were important, though she'd been getting little enough of either in the past weeks. Charlie had been doing his best to see to her needs, but she wasn't hungry, and sleep remained elusive. The effects were clear when she looked in the mirror. Her dusky skin had taken on a grayish tinge, and her eyes—always startling—appeared larger. She'd even noticed that her expertly tailored clothing didn't fit quite as well.

She saw to Emmaline's bedtime preparations, helped her into bed, and turned to leave the room.

"Mommy prays with me."

"What's that you say?"

"My mommy prays with me." Emmaline scrambled from under the covers and knelt on the floor beside her bed. "You pray."

"I have nothing to say to God."

Emmaline turned luminous eyes on her—eyes that pierced the shell she'd wrapped around herself so many years ago. "Pray."

Serepta took a deep breath and let it out with care. She crossed the room and sat on the edge of the bed. "Go ahead."

Emmaline gave her a fierce look of disapproval. "Here," she said.

Serepta wetted her dry lips. She should refuse. Be on her way. But something in the orphan child's face drew her to kneel beside her on the floor. "Very well."

Emmaline folded her hands and squeezed her eyes shut. "Dear God, bless Mommy and Papa . . ." She went on to name her brothers and sisters, a few other family members Serepta didn't know existed, and a cow that must have provided the family with milk. Then there was a long pause. Serepta began to rise when Emmaline picked up again.

"And bless this mommy and Mr. Charlie and I want a puppy. Amen."

Serepta could no more stand at that moment than she could fly. This mommy? Did Emmaline mean her? Or might she mean Ivy?

"Now you."

She looked down at the child. "I already prayed in my mind."

Emmaline blew out a bit of impatient air. "You pray in your heart." But she must have been satisfied nonetheless, because she clambered up onto the bed and slipped under the covers. "Good night."

"Good night," Serepta whispered, and then she struggled to lever herself to a standing position. Slowly, she left the room, telling herself it didn't matter who Emmaline thought of as her mother.

Colman hadn't been completely alone since he was inside the mountain. And now, standing above a rhododendron thicket, watching water tumble precipitously over rocks and down the mountainside, he had to fight a moment of panic. Yes, he was alone, but only for the moment, and after all it was solitude he'd been seeking.

He just hadn't expected being alone to bite so deeply.

Glancing up at the sky, Colman squinted against the glare of the coming summer, grateful his eyes had recovered, even if the rest of his body had a ways to go. It was hot for June. His shirt stuck to his back after he struggled up the steep hillside. He wasn't strong enough for this yet, but he'd wanted a mountaintop experience. And slipping away from Ivy's doctoring and Hoyt's watchful eye seemed needful.

He sat on a rock outcropping and closed his eyes. The roar of the creek below filled his ears, but he knew if he gave it a moment, he'd hear much more. A crow's caw. The lowing of cattle farther down the valley. Distant footsteps of a man or maybe a deer. The rustling of chipmunks in the leaves. And hopefully, the voice of God.

But no—not that. It seemed he never heard from God when he wanted to. He laughed at himself, a scarecrow perched on a rock, waiting for a sign from heaven that would tell him what to do next. He knew better.

Breathing in deeply, Colman stretched his arms wide. He still had the notion he was supposed to be doing some proper preaching, and since he wasn't hearing any voice from the clouds, he guessed he'd have to take matters into his own hands. When they started the meetings up again, he'd leave off his stories and preach a real sermon. Maybe that one on Revelation he'd been working on before he'd been redirected.

Yes sir, that was what he'd do. He stood and dusted off the seat of his britches. Lost in his own thoughts, it was too late when he registered the sounds that didn't fit the bucolic setting. A burlap bag dropped over his head and shoulders. The musty smell, sudden absence of sight, and his weakness left him scrabbling uselessly against the hands gripping him.

He moaned and bucked against whoever or whatever had his arms pinned to his sides. A low voice hissed in his ear.

"Right now it's just you, preacher-man. Don't make us drag Ivy into this."

Colman froze. Why would someone threaten Ivy? What did she have to do with anything?

"Because she's been taking care of me?" He blurted the words and received a knock on the head for it. Stars spun behind his eyes, and suddenly he was back in the cave, tumbling over stones, dizzy and sick, the illusion of light bursting into his field of vision. He choked and nearly vomited, but the bag over his head forced him to swallow the bile back down. He was pushed to his knees. He gasped for air and heard . . . what was that?

"Good thing you're a preacher-man, 'cause you're about to meet your maker," the same voice growled.

Colman had just enough time to brace himself before a mighty blow turned everything black. Blacker even than the inside of a mountain.

⁓

Blinking and moving first one arm and then the other, Colman sat up. He rubbed the back of his head and winced when his fingers found the goose egg growing there. Groaning, he looked around and saw Webb sitting on the same rock he'd used for a bench . . . how long ago? "Where'd you come from?" he asked.

"Out scouting sign of Jake McLean when I come upon the very scoundrel himself about to do you in." Webb shifted his rifle, which lay across his knees. "I had to decide whether to shoot him or save you." He shook his head. "Here's hoping I made the right choice."

Colman couldn't quite make sense of what Webb was saying, yet he chalked that up to his addled brain. "Where'd Jake go?"

Webb waved down the trail. "Run off that direction. I fired a shot after him, but I must've missed."

Colman closed his eyes against the pounding of his skull and thought maybe he did remember hearing a shot. He'd surely heard something out of the ordinary.

"Seems you've got the folks around here eating out of your hand."

Colman climbed to his feet like he was in a contest to see

how slow he could move. "You mean my storytelling? I'm entertaining a few folks, but I don't guess it's all that important. I ought to be preaching real sermons."

"Hunh. What you ought to be doing is explaining to all those no-good McLeans that they're headed for hellfire and damnation." Webb grinned. "'Course, we wouldn't want 'em to get straightened out and find salvation, would we? No sir, the wrath of God is no less than they deserve."

Colman, finally on his feet, stood a moment, waiting for the world to stop swirling around him. He stepped over beside Webb and eased down on the rock. He wouldn't say so out loud, but Webb made a good point. Did he really want his enemy to find grace with God?

The day had taken its toll on him. He was tired all the way down to his toes. "What do you want, Webb?"

His uncle slapped him on the back none too gently. "I'd say you're in a good position to get some of the McLeans to trust you. The way they keep showing up to hear you blather, they must think you're on their side. Surely some of 'em know where Jake's hiding out."

Colman laughed, and it felt like a spike sticking into his temple. "It's a long way from listening to me 'blather' to telling me where to find the heir apparent of the McLean clan."

"Yeah, well, I have faith in you." Webb picked up some loose rocks and tossed them down the hill into the creek below where their splashes were lost in the falling water. "And if you can't prove useful, I just might have to start visiting your daddy more often."

Colman jerked his attention to Webb's face. "What do you mean?"

"He and I haven't had a chance to sit and talk like we

used to. Might head on over there and visit over a glass of whiskey. Or a bottle."

Colman thought back to what Johnny and Elam said about his father's capacity to drink himself right into his grave. Apparently without ever feeling the effects. Was Webb suggesting that he'd help his father kill himself with liquor?

"I guess Dad doesn't need any booze from you."

"What he needs and what I plan to give him are two different things. 'Course, if I get what I need, then I can just leave him alone."

"What do you need?" Colman thought he knew, but he wanted to hear Webb say it.

"Vengeance." A wicked gleam shone in his uncle's eye. "And maybe an extra serving of what Serepta McLean's got. Seems to me she needs to be taken down a few notches. Losing her son would be the first step toward losing her hold on this part of the country." He stood and stretched like a cat in the sun. "We all have our weaknesses. Her son isn't her biggest weakness, but I'm thinking tracking down Jake would be a mighty fine start."

That was when a sliver of truth hit Colman like the sunlight when he first exited the cave. He didn't want Jake McLean dead. Or, at the very least, he didn't want to be part of killing him. While seeing a measure of God's justice meted out on the McLeans would suit him fine, helping to serve up the violent death of anyone's child—even Serepta's—was more than he wanted to be party to.

"I don't see how I can help you," Colman said, kneading his shoulder where it struck the ground when he fell.

"Keep telling your stories, but start buttering up some of those pious folks who come hear you. Let 'em invite you home for Sunday dinner. Pray over their sick babies. Worm your way into their lives and then keep those sharp ears of yours open." Webb turned and took a few steps down the trail. "If you can hear as good as I think you can, you'll have some information for me before long."

Colman watched his uncle stride off into the soft green leaves of early summer. Oh, he could hear all right. And he surely didn't like what his ears were telling him.

chapter
seventeen

"Where's Mack?" Serepta stomped into the kitchen, Charlie's domain, and stood with hands on her hips.

Charlie turned from sliding a pan of biscuits into the oven and wiped his hands on a towel slung over his shoulder. "Out back last I seen him."

"I need him to drive me." Charlie's face softened in that way she found endearing and, all too often, annoying. One of these days someone was going to see that look on his face and then there'd be hell to pay. "Don't make eyes at me. Just fetch Mack and keep dinner warm."

Charlie stepped closer to her. Too close. "Wait till these biscuits are done and I'll drive you."

Serepta felt the steel of her spine softening. "It would be better if Mack did. I need to see one of my buyers at the Greenbrier, and you'll only cause a stir there."

Charlie reached across the space between them and slid a hand from her elbow to her wrist. He gripped her gently. "Not so long as I keep to my place."

Serepta tried to tug away, but he held on. "Charlie, your

place is not where those fools think it is. Regardless, there are some things even I won't risk." She successfully extricated herself. "Now, please, fetch Mack for me."

Charlie gave her a saucy grin, touched an imaginary fore-lock with his finger, and said, "Coming right up, missus."

Serepta watched him go. She might have more power than any other woman in West Virginia, but there were still some battles she simply could not win. She put the starch back in her spine and recalled the advice she'd given Emmaline. When something was impossible, consider what was possible and do that instead.

Serepta tried to relax in the back seat of the car as Mack began the drive home to Walnutta. Her meeting had not gone well. She was in danger of losing her largest buyer in Pittsburgh. Too many shipments were failing to reach him, and he was threatening to find someone else who could, how did he put it, "Meet my needs with consistency"?

She was unaccustomed to being dressed down, and that was exactly what had happened in the fancy suite at the Green-brier Hotel—in her own territory no less. She unclenched her fists and folded her hands in her lap.

"I should have been part of your meeting."

Serepta startled. She was used to Charlie driving her with-out comment. "So you say. However, until you're willing to follow my lead without interjecting your own opinion, I will meet with clients alone."

"I suppose he wanted to see you about the missing liquor."

She narrowed her eyes. "What do you know about that?"

"There's been talk. And while you may not value my opin-ion, I certainly know enough to realize customers will take umbrage when they fail to receive their promised goods. Legal or otherwise."

She clenched her hands again and paused, thinking before speaking. "If you were in my shoes, what steps would you take?" She held up a hand. "And don't suggest getting out of the liquor business. That is not an option."

"I'd get to the bottom of the missing-product issue."

"And how might you accomplish that?"

Mack pulled over in a wide spot along the road where the sun dappled the car beneath lacy maple branches. He killed the engine. "I have some connections. Know some people. I think I could find out who's stealing our liquor."

Our liquor. Since when did Mack think of himself as party to her bootleg business? "Is that so? And what might these connections be?"

Mack twisted more fully around so he could look her in the eye. "You've long put too much faith in Jake and not nearly enough in me. It might be time you let me take the lead on something."

Did she detect a note of hurt in her younger son's voice? Not that she would cater to his feelings, but seeing Mack assert himself put a new twist on her dilemma. What if Mack were willing to give up his foolish idea about putting everything they had into coal and gas? What if he could succeed where Jake was failing? If he could be trained to lead her empire . . .

"What do you have in mind?"

Mack turned forward again in his seat and started the engine. "Give me two weeks to turn up the stolen whiskey. If I do, it might be time for us to talk about who's man enough to run the McLean outfit." He glanced at her over his shoulder. "Once you decide to step down, of course."

Serepta let the car sway her as Mack pulled out onto the road. Did Mack have the sand she'd been hoping Jake would develop? She'd never thought of him as a leader. People flocked to Jake's electric personality even when he acted the fool. Mack, on the other hand, kept to himself. Up until today she would have said he didn't have the tenacity to do what needed to be done—no matter what. She stared at the back of her son's head, where dark brown hair curled over his collar. She'd thought his education a waste, but perhaps he still could be shaped into what she needed.

Resting her head back against the seat, she tried to view Mack in a new light. Perhaps it was time to step back and see if he had potential. If he could do what he said, he just might be the solution she needed—at least until Emmaline was old enough to become a leader in her own right. A slow smile spread across her face. And raising Mack to the position of heir to her throne would surely put Jake in his place once and for all. It might even spur him to reformation, and if it did, she wouldn't hesitate to shift her hand of grace to his golden head once more. Mack, after all, was the second son.

⁓

Colman had made it a practice not to linger after he finished speaking at the brush arbor, but on this Friday night he stayed as Ivy led the final song. When he was a boy, the ladies of the congregation loved to linger after church and vie for a chance to invite the preacher home for Sunday dinner. He guessed if he was going to do what Webb wanted, angling for an invitation was a good first step.

It worked better than he anticipated.

He stood to the side as the final strains of the song rose toward the stars just beginning to appear through the branches above them. The congregation stirred and began rising to go home. The ladies near the front approached like they thought he might turn tail and run, yet as he smiled and shook hands, the crowd around him thickened. Soon a sort of receiving line formed, each person shaking his hand and offering their thanks or comments about what he'd said. With husbands starting to hustle their wives home, there were still quite a few unaccompanied ladies fluttering like moths to a lantern.

Lena McLean appeared before him. "You preach better than most, but it looks to me like you're not getting near enough to eat." She shot a look at Ivy, then leaned closer. "I'm the best cook this side of the mountain. You come on over to the house tomorrow at noon and I'll feed you up right."

Colman felt a surge of relief. Finally he had an invitation and could end this torture. "That would be a kindness," he replied.

The woman glanced over her shoulder. "Nell, come over here." The pretty girl with the golden hair stepped forward.

"Yes, Momma?"

"Preacher's coming to the house tomorrow for dinner. You meet him down by the crossroads and walk with him."

"That's not necessary," Colman protested. "I know the way."

Nell smiled, slow and sweet. "It's no trouble. I like to get out for a walk." She gave her mother a sly smile. "Gets me out of helping with the cooking."

Her mother cackled and patted her arm. "She's almost as good a cook as me." She gave Colman a meaningful look. "Make some feller a fine wife one day."

Nell pinked and pinched her lips. "Momma, you'll give Preacher Harpe the wrong impression."

170

"Maybe I will and maybe I won't." She poked Colman in the arm. "You meet Nell about eleven-thirty. Won't take you above twenty minutes to get on up to the house afoot." She bobbed what was almost a curtsy and left Colman to make his escape.

Nell graced him with one last sweet smile and ducked her chin. "I'll see you tomorrow."

He nodded and began backing toward where Hoyt stood, his arms crossed, watching. "You finally decide to mix with the rabble?" he asked as they started walking back to the cottage.

"I don't know that I'd call those folks *rabble*."

"Hunh. Guess I had the impression that while you don't mind telling McLeans your God stories, you still aren't what you'd call partial to 'em."

"Jesus ate with tax collectors."

"That He did." Hoyt scuffed along the darkening road. "'Course, that Nell McLean is awful purty and probably ain't never waylaid a Harpe." He grinned. "Least not yet."

"I'm just trying to follow God's call," Colman said. "I'm still not convinced this storytelling business is what He had in mind. If I spend time with folks, I can witness to them proper."

Hoyt nodded. "Well, you've picked some easy ones to start with. Lena McLean's the best cook around, and Nell's a kind, sweet girl—both believers far as I know." Silence expanded in the air between them. "'Course, won't hardly nobody court her since her daddy's prone to shoot first and ask questions later. Ain't never been anybody good enough for his Nell."

Colman tried not to groan. Somehow he'd managed to get invited to eat with the one McLean family more likely to do him in than Serepta herself. "Reckon her daddy will poison me?"

Hoyt guffawed. "If they've got a dog, see can't you sneak him a bite before you clean your plate."

The next day, Colman arrived at the crossroads ten minutes early. When preaching, he wore an old suit of Hoyt's from the man's younger days, while today he had on a shirt Ivy made for him. She'd found some flour sack fabric that wasn't too awful gaudy, and though he'd rather wear a plain shirt, at least it was clean and smelled good. He lifted his sleeve to his nose and inhaled. As a matter of fact, his shirt smelled like Ivy's garden—fresh, green, and a little spicy. He smiled to himself. Talk about making a fine wife.

Lost in pleasant thoughts, Colman heard Nell before he saw her. She was humming, a tuneless sound, and stopped the moment she saw him.

"Good morning," he said.

"Oh, you've been waiting." She fluttered to his side and grasped his arm. "Momma told me to get down here early, but I guess I walked slow—it's such a nice day."

"I haven't been here but a minute or two."

She smiled up through her eyelashes. "Well, I hope today turns out to be worth your trouble."

"No trouble," Colman said, wishing they could just go on. He started moving, and she latched on to his arm as if determined to slow him down.

"Aren't the flowers pretty this time of year? The daisies will give way to black-eyed Susans soon. And, oh, the roses have been lovely."

She nattered on as they walked. Colman tried to pay attention, but all he really wanted to know was where Jake McLean was hiding, and sweet little Nell McLean seemed interested in anything but. They finally arrived at the house where Colman could smell something frying. If nothing else, dinner smelled real good.

Lena stood on the porch, one hand shading her eyes as she watched them approach. "About time you'uns got here." She grinned, showing a gap in her teeth. "Thought I might have to send one of the boys to hurry you along." Cackling, she waved them into the plain but clean house. "Dinner's about ready. Just sit on down there while I finish dishing it up."

Two boys already sat at the table. One looked to be sixteen or so, and the other maybe twelve. Younger brothers to Nell, Colman figured. There was no sign of her gun-toting father.

Colman cleared his throat. "Will, uh, Mr. McLean be joining us?"

"Daddy's got a job riding the rails," Nell said. "Sometimes he's gone three or four days at a stretch."

Colman let his shoulders relax a notch. Maybe he wouldn't get shot right off. "That so? You must miss him."

Nell huffed a breath but didn't answer. The younger boy laughed. "Nell likes it when he's gone—she can get some sparking in." The older boy jostled his brother, although he looked like he didn't really mind his brother giving their sister a hard time.

"You boys hush," Lena said as she carried a platter of fried rabbit to the table. Colman felt a rumble of hunger, which was a relief. Maybe his appetite was coming back. Nell added a bowl of kilt lettuce, giving her brother a mean look Colman guessed he wasn't supposed to see. There was also a dish of spring peas with a pat of butter melting over the top and a basket of biscuits.

Nell batted her eyes at him again. "There are strawberries for dessert. I picked them myself, so don't go filling up on Momma's cooking."

Colman smiled, wishing filling up were something he could do. He hoped to do the meal justice, but his stomach still turned on him unexpectedly. He hitched up his borrowed britches. If only he could put some meat back on his bones.

Once everyone was seated, Colman said grace before they all dug in. Lena's cooking was indeed delicious. But after only a few mouthfuls, Colman knew he wasn't going to be able to eat enough to satisfy this good woman. She kept eyeing his plate as he moved the food around trying to eat another bite and then one more.

"You ever get in a tangle with one of the McLeans?" Tim, the younger boy, asked.

Lena reared back and looked like she was going to smack her son, but Colman jumped in before she could do so.

"That's a good question. If you're going to let a Harpe sit at your table, it's best to know what kind of man he is." Lena relaxed but stayed wary. "I don't guess I've ever really gotten caught up in the feud between our families. I've been trying to make my way as a preacher, and I'm supposed to turn the other cheek."

"But what about all your kin and the low-down way they've treated us?"

"Timothy Davis McLean, you go outside right this minute!" His mother stood and pointed at the door.

While he was grateful no one was paying attention to how much he was eating anymore, Colman figured he'd better take the reins before things got out of hand. "Now, the boy has a right to question a man who comes into his home and partakes of his hospitality." Colman pushed his chair back some. "Of course, I'd probably say the Harpes haven't done anything worse than the McLeans have." He held up a hand before the boy could jump in. "Which doesn't make either side right. Seems to me we all need to start over and let go all that business about Holy Spirit gifts."

Tim looked puzzled. "I don't know what 'Holy Spirit gifts' are, but I do know a Harpe stole a mule from a McLean and then tricked the law into letting him go free."

Nell made a face. "It wasn't about the mule. It was about the girl riding the mule who ran off with a Harpe, and he didn't do right by her. Left her alone with a child." She flushed. "And no wedding ring."

"That's enough," Lena said. "Seems like everybody's got a story." She turned to Colman. "And seems to me you must be trying to make peace, what with coming here to preach and all." She began scraping their plates into a pan. "And peace has been a long time coming. Just like these young'uns, most everybody thinks they know why we oughta hate the Harpes. I'd just as soon find a reason to turn loose of the hate and maybe even"—she nodded at Nell—"find some love in our hearts." Nell ducked her head and carried a serving dish to the kitchen.

This was not going as Colman planned.

Lena pinned him with a look. "So, you bringing peace or not?"

Colman reached for his glass of buttermilk and took a swig. "Yes, ma'am, that's what I'm hoping to do." He prayed it wasn't a lie.

She nodded emphatically and braced her hands on her hips. "Good. You go on out and sit on the porch now. Nell will bring you those strawberries directly." She glared at her boys. "You two sit out there with him. And if you can't say anything respectable, keep your mouths shut."

The three of them shuffled outside and sat on the porch steps facing the yard, hands on knees, looking straight ahead.

Tim sighed. "I still say it was about a mule, but I reckon you weren't the one to steal it."

Colman felt the corner of his mouth quirk. "Nope. I'll swear to that." He glanced at the boys sitting to his right. They were both trying not to smile.

"Probably the two of you weren't there, either."

They laughed, and soon they were talking about hunting and fishing and how Tim wanted to be an engineer on the railroad one day, while his brother Fred wanted to go to college. By the time Nell came out with dishes of strawberries and sweet cream, Colman felt like he was practically an older brother to these fine boys. And as they enjoyed their dessert, he found he didn't want to try to trick them into revealing the location of their wayward cousin Jake. He'd just have to find that out some other way.

chapter
eighteen

Serepta woke early and dressed for the day, brushing her graying hair vigorously and then twisting it snug at the back of her head. She opened a drawer to retrieve hairpins and found a slip of paper with "Song of Songs 1:15" written on it. Charlie. It wasn't the first time he'd left her this particular message, but she refused to look up the verse. She had no use for the words of a God who cared so little for His creation. She crumpled the paper and dropped it back into the drawer. Better that Charlie use his own words or none at all.

She made her way downstairs to her office. There was a shortage of workers at one of her mines, and she needed to apply pressure to the superintendent so that production would not flag. She was mentally composing the letter she would write even as she entered her office to find Jake slumped in his usual chair with soft snores rolling out from underneath the hat pulled low over his brow.

Serepta flipped the hat to the floor and circled her desk as Jake blinked and rubbed his eyes. "Why are you here?" she asked.

"Mornin' to you too, Ma."

Serepta pulled out heavy writing paper and her favorite Montblanc ink pen as though Jake weren't there.

"Yeah, well, I was just wondering if you've had any luck figuring out who's stealing your liquor."

She stilled and looked up. So, both sons knew about the missing shipments. How interesting. "What do you know about liquor being stolen?"

He yawned and scratched behind his ear. "Mack said something about it." He curled his lip. "I can't think why you'd send him after it when you've got me."

"I thought you were busy running Colman Harpe out of town. He doesn't seem to have budged an inch."

"Aw, he's not worth the trouble. I figure tracking that liquor matters more. You need to tell Mack to lay off and let me handle it."

Serepta slid the cap off her pen and smoothed the sheet of linen stationery in front of her. "You might consider partnering with your brother. If you're not careful, he just might prove more valuable to this family."

The barb landed right where Serepta intended. Jake leapt to his feet. "Mack's full of himself. He thinks all that education makes him smarter than me." Jake leaned on the desk, his breath yeasty and stale. "You tell him to back off or I will."

Serepta began carefully inscribing the day's date at the top of the blank page. *July 14, 1930.* "I'll do no such thing. Perhaps it's high time one of you took the lead and proved your mettle." She laid the pen down and folded her hands. "I'll be interested to see which one of you comes out on top."

Jake snorted like a bull, snatched his hat up from where it had fallen, and stomped out of the room. Serepta watched him go with a half smile. Finally her sons were starting to act like men. Now all she had to do was make sure she shaped one—or both—into the kind of men she needed.

"A baptizing. That's just the ticket." Ivy beamed at Colman across the table.

Colman filled his mouth with a big bite of rhubarb pie so he didn't have to answer right away. After finishing another four-day meeting, he'd told the crowd he'd speak on Wednesday evenings and Sunday mornings. No way could he keep up with speaking night after night. He'd gotten to the point where he was praying for rain hard enough to keep folks home.

They'd taken up a love offering, and talk of starting a proper church was percolating. Colman gave most of the money to Hoyt, since he knew Ivy wouldn't accept it. As for starting a church, as much as he wanted a church of his own, he wasn't sure he wanted it deep in McLean territory.

"I'm not sure I'm qualified to baptize anyone," he said.

"You're as much qualified as any of us, and the ladies around here are eager to have one." She grinned. "They figure they'd better get their men dunked before they change their minds." Ivy pushed the pitcher of cream closer, and Colman obliged by pouring a little over his pie. "You've been eating better. It's good to see you fattening up."

He finished the pie and pushed his plate away. He was feeling some better but knew he still needed to gain strength before he'd be back to his old self. "Maybe we can have a baptizing later in the summer. The water's running high right now."

Ivy's brow furrowed. "Of course. You're not well enough

yet to stand in cold water with a strong current. I wasn't think-ing." As she cleared the dishes, Colman struggled against feeling like half a man.

"That's not it. It's just that—" Colman didn't get to fin-ish his thought before Tim McLean burst through the door.

"Ma says she needs you," he said.

Ivy let a fork clatter into the dishpan. "Is she sick?"

"Not Ma—somebody over at the Dunglen. She wouldn't tell me more'n that, just said to fetch you to the house."

Ivy began stowing items in her gathering basket. "If you want to run ahead, let her know I'm coming as fast as I can."

The boy had caught his breath. "Mack'll drive us. He picked me up when I was almost here and said he'd be happy to carry you to the house."

"Mack McLean?" Colman asked, rising to his feet.

Tim looked at him as though he were a fool. "Yeah. He's my cousin."

Colman squirmed. It was one thing to see Ivy being sought out by one of the local ladies, but Serepta's son was an-other matter. "What's Mack doing around here?" The boy shrugged. "I'm coming, too," Colman said.

Ivy paused long enough to give him a hard look, then nod-ded. "Bring that sack," she said, pointing to a lumpy burlap bag in the corner. Colman lifted it, the aroma of dried plants rising to his nose. He followed the others out to the road, where Mack sat in a Model A, the engine running. He raised one eyebrow upon seeing Colman but didn't say anything as they all climbed in—Colman and Tim in the back while Ivy rode up front.

Ivy turned to Mack as they started out. "Do you know who's ill over at the Dunglen?"

Mack cast a pointed look toward Tim. "One of the *ladies*

180

from Ballyhack." Ivy's pale cheeks pinked. "She's kin. Lena will tell you the rest."

They rode in silence for a while, at last pulling up to the house where Colman had enjoyed dinner not so long ago.

Nell stood on the porch, watching them. Spotting Colman, she clasped her hands and smiled. "Oh, Pastor Harpe, God just knew we'd be needing a man of faith during this trying time."

Colman grunted. He hadn't come to offer the comfort of his faith. He mainly meant to keep an eye on Ivy while she was in the presence of that scoundrel Mack.

Lena opened the door and waved them in. "Tim, you go on out to the barn with your brother."

"Aw, Ma, I want to know what's going on."

She turned him and swatted his bottom. "Not if I can help it. Now go on, git."

Inside, they gathered around the bare table. Colman stood back, not sure he needed to be part of whatever was going on.

"Come on and take a load off, Preacher," Lena said. "Maybe you can pray Maggie's baby into the world."

Colman sat, holding himself stiff in Mack's presence. Mack, on the other hand, seemed utterly at ease. He relaxed in his chair, one foot propped on the opposite knee, his arm stretched along the table near Ivy's hand.

Lena turned to Ivy. "I guess you know what kind of girls they have over there in Ballyhack near the Dunglen. Maggie's my cousin's girl, and she had a rough go of it coming up. Guess going to work in Ballyhack was better than being around her . . . well, better than being at home anyway." Ivy nodded. "They had 'em a doctor what took care of their—" she stopped and glanced at Mack, then Colman—"female issues." She shook her head. "But he's a pure drunk and a gambler, and Maggie don't want him for this baby that's coming."

Ivy nodded and moved as though she would touch Lena's arm but then pulled her hand back before she did. She ignored the men in the room, her focus on the woman speaking. Nell sat across from her, lips pinched tight like she'd just tasted a lemon. Colman guessed she either didn't care for the topic or for the woman who'd come to help.

"She sent word she thinks the baby's about to come and she don't want that doctor tending her. She heard about your momma catching babies and asked for you." Lena looked down and fiddled with her sleeve. "She knows about your . . ." She waved at her own face. "Well, she don't care about that. Says it's better than having an old drunk who might kill her and the baby both." She looked back up. "Will you help?"

Colman marveled at the expression on Ivy's face. She looked positively luminous. "Nothing would make me happier. Helping new life into the world is the greatest blessing there is. I'll be glad to go."

Lena blew out a big breath and grinned. "Alright then. All we've got to do now is get you to Thurmond."

"I'll drive you," Mack said.

Colman jerked as though he'd been stung. Mack looked like a fox that had been offered a chance to watch over a nest of baby birds.

"It's high time I checked on my dad," said Colman quickly. "How about we take the train?"

Ivy's eyes lit up. "I've always wanted to ride in one of those beautiful passenger cars."

Colman swallowed hard. He could probably wrangle a ride in a caboose, but a passenger car might be trickier. "That can be arranged."

"When do we leave?" Ivy asked.

"First thing in the morning, if I remember the schedule right." Colman ignored the scowl on Mack's face, then whispered a prayer that God would help him make such a thing happen.

○○○○○

Rising later than usual after a restless night, Serepta walked into her office Monday morning and found several crates of liquor stacked there. Mack stood leaning on the fireplace mantel, a cigarette between his lips.

"I don't allow smoking in this house," she said.

Mack laughed. "Leave it to you, Mother, to focus on the fly in your ointment." He waved an arm toward the crates. "As you can see, I have recovered a portion of our goods."

"I do see. And will the perpetrator be brought to justice? Will the rest of *our* goods be recovered?"

Mack blew smoke toward the ceiling and smirked. "Let's just say that process is in the works."

Serepta moved around the crates to her desk and pulled out writing paper. "I would rather you share the pertinent details with me." She leveled a gaze at her son. "So that I might be certain of the outcome."

Mack stubbed out his cigarette in a crystal dish on a side table. "I know you better than you think. And I know that if I tell you the *who* and the *how*, you'll get involved and leave me out of it." He moved to the front of her desk and braced his hands against it. "Not this time." He leaned closer so that she could smell the foulness of his breath. "This time I'll do things my way so you can see once and for all what I'm made of." He stood tall. "So you will understand that sometimes I'm right"—he stepped back to slap one of the crates—"and you're wrong."

Serepta watched him saunter from the room. She wanted to tell him to get some men in here to move the crates from her expensive rug, but she didn't do it. It would sound petty, retaliatory. No, she would give Mack some room and see what he did with it. He might even surprise her by succeeding.

She shook her head and tapped her pen on the blank paper in front of her. She wouldn't go so far as to suppose Mack might prove her wrong, but she wouldn't mind if he turned out to be more of a match for her own intellect than she'd dared to hope.

chapter
nineteen

It was a miracle. Colman figured if God were going to work a miracle in his life, it would be something more important than getting Ivy into a plush coach on the C&O heading to Thurmond. Never mind that it was only because a large party had canceled at the last minute and the two other passengers moved away when they saw a working man and such an unusual-looking woman step into the car. Ivy was so enchanted she didn't notice.

Or maybe she was used to people turning away from her.

Regardless, the ride passed so quickly that Colman thought the engineer must have found a shortcut. Now they were standing outside the depot in Thurmond, looking across the wide river at the Dunglen Hotel. Colman had been there several times, while respectable folks mostly steered clear. He'd even heard the south side of the river called the Dodge City of the East due to its reputation for gambling and carousing. The only thing his mother would approve less than his going there would be his letting a woman like Ivy go there alone.

"It's not a respectable place for a lady to go," Colman told her.

Ivy tossed him a carefree smile. "I'm not going there to dine or stay—it's a mission of mercy."

Colman grunted. Mercy for a McLean woman who had clearly chosen the wrong path in life. He reminded himself that Jesus loved the woman at the well who'd been with a whole string of different men. Although that wasn't the kind of Bible story he wanted to be telling from the pulpit.

Ivy grabbed her basket and the sack of belongings she'd packed in case the child was slow in coming. Colman glanced toward the window of his room. He really should go see if the landlord had packed up his belongings, but he couldn't leave Ivy alone, and he certainly couldn't take her to his room. It would just have to wait. That and going to see his father. First, he needed to escort Ivy to the hotel and make sure she would be safe there.

Taking Ivy's sack, Colman offered her his arm. She smiled and looped her hand in the crook of his elbow. He liked the sensation of it. They headed for the rail bridge with its one lane for auto traffic and crossed over to the hotel sitting high on a bluff overlooking the river. The massive brick building was grand, and he could feel Ivy tensing as they drew near.

Maybe she wasn't quite so confident as she pretended.

Colman had an idea. He guided Ivy to the first floor of the hotel with its array of businesses. Earl Nichols sold groceries and soft drinks out of a store on the ground floor. They'd start there. Stepping into the small store was far less intimidating than the grand lobby above. Earl came out from the back and smiled like he'd been waiting for them to arrive all day.

"Well look what the cat drug in," he said and clapped Colman on the back. "I heard you run off to hunt Jake McLean and got kidnapped." He waggled his brows. "'Course, some folks said you changed sides in the feud, but I been knowing your family long enough to guess that ain't the truth of it."

Colman shifted from foot to foot. It hadn't occurred to him that there'd be rumors about his absence. Shoot, he'd been gone for two months. He should have realized folks liked a good story too much not to come up with one.

"I've been preaching over around Hinton," he said.

"That ain't near as entertaining, so it must be the truth." Earl turned his attention to Ivy. Colman was relieved that he didn't flinch at her colorless face. "And who's this pretty lady?"

"This is Ivy Gordon. She's here to look after Maggie."

The older man sobered. "Glad to hear it. Maggie's a good girl who was trying to turn her life around. It's just too bad . . . well, that's not my story to tell." Earl patted Ivy's hand. "You catch babies, do you?"

"My mother did, and I've helped." She ducked her head. "Most folks don't want me to tend them, though." One hand strayed to her cheek. "But I'm real good at treating illnesses and hurts."

Earl nodded. "Sounds like you and Maggie will do just fine together. Folks turn their noses up at her, too."

Colman felt itchy. He was uneasy for some reason he couldn't quite put his finger on. Maybe it was just having been away for so long. "Can you show us Maggie's room?" he asked.

"Cain't leave the store, but it's easy to find. Go up the back staircase to the third floor. Her room's at the far end of the hall on the back side of the hotel." He shook his head. "No need to waste the view, I guess."

Colman thanked him and led Ivy out of the store. If they were lucky, they wouldn't see anyone along the way. Earl

187

called out as they passed out the door. "Be careful if you go back into town. Like I said, there might be some who misunderstand why you've been away all this time."

Feeling Ivy tense beside him once more, he gave her hand a quick squeeze and what he hoped was a reassuring smile. Misunderstandings . . . he hadn't thought about what kind of trouble that might cause.

"What do you mean she's not at home?" Serepta looked at Charlie like he was speaking a foreign language.

"Miss Ivy and that Harpe preacher gone to Thurmond to see to a woman having a baby. Hoyt told me they might be gone a week or more."

"Who's going to look after Emmaline?"

Now it was Charlie's turn to give her a disbelieving look. "I reckon you and me are. Unless you've got someone else in mind?"

Emmaline walked in then, her dress buttoned up crooked. She marched up to Serepta. "I got dressed by myself."

"So I see." Serepta glanced down and noticed that the child's unbuckled shoes were on the wrong feet. She started to correct the error, then stopped. "And you've done a fine job. Is there anything that might need adjusting?"

Emmaline wrinkled her nose and thought it over. "My shoes feel funny."

"And what shall we do about that?"

The child chewed her lip and looked at her shoes. Then she plopped down on the floor, removed both shoes, switched them, and stood again. She grinned like she'd solved the world's biggest problem.

"Shall I buckle them for you?"

Emmaline narrowed her eyes. "I want to, but it's hard."

Serepta nodded. She knew about wanting to do things that were hard. "Then you'll just have to keep trying, won't you?"

Emmaline nodded and noticed her buttons. She sat back down and began unbuttoning, buttoning, then starting over again. Serepta lifted her gaze to Charlie. Silent laughter made his whole body shake, and she suspected it was a strain for him not to double over and slap his knees in glee. She looked back down to Emmaline, who had undone all her buttons, revealing an undershirt that was on backwards. She felt her own lips quirk.

Charlie could finally hold it in no more and began laughing in earnest. Emmaline glanced at him and smiled, but then she quickly turned her attention back to her wardrobe. Serepta firmed her mouth but knew her own amusement showed in her eyes.

"Go on then, Charlie. It appears Emmaline will be occupied for some time. And when she has completed her toilette, she can help me count bottles. It seems Mack has recovered more of our misplaced goods."

Charlie shook his head, and Serepta noticed for the first time that his ebony hair was beginning to show silver, the same as hers. Well, perhaps caring for a four-year-old would help to keep them both young a little longer.

"I'll be in the kitchen bossing Hallie around if you need me," he said. He smiled, slow and warm, like pouring boiled frosting over a cake. Serepta couldn't help but smile back at him.

━━━━━⌒⌒⌒⌒

Ivy knocked softly on the door while Colman watched up and down the hall. They'd come up a back staircase and had only passed three people, all appearing to be well-heeled businessmen. Colman didn't much like the way they looked at Ivy, then him, as though making assumptions. Ivy was so intent on her destination, she didn't appear to notice.

There was a brief scuffling inside before the door cracked open. A woman's light gray-green eye peered out at them. "Who is it?"

"I'm Ivy Gordon. Lena McLean sent me."

The door opened wider, and they could see more of Maggie, a petite woman with light brown hair swept into a messy twist and a wrapper doing little to conceal her condition. "Come on in then. I swear I might have this baby any minute." She looked Colman up and down. "You're both welcome, but your feller might want to think whether he wants to be here for the main attraction."

A laugh popped out of Ivy, and she turned to Colman, a question in her eyes.

"I need to go see my father," he said. "I'll come back to check on you after supper."

Maggie grunted. "Gets rowdy around here of an evening. Come up the back stairs."

Colman turned to leave but felt awkward just walking away. He looked back to Ivy, who was looking at Maggie with an expression of wonder. He reached out and touched her shoulder. She turned that intense gaze on him, and he felt warmth travel through him like music. "Stay in the room with Maggie. I'll be back for you."

Ivy smiled, all light and joy. "I know you will." Then she stepped through the doorway and eased it shut behind her. Colman stared at the closed door before finally giving himself a shake and making his way back out of the hotel. She'd be fine. No reason she wouldn't be.

By suppertime, Serepta wondered how she'd survived raising her own children. Or more to the point, how they'd survived it. Mack turned up late in the afternoon with another load of liquor crates. Serepta watched him unload them into an outbuilding with her arms crossed while Emmaline drew in the dirt at her feet with a stick.

"You seem to have found a regular supply of my missing goods."

"Sure did," Mack said. She was surprised by how strong he was. She would have thought he'd go soft while away at school.

"Is there more yet?"

Mack frowned. "Maybe."

"It would be more convenient if you would arrange to take these directly to the point of distribution."

"You are nothing if not practical, Mother." He shook his head and thumped the last crate. "Shall I take this one down to the depot?"

"Your brother arranged for someone to stow the goods. Ask him where it would be best to take this one." She cocked an eyebrow. "And any others."

"Jake hasn't had much use for me lately."

Serepta kept an eye on Emmaline as she began gathering rocks and building what looked like a nest out of them. "Really? Or is it you who doesn't have much use for him?"

Mack laughed, leaned against his truck, and crossed his arms. "It goes both ways. You know he's a wastrel."

Serepta smiled without it reaching her eyes. "Perhaps you could guide him. It would be ideal if the two of you learned to work together. If this family enterprise continues to grow, there will be plenty of responsibility—and income—to go around."

"Would that please you?"

Serepta hesitated at the unexpected question. Please her? "It would please me to know what I have built is in good hands." She continued to watch Emmaline's hands as they stacked stones with surprising dexterity for one so young. "It's late to start training someone else to take over." She looked into Mack's eyes and saw his expression harden.

"I agree," he said. "Maybe I will have a talk with Jake. Perhaps we have more in common than we realize."

chapter
twenty

The hike up the mountain to his father's house seemed steeper than Colman remembered. He was panting by the time he reached the porch, the July sun too hot against the top of his head. He thought his father would be outside, but the single chair on the porch sat empty and the house felt too quiet.

"Dad? You here?" Colman called out as he leaned against the doorframe to catch his breath.

From the darkness of the front room he heard a stirring. "'Bout time you came around."

"You got word, didn't you?"

"Eventually. You know Webb. He does things in his own time."

Colman flinched. This was as close as his dad would come to accusing him of causing worry. He could have written. He could have sent word another way, but he'd been too wrapped up in his own troubles. In the dim room he could just make out his father sitting in a sprung armchair with an old towel draped over the back of it. His dad looked thinner, more worn. Or maybe he'd always looked that way and Colman was just now noticing.

"Sorry about that."

Dad raised one hand and let it fall back to the arm of the chair. "No harm done. You back to stay?"

"Not sure. I brought Ivy—she's a healer—to tend one of the girls over at the Dunglen."

His father coughed. "You been over there? I ain't been since before I married your ma." His grin came fast, out of nowhere. "She didn't think that place was suitable for a married man. I told her how Jesus spent plenty of time with shady folks, but she didn't buy that argument." His grin faded. "Can't say as I minded doing what she wanted." He sighed and thumped the arm of his chair with a fist. "Your plunder's in there in the bedroom."

Colman furrowed his brow. "My things? What do you mean?"

"When you didn't come back, Walt down to the bank cleaned out your room and rented it to somebody else." He levered himself to his feet. "He could've just tossed it all. Guess it was a kindness that he brung it to me. Some of the Harpes ain't too happy about you running off to the McLeans. Guess they don't quite believe this preaching business."

Colman followed his father into the one bedroom in the house. He hardly ever came in here. The covers were rumpled, and the mattress was sunken on the right side where he supposed his father slept. The left side that would have been his mother's was perfectly smooth, her pillow covered with a lacy sham. Colman felt a lump form in his throat but pushed it back down. A pasteboard box sat on the dresser holding his spare clothes, one pair of dress shoes, two books, a wheel-tapping hammer, a picture of his mother, and a pocket watch. Colman had never seen all his worldly goods gathered together before, and he was surprised at how few there were.

"Can I leave this stuff here?" he asked.

"Sure. Where're you staying?"

Colman hadn't thought that far. Somehow he'd had the idea his room would still be waiting for him. "I don't know."

"You're welcome to stay here. I've slept on that sofa more'n once. It ain't bad."

Colman nodded, took out the photo of his mother, and set it on the dresser. "Appreciate it. How about I rustle us up some supper? And then I'd better go check on Ivy over at the hotel." His father's answering smile brought the lump back to Colman's throat.

Colman approached the hotel in the gathering dusk. A whippoorwill called from the tree line, and he heard another—probably on the far side of the river—return the call. He swung wide to avoid the steps, angling up to the broad wraparound porch.

"I heard you brought a healer to look after Miss Maggie."

The deep voice seemed to fall from the sky, but when Colman looked up, he saw it was the hotel manager, Alden Butterfield, leaning on the porch rail and looking down at him.

"I guess Maggie's not so wild about that doctor you keep on hand," Colman said.

Alden snorted. "I wouldn't let him touch me with a ten-foot pole, but his price is reasonable." He motioned with his head toward the back of the hotel. "I'll meet you at the back door."

Colman grimaced and trudged on around. He would have preferred that his comings and goings went unnoticed. But while Alden wasn't in the running for citizen of the year, he always knew what was happening in his hotel.

Alden stood holding the back door open. "I'm disappointed that you didn't come see me when you first arrived. I imagine you meant to set that to rights this evening."

Colman rubbed the back of his neck. "How's business?"

"Terrible." Alden let the door swing shut behind them and steered Colman to a staircase he hadn't used before. It was almost as if he wanted to make sure Colman avoided certain parts of the hotel's storage area. And that was fairly likely with all the nefarious goings-on at the Dunglen.

"Sorry to hear that."

"I'll bet you are. You and all the self-righteous Harpes." The fair-haired man's eyes gleamed. "Even the ones who come around when they think no one's looking."

Colman flushed, but let the gibe slide away. "Folks around here losing their taste for sin?"

Alden barked with laughter. "Not likely. The problem is automobiles. That and how I hear some of the mines are playing out. It's easier to drive to Glen Jean or even Oak Hill for entertainment."

"Guess you'll have to consider becoming respectable." They reached the top of the stairs, and Alden held the door open for Colman to enter the hall.

"Respectability is overrated." Alden flicked a speck of something from Colman's sleeve. "I'm not too worried. Seems like there's always a new opportunity to serve the world's vices." He winked, then disappeared back down the staircase.

Colman shook off the feeling he'd just been escorted to a cell by a warden. He stepped down the hall and knocked softly at the door to Maggie's room. It opened a crack, and Ivy peered out at him, the paleness of her sparse lashes making her eyes seem even bluer. She opened the door wider, inviting him into a small sitting room.

"Come in, but you can't stay more than a minute." Her eyes were gleaming with life, her complexion almost rosy. "Her labor's started, but she has a ways to go yet."

Colman blanched. He hadn't thought about actually being present when the time came. He knew almost nothing about childbirth and had no desire to learn. "I'm just here to check on you."

"Oh, I'm fine." A soft moan came from behind an interior door, but Ivy didn't appear to hear it. "One of Maggie's friends brought us some food, although Maggie's not very hungry. I've given her some raspberry leaf tea to help move things along."

Another groan emanated from behind the door. This time Ivy turned her head toward the sound. Then came a deep, guttural cry, and Ivy flew into the next room. Colman had begun backing toward the exit when Ivy suddenly reappeared and grabbed his arm. "I need your help," she said, pulling him into the bedroom.

⁓

Serepta couldn't remember the last time she ate a meal with both of her sons. Charlie brought in a platter of deviled eggs and added them to the pork roast, creamed potatoes, and a salad of fresh cucumbers from the garden. The thought that she should invite Charlie to eat with them flitted through Serepta's head, but she dismissed it with a half smile. This meal was likely to be difficult enough without intentionally adding to it.

"Is Emmaline asleep?" she asked Charlie.

"I doubt it. She kept asking for you."

The comment pleased her. It was good that Emmaline asked for her rather than her mother or even Ivy. She would go look in on the child once this meal was concluded. She nodded to Jake. "You may serve as the eldest."

Jake looked at her as though she'd sprouted horns. He sighed heavily, stood, and began carving the roast. He slapped two slices of pork on her plate, cut some more, added them to his own plate and sat back down.

Mack picked up the knife and pointed it at Jake. "Don't mind me, brother, I can help myself."

"I reckon you can," Jake said, piling sides onto his plate.

Dishes made the circuit around the table. Only the click of serving utensils and the soft splat of food hitting china disturbed the silence. As they began to eat, Serepta looked from one son to the other. "To what do I owe this unexpected pleasure?" she asked. "It's rare for both of my boys to sit at my table of an evening."

"You suggested I talk to Jake about working together to further your empire," Mack said.

Jake grunted. "Guess my little brother wants to make sure he gets a piece of the pie. 'Course, I don't exactly need his help."

"Don't you?" Mack curled his lip as he moved to sip from his water glass. "And who's responsible for recovering the bulk of our missing shipments?"

Jake's head jerked up. "What?"

"Oh? Hasn't Mother told you? I've managed to find quite a bit of the missing liquor and have either returned it here or arranged for it to be shipped by rail as originally intended."

Serepta watched the interaction between the two men. There was an undercurrent that seemed to go deeper than sibling rivalry. Her sons might as well have been having a fistfight with their words, and yet she couldn't quite read the undercurrent.

Jake clenched his hands and flexed his fingers. "Well, aren't you the golden boy. Want to tell me how you managed to *discover* the missing goods?"

Mack popped half an egg into his mouth and chewed, his eyes sharp on his brother. Once he swallowed, he patted his lips with a napkin. "You could say a little birdy helped me find the missing crates."

Jake looked as if he were going to explode. Could he be so angry simply because his younger brother had succeeded where he failed?

"And did you find the thief?" Jake asked.

"He's being taken care of as we speak."

Jake glared at Mack, then looked to Serepta. He opened his mouth, then snapped it shut. The tension that had been building suddenly melted. Jake relaxed, reached for a biscuit, and began buttering it. "Well then, sounds like we might should work together to make sure something like this doesn't happen ever again."

Mack chortled. "That sounds like a fine idea." He raised his glass in mock salute. "Partners."

Jake forced his lips into a smile. "Yup. Partners."

Serepta narrowed her eyes at her sons. There was more to their talk than she understood. Sometimes the first step to learning what one most needed to know was realizing what one didn't. While she was glad her sons seemed to be willing to take on a measure of responsibility, she didn't trust them. Not fully.

She'd talk to Charlie tonight, after everyone had gone and she was certain Emmaline was asleep. The thought was so pleasant it almost brought a smile to her own face.

chapter
twenty-one

Colman sometimes found his keen hearing to be a blessing, but this night he wished he were deaf. Maggie's cries were loud enough for someone in the farthest corner of the hotel to hear. Shoot, his father might could hear her on the far side of the river.

Sweat popped out on his forehead and trickled down his cheek to slide into the collar of his shirt. He was sweating almost as much as Maggie. Almost. Ivy, on the other hand, looked like she was out for a Sunday stroll on a cool summer evening. She was calm, serene, and perfectly in control. Maggie, eyes wide and mouth gaping, seemed to be trying to breathe in Ivy's peace with each gasp.

"I cain't do this much longer," she panted.

"'Course you can. Just think about what a gift you'll have when you're done." Ivy motioned for Colman to wipe the girl's forehead with a cool cloth. He dipped the fabric, wrung it out, and dabbed at Maggie's face.

Then she threw her head back and hollered. Colman felt as though his innards were curling in on themselves. He summoned every ounce of his strength to force himself to relax and tend to his duties. "Is she gonna be alright?" he whispered to Ivy.

"Maggie's going to be fine," Ivy said with a stern look. She then grinned. "And if I'm not mistaken . . . come on Maggie, one more push. You can do it."

Maggie gritted her teeth, screwed up her face, screamed loud enough for folks in Glen Jean to hear, and just like that a child entered the world. Colman froze as he watched Ivy lift the babe in the air. He'd seen cows and pigs give birth and had seen many a chick hatch, but this . . .

The child's face wrinkled, its eyes squinched tight, and then the little chest rose and a cry filled the room. It was the most beautiful sound Colman had ever heard. More beautiful than the ping of a perfect train wheel. More beautiful than Ivy's singing the day he escaped from that dark cave. More beautiful than his mother's voice. It was perfect, and he was pretty sure he'd never heard perfection before.

Ivy smiled at him, and it occurred to him that he'd never seen perfection before either, but this might be as close as he'd come. He no longer saw her as different. All he could see was pure joy in her smile, her eyes, and . . . he could swear he heard singing somewhere in the distance.

"Let me hold my babe." Maggie lifted her head and watched Ivy. "Is it a boy? I had a notion it would be a boy."

"Yes indeed, a healthy boy." Ivy laid the child across his mother's breast, and Maggie stroked his little head, examined his hands and feet, and snugged him close.

Colman took in a deep breath and let it out slow. "Looks like a fine little man. And with a fine head of red hair."

Maggie shot him a look. "What of it?"

"Nothing. Just haven't seen that much hair on a newborn before."

Ivy giggled. "How many newborns have you seen before today, Preacher Harpe?"

Colman flushed. "This would be one," he said, and grinned big enough for them all.

⁓

Mother and babe slept while Ivy kept watch over them. Colman eased from the room into the hall. He supposed he should go on back to his dad's knock-kneed house clinging to the mountain across the river, but he was too wide awake to rest. And he felt a connection to the three souls in the room behind him that made him reluctant to stray far.

He crept down the back stairs thinking he'd just step outside for some fresh air. In the darkness he got turned around and realized the exterior door he was looking for was somewhere to his left. He stopped to get his bearings, and in the stillness he heard . . . mumbling. He moved closer to the sound coming from a door and stopped again. While there was likely to be gambling, drinking, and other nefarious goings-on in the Dunglen at just about any hour, this sound was different.

Colman closed his eyes and listened. It was a man's voice, slurred some and growing a bit louder. He eased back into an alcove and watched as the door to what he figured was a storeroom opened. A man stumbled through the doorway, bottle in one hand, the other hand bracing against the green plaster wall to catch himself from falling.

"Stealing the same liquor I stole. Ma always did like him better." A bitter laugh. "Well, I ain't played out yet. She don't really like anybody, 'cept maybe that orphan child." The man grunted and pushed himself to standing. As he peered owlishly into the dark hall, Colman realized it was Jake McLean.

He was standing not twenty feet away from the man who'd

murdered Caleb. He tried to think what he should do. Tried to remember the burn of anger he'd felt the day he learned of the killing. But he found the sharp edges were worn now. Hate had given way to sorrow and regret. He was sorry for Jake, standing there drunk and mumbling about who-knew-what. He seemed more pitiful than evil.

Jake took a couple of steps away from Colman before veering back into the wall. He stopped, slid down to a sitting position, and thumped his head against the plaster several times. "Gotta get back on top. Can't let Mack win. Think, think, *think*." He bumped his head each time he said the word.

Colman replayed what Jake had been saying. Had Jake stolen his own mother's liquor shipments? Could the sons of the most powerful person in southern West Virginia be undermining her strength? And to what end? He'd never thought Jake was smart enough to take on his mother's empire, but Mack . . . that one was sharp. What were Serepta's sons up to? And did it even matter? If they all turned on each other and destroyed the McLean hold on the region, that would be a good thing.

Or would it? Who would step into the vacuum left behind—Webb? Colman wasn't sure that would be any better.

Jake was snoring now, whatever plan he'd had when he left the storeroom lost in his drunken brain. Colman went to the door Jake exited and pushed it open. It was a storage space sure enough, blinds pulled down over the tall windows letting in dim light. One corner had a bed and chair in it, along with a crate of McLean liquor that had clearly been sampled. Repeatedly. Looked like Jake had been hiding under the Harpe family's nose for some time.

Colman walked back out, found another exit door, and

stepped into the predawn morning. Rain crows called from the trees on the steep mountainside beyond, and the dew covering the grass wet his boots as he strode along. He watched the last of the stars fade as the sun rose higher. He'd just witnessed a miracle of life, followed closely by one of circumstance. What were the odds of his stumbling upon the hiding place of Jake McLean in addition to learning some powerful information even Serepta didn't likely know? Now he was going to have to do some thinking and praying about what, if anything, should be done about it.

Mack had taken to working at a table in the far corner of Serepta's office. She hadn't wanted him there at first, but after a few days his quiet presence and the scratch of his pencil became, if not welcome, then familiar.

It was time for Charlie to take cash payments to some of the men who helped smuggle her liquor. She unlocked her right-hand desk drawer and started to pull out the cashbox when her eyes flicked to her younger son bent over a ledger, recording coal shipments for the month. She'd never had anyone present while she was counting out cash, not even Charlie. She thought to ask Mack to leave the room, then changed her mind. She thumped the metal box onto the desktop. Mack glanced at her and then quickly focused on the ledger again. She lifted the lid and began counting out bills into three stacks—no, four now that Jake's man Ellis was part of the group. She took out four envelopes and tucked the money neatly inside them, noting that she would need to replenish her coffers soon.

"Mack, will you take these to Charlie for delivery? He knows who they go to."

Mack set down his pen, stretched, and rose to join her. "Charlie's gone to town."

Serepta frowned. Charlie never went anywhere without telling her first. "What for?"

Mack shrugged. "Didn't say. He just said to tell you, and I guess I forgot."

She frowned more deeply. "He knew I needed him to deliver these payments."

"I'll take them." Mack leaned on her desk. "I'm assuming you're paying whoever helps you get our liquor where it needs to go. Jake mentioned a fellow named Ellis—who are the others?"

Serepta tapped the stack of envelopes against the desktop, thinking. It wasn't a good idea for too many people to know her business. Then again, if Mack really was going to step up and take a leadership role, it just might be time to begin letting him in on a few details. "Fine." She listed the names and explained where he would find the men and how the transfer took place. Mack listened attentively, tucked the payments inside his jacket pocket, and set off, whistling. Serepta watched him go, eyes narrowed. She'd consider this a test, and if Mack failed her, she'd cut him off without thinking twice.

Colman headed across the bridge toward his father's house once he made sure Ivy and Maggie had breakfast. He'd feel better if Ivy came with him and left the Dunglen behind, but he guessed being alone in a rickety house with two single men wasn't a whole lot better. He got her to promise she wouldn't leave the room until he came back for her. He could tell, though, she thought he was being silly.

A train thundered into town, and soon a handful of folks

disembarked at the station. One of them looked a little like Mack McLean, but that wasn't likely. Or was it? Colman adjusted his path, heading toward the station. If Mack had come to town to meet up with Jake, he wanted to know about it.

"Well if it ain't the turncoat."

Colman had little choice but to stop when Don Fenton stepped in front of him. He hadn't seen his cousin by marriage since Caleb's funeral.

"I didn't think you'd have the nerve to show your face around here after running off to join the McLeans."

"I've been preaching to them."

"Hunh. Is that what you call it?" Don fished a packet of snuff out of his pocket and deposited a pinch inside his lower lip. "Way I heared it, you been consorting with the enemy pretty hard since you went missing."

"The Lord loves them the same as you and me." Colman wasn't altogether certain he believed that, but he knew he was supposed to say it. He tried to move around Don, but the other man wouldn't let him.

"I'd say the devil loves 'em even more." Don grinned, liking his own joke. "Why are you back here anyhow? They've done replaced you down at the station. Johnny and Elam tried to put in a good word for you, but everyone knows they're tetched, too."

Colman peered toward the depot, trying to catch a glimpse of the man who looked like Mack. Surely a McLean wouldn't be so bold as to show his face in the middle of Thurmond.

"You lookin' for somebody?" Don spit onto the sidewalk.

"Webb still got men out hunting Jake McLean?" Colman figured if he couldn't get past Don, maybe he'd get some information from him.

"Like I'd tell you anything about what Webb's up to. Now, there's a man who knows what *family* means."

Colman considered how Webb had treated his own brother. Shoot, he'd been awful rough on Caleb growing up. It was only after he died that Webb began talking about him like he was a saint and the best son who ever lived. Colman pictured Caleb the way he'd seen him last—laughing and a little bit drunk, with his arm around a girl and his ever-present hat tilted way back on his head . . .

Colman's eyes widened. "Don, it's good to see you. I've gotta run." He whirled and began trotting up the steep hillside toward his father's house, leaving Don Fenton to scratch his head and watch him go.

chapter
twenty-two

"Red hair you say?" Colman's father rinsed the pan he'd fried eggs in for breakfast. "Not many redheads round these parts."

"But there was one in particular."

Dad frowned. "Oh. You mean Caleb? You saying he's the daddy?"

"I don't know. Just seems like a fair chance. What with him spending so much time over at the Dunglen." Colman yawned. He needed some sleep. "And the girl was real touchy when I mentioned that young'un's hair."

His father shrugged. "What of it? He ain't around to take responsibility."

Colman rubbed his gritty eyes. "That babe might be a Harpe, though. Seems like that'd matter to some folks."

"And not to some others." Dad wrung out his dishrag and hung it on a hook. "Son, whyn't you get some sleep? You look like something the cat drug in."

Colman laughed. Maybe he would lie down for a minute. He trailed into the bedroom, kicked his boots off, and stretched out. He'd just rest a little while and then he'd go back and check on Ivy.

———

Voices woke Colman. In spite of his keen hearing, living alongside the tracks had given him the ability to sleep through dynamite. But there was something in the cadence of the lowered voices that had jarred him awake.

"My son wouldn't take up with a common whore."

Colman sat up and swung his legs over the side of the bed. If he didn't miss his guess, Uncle Webb was sitting at the kitchen table.

"Guess you don't remember what it was like to be a young buck." That was Dad.

"Don't try to tell me what I was like twenty years ago," Webb hissed. "And don't try to sully my son's—your nephew's—name."

"Can't see how bringing new life into the world is sullying anything." Dad's voice had risen to a normal level.

Webb cursed. "Where's that turncoat boy of yours?"

Silence.

Colman pulled on his boots, finger-combed his hair, and eased out into the sitting room. "Howdy, Uncle Webb."

His uncle draped an arm over the back of the kitchen chair and looked Colman up and down. "You have enough of running with the McLeans? Come crawling home on your belly?"

Colman straightened his spine. "Do I look like I'm crawling?"

Webb snorted. "You look like you been rode hard and put up wet." He turned away. "Guess you aren't quite as pitiful as you was the last time I saw you."

Colman straightened his shirt collar—the shirt Ivy made him. "What if that child is your grandson?"

Webb whirled back toward him and squinted. "What do you care?"

"Caleb and me used to be real close when we were young'uns." He lowered his head. "I guess our lives went different ways as we grew, but the notion that he has a child . . ." Colman looked up again, straight into his uncle's eyes. "That notion is a comfort to me now that he's gone."

Webb turned away. "If that's so, then you and me have different notions of what brings comfort."

If Colman wasn't mistaken, tears glistened in the older man's eyes. "The only thing that would bring me comfort is having my son alive and well." He stood, pushing his chair back with such force that it almost fell over. "You can tell that woman over at the Dunglen that she won't get anything out of me." He stalked out the door and soon disappeared down the side of the mountain.

Colman looked at his father, who pushed a glittering bottle of liquor toward him. "Want some?" Colman snatched up the bottle and threw it out the open back door, where it shattered against a tree trunk. He watched the liquid as it ran down the bark and soaked into the soil.

Serepta took Emmaline's hand and disembarked at the Thurmond train station. She held her head high here in her enemy's camp. She felt confident no one would trouble her while she walked hand in hand with a four-year-old child . . . with a black man trailing behind them. Charlie had protested the whole way. He'd tried to persuade her to make her cash withdrawal at one of the other banks where she held accounts. But Serepta had made up her mind, and Charlie of all people knew she was unlikely to change it.

Eyes and frowning faces tracked her as she strode past the Mankin Drug Company building and Standard Dry Goods to the National Bank of Thurmond, where she kept significant funds mostly because it amused her to know that withdrawing them had the potential to cause a business in Harpe territory a measure of difficulty. She let the ghost of a smile hover. The bank manager would have to walk a fine line in order to cater to an important account holder without offending his local constituency.

Charlie mumbled something behind her, but she ignored him. Emmaline had been enchanted by the train ride and was even now gawking at the narrow town teeming with life. They'd stay at the Dunglen Hotel once she'd finished her business at the bank. Not only was it friendlier to McLeans, but she could check on Ivy. While the hotel wasn't quite what it had been in its heyday, Alden Butterfield would ensure they had the best room in the quietest corner. Of course, Charlie would have to bunk in nearby Ballyhack. Although such treatment made Serepta bristle, she knew better than to stir that particular pot.

Gliding beneath the grand stone pediment into the bank, Serepta enjoyed the stir her entrance caused. Charlie stood outside the door, back pressed against a pillar where he could keep watch. She felt a surge of pleasure at the thought that he was looking out for her. It was a sensation she'd never experienced until Charlie came into her life, and she relished it now.

She sailed past the marble check-writing stand, as well as the tellers behind their ornate windows, and approached the bank manager's desk. The obsequious banker treated her as she expected—like a customer who could impact his bottom line if she chose to. Finished with her task, she ushered Emmaline back to the door, tugging at the crocheted gloves she wore as she stepped outside.

Charlie was not in his spot.

She looked up and down the row of buildings and across the tracks, frowning. It was unlike him to leave his post. She pinched her lips and took Emmaline's hand. She raised her chin and started back toward the depot, so they could cross the New River to the Dunglen Hotel.

As she passed the Mankin Drug Company, Police Chief Harrison Ash stepped onto the sidewalk. He grinned, swept off his Stetson, and bowed. "Well howdy there, Mrs. Mc-Lean," he drawled in what she supposed was an imitation of a cowboy. "To what does Thurmond owe the honor?"

She stared at him long enough to make him plop his hat back on and dial that grin back a few notches. "I am here to do some banking. I had thought to hear from you before now in regards to the question I posed some time back."

Harrison motioned for her to continue walking and darted a look around as he fell into step beside her. "Best I escort a fine lady like you traveling so far from home. Not everyone around these parts knows to make you welcome." He spoke loudly enough that passersby could hear him.

Serepta gave Emmaline's hand a tug and proceeded toward the station.

Harrison lowered his voice. "I might have a lead for ya, but it seems like the man who stole your liquor is being stolen from himself."

Serepta didn't spare the lawman a look, but she did furrow her brow. "Well, that is unusual. Give me a name, and I will take the matter from here."

"I'm not quite ready to do that just yet."

She turned and glared at him.

"Yeah, yeah, I know. You've got me right where you want me. Thing is, I need to get clear myself before I make a mistake and toss a rabbit into the briar patch he came from to start with."

"Whatever do you mean by that?"

"Just that whatever's going on might hit awful close to home for you, and I need a little more time to"—he fingered the brim of his hat—"let some chickens hatch."

As they arrived at the station, Serepta had yet to see Charlie. "You speak in nonsensical riddles. Did you see my man Charlie waiting outside the bank?"

"Black feller? No, but then I haven't been by the bank today."

Serepta wanted to press the man harder to tell her what he knew, but Charlie's absence was distracting her.

"If you do, send him to the Dunglen. And I will give you two more days for your . . . chickens to hatch. Then I shall expect a full report."

Harrison tipped his hat. "Ma'am," he said and walked away.

Thankfully, Charlie had arranged for porters to carry their luggage to the hotel before he disappeared. Which made Serepta think that perhaps Charlie had gone ahead to make sure their room was ready. Well. She'd give him a piece of her mind when she saw him. He was to stay with her—and the child—at all times.

Emmaline lagged and tugged at her hand, wanting to look at the tracks and the river and the people and everything else she encountered. Serepta finally snatched the little girl up and carted her across a wooden walkway over Dunloup Creek to the hotel. Emmaline protested and pushed, but Serepta had an iron grip. By the time she came to the double-decker porch with its stairs leading up to the lobby, Emmaline was screeching and kicking. Serepta dropped her to the ground, and the child exploded into howls.

Jake and Mack had given her trouble a time or two when they were boys, yet she'd never had to deal with anything like this. She stood, hands on hips, watching the child she'd begun to think of as her own turn into a demanding, red-faced tyrant screaming to have her way. Where was Charlie when she needed him? Where was Ivy for that matter? She'd only dared to trust a few people in her life, and they had abandoned her to deal with this impertinent child.

"Get up."

Emmaline continued her wailing.

"Get up and come inside."

"I want my mommy!" she screeched, then lay down full length in the dirt and kicked her heels, pounding them against the ground and likely ruining her shoes.

Serepta paled. "You will not find her here or anywhere, but you are free to go looking." She tugged her gloves into place once again and marched up the stairs. By the time she'd reached the first landing, the tirade below had faded to sobs and hiccups. By the time she reached the porch, the crying had stopped. And by the time the front door was opened by a bewildered-looking doorman, she could hear little feet pounding along behind her.

She stepped into the lobby as a small body crashed into her legs. She ignored the child and strode to the front desk where she asked for her room key and made sure her luggage had preceded her.

"Have you seen my man Charlie? I expected him to come and make certain everything is in order."

The clerk shook his head. "Nobody's been here checking on your room." He smirked and waved at Emmaline. "Maybe that one scared him off."

Serepta managed to look down her nose at the man even though he was taller. "Nothing frightens Charlie." She spun on her heel and made her way to her room, Emmaline bumping into her every other step. Once inside the spacious room with its view of the river and mountains beyond, she noted that her luggage was present, but still no Charlie.

Sighing, she sat on a small settee and tried to think where Charlie might have gotten to. Maybe . . .

"Momma?"

Serepta froze, her heart in her throat. She stared at Emmaline's tear-stained face. The child looked terrified. Had she caused that? "What did you say?"

"I'm sorry, Momma."

Serepta felt a powerful urge to scoop Emmaline into her arms and onto her lap. To hold her until all was well again.

But she resisted. Emmaline did not need coddling. She needed to develop a spine of steel. "For what are you sorry?"

Emmaline looked down, then up, then scrunched her face. "For making you go away."

Serepta's heart caught again. It was a sensation she hadn't experienced in a long, long time. She patted the settee, and Emmaline climbed up next to her. "You must do as I say." She reached out, drew her hand back, and then reached forward again, pushing dark curls from ruddy cheeks. "I will always ensure your safety, but you must trust me. If I say 'no,' or 'come,' you must obey. Do you understand?"

Emmaline nodded. "Mommas go away."

Serepta closed her eyes and put one arm around the child, allowing her to lean into her side. "I will neither fail you nor forsake you." Now, where had she heard those words before?

Emmaline sighed, clearly exhausted by her fit of temper. Serepta knew how that felt. She tilted her head back and released a pent-up breath of her own. Now if only she could discover why Charlie had left, though hopefully not forsaken, her.

chapter
twenty-three

Ivy wouldn't leave Maggie and the as-yet-unnamed baby. Colman tried to persuade her to come with him back to Hinton, but she wouldn't budge. "Maggie needs my help a while longer," she said.

Colman asked how long "a while" was. Ivy just shrugged and grinned at him. So now he sat on a stool at the counter in Mrs. McClure's restaurant, drinking coffee and eating a slice of peach pie. He was just about finished when he caught sight of Elam trotting across the tracks toward the restaurant. He looked worried as he peered through the plate-glass window. Colman lifted a hand, and Elam perked up. He jerked the door open and hurried to Colman's side.

"You'd best come go with me," he said.

Colman felt a knot tighten in his gut. "What's the matter?"

"Just come on. Johnny's keeping an eye out, but we need to do something quick." He flashed a smile. "I saw you with my second sight. I didn't hardly believe it until I looked through that window."

Colman didn't like the sound of this. He dropped some

coins on the counter and followed Elam outside. His cousin looked up and down the sidewalk before hustling Colman past the Lafayette Hotel and Armour meat-packing plant and turning up the steep hillside to the small foursquare house he and Johnny shared. Finger to his lips, he pointed to the back room. Colman pushed the door open. The windows had been covered with feed sacks. In the dim light he could make out Johnny. He was sitting where he could peek out a window by pushing back the makeshift curtain. There was also a figure lying on the narrow bed.

Elam eased up behind him. "It's that colored feller what trails along after Serepta McLean."

Colman moved closer as his eyes adjusted and saw that it was indeed Charlie, although if it hadn't been for the color of his skin he would be unrecognizable. One eye was swollen shut, his nose looked crooked, and his lips were bloodied, split, and swollen. "What happened?"

"Some of Webb's crew got ahold of him. Guess they didn't dare snatch Serepta herself but figured whipping her man would be a close second."

Colman finally tuned in to a low sound he'd been hearing since stepping onto the front porch. It was a soft keening rolling off Charlie. He stepped closer and noticed the men had a bowl of water and a cloth on the nightstand. "You try to doctor him?"

"Some. He weren't too cooperative. Wouldn't have thought there was much fight left in him, but he held us off till we give up."

Colman looked the beaten man in his one good eye and saw agony there. Still, he had a notion it wasn't physical pain so much that was troubling him. "There's a woman named Ivy at the Dunglen. She's tending to a newborn babe there. Fetch her."

"We was hoping you might take him out of here," Johnny said. "Couldn't leave him after we saw what'd been done to him, but it won't sit well if Webb's bunch finds out we helped."

"The quicker you get Ivy, the quicker she'll have him in shape to leave on his own." Colman glanced at the light still filtering through the feed sacks. "And he can't go anywhere in daylight."

Johnny grunted. "I'll go."

They all sat in silence for a while, then Colman picked up the cloth, dipped it in the basin of water, and wrung it out. He looked a question at Charlie and, not seeing anything that looked like refusal, began cleaning blood from his face.

"Serepta." The name was little more than a breath on Charlie's swollen lips.

"Word would be out if anything had happened to her," Colman said. "She in town?"

Charlie nodded, then flinched.

"Seems like the last place she'd want to turn up," Colman said.

Amusement lit Charlie's good eye. "Stubborn," he whispered. "Willful." Then so soft no one but Colman could possibly hear, "Wonderful."

Colman frowned and continued cleaning. Though he didn't know Charlie well, he did know him to be hardworking and had never heard a word spoken against him. His loyalty to Serepta made Colman wonder what he saw that no one else did. He opened his mouth to ask but stopped when he heard footsteps coming up the path—Ivy's, if he wasn't mistaken. Fancy that . . . recognizing the sound of her step.

Charlie reached up and grasped his arm with a battered hand. "There's more to her than you know."

Colman stared at the broken man and then turned to see Ivy enter the room with a bag in her hand. "Oh, Charlie . . ." Tears welled in her eyes, but she shook them away. "Serepta's at the Dunglen, and worried about you. We'll get word to her soon as we can." She darted a look at Colman. Did she mean for him to go tell Serepta?

But Ivy wasted no time, calling for clean water, bandages, and a bowl for mixing. She set Johnny to boiling water and making a tea so pungent, Colman was grateful it hadn't been the cure for what ailed him. He gradually backed out of the room, leaving her to her ministrations. He found Elam on the front porch, feet dangling as twilight descended and lightning bugs began rising into the air.

"Anybody else know he's here?" Colman asked, settling beside his cousin.

"Don't think so, but you know how word gets around." He nodded down the hill at the closest house. "Estelle's been twitching her curtains back all day. She may not know who's here, but she knows there's something going on. Only a matter of time before she butts in and tells the whole valley." He laughed. "Don't need the second sight to know that."

"Maybe we can get Charlie over to the Dunglen. Ivy said that's where Serepta is."

Elam looked at him like he'd lost his mind. "You want to tote one of the McLeans' men through town past who knows how many Harpes, some who tried to kill him last night, across the bridge, and then march into the Dunglen, where you know they don't cotton to coloreds, and knock on Serepta's door?"

Colman nodded. "Sounds about right."

Elam snorted. "I'm betting you can hear what I'm a-thinking right now."

"I believe I can." Colman grinned. "But I'm going to do it anyway."

Serepta had intended to be home by now, yet she could not leave without Charlie. She'd found Ivy, who introduced Emmaline to a squalling infant she'd helped into the world. Normally, Serepta would have no use for such things, but the distraction for Emmaline was convenient as she made queries about Charlie. No one had been helpful. As a matter of fact, several hotel denizens had seemed particularly shifty. Alden kept asking after Jake in a way that aroused her suspicion. Perhaps there was a price on her son's head. She wouldn't put it past the oily hotel manager to sell her son out to the highest bidder.

Now she was back in her room preparing for a second night. Emmaline had gone to bed after supper, exhausted from a day spent running wild and fawning over that father-less child. It wasn't how she preferred her protégé spend her day, but until she learned what had become of Charlie, she'd allow it.

She stood at the window staring into the darkness and chewing her lower lip. In the morning she'd leave Emmaline with Ivy and talk to every person with any authority in Thurmond. She wished she'd brought along her pistol. Perhaps Alden could provide her with one. While she didn't trust the man, she knew he'd never refuse her anything he could do as easily as that.

There was a scuffling sound at the door. She whirled and longed for the pistol even now. Moving between the door and the room where Emmaline slept, she waited, listening so hard her ears throbbed.

A light tapping sound.

Drawing close to the door, Serepta spoke low. "Who is it?"

"We've got your man."

She didn't recognize the voice, but then Ivy said, "Serepta, it's alright, let us in."

Pulling the door open, Serepta struggled to remain calm as Colman Harpe, a second man she didn't know, and Ivy helped a battered Charlie inside.

"What happened?" she hissed as she whisked the door shut behind them.

"Some of the fellas in town gave Charlie what they wished they could give you." Colman's look told her she'd been judged and found guilty.

"Put him on the sofa." If nothing else, she knew how to give orders.

Ivy slipped up beside her. Serepta had the impression the younger woman thought to put an arm around her but withheld the gesture. "His ribs are bruised, but I don't think they're broken. I wrapped the fingers on his left hand—they most likely are broken. Everything else will heal given time."

Serepta nodded.

"I gave him a tincture for the pain. He should sleep now."

Serepta turned to the men who'd returned Charlie to her. "Did anyone see you?"

The older man—not Colman—ducked his head. "Most likely. We was real careful, but they's folks everywhere. If no one saw us it'd be a miracle."

Colman stepped forward. "I'd recommend heading out in the morning. There's an early train, if you can get Charlie up and on it. He might be hurting bad, but he's got more grit than most men."

Serepta gave him her steeliest look. "McLeans don't run."

Colman glanced at Charlie, who had subsided into the sofa with a groan. "I don't guess Charlie's a McLean."

She looked at the only man she'd ever trusted, laid low because he was associated with her. "That he is not," she said. "And never can be."

***

Colman held Ivy's hand tight in his. Something about the day's events made him feel protective of her. "Maggie's alright, and we've done what we can for Charlie. We could take a late train back to Hinton. Sleep all the way."

Ivy shook her head. "I want to give that mother and child every chance I can. Maggie needs one more night of rest before I leave her on her own."

Colman sighed and squeezed her hand before releasing it. "I'll stay the night with Dad. Be looking for me first thing tomorrow. Maybe Elam's rubbing off on me, but I have this notion you need to put Thurmond behind you."

Ivy laughed and patted his shoulder. "I've done more good for folks the past two days than all last month back home. It's fine to hand out tonics and ease aches and pains, but Maggie and Charlie truly needed me." She lowered her gaze for a moment and then looked at Colman again in a way that set his pulse to racing. "It's the best feeling I've ever known."

Colman swallowed a lump in his throat. "Well then. You see to Maggie. I'll be back in the morning." He left and made his way onto the bridge crossing the New River, pausing out in the center to be still for a moment. The moon was little more than a sliver in the inky sky, yet what showed caught its reflection in the river beneath him. Often he'd tune out the abundance of sounds that came to him. At this moment, though, he really listened.

223

A dog barked. Someone spoke, soft and quiet, maybe a mother to a child or even one lover to another. The wind sighed, and the river whispered against the bank. A train whistle sounded so far off that even Colman could barely make it out.

Then there was a sound that didn't quite fit. It was a rough scraping sound, maybe from the direction of the hotel. Colman tuned in to footsteps and turned to see a man approaching from the Thurmond side of the bridge. He moseyed along, in no hurry, and his shape and height put Colman in mind of his father. But it wasn't Dad; it was Uncle Webb out for a late-night stroll.

"Hear you've been busy," Webb said, drawing closer.

Colman tried to look relaxed. "That I have."

"Doing the Lord's work?" Webb leaned on the railing beside Colman and spit into the water below.

Colman pondered how to answer. "You know, I believe I have been."

"Hunh. Always did find God to be meddlesome." Silence hung between the two men, thick as the night. Webb shifted. "Your work wouldn't have anything to do with Serepta's houseman, would it?"

Colman held his tongue.

"'Cause if it did, I might take exception to that. It's one thing to go into enemy territory to *preach*"—the word sounded like a curse on Webb's lips—"but it's something else altogether to aid the enemy in your own town."

"Charlie didn't shoot Caleb."

Webb straightened and turned to face Colman. "You think that's what this is about? That was just the straw that broke the camel's back. I've tolerated the McLean hold on this whole territory for as long as I intend. It's time power shifted, and Serepta's days are numbered." He leaned closer. "As are the days of anyone who sides with her."

Colman threw his hands into the air. "So, it's about power? And money, and who's stronger? Do the men you've got helping you know that? Do they know you're just using the murder of your son as an excuse to wrestle the reins of control from Serepta McLean?"

He didn't see the fist coming, just landed on his hind quarters on the bridge. Webb stood over him, breathing heavily as Colman rubbed his jaw. "If you think I don't mourn my son every day, then you've got—"

"If you mourn him, why don't you march over there to the Dunglen and claim his boy? Help the mother of your grandson build a life for herself and that child." Colman stayed down, figuring he'd be harder to hit at this angle. He could see that his uncle had a pistol tucked into his waistband.

"Why you—"

Whatever Webb was going to say was cut off by a flash of light and a burst of voices behind Colman. He scrambled to his feet and glanced back toward the Dunglen. Flames shot into the sky, reflecting in the fast-running water of the river. He and Webb stood slack-jawed for a moment before breaking into a run toward the burning building.

chapter
twenty-four

Once Charlie had settled into a deep sleep, Serepta went into the adjoining bedroom and checked to see that Emmaline was also sleeping. Seeing she was, Serepta turned away, pressed a pillow to her face, and wept. She couldn't remember the last time she'd shed tears for any reason. Even now they were no comfort to her, but felt like acid pouring from her eyes and burning her cheeks. She wondered that the pillow didn't dissolve in her hands.

If someone had asked, she would have had difficulty telling them why she was crying. It might be for the suffering forced upon the only man she'd ever thought good. It might be for the orphaned child splayed in the bed behind her. It might be for the way her sons had disappointed her. It might even be for the life she had been denied . . .

Serepta forced herself to gain control. She'd never allowed emotion to sway her or sidetrack her before. Now was not the time to begin. She wiped her face with a handkerchief smelling of rose water and took a shuddering breath. Moving to the window, she raised the sash wide and leaned out into the night air. It must be after ten by now. She took in the starry sky, then allowed her gaze to roam over the trees and mountains beyond. She almost wished she had the heart to find it beautiful.

A figure darted out of a door below, looked all around, and then sprinted for the tree line. Serepta furrowed her brow. If she didn't know better, she would say the man looked a great deal like Mack. But that couldn't be. He was back in Hinton overseeing business while she was away. Suspicion twisted her gut. If she learned later that he'd broken the trust she was beginning to give him . . .

Someone cried out from inside the hotel. Then another shout. Serepta could just make out the sounds and assumed it was an angry gambler or a drunk. She turned back toward Emmaline to make sure the child continued to sleep, then peered into the sitting room where she saw Charlie's eyes were open, starkly white against his dark skin. She knelt beside him and took the hand that wasn't injured in her own.

"I don't often say I'm sorry, but I regret that you were placed in a position to be so badly hurt."

Charlie started to laugh but it clearly pained him. "Did I just hear the great Serepta McLean admit she made a decision that might not have been for the best?"

Serepta scowled at him. "Make light of it if you will, but I do not like seeing you laid low. I will discover who is to blame and—"

Charlie squeezed her hand and interrupted her. "No, you won't. I don't often contradict you, but tonight I hurt too bad to dance. I'm tired of people hurting each other. Let's not pay back evil with evil."

Serepta stood and stepped away. "You always were the most infuriating man. If I didn't . . . ." She hesitated.

"Didn't what?" Charlie tried to smile, but his fat lip wouldn't allow it.

Serepta cleared her throat. "If I didn't want the best for you."

"Hunh. Thought you were gonna say something else."

Serepta closed her eyes and exhaled long and slow. "Charlie, I bow to no man. But even I know there are some rules you don't break."

"Seems to me we've already broken a few."

"And no one need ever know that."

Another cry came from downstairs, louder this time. Serepta moved to the door, cracked it open, and glanced into the hall.

"Fire!" This time the cries were clear. Serepta stepped into the hall and saw a man surge up the stairs, taking them two at a time. "The hotel's on fire! Everybody get out as quick as you can!" He tore off down the hall, pounding on doors as he ran. Guests began to appear, doing up buttons and wrapping robes around themselves.

Serepta stepped back inside and looked wild-eyed at Charlie. "We have to leave," she said. "People will see you."

Charlie was already struggling to rise. Serepta moved to help him as he grunted and groaned. "Get Emmaline. I'll turn my collar way up and pull a hat way down. No one will pay attention in the hubbub."

Serepta nodded and roused the child, who was still sleeping soundly. Once her shoes were on, she hurried her toward the door. Charlie waved them on. "You go ahead. I'll come after you so's folks won't know we're together. I'll go around back and mix with the help."

It angered Serepta to be forced to leave Charlie to sneak out on his own, although she saw no other way around it. She started toward him one more time, but he waved her on.

So she grabbed Emmaline by the hand, and they scurried out of the room.

She saw flames as she rushed her charge through the hotel lobby but was soon outside and on the front lawn where a crowd had gathered to watch the growing inferno. She examined the shape of every person who exited, hoping to see Charlie, but he would likely find a different exit. She cursed the fire, the men who hurt Charlie, the circumstances, and the fact that all she could do right now was stand and watch. If her purpose in life was to never feel powerless, then she had failed.

By the time Colman and Webb reached the hotel, people were spilling out into the grass in a chaotic mess. Colman examined the face of every woman he saw, searching for Ivy. He'd lost track of Webb, and good riddance. He saw Serepta and Emmaline standing back from the flames, watching the crowd as intently as he was.

"Where's Ivy?" he yelled as he grabbed Serepta's arm. He'd never been this close to the woman before, and he was shocked by the ice in her eyes gleaming in the firelight.

There was a flicker of emotion before she stiffened and replied, "How should I know?"

Colman released her and began pushing through the crowd, looking for Ivy, Maggie and the baby, but failing to find them. He drew nearer to the building. One side of it was engulfed by the fire now. He spotted Webb, pistol in hand, his eyes on . . . Jake McLean, staggering out of the smoke-filled lobby with a baby in his arms and a woman clinging to his side. They practically fell down the stairs. Jake shoved the baby at the woman—Maggie, Colman realized—then turned and ran back inside. Seconds later, he came out carrying another woman, nearly falling before he reached the grass and set her down.

Colman ran forward and dropped to his knees beside Ivy, who was coughing and covered in soot. The hem of her dress was scorched, but other than that, he could find no damage. "Are you alright, Ivy?"

She coughed and smiled. "I think I will be. Good thing . . ." She coughed some more, then caught her breath again. "Good thing I know how to treat a cough." She looked around. "Where'd Jake go? He saved us. Maggie fell, and we were afraid for the baby—"

Colman spotted Jake just as a shot rang out above the bedlam.

～～～

Serepta saw it but couldn't make sense of it. Jake was here. And he'd helped two women and a child escape the fire. She would have assumed Jake would save his own skin rather than risk it for anyone else's. And then she saw Webb Harpe. He was pointing a pistol at her son. She almost closed her eyes, unwilling to watch her flesh and blood gunned down while she stood helpless. Instead, she steeled herself to witness what she would surely avenge.

Webb seemed to be taking a long time. Serepta began to think she might be able to reach him, to stop him. Then he shifted his aim and fired the pistol.

～～～

Colman spun in the direction of the shot. Webb stood, pistol in hand, his expression an unreadable mask. He then stalked off into the roiling crowd.

Jake glanced at Colman, a surprised look on his face. "He missed!" Patting himself all over, Jake looked around. They were standing near an outbuilding. Jake pulled out his pocketknife and dug at a spot in the wood. He held up a slug, glinting in the firelight. "He missed by more than a little."

Colman, arm around Ivy's shoulders, couldn't make sense of what had just happened. Webb was a crack shot. No way would he miss at such a range, even at night with all the chaos around them. He locked eyes with Jake again, and something passed between them. It was almost as if Colman could hear the other man's heart begging for forgiveness . . . and hoping it might look like a slug buried in a piece of wood.

But where was Charlie?

Serepta and Emmaline stood watching the fire until after midnight. The Mount Hope and Oak Hill Fire Departments finally arrived on the scene after winding their way down the precipitous mountain into the gorge, but it was much too late by then. The building had been largely destroyed. Eventually, everyone made their way to the Lafayette Hotel, with its veranda extending to the tracks in Thurmond. Ivy met Serepta out front.

"They have Charlie," she said.

"What do you mean 'have' him?" Serepta was exhausted mentally and emotionally, and poor Emmaline needed a bath and a bed.

"They're talking like . . . well, I don't care to say it." Serepta wouldn't have thought it possible, but Ivy looked even paler than usual.

Serepta had no patience for this. "Just tell me."

"Like he was staying with you." Ivy paused, and a hint of color washed her cheeks. "In your room."

"So he was," Serepta said. "Take Emmaline." She brushed past Ivy and stalked into the lobby as though ready to brace a pride of lions. But when she saw Charlie, she stopped.

He stood, head hanging low, his wounds painfully obvious in the well-lit room.

"What's the meaning of this?" she asked in a voice that carried to the farthest corner.

Douglas McIver, the hotel manager who was married to a Harpe, stepped forward. "Several witnesses saw this man exiting your room during the fire."

Serepta raised her chin, grateful she hadn't changed into her nightclothes. "And they say they saw this in the chaos of a hotel emptying?" She looked around the room. "Let them step forward and say so to me."

Douglas flushed. "They'd just as soon remain anonymous, but I can vouch for them."

She looked daggers at him. "Can you?"

"Now see here, it's been a difficult night, but we can't be having any . . . untoward situations at the Lafayette." He tugged at the lapels of his jacket. "We run a respectable establishment."

Serepta snorted and braced her hands on her hips. "Charlie is a man in my employ, and *I* can vouch for him. I'll thank you to let us all retire and get what sleep we can before sunup."

A low drawl came from the far corner of the room. "But who can vouch for you?"

She turned and saw Webb Harpe separate from the crowd. The wild-eyed man she'd seen miss shooting down her eldest son looked calm and collected now. She kept her peace. She had nothing to say to him.

Webb stepped closer. "We may not be the most upstanding town in southern West Virginia, but even the Dunglen has standards."

"Had," Serepta corrected. "The Dunglen Hotel is no more."

Webb colored, but quickly regained control. "If we had any notion something—" he paused, the gleam in his eye sharpening—"unnatural were going on, we'd have to take steps to remedy the situation."

Serepta felt the emotions she'd tamped down after her fit of tears begin to rise and bubble. She prided herself on her ability to hide what she was feeling at all costs, but in this moment she was precipitously close to showing her hand.

"I snuck in there."

Every head in the room swiveled to stare at Charlie where he stood, feet planted wide as if to keep from toppling over.

"What's that you say?" Douglas asked.

Charlie lifted his head and met Serepta's eye. "I figured with everybody running around like headless chickens, it was my chance to sneak in and steal the missus' purse."

Serepta felt her mouth gape open and snapped it shut again.

"Figured it was a good opportunity to get some of my own back from her."

Words failed Serepta. She gave her head a shake, but Charlie's gaze didn't waver.

"You'uns can't be thinking I'd be there for any other reason."

Someone in the crowd snickered, and Serepta felt heat tinge her ears. Webb moved closer still. "Don't let—"

Serepta whirled on him, breaking her connection to Charlie.

"You may not speak," she hissed. "I will take my man home and deal with him my own way."

Webb's eyes narrowed, and he spoke low so that no one else could hear. "Don't be too sure about that." He raised his voice. "If he was stealing from his own *mistress*, who's to say he wasn't stealing from others in the hotel? Search him."

Several men laid hold of Charlie, reaching into his pockets, touching every inch of him, and finally ripping his shirt open. And there, against his bare chest, hung a ring on a chain. Serepta gasped. It was the ring she'd given him years ago, a simple Art Deco design with a single diamond. Not ornate or even very valuable. She'd given it to him almost as a joke—probably the only sentimental thing she'd done in all her life.

Webb surged forward and snatched the ring, breaking the chain. "What's this? Looks like a lady's ring." He glanced around the room. "Anyone missing a ring?"

One of the girls known for servicing the Dunglen bit her lip, glanced from side to side, and raised a tentative hand. "I'm missing a ring."

Webb grinned. "Well now, missy. Step right up and see if this ain't the one." The girl eased forward, and Webb slid the ring onto her finger with a flourish. "Perfect fit. Looks like we have a thief in our midst."

Serepta opened her mouth to speak, then quickly snapped it shut. If she said she'd given the ring to Charlie, it would be as good as admitting they had a relationship deeper than employer and employee. And this crowd would be happy to think the worst. Which was no more than the truth. And that would be the end of any respect they had for her. She turned to Charlie, but his head was back down. He swayed, and a man put a rough hand out to steady him.

"Guess we've had enough excitement for one night," Webb said. "I'll take custody of the thief until we can turn him over to Chief Ash." He took Charlie by the arm and jerked him across the room. "You good folks try and get some sleep now." Before he left, he caught Serepta's eye and touched his forehead with a knuckle. Then he grinned like the cat that ate the cream and hauled Charlie away.

chapter
twenty-five

Colman made sure Ivy, Maggie, and the baby were safe, then staggered to his father's house and collapsed on the sofa where he stayed until morning's song woke him. Dad was in the kitchen frying eggs and sausage. Colman washed his face and poured himself a cup of coffee.

"Webb had a chance to kill Jake McLean last night."

Dad flipped an egg.

"He didn't, though," Colman added.

Dad pulled two plates down and began loading them with food. "Don't have any bread this morning."

Colman accepted a plate and sat at the kitchen table. "I can't figure out why he didn't do it."

"Can't you?"

"Well, Jake just pulled two women and a baby out of a burning building, but I didn't expect Webb to go soft just because of that."

"Ain't that the baby you think is Webb's grandchild?" A look of wonder flitted across Dad's face. "That'd make him my grandnephew. How about that?"

"But Webb said it's not Caleb's child."

Dad laughed and began eating. "Since when did what comes out of Webb's mouth have anything to do with what's going on inside his head?"

Colman mulled that over as he ate. "You think he'll claim the boy?"

Dad shrugged. "I think Webb's madder than a wet hen because he wants what Serepta's got and he can't figure out how to take it from her."

They ate in silence a while. Finally, Dad spoke again. "You there for the to-do over Serepta's man?"

"The what?"

"Guess since Webb couldn't lay hands on Serepta, he turned some of his boys loose on ole Charlie and then accused him of being shacked up with his boss lady and stealing some girl's ring."

"I know they beat him up, but what's this about stealing?"

"Johnny come by early and filled me in. Said you'd want to know about it. Webb hauled Charlie off. Said he was gonna turn him over to the authorities."

"And Serepta let him?" Colman was dumbfounded.

"Guess she didn't have much choice, unless she wanted to tell folks she had a black man in her bed. Way Johnny told it, she just let Webb march Charlie on out of there."

Colman pushed his chair back and stood. "That's pure crazy."

Dad shrugged and put their plates and silverware in the dishpan. "Maybe. But there's not much anybody can do about it."

Colman frowned. "It's getting to where I can't tell whose side I'm supposed to be on. Nobody's acting right."

"Son, that's been the way of the world since Eve plucked that apple."

"Yeah, well, I don't care if Webb takes on Serepta, but he ought to leave poor Charlie alone. I'm gonna see if I can't do something about this."

Dad nodded, then went to cleaning the dishes.

⌒

The last person Serepta expected to see when she walked down the stairs to talk to that good-for-nothing Harrison Ash about Charlie was Colman Harpe. And yet there he stood, glaring at her as though she were late for an appointment with him.

"Can I help you?" she asked.

"You can help the only person who'd give more than a dime for your hide."

She raised her eyebrows. "I suppose I know who you mean."

"It's not a long list of possibilities. How could you let Webb haul Charlie out of here like that?"

Frustration fizzed beneath her skin, but she wouldn't let it show. "I chose to bide my time. I will tend to the matter this morning now that tempers have cooled."

"Well, your time is up. I checked before I came over and Charlie's long gone."

A feeling as hot as last night's fire shot through her. "Gone? Gone where?"

"Webb and his gang put Charlie on a coal train headed west before dawn. And from what my cousin tells me, he went willingly. Like maybe he was glad to finally get shut of this mess."

Ice ran through Serepta's veins, and she could hear a buzzing in her ears. Charlie gone? It couldn't be. "But Chief Ash—"

"Harrison Ash claims he was still at the Dunglen when they ran Charlie out of town. Says he didn't have a chance to stop them. Seemed real keen on you knowing that." Colman narrowed his eyes. "I'm of a mind to tear this up, but I guess Charlie wanted you to have it. Elam asked me to pass it on since you and him don't run in the same circles." Colman practically spit the words at her as he handed over a folded piece of paper. "If anybody ever needed the Lord, it's you." He spun on his heel and headed up the stairs—probably to check on that loose woman and her child.

Serepta didn't remember walking back to her room, but she was suddenly there, checking to see that Emmaline was still sleeping. The child had been exhausted after their or-deal, and Serepta spent most of the night watching her sleep, wishing she could do the same. She sagged into an armchair and unfolded the paper. She'd helped Charlie learn to read and write, and he had a nice hand.

S, I've been a fool for too long. I thought if anyone had the courage, it would be you. I know you had to choose and I can't say you chose wrong. Time I headed on. —C

Serepta stared at the paper until the lines blurred. Her only friend. Her only trusted companion. She crumpled the paper in her hand. Well, maybe she'd chosen wrong after all—back when she chose to trust someone. Maybe Charlie had never been what she'd imagined. She stood and began gathering their few things for the trip home, cursing the traitorous tears dripping from her chin.

Colman had never been so glad to see Thurmond disap-pearing behind him as he was this morning. It was hard to say why he was so mad about Charlie being run out of town—he hardly knew the man—but something about the way Charlie had been treated galled him.

He settled Ivy in her forward-facing seat and sat across from her. He wanted to sit right beside her and protect her from any comers, but he didn't think she'd appreciate it. As disgruntled as he was, she was all sunshine and light. She jabbered on about that baby and how she'd been able to give folks who breathed in smoke tonics that helped them. He tried to listen, but instead he was stewing over Charlie's treatment, the way Webb had missed shooting Jake, and the way Jake had looked at him . . . almost hopeful. His mind was a whirl, and he didn't know what to think about any of it.

"Please do."

Colman jerked his head up. Ivy was speaking to someone. He looked around, and there was Mack McLean settling into the seat beside her. He just stared. It seemed like he ran into a McLean everywhere he went these days. "Where'd you come from?"

Ivy frowned at him.

"I'm traveling from Cincinnati home again. What a coincidence that we should meet." Mack smiled at Ivy. And she let him. "I heard there was quite a commotion in Thurmond last night. Shame about the Dunglen burning, but I'm glad no one was seriously hurt."

"Charlie Hornbeck surely was." Colman glared at the man sitting too close to Ivy.

"Not in the fire, as I understand it. The stationmaster mentioned that Mother left on an earlier train this morning, alone except for the child. Apparently, Charlie was waylaid by"—he looked Colman up and down—"some of your kin, I believe." Colman felt heat climb his neck. "Shame. Charlie was a good man and loyal to my mother."

"Do you think he'll come home again?" Ivy asked, touching Mack's sleeve.

"I doubt it. Mother's unlikely to forgive him for leaving, even though he had little choice." Mack laughed and laid a hand over Ivy's. "She's shrewd, and she never doubts her decisions. I'm sure she'll find another helper to see to her household needs."

"I hope Charlie's alright. He really shouldn't be traveling with his injuries." Ivy frowned, and Mack squeezed her hand. It was all Colman could do not to reach over and push Mack away.

Colman suddenly stood. "I'm going to the dining car. Want anything?"

Ivy looked at him with wide blue eyes. "I'm fine, thank you."

"Why don't you walk with me?" Colman said to Mack.

Mack shook his head and worked his shoulders against the back of his seat. "I'm fine as well. But thank you for asking."

Colman stomped down the aisle. Though he didn't want to leave the pair of them alone, he needed some fresh air and a few quiet moments to think.

Serepta stared out the window, watching the scenery go by all the way to Hinton. She disembarked and was handed her luggage. She stared at it, thinking how Charlie would have whisked it away and home without her ever having to think about it. She clenched her jaw, hired a man to drive them to Walnutta, and sealed her heart up tight against any emotion. Even Emmaline seemed to sense her mood, remaining quiet and subsiding into the back seat of the car.

When she arrived at the house, no one greeted her. She had thought Mack at least would be around. Her mind flashed back to that figure the night of the fire. But no. Mack had no reason to visit the Dunglen Hotel.

She dragged her bag up the wide front steps, Emmaline trailing behind her. Hallie, the girl who helped in the kitchen, finally clattered into the front hall, fear painted across her dark features.

"Mr. Charlie ain't sent word of your comin'," she said. "You wanting supper? Where's Mr. Charlie at?"

Serepta let her bag thump onto the hardwood floor. "Mr. Charlie has left us to fend for ourselves. I would be grateful if you could manage a simple meal." She looked around the silent hall. "Is Mack here?"

Hallie got a cagey look. "He say he be back today." She looked up at the ceiling. "He say he go to Cincinnati. Say you're not to worry."

Serepta nodded. What in the world had carried her son off to Ohio? "Emmaline and I will be upstairs resting from our journey. Please call us when supper is ready."

Hallie made a motion that was almost a curtsy, then scurried back toward the kitchen.

"Come, Emmaline." Serepta abandoned her bag in the hall and led the way upstairs, the child trailing along behind her. "We will refresh ourselves and look forward to something good to eat."

As they reached the upstairs landing, Emmaline tugged at Serepta's pant leg. "Momma?" Serepta froze. She'd almost forgotten that Emmaline had called her that before all the chaos. "Yes?"

"Where's Charlie?"

Serepta closed her eyes and breathed slowly, in and out. She took the girl's hand and led her into her own chamber. They settled on a chaise lounge positioned to enjoy a view of the rolling fields and hills beyond the window. Serepta drew Emmaline close.

"I will tell you a story," she began. "Once upon a time there was a wicked queen who ruled the land with a fist of iron. A king came to her, but he was disguised as a peasant. No one, least of all the queen, saw him for what he was." Emmaline leaned into her, and she stroked the girl's silky curls. "But the queen began to sense that there was something special about the peasant. He was kind, generous, faithful, and always trustworthy. The queen began to care about the king in disguise, not realizing she was not worthy of him." Serepta fixed her eyes on the distant hills where the sun chased shadow clouds. "Then one day the common people of the land captured the king in disguise. They didn't know what he was either. They were cruel to him. Hurt him and banished him from the land."

Emmaline stirred and tucked her little hand in Serepta's. "Where did he go?"

"I don't know," she whispered.

"Why didn't the queen stop them? Why didn't she bring him back?"

"I don't know," Serepta repeated, "but maybe it's better that she didn't. Maybe it's better that he goes to a country where his worth can be known."

"What about Charlie?" Emmaline tipped her head up to look at Serepta with dark eyes.

"He went with the king, who needs his help more than we do."

Emmaline looked back down and snuggled against Serepta's side. "I miss him."

"So do I," she said as she watched the clouds chase nothing, going nowhere.

chapter
twenty-six

As Colman escorted Ivy back to her cottage, he felt a conviction that would not leave him alone. Preaching, telling stories, and ministering to the McLeans who came to his meetings wasn't enough. He needed to strike at the heart of the darkness that had weighed on the region for too long.

It was time to witness to Serepta McLean herself. He'd rarely felt so certain about anything in his life. When he'd confronted her about her treatment of Charlie and her need of God, he'd spoken a truth deeper than he'd known. If he could win her to faith, surely the rest would follow. If he could lead her to peace, their struggles would come to an end. It was the only answer—the surest, fastest way to salvation for the Harpes and the McLeans.

Then maybe he could go home and stay there. And maybe he could take Ivy with him.

For the first time since leaving the cave, Colman felt strong. The knowledge of what he needed to do filled him with a vigor he'd been missing for too long. It was like hearing the ping of a perfectly balanced wheel that he knew would carry that train all the way to its destination.

The only question was how to begin. That would take some thinking, but first he would deliver Ivy home.

Hoyt was there to greet them as they crossed the stream and started down the path to Ivy's garden. "'Bout time you two got back here. I've lost ten pounds eating my own cooking." He wrapped Ivy in a hug. "And the hearth is a lonesome place of an evening when you're not there to grace it."

Ivy hugged him back and began chattering about her adventures. "Oh, but the garden. Have you been tending it?"

Hoyt shook his head. "Not as good as you. Go on and look after your plants." Ivy darted ahead and began walking up and down the rows as if greeting old friends.

Hoyt turned to Colman, his expression of joy gone dark. "They's rumors that a Harpe set fire to the Dunglen Hotel since it's mostly used by the McLeans. Your name ain't come up that I know, but it might."

Colman tried to smile. "I thought I'd turned traitor by running off to preach to the McLeans."

"Well, it just might turn out both sides think that about you. Could put you in a pickle."

Colman nodded. "I've been thinking—"

Hoyt interrupted. "So have I. As much as Ivy and I enjoy having you around, I think it might be time we found you other accommodations."

Caught flat-footed, Colman couldn't think what to say.

Hoyt lowered his voice. "Ivy has a hard enough time as it is, what with people thinking she's different. I couldn't stand it if more trouble came to her door."

"Neither could I." Colman forced another smile. "You know of a good boardinghouse around here?"

"No." Hoyt chuckled. "But there's a cabin over near the salt spring that's been abandoned for the past five years or so. Fella what lived there took to gambling up and down the line and quit coming home." He made a face. "Either he hit it big or . . ."

Colman nodded. "Let's hope he hit it big." He rubbed his hands together. "Alright then, show me this cabin and I'll see if it won't suit me fine."

Hoyt slapped him on the back. "Sure thing. Come have some supper first and then we'll walk over there together. Ain't far."

"You do the cooking?"

Hoyt moved ahead, shooting Colman a look over his shoulder. "I did, and if you want to know the truth, I gained five pounds while you'uns was gone. I'm a better cook than Ivy." He winked, and Colman followed him into the cottage.

Mack arrived at Walnutta just in time to sit down to the simple meal Serepta and Emmaline were eating.

"What took you to Cincinnati?"

"Skipping the niceties, Mother?"

She speared him with a look.

"Mind if I join you?" he asked.

Serepta called for Hallie to bring a plate and waved Mack into a seat. He added cold ham and sliced tomatoes to his plate. "I had some suspicions about who was stealing our liquor. Unfortunately, they didn't pan out."

Had Harrison said something similar about suspicions? Serepta's gut tightened. "I don't suppose you stopped over at the Dunglen Hotel on your way home."

Mack swallowed a bite of food. "I did not, but I certainly heard about its burning and I'm relieved to see that you and

Emmaline are well." He smirked. "Some people think Webb Harpe had something to do with the fire."

Serepta tapped a finger against the edge of her plate. "He was there that night."

Mack raised his eyebrows. "Was he? You saw him?"

"He had the opportunity to shoot your brother down in cold blood." She paused, watching for her son's reaction. "And apparently he chose not to take it."

Mack set down his fork and rested his elbows on the table. "That's strange. What was Jake doing in Thurmond?"

Serepta had a hard time reading her younger son. "I don't know. I thought you might have a notion." She lifted a slice of buttered bread. "Since you and he are working together now."

Mack leaned back in his chair and blew out an exaggerated sigh. "I wanted him to come to Cincinnati with me, but he claimed he had other business to attend to. Sounds like that business might have been in Thurmond." Mack sat forward again. "You know, with Colman Harpe hanging around, I wonder if the pair of them might not be cooking something up. Colman's people don't trust him anymore, and with him taking Ivy to the Dunglen . . . well, it seems suspicious."

Serepta frowned. It was befuddling that Colman had been so ready to take Ivy to Thurmond, and that Jake should be there at the same time. Still, she couldn't quite think what scheme they might have up their sleeves. Even if Jake wanted to undermine her power by siding with the Harpe clan, they wouldn't allow Caleb's murderer to join them. Unless Jake and Colman were up to something neither clan would like.

"I have much to think about," she said. "I'll put Emmaline

to bed and then retire myself. Will you still be here in the morning?"

Mack reached across the table and patted her hand. The gesture was so unusual between them that Serepta nearly jerked her hand away. The tenderness of it cracked her heart.

"Charlie is gone," she blurted.

"I heard about that, too." Mack looked sad. "I'm sorry, Mother. I know he'd been with you a long time."

She stood, pulling her hand out of reach as she did so. "And now that he is not, I will need your help more than ever."

"You shall have it," Mack said.

Serepta nodded, then herded a drowsy Emmaline upstairs. She thought she should be comforted by her son's statement . . . and yet she felt cold and alone instead.

~~~~~

The cabin had seen better days. Even so, it felt like a place where he belonged as soon as he walked inside. It was little more than a single room with a fireplace in one end and a narrow iron bedstead in the other. He tested the thin mattress with one hand and was surprised to find it acceptable. Ivy walked with them to see the cabin, and she flitted about like a moth talking about chairs and a table and kitchen things. Hoyt finally rounded her up, handed Colman a bundle with blankets and a flint, thumped him on the shoulder, and left him in peace.

After making his bed and laying a fire for the morning, Colman settled on the crooked porch to watch twilight fall. In town he would have tuned out the cacophony around him—people, animals, machines, and most of all trains. But here the sounds invited him to sit and take them in. Crickets, a nearby brook, the scurry of tiny feet hurrying home, a sighing breeze, and maybe, just maybe, he could hear the stars flickering to life.

Then he heard a more certain sound. Footsteps coming slow and tentative. Like someone was hurt or maybe sneaking along. He eased to his feet and moved to where he could press his back against the side of the cabin. There was just enough light to see the shape of a man separate from the trees and head for the porch. He stopped at the slab of fieldstone serving as a step and took a deep breath as though he'd been a long time getting here. Colman wondered if the gambling man had finally made his way home.

"This your place?" Colman kept his voice low. The man jumped like he'd been snakebit.

"Who's there?"

That voice . . . from where did Colman know it? "I was planning to spend the night here, but if the place is yours . . ."

The man turned toward him and peered into the twilight. "Colman Harpe?"

That was where he knew the voice—Jake McLean. "You're a long way from where I saw you last."

Jake took a step closer. "So are you. 'Course, this time you're the one who's strayed from home. Thought maybe you'd gone back to Thurmond to stay—give up on converting folks around here."

"Not yet."

"Hunh. I'm starting to wonder if we're worth the trouble myself."

Colman walked out and sat on the edge of the porch again. He guessed he was supposed to want Jake dead, but after seeing the man help save two women and a child from a fire, he was mostly curious. "That was a narrow escape back at the Dunglen."

Jake settled on the porch about ten feet away. Tension thrummed the air, yet there also seemed to be a truce. "Which escape would that be? From the fire or from Webb Harpe?"

"I'll admit I was surprised by both."

Jake laughed but without mirth. "Yeah. If I'd stopped to think, I doubt I'd have risked my skin to pull those gals out of there. But I heard that baby cry and . . ." Colman could hear the shrug. "Then I reckon Webb missed me a-purpose. Can't say why."

Colman let silence settle before speaking. "There's a fair chance that young'un's his grandson."

When Jake spoke next there was a tightness—a thickness—to his voice. "Caleb's boy?"

"Seems a fair guess considering where Caleb spent his time and the thatch of red hair the child was born with."

"You don't say." This time neither man broke the silence, until finally Jake stirred and fished the makings for a cigarette out of his pocket. "Mack set that fire."

Colman jerked at the unexpected comment. "Why would he do that?"

Jake finished rolling his cigarette and flicked a match aflame against his fingernail. He took a puff and exhaled. "I been thinking on that. The thing is . . . he might've known I was holed up there."

Colman kept his peace. No need to admit he'd known as much himself.

"The fire started right outside the room I was sleeping in." He shifted and inhaled smoke deep into his lungs, coughing a little as he let it out. "I ain't been sleeping so good. Bad dreams. Just so happens I woke up in time to smell gasoline and cracked the door open right before Mack threw the match."

Colman nodded but didn't say anything.

"Guess maybe Mack wants to be next in line if anything happens to the queen of the McLeans." His voice twisted at the end. "Looks like your uncle and his men aren't the only ones who want me dead."

Colman pondered Jake's words. He didn't like the man, but right now he felt sorry for him. And maybe he felt a touch of empathy. He didn't think anyone was trying to kill him, but neither was he entirely welcome in either the Harpe or the McLean camp. He was an outsider in both places. "Sounds like you're in a tough spot."

Jake laughed, then choked on smoke as he stubbed out the glowing cigarette on the edge of the porch. "That I am. You want to know the worst of it?"

Colman angled himself toward Jake and leaned against the rough post holding up the roof. "Sure. Since we're getting on to be friends here in the dark."

"Mack's pulling the wool over Ma's eyes."

Colman felt his own eyes widen in the deepening night. Was Jake betraying his family? Well, why not? They hadn't exactly watched out for him. "What do you mean?"

"She thinks he's helping her with the business, but I heard from Alden at the hotel that Mack's been talking to some of the high rollers who come through there about natural gas. Says coal's on the way out and he knows where they can get their hands on a well that won't run out maybe ever."

"He telling the truth?"

Jake leaned back and tilted his head toward the stars blanketing the sky. "Probably. The fellas he's trying to team up with wouldn't take kindly to being lied to."

"Neither would Serepta."

"Ain't that the truth. Thing is, I can't figure out where Mack's getting his bankroll. He's been living high, showing off for the big wheels. Ma sure wouldn't give him that kind of money. And if he stole it, she'd know in about thirty seconds."

Colman looked at the stars too, marveling at this unlikely conversation. "Jake, did you come out here looking for me? Did you think I might could help you figure things out?"

Jake blew out a puff of air. "Crossed my mind. When I saw you back there at the Dunglen, it came to me that you're about the only person who goes back and forth between Thurmond and Hinton without folks taking offense. People trust preachers."

"Some do. Not sure it's always a good idea. The question is, can I trust you? I'm not quite over that time you knocked me on the head."

Jake was silent for a moment. Then he asked, "How drunk was I?"

"What?"

"I don't quite recollect knocking you on the head, so I guess I must have been awful drunk."

"How should I know? You snuck up and threw an old sack over my head first."

"Well now, you must have me mixed up with somebody else. I'd remember doing that, and if I was drunk I know I couldn't sneak up on your eagle ears."

Colman snorted. "It was up on the ridge above the creek near Ivy's place. I was sitting up there when you came along, threw a bag over my head, and knocked me cold. When I came to—" he paused—"Webb was there and said he'd chased you off."

"Are you funning me?"

Colman shook his head. "No, but I'm starting to wonder if Webb was funning me."

"How's that?"

"He got after me about helping him track you down. Said something about wanting vengeance and 'some of what Serepta McLean's got.'" Colman thought back through the encounter. "That's when I started trying to get on the right side of the folks around here, hoping they could tell me something I could pass on to Webb."

Jake guffawed. "You mean like Nell McLean? Watch out. If that girl sets her cap for you, it won't matter if you're a Harpe or not."

"That's not the point. Point is, you say you weren't there, and I know Webb was."

Jake sobered. "You think he bushwhacked you? Why would he do that?"

"To get me to do what he wanted. Webb's always known how to get under a person's skin. He threatened my father."

"His own brother?"

"Well, you think your own brother tried to burn you out."

Jake shifted. "Guess blood ain't always thicker than water. We know why Webb would want vengeance, but what d'you think he would want from my mother?"

"Power."

Jake nodded. "Just like Mack."

Colman ignored that. "Funny thing is, I could swear I heard two men when they dropped that burlap bag over my head."

chapter
twenty-seven

Serepta didn't make a habit of expressing her appreciation, but she was so grateful for the calm, steadying presence of Ivy that she squeezed the other woman's hand and said, "Thank you for coming."

Ivy took the gesture in stride, likely accustomed to kindness. "I'm glad to have Emmaline to take care of again. I'm missing that babe of Maggie's."

Serepta pinched her lips and left the pair to collect baskets and go berry picking before the sun was too bright for Ivy. She said the blackberries were thick and it would be fun for them to bring back enough for a pie or some jelly. *Fun*. When was the last time Serepta had any of that?

She spent the morning going over production numbers for the mines on the C&O's Loup Branch line. They'd built the branch to make it easier to get the coal out of the mines along the creek. She was worried the Meadow Fork mine was played out but had high hopes for the Prudence and Red Star mines. Maybe she'd send Mack to observe the operations and make recommendations about possible improvements.

Taken with that idea, she gathered some notes and went in search of her son. He'd worked at his desk on the far side of the room for a time that morning but had disappeared an hour or so ago. She ghosted through the house, hoping he hadn't left. She wanted to move forward with her idea right away.

Voices from the kitchen drew her.

"And the leaves make a tea that's wonderful for a sore throat." That was Ivy speaking.

Mack responded, "You sure do know a lot about plants."

Serepta peered through a crack on the hinge side of the door. Her son stood close to Ivy while Emmaline dug into a bowl of berries and cream, her mouth stained purple along with her fingers. Ivy flushed, giving her pale cheeks a hint of color. Mack reached up and brushed a finger along her jawline. Serepta jerked as if he'd touched her. Ivy froze.

"You know you're special," Mack said.

Ivy moved away and busied herself gathering ingredients for what looked like piecrust. "There's not much special about me. Different maybe, but not special."

Mack stood and watched her. "There's a great deal special about you. You're kind, knowledgeable about plants and cures, you're gentle . . . and you're lovely."

Ivy looked like she'd dabbed circles of rouge on her cheeks. "Mack McLean, you stop talking like that. I know when I'm being buttered up. You just want some of this pie when it's done." She reached over and wiped Emmaline's face with a rag. "Child, you're going to need a good scrubbing." Emmaline giggled and scooped up the last bite of berries.

"I've always thought highly of you—even when we were children," Mack went on. "You know that."

Ivy stopped her bustling and got a faraway look. "I know

you were kind to me when hardly anyone else was." She looked sad. "It's only natural that children tease someone who looks . . . different." She raised her eyes to gaze at Mack. "But you never teased me. You even stood up for me a time or two."

Mack shrugged. "I might have been given a hard time once or twice myself. Jake was always the golden boy, and when you prefer reading and studying to running with the other fellows . . . well, I guess I had some notion of how it felt to be left out."

Ivy reached over with floury fingers and gripped Mack's hand. "Thank you for being kind." She laughed when she realized she'd dusted Mack's hand with flour. "But you don't have to defend me anymore. I'm a grown woman, and there's no need for idle flattery."

Mack turned his hand and twined his fingers with hers. "You *are* a grown woman, and it's *not* idle flattery."

Emmaline chose that moment to hop off her stool and nearly topple a basket of berries from the table. Ivy lunged to catch it, and whatever spell Mack was weaving broke. Serepta watched long enough to be certain the tête-à-tête was over before making her way back down the hall. Now she had more reason than ever to send Mack to check on those mines.

~~~~~

The next morning, Colman left Jake snoring on the floor of the cabin, tangled in a worn quilt. He'd used the house before as a sort of hideaway when he needed to sleep off a drunk. He'd been sober enough the night before but seemed exhausted. In the light of day he looked as gaunt and hollowed out as Colman had been when he'd emerged from the cave. It was almost enough to make a man feel sorry for him.

Making his way to the Gordon cottage, Colman had the notion that if Ivy were still looking after that orphan child Serepta took in, tagging along might be his way to speak to the woman. Of course, if Ivy offered him breakfast, that wouldn't hurt his feelings.

He crossed the creek and saw smoke curling up from the chimney, and he heard the promising clack of a spoon against a bowl.

"Halloo," he called as he drew near. After a moment, Hoyt appeared in the open doorway and waved him over.

"You turn up as regular as a hungry hound dog."

Colman grinned. "Now that I have my appetite back, I aim to take advantage of the fact. Who's cooking this morning?"

"We're having blackberries and cream along with last night's leftover biscuits. If you was looking for meat, you're out of luck this morning."

"I've learned not to be particular when I barge in uninvited."

"Wise man," Hoyt said, following Colman inside.

Ivy's smile was like the song of a bluebird on the first day of spring. Colman felt his own smile widen in response. Dang if she didn't look awful pretty this morning.

"I knew I made extra for a reason," she said. "You're a pleasure to feed now that you're hale and hearty again."

Colman puffed his chest out a notch, pleased by her comment. "You headed over to the McLean place today?"

"That I am. Emmaline and I have blackberry jam to make."

"Mind if I tag along?"

The smile dimmed. "No, I suppose not. But do you think Serepta will be glad to see you?"

Colman sat at the table and accepted the bowl of fruit Hoyt passed to him. "If I'm going to be a proper preacher,

257

I need to visit folks in the community. Seems like Serepta's house is a fine place to start."

Hoyt butted in. "I thought you already started over at Lena's place. On a day when Nell's daddy weren't around to mind, as I heard it."

Colman made a face like his first bite of berries had been sour. "You know they invited me to dinner, so I went."

Hoyt nodded. "Un-huh. And sweet Nell's been talking you up ever since."

Colman flushed. "I can't help what people say."

"True enough," Hoyt agreed.

"Grandpa, stop teasing Colman," Ivy said. "If he wants to come visit Serepta, I'm proud of him. Goodness knows she needs some kindness and understanding."

The pleasure Colman felt in her praise quickly faded. His intent wasn't to be kind or understanding. He wanted that infernal woman to see the error of her ways so he could count this job done and go home. He had the uncomfortable feeling that might not have been God's intent in sending him.

Hoyt huffed and sloshed coffee into Colman's cup. "Girl, you always did have a knack for seeing the best in everybody."

Ivy smiled. "I'd rather look for the best. The worst usually makes itself known soon enough."

Colman shook his head. The woman was a wonder. And if he were being honest, he would have to admit that coming here had a fair amount to do with his spending time in the same room with Ivy.

"Finish your breakfast. The car from Walnutta will be here any minute. You can ride with us over there."

Colman used a biscuit to push berries and cream onto his spoon. Serepta sent a car, did she? He wondered who would be driving now that Charlie was gone. The thought of Charlie soured his mood briefly, but he reminded himself that Serepta's treatment of her only ally was one more reason he needed to win her to faith. Maybe she'd repent of her actions and bring the hired man back.

The sputter of an approaching car set them into motion. Colman slurped the last of his coffee while Ivy took up her gathering basket, donned her hat and gloves, and kissed her grandfather on the cheek. "I'll be home in time to make supper," she said, then gave Colman a coy look. "Which means this fellow may follow me home again."

"Well, if you're extending an invitation . . ."

"You're always welcome here," Ivy said, wrapping her hand around his elbow and tugging him toward the door.

Her touch set off something inside him. It was like music but without specific notes. It tickled up and down his whole body and finally reached his head, where it was like light filling his mind. He was so surprised he could hardly put one foot in front of the other. Then she released him to hurry ahead across the creek and on to the car. Whatever music had been playing stopped as abruptly as it began. He blinked after her, then reminded himself to follow, trying to shake off the odd sensations still echoing through his spirit.

Once he reached the car, though, any pleasant thoughts left him. Mack was driving, and he didn't look any too pleased to see Colman tagging along.

"Colman is coming with us today to visit Serepta," Ivy explained.

"Well that's a terrible idea," Mack said. "You know she doesn't much care for the Harpes." He sneered at Colman. "Although I suppose this one is harmless enough."

Colman held his tongue as he slid into the car beside Mack. Ivy clambered into the back seat. No one spoke until they pulled up at Walnutta. Mack turned to Colman. "What is it you plan to say to my mother?"

"Just a local pastor paying a call," Colman said.

"Mother isn't a member of whatever congregation you've managed to cobble together."

Colman grinned at the man scowling beside him. "No. But she could be." He then hopped out of the car and started up the walk, his heart thudding in his chest. Doggone if he wasn't nervous about this.

Emmaline came flying out the front door and clattered down the steps. "Ivy, Ivy, come see! The cat had kittens in the barn."

And just like that, Ivy and the child disappeared, leaving Colman alone with Mack and Serepta, who had followed Emmaline onto the porch. The older woman stood with her feet wide apart and arms crossed. Her blue eyes glinted.

"To what do I owe the pleasure?" she asked.

Colman swallowed hard. "Making the rounds of the neighborhood. Visiting is an important part of the Lord's work."

Serepta's gaze didn't flicker. "Come in." She turned and disappeared inside.

Colman wasn't sure who was more surprised, him or Mack. But he didn't stop to ponder the invitation, just hurried up the steps and into Serepta's study. Mack followed close behind.

"Sit." Serepta waved him toward a chair while she settled behind a large oak desk. She folded her hands and waited for Colman to sit down. "What would you like to share with me?"

Colman felt like he'd been caught in the outhouse with his pants down. He'd assumed Serepta would refuse to listen to him and wasn't exactly prepared with a speech. He flung a prayer toward the ceiling and hoped something would come to him.

"The Lord sent me here to say you're in a bad way. Keep up misbehaving and He'll do something about it eventually."

A look of honest amusement flashed across Serepta's face. "Is that so? What do you suppose God will do to me?"

"Punish you." Colman thought he'd be better at this.

"More than He already has?" Serepta sat even straighter. "He's been punishing me since the day I was born. Are you suggesting that if I stop *misbehaving*, God will suddenly shower me with blessings?"

"Well, He sure won't the way you've been doing." Colman almost flinched at his own words. No one talked to Serepta like this.

"What about all the misbehaving others are up to? That girl at the Dunglen having a child without being married. Some rapscallion burning down the hotel." She pressed her palms to her desk and stood, eyes sparking like sunlight on ice. "What about a gang beating an innocent man nearly to death merely because he's associated with me?" Moisture glistened in her eyes. Colman wasn't sure if they were tears or the oil of anger. "What about mothers who refuse Ivy's ministrations because they fear her paleness? Think she's the offspring of the moon-eyed people?" Serepta seemed to grow brighter and stronger with each word. "What about self-righteous fools who cannot see the beams in their own eyes?"

That last was like a slap. Had she just quoted Scripture at him? He was supposed to be using Scripture to sway her—not the other way around. "Look, I'm just passing on the message. God wanted me to come here and tell you He loves you. That's all. I don't know about all the rest. None of this makes sense to me, either." He stood and wished he had a hat to slap on his head. "I'll be on my way now. I appreciate your time." Then he scurried from the room feeling like a dog with its tail between its legs.

chapter
twenty-eight

Serepta watched her enemy flee. She'd routed him sure enough. Sometimes the best way to handle a foe was to let him think he had the upper hand. So why didn't she feel pleased? And where had that bit about the beam in the eye come from? She vaguely remembered it as a snippet of Scripture having to do with harping on about a minor flaw in someone else while ignoring your own mighty flaw. Well, she had mighty flaws aplenty and no time for fussing over the flaws of others. But that last piece Colman said . . . God sending her a message of love? That was the least likely thing she'd ever heard, and yet something in her strained toward it.

She realized Mack was still in the room. "Why did you bring that buffoon here?"

"He came with Ivy."

"Be certain he returns without her, then come see me. I have a job for you." Mack nodded and started toward the door. "Wait." Serepta stopped him. "Where is your brother?"

Mack's shoulders tightened. "What makes you think I'd know?"

"The two of you were planning to work together for the good of the family business, remember?"

Mack curled his lip. "Was that the plan? You know he can't stay steady. Probably drunk somewhere, or he's shacked up with a woman."

Serepta dismissed her son with a flick of her wrist. One more disappointment. God's love indeed.

⁓

Colman hiked all the way back to the cabin from Walnutta. It had been abundantly clear he wasn't wanted there, although he'd circled around the house to check on Ivy before he left. And a good thing, too. After Mack gave him his walking papers, he'd apparently gone to find Ivy. Colman rounded the house just in time to hear their exchange outside the barn. He pulled back and pressed in under the eave.

". . . wish you'd consider my proposition."

Ivy glanced at Emmaline, who was busy petting the tomcat that had likely fathered the newborn kittens. "I had hoped to marry for love."

"That will come. You care for me, don't you?"

"Of course I do. But I care for a great many people. It's a long way from there to spending a lifetime together."

Mack reached out and brushed her cheek with the back of his hand. "Is there someone else you're thinking to spend a lifetime with?"

She lowered her head. "No. No one who would have me."

Mack tucked a finger under her chin and lifted it. "I'd be glad to have you."

A wash of color rose from the neckline of her dress all the way to her hairline. "Out of pity," she said.

"Not that. No. Practicality maybe. Good sense certainly. But pity? Never."

Colman realized that his fists were clenched, and he was leaning forward as though into a stiff wind.

"For the land that will come to me one day then."

Mack let his hand fall away. "Not for it, but you have to admit that combining our resources would offer a way to break the feud between the Harpes and McLeans. You want that, don't you?"

Ivy sighed and watched Emmaline with a wistful expression. "I do want that. And I like you, Mack. It's just that I hoped . . ." Mack pressed in close to her. Too close.

"Hope in me," he said.

With that, Colman had fled.

Now, walking along a rushing creek, he tried to pin down exactly what had disturbed him so. He cared about Ivy and wanted to see her happy. He guessed she could do worse than marry Mack. Was it simply the fact that he was a member of the family that had been feuding with the Harpes for so long? Or had it been Mack's hint that there was something more to a union between him and Ivy—that "breaking the feud" business? Or might it have something to do with the soreness he was feeling around his heart?

Colman was still stewing when he stepped up onto the lopsided porch of the cabin around lunchtime. He'd noticed wild grapes growing out back when he left that morning. Maybe they'd be ripe. He went inside to see if he could find a bowl for collecting the fruit. Instead, he found Jake reclining on the bed, humming, an empty bottle on the floor beside him.

"I see you've been drinking your lunch," Colman said.

Jake hiccupped. "Breakfast too. Nectar of the gods."

Colman kicked the empty bottle. "That's not one of your mother's."

"You're right. It wasn't nectar. Mother is a shrew, but she makes exceptional whiskey." Jake raised up on one elbow. "That was the spit of the gods." His sides shook in laughter at his own wisecrack. "But it got the job done."

"Would that job be rendering yourself useless?"

Jake flopped back down. "Oh, I'm useless on my own. What that stuff does is make me not mind so much."

"Since when is your brother interested in Ivy Gordon?"

Jake laced his hands behind his head. "Didn't know he was."

"If what I heard's any indication, he wants to marry her."

Jake snorted. "Been eavesdropping, have you?" He rolled onto one side and swung his feet to the floor as though checking to make sure it was still there. "She's not bad looking, so long as you ain't looking for color."

Colman balled his hands into fists. "Would Mack do right by her?"

Jake rubbed his face with both hands. "I doubt it, but who knows? Say, are those tins of pork and beans still in the cupboard? I need to put something in my belly to stop the sloshing."

Colman checked the cupboard on the wall next to the fireplace. There were three cans of beans, one of peaches, and some tobacco.

"Hand me one of them cans." Jake dug out a pocketknife and worked the blade around the rim of the can. He used the knife to scoop beans into his mouth. Colman hesitated, then decided it beat wild grapes and did the same with a second can. They ate in silence for a while.

"You don't reckon Mack's after more than Ivy's"—Jake flicked a look at Colman—"attentions, do you?"

"What do you mean by that?"

"I mean what else has she got that he'd want?" Jake tossed the empty can toward the cold fireplace and missed. "Hoyt ain't gonna live forever. I'm guessing she'll get that house and the land it sits on when he goes."

Colman wiped his mouth with the back of his hand, deciding to keep Mack's other comments to himself. "How much land?"

"Something like eighty acres if I remember right. Got one of them smelly springs on it, too. The kind the tourists like."

Colman smirked. "You think Mack wants to open up a resort?"

Jake scooched to the head of the bed and leaned back against the wall, hands folded across his belly. "Can't see that, no. But there's some timber might be worth something, once it grows some more." He closed his eyes, and Colman thought he might be going to sleep. "'Course, there's that cave he stole my liquor out of. Guess there could be coal or something in there."

"What liquor? What cave?"

Jake's eyes blinked open, and he stared at Colman like he'd forgotten someone else was in the room. He got a cagey look, then shrugged. "Don't matter now. I'm the one who was stealing Ma's liquor. I'd hide it in the cave, find a buyer, and then smuggle it out. 'Cept Mack caught on and stole every last crate to take back to Ma." He grunted. "Just to make himself look good."

"Did it work?" Colman couldn't believe he was having this conversation with Jake. But the more they talked, the more he suspected this was bigger than a simple feud.

"Yeah. Reckon it did."

"And then he decided to burn down the Dunglen Hotel, with you inside it."

Colman watched the other man intently. Was he following right?

Jake straightened up, his eyes widening. "He's trying to take over my birthright." He snapped his fingers several times. "Like that feller in Genesis—what was his name?"

"Jacob. He tricked Esau into giving up his birthright."

"Doggonit. You reckon that's what's going on? Mack's trying to get in good with Ma, so he can run the family business when she gives it up?" He frowned. "If she ever does. Probably live forever."

"Sure looks that way," Colman said with a nod. "About that cave—sounds like maybe it's the one I got lost in."

Jake shook his head. "Fool thing, getting lost in a cave. Heard you popped out of there looking like you'd been drug through hell and then rolled in the mud for good measure."

Colman frowned. Something was niggling at his memory, something from his time in the cave. "Could there be anything of value in there? If it was coal, you'd think somebody would have dug it out by now."

"I've never gone far into it, but maybe there's pirate's gold or gems in there." Jake had a faraway, dazed look on his face. "We could go hunting it."

Colman shuddered at the notion of going back inside that cave, and an image popped into his mind. "I dropped a match while I was in there. It flared like catching lamp oil. Smelled of sulphur."

"Half the water round these parts smells of sulphur." Jake closed his eyes. Colman figured he'd be asleep any minute now.

"Water doesn't burn, though. Not even sulphur water."

"Gas sure as shooting does," Jake murmured and began to snore.

Colman picked up Jake's tin can along with his own and took them out to the rain barrel to rinse. True, gas would burn. In fact, he remembered hearing about how Burning Springs to the north had been named for two springs that could catch fire because of the natural gas bubbling up through them. Is that what he'd seen inside the cave? Had he ignited gas with the match? If that were the case, it just might be that Mack was after the gas and maybe even oil located on the Gordon family property. And if he married Ivy . . . Colman dried his hands on his pant legs and began trotting toward the Gordon cabin. He needed to talk to Hoyt right away.

***

Serepta was distracted. She ought to be tending to business, but Mack's behavior had left her unsettled. He was far too attentive to Ivy. She would be glad if he had the sense to make such a practical choice for a wife, but she knew enough about men—including her sons—to be suspicious of Mack's intentions. And she would not tolerate him trifling with Ivy.

Her son finally reentered her office, his head down, hands clasped behind his back.

"You've been gone quite some time. Did you escort Colman Harpe back to wherever he came from?" she asked.

Mack jerked his head up at her voice. "No, Mother. Colman found his way off our property on his own."

"Where have you been then?"

Mack drew himself up to his full height, which had never been equal to his brother's. "I've been minding my own business. And you?"

She glared at him. "You mean minding Ivy's business. What are your intentions toward that girl?" She was pleased to see she'd surprised her son.

269

"Intentions?"

"Yes. I've seen you pursuing her, and while I wouldn't disapprove of the choice, I will confess to a measure of surprise."

Mack flushed and looked away. "I don't have any intentions. You're mistaken."

Serepta raised her eyebrows and remained silent. Finally, Mack strode over to his small desk in the far corner. "Jake's the one who pursues anyone in a skirt. I'm just being kind."

Serepta pursed her lips and waited.

"You said you had a task for me. Do you intend to tell me what it is?"

Serepta touched the tip of her tongue to her upper lip and let the silence linger for another moment. "Yes. I need you to go check on some of the Loup Branch mines. We need to ensure they're operating at maximum efficiency."

Mack frowned. "Don't you have men for that? I thought I was working here, with you, focusing on the liquor side of the family empire." She didn't care for the way he said "empire."

"The mines and the liquor are all part and parcel of our *empire*," she said, matching his inflection. "But if you would rather not go, I certainly can find someone else. I can find someone else to do a great many things."

Mack thumped into the chair at his desk. "Fine. I'll leave on this afternoon's train."

She smiled but knew it was a chill expression. "Excellent. I'll expect your report day after next."

Mack mumbled something, grabbed some papers off his desk, and stomped out of the room. Serepta watched him go, wondering if trying to shape him into a better man was worth the trouble. Maybe she should give up on her sons and put her faith in little Emmaline instead. It would be years before the girl was ready to take on any responsibility, but Serepta could hold on that long. And perhaps, knowing what she did now, she could be more intentional in how she raised the child.

She half stood and then sank back into her chair. She'd been going to find Charlie and ask what he thought. She felt her eyes prickle and stiffened her spine. She was on her own now. When she told Mack she could find someone else to do a great many things, she'd been lying. She really ought to send for Chief Ash and press him for the information he'd been withholding in Thurmond, but there was too much else for her to do. Charlie was the one who managed people—even the police chief—for her. She had no doubt she could still strike fear into the hearts of the men who worked for her, but she was less confident of her ability to inspire loyalty. It was Charlie who had that knack.

She sighed and pressed her fingers to the bridge of her nose. She would have to conduct her work through her sons. They were all she had left. And if Jake didn't turn up soon, she might have only Mack. She rubbed at the ache centered between her eyes. Perhaps Ivy could give her a tonic. But no. That would be showing weakness. She would simply have to will the pain away and give her full attention to transforming Mack into the man she needed him to become.

chapter
twenty-nine

Colman reached the Gordon cottage well before Ivy re-turned, just as he'd hoped. There was no need to draw her into whatever schemes Mack and Serepta were hatching. He found Hoyt outside, stacking firewood.

"You ever been in that cave I was lost in?"

"Well hey and howdy to you, too." Hoyt dusted his hands and ambled over to his favorite chair in the shade of a maple tree. "Sit a spell and tell me what's got you riled."

Colman took a breath and set a block of wood on end for a seat. "I think Mack McLean's after your land, and it has something to do with what's inside that cave."

Hoyt's smile was half hidden by his beard. "What, lost treasure? Gold? Silver? Or maybe the liquor that's been hid in there a time or two."

"You know about that?"

Hoyt chuckled. "Jake McLean ain't half so clever as he thinks he is."

"Why'd you let him get away with it?"

Hoyt shrugged and dug out a pocketknife. He picked up a piece of wood and began carving at it with the blade. "Weren't no skin off my nose. Anyhow, I'm pretty sure Mack's already *recovered* all the liquor Jake stashed in there."

Colman shook his head. "I'm not talking about booze. I'm talking about gas—natural gas bubbling up inside that cave."

Hoyt's knife stilled, then resumed its motion. "Gas, huh? Guess that wouldn't be a surprise. Other folks around here have found it."

"Well? What should we do about it?"

Hoyt grunted. "Nothing."

"What do you mean? We have to stop him."

Hoyt stopped his whittling and cocked his head to one side, considering Colman. "Stop him from doing what? He's not getting my land."

Colman felt his face going red. "But he's trying to court Ivy so he can get his hands on the land."

A rumble of laughter rose from the old man's belly. "Won't do him much good since Ivy won't get the land. The cottage and the garden are already hers, and the rest belongs to the federal government."

Colman couldn't make heads or tails of what Hoyt was talking about. "I don't understand."

"Weeks Act of 1911. Federal government's been buying up land to make what they're calling national forests. The notion is to save some of the land around here"—he let his gaze take in the scenery around them—"so the coal miners, loggers, and everybody else don't strip it bare. They paid me a fair price for it, and Ivy won't need more than a place to live and her plants to tend." He grinned. "It'll make folks like Serepta McLean and Webb Harpe madder'n hornets when they find out."

"But you come and go on the land like you own it."

"Those government boys don't care. Guess they might

come in here and do something one of these days, but for now it feels just the same to me."

Colman shook his head. "I think you just threw a big ole wrench in Mack's plans. Does Ivy know?"

"She knows the house and garden are hers. And she knows I sold some land. Don't guess she knows exactly how much or that the cave is on that land."

"Maybe we need to tell her before she goes and lets Mack talk her into something foolish."

Hoyt slowed his whittling. "Mack was always nice to Ivy when they were young'uns. Never teased her about her being fair and kept her company when no one else would. What makes you so sure he doesn't really care for her?"

"The way he was talking—it wasn't like a suitor. It was like he was trying to get her to agree to a business plan. I don't trust him."

Hoyt cocked an eyebrow. "You sure it ain't because you can't see how a man would want a woman like her?"

Colman flushed deeper. "Of course not. Ivy's . . . special."

Hoyt held up the shape of a roughed-out bird. "This has potential," he said. "And so does Ivy. About time you noticed." With that, he stood and walked into the cottage.

⁓

Emmaline and Ivy were layering flowers in tissue paper and pressing them between heavy books. Serepta stood watching for a few moments before the child noticed her.

"Momma," she said, and rushed to wrap little arms around her legs. "Come see the flowers."

The warm look on Ivy's face reflected the emotion Serepta wished she could find a way to show. She adored this little imp who had been thrust into her life, but she felt ill-equipped to express what was stirring inside her. Why did acts of love and caring come so easily for Ivy? Serepta felt like someone who had never been taught to swim suddenly thrust into deep water.

She disentangled herself from Emmaline and joined Ivy at the table strewn with wildflowers. She picked up a spray of virgin's bower. She'd noticed the white flowers cascading over fence posts and roadsides as summer waned, but she'd never thought to pluck any. Flowers weren't something she troubled herself with.

"It would seem my son is expressing an interest in you," she said.

Ivy's eyes widened. "I don't think he's serious. Just a passing notion."

"What if it were not?" She began to fashion a crown of flowers for Emmaline's curls. It surprised her that she knew how.

"How could it be anything else?" Ivy blinked those seemingly lashless eyes at her. "I'm not generally considered desirable."

Serepta stilled her hands. "Men are fools, and unfortunately my sons are no exception. But if Mack were wise enough to want you for his own, I would be . . . pleased." The last word felt round and solid on her tongue. When was the last time she was pleased? Ah yes, with Charlie before they left for Thurmond.

"Thank you." Ivy spoke so softly, Serepta leaned toward her. "I have considered . . ."

"Yes?"

Ivy lifted her chin. "It's unlikely that anyone else will want to wed me, and while I don't really know Mack anymore, he was kind when we were children." She paused and cast Serepta a sidelong look as though calculating her next words.

"He thinks our union could help end the feud between the Harpes and the McLeans, but I don't understand how."

Serepta hid her surprise. Mack wanted to end the feud? Why?

"Is that what he thinks? Well, perhaps because you are so well acquainted with Colman Harpe."

Now Ivy's gaze grew wistful. Her eyes lost their focus, and she began to gather flowers until she was holding a bouquet that she seemed unaware of. "Perhaps," she echoed. "I wish I could be more certain that"—she flushed again—"a deeper affection would grow."

"Pah. Affection, by which I assume you mean *love*, is something fools long for. If you can win a man who will treat you with the respect your intellect and good sense demand, it should be more than enough." She placed her circlet of flowers on Emmaline's head, much to the child's delight. "And if you were to wed Mack, I would ensure he gave you that respect—of that you may be certain."

~~~

When Colman arrived back at the cabin, Jake had disappeared, leaving a half-empty bottle of cheap whiskey and not much else. In frustration, Colman wiped the mouth of the bottle on his sleeve and took a swig, then spit it back out. Burned like fire. He'd stewed over Hoyt's reaction to his news about Mack's intentions toward Ivy all the way here. And he had yet to puzzle it out. The nerve of Hoyt. Suggesting he didn't recognize Ivy's potential.

He might be able to hear a mouse whispering in the far corner of the barn, but some words plainly spoken were beyond his understanding. He lit the kindling he'd piled in the fireplace and got a cook fire going. He'd set a snare the day before and had a fine rabbit to show for it. He spitted it and set it to roast near the flames. He'd also "borrowed" some ripe ears of corn from a field he passed along the way. He peeled the husks back, stripped out the silks, wrapped them back up, and buried them in embers beneath the flames.

Hoyt had given him a pack Ivy left for him—cornmeal, some coffee, dried beans, cold biscuits, and several little packets of her herbs. With all this bounty, he almost wished he had someone to eat supper with him—even Jake.

He cocked an ear when he heard voices. It was early evening and full daylight still, so when he peered into the distance he could see two men coming from a long ways off. He soon recognized them—Johnny and Elam. They were talking and laughing like two old gossips. Colman rolled his eyes. After turning the rabbit and making sure the corn wasn't going to burn, he stepped out onto the crooked porch and waited.

His cousins were having a lively discussion about the merits of pipe tobacco over snuff. Johnny was a proponent of pipe smoking—cleaner, he said—while Elam preferred snuff—less polluting of the air. Colman smiled and shook his head. He should've gotten better acquainted with his family a long time ago.

"Howdy, Colman. Heard you was staying here," Johnny said, brushing a hank of hair off his forehead.

"Word sure does get around. Somebody send you a telegram?"

"Naw—they's a wanted poster with your picture down at the station." Elam grinned almost as wide as his ears and then spit, demonstrating his preference for snuff.

"Well, I guess you two must be able to smell as good as I hear, since you've arrived just in time for supper."

"Now, that's the kind of greeting makes a man glad. What you got?" asked Johnny.

"Rabbit and sweet corn, with some of Ivy's biscuits I'll toast over the fire."

"That'll do," said Johnny.

They trailed inside behind Colman and settled on the floor while he tended their meal. Lacking plates, Colman spread the husks out around the soft, lightly charred corn, and laid pieces of roasted rabbit there. He used a forked stick to toast the biscuits and handed those around, as well. To drink, they had cold well water.

"There's some whiskey if you want it, but it's pretty bad," Colman said.

Johnny shook his head. "Gave the stuff up some years back, and Elam here never touched it. So, you want to say the blessing since you're a preacher now?"

Colman bowed his head and gave thanks for the simple food. They ate with their hands in silence for a few moments. Finally, Johnny cleared his throat. "We come for a reason, Colman."

"Did you? I figured you were just hungry." Colman aimed for levity, but he'd sensed his cousins hadn't come all this way just to be sociable.

"Webb's been worse than ever lately. Going around telling anyone who'll listen that Maggie's child can't be Caleb's. Says he run Charlie out of town, and he'd be glad to show anyone who has sympathy with the McLeans the same door." Johnny leveled a look at Colman. "I think he means you mostly."

"I'm not in town," Colman said. Although getting back to Thurmond and leaving Serepta and the rest of the McLeans behind did have its appeal.

Elam picked up the thread of conversation. "Webb's been

wanting to stand taller than Serepta McLean ever since her man died. Thing is, we think he's been consorting with the enemy."

Johnny held up his hand. "Well, not exactly. What's that saying, 'the enemy of my enemy is my friend'? Guess he thinks Mack McLean is his friend."

Colman perked his ears. "Mack? What's Mack got to do with this?"

Elam licked his lips and leaned in like he was afraid someone outside might hear. "I seen 'em. Webb and Mack been meeting out at Loup Branch." He shot a look at Johnny. "I've got a fishing hole out there."

Johnny snorted. "What he means is, he's got a place to hide when he lays off work."

Elam rolled his eyes and tugged at his oversized ear. "Says you. Anyhow, I've seen the pair of 'em out there twice. Don't know exactly what they're up to, but it seems mighty peculiar."

"Whyn't you use your second sight to see what they're up to?" Johnny smirked. "Or don't it work like that?"

Elam stuck his chin in the air. "It's a gift. I don't get to command it like calling a dog."

Colman jumped in before the pair of them got carried away. "You're telling me Webb Harpe and Mack McLean have been meeting in secret?"

Elam nodded. "Sure enough."

"What I think is," Johnny chimed in, "Mack, being the second son, figures he can sell out Jake and his ma so's he gets a bigger piece of the pie. Webb, he'll cozy up to anybody who can help him knock Serepta off her tree stump. And who would be better to do that than her own boy?"

Colman tried to put all the pieces together in his mind. If Mack was after the gas on the Gordons' land, that would be a big step toward gaining money and power. And if Jake were out of the picture, Serepta would likely include her younger son in business matters that would give him the insight he needed to undermine her. Shoot, he wouldn't even have to undermine her. He could just weasel his way into her business, and she'd probably let him.

"What's in it for Webb?" he asked.

"Aw, he's wanted to have a corner on the illegal liquor business since he was a young pup. He wants to put on fancy duds and lord it over the rest of us. He thinks he can get in with the high society folks up there at the Greenbrier Hotel."

Colman closed his eyes and tuned his ears. Something about that last comment rang a bell . . . What had he heard?

That's it.

The day he'd been knocked in the head and had woken to find Uncle Webb watching over him, he'd heard something out of the ordinary. Hushed voices—Webb's and . . . not Jake's. Whose voice had it been? "Mack McLean," he whispered.

"What about him?" Johnny asked.

"When I was coming to that day, I heard Mack telling Webb he'd let him use the McLean suite at the Greenbrier. He sounded mad about it, too. Doggone, I think it was Mack who shoved that sack over my head. Or maybe even Webb, but the two of them were in it together."

Johnny and Elam exchanged looks. "What in tarnation are you going on about?"

Colman closed his eyes and scrubbed his hands over his face. "I can't quite call it to mind, but I'm pretty sure Webb and Mack were making some kind of deal so Webb could get me to do his dirty work for him." He tossed his corncob in the fire. "And I let him do it."

chapter
thirty

The letter lay in the center of her blotter, the handwriting all too familiar. Serepta stared at it. Finally, she picked up the envelope and slit it open. She wasn't going to let a bit of paper and ink best her. A single sheet slipped out, and for the briefest moment she thought she caught Charlie's scent—a mix of woodsmoke and fresh air. She closed her eyes and pushed down the emotion welling inside her.

Her hand shook as she lifted the paper, and she willed it to steady. She could hardly read, her eyes were so eager to take in the words printed there. She drew a deep breath and forced herself to take the letter in, word by word.

S, I have arrived in Gauley Bridge. There is work here, building a tunnel for the river. I don't understand what they mean to do with it, but they're giving colored men jobs, so I took one. I've healed up good. Don't worry about me. We knew it couldn't last. Revelation 3:19–20. Look it up this time. —C

Tears burned her eyes, yet she would not let them fall. What had she expected? That Charlie would return to her after she had failed him? He would never ask her to follow him—he knew she'd worked too hard to throw everything away when there was no place for them to be together in this world.

He hadn't gone very far. Gauley Bridge was just a few stops north of Thurmond on the C&O. Of course, he might as well have gone to Mexico for all it mattered. She could no more go see him or fetch him home than she could marry him.

She crumpled the paper, then smoothed it out again. Even if she were willing to sacrifice her position, her power, and wealth for Charlie, it wouldn't matter. The world simply would not allow him to ever be more to her than a servant. Anger rolled deep inside her. No matter how hard she worked, no matter what she sacrificed, some things remained beyond her reach. And what did Charlie say to that? He sent her yet another Bible verse.

Well. She would look this one up, only because she supposed it would be Charlie's last request of her. She looked around for a Bible. She thought there was one somewhere on the bookshelves lining the far wall, but she failed to turn one up. Then she remembered. Charlie's room. She rarely entered the narrow space in back of the house. As she walked through the kitchen, Hallie froze in the midst of pulling dark purple grapes from their stems and gave her a look of veiled terror.

"You need anything, missus?"

"I intend to clean out Charlie's room now that he's gone."

"I can do that." The girl moved toward the doorway, but Serepta stopped her with a look.

"That's not necessary. I'll call you if you're needed."

Hallie nodded and went back to her fruit. Making juice or jelly, Serepta assumed. She hesitated at the closed door, then stiffened her spine and pushed it open.

Inside, the space did smell like Charlie, a hint of cedar rounding out the aroma she'd imagined earlier. She breathed it in and told herself it was enough that she'd known at least one good man. A clean shirt hung on a nail on the wall, as well as a coat. A straw hat lay on top of a chest, and there, on a rickety table beside a narrow cot, was Charlie's Bible.

Serepta lifted it, the worn leather cover soft in her hands. She feathered through the pages and saw that Charlie had plied his pencil on every leaf. Words and phrases were underlined. He'd written things in the margin, like *truth* and *hope*. Remembering some of his earlier notes to her, she found the Song of Songs. There on the first page he'd written *Love her this way*. The words shot through her like a bolt of lightning, and she sagged to sit on the edge of the cot. Did he mean . . . ? No. She would not torture herself like this.

Slamming the book shut, she started to set it down, then tucked it under her arm and reentered the kitchen where the aroma of grapes made the air sing.

"Hallie, I've changed my mind. You may clean out the room. Pack it all up, and I'll give you an address to send it to."

Hallie nodded. "Yes'm. You want me to do it now?"

"You may finish what you're doing first." Hallie looked relieved, and Serepta swept from the room intending to crush any remaining emotion the way Hallie was crushing her grapes.

***

Colman had to get to Ivy to warn her that Mack was up to no good. Johnny and Elam had spent the night, and by the time Colman made it back to the Gordons' cottage, Ivy had already left to watch over Emmaline for the day. Now he was making the trek to Walnutta on foot. And while he had made strides in regaining his health, he'd been doing an awful lot of walking the past few days and worry had been stealing his sleep.

When he saw a fallen tree near the road, he sat to dig a pebble out of his left boot. It had been boring a hole in his foot for the past twenty minutes, and he could bear it no more. Stone removed, he was lacing his boot back up when he heard the rattle of a horse and cart approaching. His first instinct was to duck back into the brush, but maybe whoever it was would give him a ride.

As the cart drew nearer, Colman saw that Lena and Nell were braced on the rattling board that served as a seat. Nell drew back on the reins and brought their stout workhorse to a stop.

"Hey there, Preacher. Been too long since we seen you last," called out Lena. She didn't look altogether pleased to be seeing him now. "Thought you would have called on us again by now."

Nell gave him a pouty smile. "I thought there was going to be a baptizing. I was so looking forward to it."

It occurred to Colman that Nell might not be anticipating her baptism for all the right reasons. Of course, his motives hadn't exactly been pure since he came to Hinton, either.

"I've been busy back in Thurmond," he explained, "helping Maggie with her baby."

"We heard the hotel burned down over there." Lena looked Colman over from the crown of his head to the toe of his boot. "Some folks say it was a Harpe what started the fire."

Colman opened his mouth to protest, then snapped it shut again. He had no proof Mack had set the fire beyond what Jake told him, and these two ladies weren't likely to believe that he and the man who killed his cousin had been going over recent events together. It seemed preposterous even to him.

"Well, if it was, I hope they catch him. That fire could've killed somebody."

"Un-hunh." Now Lena looked like a cat with some cream. "Guess maybe the Harpe name's come up around that babe of Maggie's, too. Anybody claim him yet?"

"I wouldn't know about that," Colman said. "Say, I'm on my way to see Ivy at Walnutta now. Don't suppose you could give me a ride?"

"Walnutta?" The older woman's eyebrows climbed her forehead. "I wouldn't have supposed you were what you'd call welcome over there."

Colman shrugged. "I'm probably not. But I need to talk to Ivy, and that's where she is."

Lena gestured toward the back of the wagon. "Climb aboard. This sounds more interesting than visiting Maude."

Nell perked up and dimpled at Colman as he scrambled up onto the rough planks. "You can sit on up here between us if you like."

"That's alright, don't want to crowd you," Colman said, trying to settle himself comfortably.

She narrowed her eyes and slapped the reins, starting the wagon moving again with a jerk. Colman grabbed the side and felt a splinter stab his finger. He stuck it in his mouth and nearly fell off with the next lurch of the wagon.

Soon enough, they were approaching Walnutta. The wide front porch looked welcoming, but Colman knew better. Nell pulled the horse to a stop just as Serepta stepped out onto the porch. He saw a pistol tucked into the waistband of her slacks.

Serepta nodded. "Lena. It's been quite some time since we last visited."

Lena snorted and muttered, "We ain't never visited." She raised her voice. "Brung you a preacher." She pointed a thumb toward Colman.

He scuttled to the back of the wagon and dropped to the ground. His finger throbbed, but he ignored the pain.

Serepta eyed him. "Why would you bring that man to me?"

Nell piped up. "He's hunting Ivy." She glanced at him. "Although he didn't tell us why."

Serepta traced the butt of her pistol with her thumb. "Ivy is occupied at the moment. Perhaps you could call on her once she returns to her own home."

Colman took several slow steps toward the porch. "My business with her is . . . urgent. I'd sure like to talk to her now."

"Urgent, is it? Well, why don't you tell me, and I'll pass the information along."

Colman squared his shoulders and tried not to look at her gun, though looking her in the eye was equally uncomfortable. "I need to warn her that your son is trifling with her."

Something flickered in Serepta's icy eyes. "Is that so?"

"It is." Colman swallowed hard and figured in for a penny, in for a pound. "He might be trifling with you, too."

Serepta threw back her head and laughed. It was a deep belly laugh that sounded genuine. Colman didn't know what to think. Finally, she drew in some air and took a step closer to him. "God must be on your side to give you the courage to suggest such a thing to me right here on my front porch." A strand of hair worked loose and fluttered against her cheek, softening the look of her. "Why don't you step into my office and tell me just exactly how it is that my son is trifling with Ivy." She turned to go inside, then paused and looked over her shoulder. "Not to mention trifling with me."

Colman moved up the steps feeling like he'd just been invited into the lions' den. He prayed that God would shut up this particular lion's mouth while ensuring that his own tongue didn't get the best of him. Inside, he noticed a stillness to the house and wondered where Ivy and Emmaline were. If he could just see Ivy, he thought it would give him the courage he needed. He tuned his ears to hear any trace of her, but all he heard was the throbbing of his own heart.

Serepta swept into her office and stood behind her desk. Colman figured he'd best stand on the other side of it, facing her. He realized his hands were shaking and clasped them behind his back. Serepta stood staring at him, giving him the feeling she could wait a month for him to speak, if that was what it took.

He cleared his throat. "There's gas in the caves on the Gordons' land." Her eyes threw a spark. "We . . . that is to say, I think Mack is trying to win Ivy so he can have access to the gas. Market's strong for it right now, except Hoyt's deeded that land over to the federal government, so it won't do him any good."

The skin along Serepta's jaw tightened. Colman could hear her teeth grinding. "Well now, sounds to me like Mack's working to expand the McLean family holdings. And I approve of Ivy, so even if his plan is flawed, I see no reason to stand in his way."

"There's more to it," Colman said. His instincts told him to cut and run, but he decided to stand his ground regardless. "I heard Mack talking to Ivy about breaking the Harpe-McLean feud." He flinched at his own words.

Serepta flinched as well. It was a small movement, but

Colman was watching her as though his life depended on it, because he feared maybe it did. She frowned. "Been eavesdropping, have you? That's an excellent way to misunderstand a conversation."

"It's also an excellent way to hear uncomfortable truths."

Serepta crossed her arms and drummed her fingers. "Well. I have long believed that sleeping dogs should be awakened. Let's fetch Ivy, shall we?"

Colman felt his mouth go dry. He really didn't want to share Mack's duplicity with her in front of Serepta.

"Hallie," Serepta called in a voice with more power than volume. A young colored girl popped in through the door. "Go fetch Ivy and watch Emmaline for her until we've finished."

Hallie looked like she was going to protest, but one look into Serepta's stormy eyes and she nodded and ran from the room. Serepta settled into her chair as if settling in for a cozy chat after dinner. She nodded to the chair nearest Colman, and he took a seat finally.

They waited.

The ticking of the clock began to sound like a great beating drum. It chimed the quarter hour, and Colman nearly jumped out of his skin. He gave Serepta a nervous smile without thinking, but when she continued to sit stone-faced, he let the smile fade.

Another excruciating five minutes passed. After ten minutes, Serepta stood so suddenly that Colman yelped. She glared at him and exited the room. In her wake, Colman felt like a physical weight had been lifted from his shoulders. He wondered for the first time if Lena and Nell were still outside. He slipped over to the window, feeling like a boy escaping his school desk while the teacher wasn't looking.

Outside, the two women had pulled their wagon into the shade and were talking. It appeared they had decided to stay in case there was going to be a show. He hoped they would be disappointed. He went back to his chair and sat again, thinking it was good he hadn't been caught. Then he shook his head—caught doing what? He was certainly free to come and go, to move about the room as he pleased. Serepta had the strangest ability to make him feel like a child. He stood and walked to the office door, peering out into the hall. While he didn't see anyone, he could hear voices out back. He followed them.

Hallie and Serepta stood on the back stoop. The girl alternately waved her hands in the air and wrung them while talking animatedly. Colman thought Serepta looked stern before, but now her face was a thundercloud and her eyes shot lightning.

"I don't know, I just don't know," the girl was saying.

Serepta planted her hands on her hips and glared. "They were in the garden not thirty minutes ago. Did they take a wagon? Did they set out on foot?"

"Wagon's still here. They could've wandered off down to the crick."

Serepta heaved a sigh. "Did you look?"

"Yes'm."

"And were they there?"

"No'm."

"Well then, it's not likely that's where they've gone, is it?"

The girl burst into tears, burying her face in her apron. Serepta spied Colman and turned to him. "It would seem Ivy and Emmaline have gone exploring, even though I expressly told Ivy to remain near the house." She pursed her lips. "And it's not like her to disregard my wishes."

289

Colman felt a nudge of worry. "It's not like her to ignore anyone's wishes. Do you think—?"

Serepta jerked the apron from Hallie's face. "When did you see them last? What were they doing?"

The girl sniffled and rubbed at her eyes. "Miss Ivy come in for a basket to pick beans in. Said she was going to teach the little one to make leather britches."

Serepta's frown deepened. "And she didn't return?"

"No'm. I ain't seen her since."

Serepta shot a look at Colman that he decided to take as an invitation as she strode across the yard into the garden. They walked down tidy rows, and Colman had the passing notion that even weeds knew better than to cross Serepta McLean. When they got to the bean arbor, Serepta stopped so suddenly Colman nearly crashed into her. He peered over her shoulder.

A basket of beans lay on its side, vegetables tumbled into the dirt. Nearby squash plants were trampled, and there were scuff marks. Colman's stomach clenched, reminding him of how he felt before Ivy cured whatever had sickened him when in the cave. He swallowed down the bile rising in his throat.

"What happened?" he asked, not expecting an answer.

Serepta shook her head. "Nothing good. It appears to me that Ivy and Emmaline have been taken."

"Who would do that?" Colman felt shock and horror in equal parts. "And why didn't I hear them?"

The sturdy woman before him looked like she would as soon spit on him as answer that question. "They must have been abducted before you arrived. Perhaps this is a clue," she said with a sneer and bent to pick up a ragged, dirty scrap of paper weighted down with a stone. She looked at it, her expression blank.

"What does it say?" Colman wanted to snatch the paper from her hand.

She thrust it at him and strode back toward the house. It held just three words. *What matters most?*

Colman darted after Serepta, but then paused when he noticed larger, deeper footprints in the soft garden soil. Men's boots and shod hoofprints. A wave of weakness washed over him as though the illness he'd fought for so long were returning. But he stiffened his spine and determined not to succumb to it. He hurried on to the house, wondering what Serepta intended to do.

chapter
thirty-one

Serepta considered taking a glass of whiskey to steady her nerves but decided it would not do for Colman to see how unsettled she was. There was only one person—except for maybe Charlie—who could have any inkling about how much Emmaline meant to her.

Webb Harpe. It had to be.

It wasn't enough that he'd robbed her of Charlie. Now he had stolen Emmaline knowing it was the only way he could hurt her. She supposed Ivy had simply been in the wrong place at the wrong time. Anger at Ivy spiked briefly. How dare that woman allow Webb to steal the child? She pushed the thought away. Ivy was the closest she had ever come to having a friend. Other than Charlie. He would know what to do. She pushed that thought away, too. How had she allowed herself to care about anyone, much less three people? She knew better. And now she was paying the price.

She went to her gun cabinet and pulled out a rifle. Colman Harpe was still trailing along after her. She handed him a Winchester 30.06, Model 54, then took up a Model 94 for herself. His eyes widened as she thrust a box of cartridges at him, but he took them and quietly loaded the gun.

"Fine rifle," he said.

"Of course it is," she snapped.

"Who are we hunting?" His voice was low and hoarse.

"Most likely your uncle Webb."

Colman swallowed hard. "I saw prints—a man and a horse."

That made her pause. "I suppose he needed a way to carry them off. Which means he's taken them some distance." She glared at Colman. "Are you too much a man of God to do what must be done?"

"I don't plan on shooting anyone."

She snorted. "I do."

The infernal man gnawed at his upper lip and then handed the rifle back to her. "Guess that's between you and God. I'll come with you, but I'm not shooting anyone."

"God has no more use for me than I do Him. Go unarmed if you choose, just know I'm planning to defend my own and you aren't counted among those."

He almost smiled. "Can't say as I'm surprised."

She spun on her heel and was confronted with Mack, standing in the open doorway. "What are you doing here?" she spat at him. "You're supposed to be checking on my mines."

He walked over and picked up the rifle Colman had surrendered. "Came back for something. And a good thing, too. Seems your enemy has stolen Ivy and Emmaline out from under your nose."

Rage set her veins to humming, and she wanted to strike Mack the same way she had Jake, only she wouldn't make that mistake twice. Instead, she narrowed her eyes and spoke through gritted teeth. "We shall discuss this later. For now, your assistance may very well be welcome." She flicked a look at Colman. "You're certainly likely to be more help than a pacifist Harpe."

She stormed out of the house, passing those two meddling women along the way. Colman paused and spoke to them as she threw open the barn doors to reveal her car. Colman hurried to the passenger seat and climbed in while Serepta slid behind the wheel, forcing Mack to sit in the back, which clearly perturbed him. Her son's dissatisfaction allowed Serepta to gloat for a moment. She was still in control.

She glared at Colman, wondering how her world had come to this—chasing after Webb Harpe while his nephew rode shotgun. "If you give me the slightest hint you're siding with your uncle in any way, I'll shoot you as well."

She saw his Adam's apple bob. "Yes, ma'am."

She laughed without humor and started the car.

~~~

Colman wondered what kind of idiot he was. He should have at least carried the rifle. Even if he didn't plan to use it, a gun would give others the impression he might. And knowing Mack was behind him with his own rifle was no comfort at all.

But no. He'd have to trust in something more than bullets to resolve this mess. Of course, Serepta might be wrong. Maybe it hadn't been Webb who took Ivy and the child. And he was still trying to figure out how Mack was mixed up in things. At least he could keep his eye on him in the back seat.

What would happen if Mack were indeed working with Webb? Would Serepta choose her son over the child she'd taken in? Over Ivy, who had shown her such unmerited kindness? He prayed with a desperation he'd never felt before.

294

Serepta reversed the car out of the barn, then slammed on the brakes, nearly sending Colman into the windshield. He twisted around to see what the problem was. Webb stared at them from atop his silver sorrel. Serepta cursed softly and got out of the car. Colman followed.

Serepta strode toward the horse and rider, making the animal shy. "Where are Ivy and Emmaline?"

"Tucked up someplace where you won't find them anytime soon."

"Fetch them back this instant."

Webb began to shake, and Colman realized the man was laughing. "Why would I do that?"

"I can make it worth your while," Serepta said.

"Well now, that's more like it. Making this worth my while has been my intent all along." With a smile, he slid off the horse and dropped the reins to let the animal graze freely. "Might be we could come to an understanding right here and now. Work everything out to both our satisfactions."

Colman looked over his shoulder to see what Mack thought of this exchange, but Mack was nowhere to be seen. Which made Colman nervous. If he were in cahoots with Webb, he might even now be doing something underhanded.

Serepta waved her rifle at Webb. "Don't get any high-minded ideas about what those two are worth to me. Name your price carefully."

Webb sauntered toward them. "Oh, I've got a particular agreement in mind."

Colman decided it was time to throw out some bait and see who went for it. "I thought you'd already come to an agreement with a member of the McLean clan."

Serepta furrowed her brow and frowned, clearly unaccustomed to having anyone insert himself into her negotiations.

Webb grunted and hooked his thumbs in his belt. "Thought that myself but turns out all the McLeans are lower than snakes." He stepped closer to Serepta, jabbing her breastbone with his index finger. "Your boy Jake shot my Caleb because his brother roped him into it. You think you're so smart? You've got no idea how your own boy's been taking you for a ride."

Serepta looked like she'd been slapped. For the first time, Colman thought he saw something other than anger in those icy blue eyes.

Webb looked pleased. "That's right, Miss High-and-Mighty. Your boy Mack's been siding with me, a Harpe, to take over your bootleg business. Jake stole from you." He shook his head and started laughing. "Then Mack stole from Jake and gave all that liquor to me. You thought he was sending it on to your men for delivery . . ." He swiped tears of laughter from his eyes. "But I was selling it and splitting the proceeds with Mack so's he could grease the palms of the fellers running your mines." He threw his head back and laughed some more, long and loud.

Serepta felt her confusion give way to a gnawing anger at her own blindness. Is this what Harrison had been hinting at? She had sworn she would never experience such a feeling of helplessness again. She pointed her rifle at Webb's chest and levered a round into the chamber.

Webb stopped laughing, cocked his head to one side, and considered her. "You shoot me, and that woman and child will surely die." His eyes glinted. "Especially since they got scraped up a might in all the hubbub. Smell of blood might make 'em easier for critters to find."

Serepta's own blood ran cold. What was happening? When had she so utterly lost control? Every beat of her heart demanded that she regain the upper hand. "What do you want for them?" She spoke through bared teeth.

Webb reached out and gently pushed her rifle barrel down. She allowed it. "I'm not asking for too awful much. Just turn the bootleg business over to me. I don't want all the work of messing with coal." He grinned. "Although seems to me Mack owes me something for the trouble he's caused. Guess I'll take an outright payment from him." He closed one eye and looked toward the sky. "His share of the sales from that liquor he stole from you oughta do it."

Serepta tapped her right index finger on the outside of the trigger guard. She waited just long enough to see Webb begin to fidget. "I could do that," she finally said. "I could probably even make Mack give you the money." She raised the barrel again. This time the rifle pointed just south of Webb's belt. "Or I could shoot you right now, forget about that ghost of a woman and the motherless child, and send my two worthless sons packing."

She heard Colman's sharp intake of breath behind her. Webb's eyes flickered, and he moved his hands in front of himself slowly, as though she couldn't shoot right through them. "You are a hard woman, Serepta McLean. But I think you're bluffing. I usually have a pretty good idea about folks' weaknesses, and yours has been a long time coming." He licked his lips. "And it's that child."

Serepta felt herself choking on frustration. Webb was right, and there was nothing she could do to change the fact that losing Emmaline would be more than she could bear. Losing Charlie had been a terrible blow, but the little girl who called her Momma had shattered the wall Charlie had begun to wear down. She could feel herself shaking as if she might tear in two. She could not give up her power, but neither could she sacrifice Emmaline.

She wished the God who surely hated her would strike her dead and be done with it.

chapter
thirty-two

Colman couldn't stand it another minute. Webb had gone too far this time. Even Serepta McLean deserved better than this. "But why Ivy?" he blurted.

Serepta and Webb jerked around to stare at him as though they'd forgotten he was there.

"You took Emmaline because she matters to Serepta, but why take Ivy?"

Webb blinked. "Because she matters to Mack."

Colman wanted to stomp his foot in frustration. "Well, I'll bet as soon as he finds out the natural gas inside that cave doesn't belong to her, she won't matter to him anymore."

"What's that you say, Harpe?" Mack stepped out from the barn, his mother's rifle cradled loosely in front of him.

"Hoyt signed the land away. It belongs to the federal government." Colman waved his hands in the air. "It's a national forest or something like that."

Webb began to laugh again. "Outsmarted by an old man and an unnatural woman. Son, you're as dumb as a bag of hammers."

Mack growled and pointed his rifle at Webb. "You think

I'm dumb? Colman there just guaranteed I don't care whether Ivy Gordon's ever found." He sneered at his mother. "And as for the child, why would I care about someone my mother prefers to her own flesh and blood?"

Colman could see Mack's finger tightening on the trigger. He thought he should probably lunge at him or throw himself in the path of the bullet, but he felt paralyzed. He closed his eyes, not wanting to see his uncle die, no matter what terrible things he'd done.

There was a sharp crack, and a man cried out. Colman opened his eyes. Webb looked surprised, while Serepta was pointing her rifle off toward the house. Mack gripped his arm, the gun awkward in his hand and blood seeping between his fingers. Had Serepta fired on her own son?

Serepta lowered her rifle, and Colman followed her gaze. Jake stepped out from behind a rose-covered arbor, pistol in hand. "I'm thinking there's been enough killing, enough dying. This feud's never done anybody any good." He looked at Serepta. "Ma, I've been trailing after Webb, figured I'd best know my enemy's whereabouts." He paused and shook his head. "Can't we just let it go, Ma? Can't we just get Webb to give us that child, take some money, and leave this place? Everything's tainted. Poisoned. None of it's worth having anymore."

Serepta snorted like an angry bull. "No. There's no one left to trust. You lied and stole and killed. Mack has been playing all the angles, manipulating everyone to try to get his way." She gestured toward Colman. "This sorry excuse for a preacher is the only one who hasn't crossed me, and I certainly don't plan to start trusting a Harpe."

Colman heard a deeper sound and tilted his head to look toward the sky. He'd heard that voice before. "No," he said. "Not now."

Serepta glanced at him but kept her focus on the other men—the ones with guns. "That's right," she said. "Not now, not ever."

Colman sighed. This was not how he'd imagined winning Serepta McLean to faith. "Trust God," he said.

"What?" This time Serepta didn't spare him even a glance.

"When you can't trust anyone else, trust God."

She turned to him with a look of astonishment on her face. "You're preaching to me?"

Colman hung his head. "I heard it in the wind. I heard a command to trust God. Guess it might be for you, but more likely it's meant for all of us."

Mack cursed and struggled to raise his rifle with his injured arm. He cursed again, but before he could take aim, another shot rang out and he crumpled to the ground, blood pooling beneath his body.

Webb stood, the Smith & Wesson he always kept tucked in his waistband now smoking in his hand. He pointed it at Jake, who held up his hands and took a step back. "Move on over here next to your ma and Colman. I want all of you where I can keep an eye on you. This party's getting out of hand."

Jake did as Webb commanded, mournful eyes fixed on his brother's body. "Too much dying," he muttered.

* * *

Is this what it's come to? Serepta hoped Mack wasn't dead, but she knew better. Yet the knowledge of his loss wouldn't sink in. He'd crossed her as well as Webb, and now he'd paid the price—it was no more than he'd deserved. She'd have to acknowledge his death at some point, but not now. Not while Emmaline was still at risk. She kept her rifle trained on Webb.

She jerked when she felt a hand settle on her shoulder. Hardly anyone touched her now that Charlie was gone. It was Colman's hand, and his voice followed, soft in her ear. "There's been enough dying today. Don't let Ivy or Emmaline be next."

The barrel of her rifle began to drop, and she felt the fight leaving her maybe for the first time ever. A slow smile spread across Webb's face. "You ready to give me what I want?"

She raised the rifle back up, pushing herself to hold on to the pain and anger that had driven her for as long as she could remember. "I suppose you mean to kill Jake now."

Webb crossed his arms, letting the pistol dangle from his right hand. "I'll count that one over there as payment for Caleb." He nodded toward Mack's motionless body, then leveled his gaze on Jake. "Way I heard it, your boy was too drunk to do much harm, and Mack egged him on. Pushed him to do his dirty work to keep this feud from dying down." He heaved a sigh. "Guess the real troublemaker's chickens have come home to roost."

If Serepta didn't know better, she'd say Webb looked sad. "Now what?" she asked.

"Deal ain't changed. You keep your coal, and I'll take on the bootlegging." He grinned, but it looked forced. "Gonna get me a double-breasted suit and set up at the Greenbrier. Show those high rollers how it's done."

Serepta felt herself waver. She was as tired as Webb looked. What if she did just throw in the towel? She felt Colman tense behind her. "Someone's coming," he whispered. "Webb hasn't heard."

She wet her lips and waited. "Sometimes getting what you want leads you to discover it's not what you wanted after all."

Webb knit his brow and started to speak, but before he

could, they all heard the sounds of people approaching—quite a few people it seemed. "What . . . ?" Webb took several steps toward the group. It was led by Lena and Nell in their wagon, with Hoyt and a whole crowd of others in the back. Harrison Ash rode on horseback, as did several other men.

Serepta realized some of the newcomers were helping Jake carry Mack's body away. She recognized both McLeans and Harpes in the group. Tears washed Jake's cheeks, and he didn't look toward her even once. She had the notion she'd just lost both of her sons.

"Hey there, Webb, Colman. Heard you fellers were having a dustup," said a lanky fellow with blond hair flopping across his forehead. He was shadowed by another man whose ears set him apart. Serepta recognized him as the one who'd helped bring Charlie to her the night the Dunglen burned down.

"Johnny, what in tarnation are you doing here?" Webb asked. "And with McLeans to boot."

The fellow called Johnny wrapped an arm around Lena's shoulders. "I guess you could say we've realized we have something in common with the McLeans."

Webb glanced from person to person. "Yeah, what's that?"

"We're tired of this feuding," Johnny said. "Wore slap out with it. Too much dying and not enough living."

The second fellow pushed forward. "You act like this feud is the only thing that matters. Family against family. But everybody knows you got a grand-young'un back there in Thurmond, and you won't even claim your own blood. That ain't no way to take care of family." He spit and wiped his mouth with the back of his hand. "Nobody's backing you this time around." He jerked his head toward the bloodstained earth where Mack's body had lain. "Seems to me enough damage's been done. Whyn't you fetch that woman and child and let's all be done with this business."

Webb's jaw looked like it had turned to stone. "I'll be cursed if I will, Elam. My own kin turning against me. You just wait till I get back to Thurmond."

Elam shook his head. "Won't have any better luck there. Word's out you only care about the feud so long as it suits your purposes." He closed his eyes. "I seen it in the water barrel yesterday. You and that woman over there have lost your hold. Times are a-changing and you'uns ain't changed with 'em."

Serepta had no idea why the man was blathering about water barrels, but losing her hold—that was something she could see herself. The iron will she'd exerted for so long had cracked when they sent Charlie away, and now she'd been broken. Not by Webb or Colman or even her own son now growing colder by the minute. It was Emmaline who had broken her, and she wanted the child back more than anything else.

"Please," she whispered.

Webb whipped his head around. "What'd you say?"

She cleared her throat and lowered her rifle barrel until it pointed into the dirt. "Please fetch Emmaline for me. Please don't punish her on account of me."

Webb stared at her like she'd grown horns—or maybe lost them. Then he threw his head back and laughed. "Well that tears it," he said. "The lot of you can go jump in the lake of fire. I'm done here. Good luck finding them girls." He spun on his heel, mounted his horse, and trotted off into the trees.

Serepta thought to shoot him in the back but didn't have the energy to raise her rifle again. She watched him go, dread settling in the pit of her stomach. What now? "We have to find them," she said to no one in particular.

Colman's hand settled on her shoulder once more, warm and solid. "We'll find them. All we have to do is listen."

~~~

"Want me to go after him? Haul him in for kidnapping and murder?" Harrison rested a hand on his notched pistol.

Colman shook his head. Only in Thurmond would the chief of police ask if he should arrest someone for kidnapping a woman and a child, then shooting a man down in front of his mother. But then Harrison always had applied the law when and how it suited him. And Colman suspected his actual salary was a pittance compared to what Serepta paid him.

"What good would it do?" Serepta asked. "I doubt you can force him to take us to Emmaline, and arresting him certainly won't bring my son back." She squeezed her eyes shut and pinched her nose. "I suppose you had some inkling about all of this and neglected to tell me. I'm beginning to think your usefulness is at an end."

Harrison opened his mouth—to protest, Colman assumed—but before he could speak, Colman held up a hand and put a finger to his lips. "You hear that?" he asked.

Colman closed his eyes and listened. He listened to the murmurs of the people gathered at Walnutta. He listened to the insects in the nearby pasture, to the stirring of animals in the woods beyond, and to the creek that flowed even farther away. The people hushed, and Colman could feel their eyes on him.

"Listen," he said.

And they did.

It was almost as though they were helping him hear farther and wider than he'd ever heard before. He could hear the

clopping of a horse's hooves on a distant road and the put-
tering of a car somewhere beyond that. He thought maybe
he could even hear the gurgling of the sulphur spring in Ivy's
makeshift bathhouse.

And there it was—a song.

"Softly and tenderly Jesus is calling,
Calling for you and for me;
See on the portals he's watching and waiting,
Watching for you and for me . . ."

"I just want her to come home."

Colman's eyes flew open, and he looked at Serepta, whose
own eyes pleaded with him.

"I'm so very weary," she said. "Is it too much to ask God
to do this one thing?"

"They're in the caves," Colman said. "Let's go get them."

───── ⁓ ─────

Colman had known fear, but he'd never willingly walked
into a situation that scared him like this. Going back into
those endless tunnels seemed foolhardy, but what else could
he do? A woman and child were in there somewhere. A very
special woman.

The whole crew—McLeans, Harpes, and even Chief Ash—
trekked over to the caves near Ivy and Hoyt's cottage. They
gathered lanterns and ropes and were even now dividing into
two search parties of three each. Colman would go with
Johnny and Serepta, while Hoyt, Elam, and another McLean
family member would form the second party.

Hoyt explained that while there were plenty of tunnels,
cracks, and crevices, there were also two main tunnels. "You
fellers take the one to the right. It's narrower and you're a
skinnier lot."

Colman shuddered at the thought of being stuck in a narrow passage with jagged rock all around him. He checked his pocket for the full box of matches one more time. In addition to his lantern, he carried two candle stubs, chalk to mark their way, and a wad of rags he figured he could make into a torch. He would not lose the light this time.

"Can you hear her?" Hoyt asked.

Colman nodded. "She's humming now. Guess her voice is giving out. She's bound to be tired and thirsty."

"Well sir, she won't be much longer," Johnny said. He patted a canteen of water he'd brought along. "Lead us to her, Colman."

They ducked inside the cave, where Colman paused for only a brief moment, tamping down the wave of panic that washed over him. He closed his eyes and listened. He could still hear Ivy, but he knew sounds would bounce around and echo inside this mountain. He looked at Serepta's stony face, shrugged, and began picking his way into the narrow passage.

chapter
thirty-three

Serepta couldn't believe her world had come to this—following two Harpe men deep into the bowels of a mountain. She knew they thought she should stay behind with the women, but she'd rarely let what anyone else thought stop her before. She wasn't sure she believed this nonsense about Colman being able to hear Ivy singing, but neither did she have a better plan for finding Emmaline. And she *would* find her.

Scrambling over a tumble of rocks, she bumped her head and bit her lip to keep from crying out. She touched the spot and felt moisture. Blood, but not enough to slow her down. She pulled out a handkerchief and pressed it to the cut as they pushed farther into the cave.

"Don't think I can squeeze through that there gap," Johnny said. Long and lean, the man was clearly too tall for the space. "Want I should go back and send someone else?"

Colman huffed air through his nose. "Don't bother. We'll be fine." He darted a look at Serepta. If he thought she would return with Johnny, he'd better think again. She nodded once and waved him on.

Colman moved ahead, slow but steady, contorting his body

to fit through what passed for a tunnel. His face was pale and his eyes wide in the lantern light. She supposed this must be hard for him, having been lost here once. Well, almost every moment of every day of her life had been hard. If she could continue on, surely this supposed preacher could, too.

"Where is your God now?"

Colman paused and looked back at Serepta. "What?"

"Your Almighty God—where is He when children are kidnapped? Where is He when men shoot one another down?" She sneered. "Where is He when the world is nothing but darkness and you're buried inside a mountain?"

Colman shook his head. "Woman, you want to talk theology now?"

"Ah. I see. God can only be found in the comfort of a congregation in the light of day. Don't trouble yourself. I did not suppose He was really here."

⁓

Colman wanted to scream with frustration. *Now?* God was opening the door for him to witness to Serepta McLean now? He slumped against the stones surrounding him. Well, why not? Ivy had stopped singing, and it wasn't as if he knew what he was doing. He'd probably muddle things again, but surely God would sort it out.

"God is everywhere," he began.

Serepta crossed her arms, her eyes sparking in the flickering light. "Not where I am. He left me a long time ago— maybe even before I was born. And I have managed just fine without Him."

Colman ran a hand over his face. "It's right there in Psalm 139. 'Whither shall I go from thy spirit? Or whither shall I flee from thy presence?' King David knew he couldn't go anywhere God wasn't. If He's not with you, then He's not the one who left."

Bitter laughter burst from Serepta. "Such pretty words. Was He with you when you were lost inside this cave? Was He with Ivy and Emmaline when they were taken?" Her voice caught and her eyes gleamed. "Was God with Charlie when he was beaten, or with my son when he died?"

Colman swallowed hard. "Yes."

"How can you say such a thing? How can you believe God gives any of us more than a passing thought when such horrors befall good people every single day?"

"Because none of us are good, and there's more to life than today."

Serepta looked like she wanted to pace back and forth, but the tight space prevented her from doing so. The tension rolling off of her made the space feel even smaller. "There is nothing but today," she countered.

"That's just it, Serepta." Colman felt an unexpected tenderness for this hard woman welling up within him. "There's eternity. And everything we suffer here will seem like nothing once we arrive there." He slapped a chunk of fallen stone. "I've done my fair share of complaining. I've cried out to God more than once, and He answered me. It sure as shooting didn't sound like the answer I wanted to hear, but I know He's smarter than me." He stood and held the lantern in front of him. "We should keep moving. Those girls need our help, and it just might be that God will use us to rescue them."

Serepta frowned and muttered, but Colman could hear her just fine. "If He does, perhaps I will give Him another chance."

Serepta pondered what Colman had said. She didn't want to believe in a God who had allowed such grief to befall her over and over again, and yet it would be a comfort to suppose there was more to her existence on earth than this never-ending struggle. The cut on her forehead throbbed with each beat of her heart. She steeled herself and offered up something like a prayer—or perhaps it was a negotiation.

If you are there, God, you are a mean-spirited, vengeful sort, but then so am I. If you would have me believe in you—if you would have me look to you for anything other than pain—then you will restore Emmaline to me. For her sake I will make a concession and allow that if you can be trusted in one thing, then perhaps you can be trusted in others. I do not suppose what I am offering is enough, but it is all I am willing to give. You may take it or you may leave it.

She considered adding an amen, but it felt insincere. If God was all that He claimed, then He would not wonder to whom she was speaking.

Colman slid down an incline where a trickle of water ran. Serepta stepped forward to follow him but then saw another opening to her left. Hope blazed up in her so unexpectedly that she froze. It was as though a warm breeze pushed her toward the other tunnel. She glanced at Colman, who was fussing with a wet pant leg, then turned and slipped into the passage.

Where in tarnation had that woman gone? Colman called out, but she didn't answer. Though he could hear movement, he couldn't see her. Had she gone back? Had she gotten turned around and lost? She'd been carrying a second, unlit lantern, so wherever she was, she wouldn't be in the dark.

Maybe if he extinguished his own lantern, he'd be able to see hers. He pursed his lips to blow out the flame, then hesitated. The thought of being thrust into darkness was hard to bear. What if he didn't see Serepta's light?

"Why, you'll just relight this one." He said the words aloud to reassure himself.

Sweat popped out on his forehead in the cool of the cave. He swiped at it, forced a laugh, and blew out the flame.

Darkness wrapped around him so suddenly he thought he was suffocating. He took a few deep breaths to calm himself and strained his eyes against the dark. No light. Well then, he'd best get this lantern relit. He'd just go on without that hardheaded woman. If she was lost, let someone else find her. And if she'd turned around without telling him—well, that was the sort of trick he'd expect of her. It would be simple enough for her to follow the chalk marks back to the entrance.

He dug in his pocket for the matches. His fingers closed around them just as he heard a shout from somewhere deep in the cave. It was a joyful sound, and his heart leapt. Had the other team found them? Were they even now returning to sunlight and fresh air? He fumbled with the matchbox and heard it fall. Lunging toward the sound, his head came in contact with rock, and a deeper darkness closed over him.

⁓

They were found. Serepta didn't know what to make of it. The passage she'd turned down led straight to Ivy and Emmaline—cold, weary, tired, but altogether intact. Moments after she'd found them, Elam appeared and gave a whoop of delight. She almost joined in, almost allowed a smile to stretch her lips wide with joy.

Emmaline flew into her arms and burrowed her tangled curls against her shoulder. Serepta closed her eyes and breathed in the grubby little girl smell of her. Had God heard her? Or was this a mere coincidence? She was afraid to trust anyone—much less a God she could not see—and yet denying Him now felt like an even bigger risk.

"The fear of the Lord is the beginning of wisdom."

Now where had that come from?

"Momma, you found me."

Serepta cradled the child closer. "Did I not tell you I would never fail you?"

Emmaline nodded her head and sighed, relaxing as though all her worries were at an end forever. And in that moment Serepta envied this helpless child who trusted her so completely. She did not deserve such trust, and yet here it was. What a relief it would be to trust someone like that. What was it Colman said? *"Trust God."*

Well, she wasn't convinced just yet, but she could at least understand why people wanted to believe in a God who would provide for them. She wanted that, too. If only life had not taught her how useless wanting was.

"Let's get you'uns out of here and cleaned up," Elam said. "I expect you're ready to see the light again. Hoyt had to turn back when we was forced to crawl on our bellies, but he'll be awful glad to see ya."

Ivy laid a hand on Serepta's shoulder. "Thank you for finding us," she said in a raspy voice. "I was running out of songs."

"Colman is the one who heard you and brought us here." Serepta was surprised at herself. She had not intended to praise that fool of a Harpe.

"He did?" Ivy looked around. "Where is he?"

"In the passage behind me. I expect if we call to him, he will hear and meet us." She looked Elam up and down, taking in his filthy clothes. "And the way I came did not require crawling on my belly."

Elam chuckled. "No, ma'am. I don't expect you've ever crawled for anybody."

Serepta pursed her lips but let the gibe pass. She turned and led the way, putting Emmaline down so they could navigate the rough passage. Elam called and hallooed for Colman every few feet. She assumed they would meet him in short order, but instead they found themselves back at the entrance to the cave. Everyone cheered when they saw the missing girls, and there was much excitement for a few moments. Finally, Johnny approached and asked where Colman had gotten to.

"Is he not here?" Serepta asked.

The joy of the crowd faltered as others began to realize that one was still missing from their group.

Johnny looked at her like he thought she was responsible for Colman being missing. "He was with you. Do you mean to say he's still in there? How'd you get separated?"

"I followed my instincts while Colman followed his ears," she snapped. The nerve of them behaving as if she were responsible for the man.

Johnny flapped his hands. "We've gotta go after him. Poor feller's been lost in there once before—he might've gone off his head or something."

"Ivy's gone back for him." Hoyt stepped forward and chuckled. "Guess she's more comfortable in the dark than most of us. I told her someone would go with her, but she just went on ahead. Said she'd be right back." The old man smiled. "And I believe her."

chapter
thirty-four

It seemed no one would leave the cave entrance until everyone was out again. Serepta frowned. She supposed it was the correct thing to wait, but she'd never paid much attention to societal expectations. Emmaline had fallen asleep against her shoulder and was growing heavy, but Serepta was loath to put her down.

She drew farther back, moving toward a burbling stream. She'd never fit in with people, least of all this ragtag band of feuding families united in Ivy's and Emmaline's—perhaps even Colman's—rescue. She sat, settling Emmaline more securely on her lap, and bent to the side so she could wet a handkerchief in the water. She used it to wipe her face. Then she scooped some water in her hand and lifted it to her mouth.

"Feels good going down, don't it? Better than that hooch you make."

Serepta stilled, then scooped more water.

Lena sat down on a gnarled root at the edge of the stream. She kicked off her shoes and slid her feet into the cool water. "Oh my, that does feel good. A woman oughtn't ever be too old or too proud to put her hot feet in a crick."

Serepta sighed. "You needn't keep me company."

"I'm cooling my feet. You just happened to be at a likely spot."

A ghost of a smile flitted across Serepta's face. "Your husband was cousin to mine, wasn't he?"

"Best I know. Don't think they ever spent much time together. Didn't run in the same circles, even if they were part of the same family." Lena sloshed her feet back and forth. "Funny how people run in packs."

"Unless they run alone."

"You like being on your own?"

Serepta looked toward the cave and the people gathered there waiting. One of her boys was dead. The other had left without a backward glance. Charlie had been run off, and the child she'd begun to think of as her own had been stolen, if temporarily. "I thought I did." She fingered her pearls. "But I don't suppose I was quite as alone as I imagined."

Lena nodded. "Life has a way of teaching you lessons you thought you'd already learned." She nodded toward Nell. "That one there's fixing to learn a hard lesson right now."

Serepta looked at the pretty young woman, glad to have the attention diverted from herself. "Why do you say that?"

"She's set her cap for that preacher. Guess I might have encouraged her in it. He seems like a fine fella, and I figured it might be a step toward ending this danged feud." She watched Serepta like she expected her to protest. When she didn't, the other woman continued. "But he don't have eyes for my Nell." She chuckled. "Best I can tell he's sweet on Ivy, though I'm not sure even he knows it."

"Ivy?" Serepta eyed the cave again. "Is that why he went in there?"

"I expect so."

316

"It has been my experience—" she hesitated to finish the thought—"that men prefer women who are more . . . traditionally attractive."

Lena laughed and pulled her feet from the water, resting them on plush green moss. "Ain't that the truth. My Nell could have had a husband three or four times over, but she's particular." This time her laugh sounded hard. "Wants what she cain't have, that one. Makes the preacher-man awful tempting to her."

"And you, what do you want?" Serepta had no idea where that question had come from. She'd never been one for idle conversation.

Lena cocked her head to the side. "Well now, mostly it don't matter what I want. Wanting don't put food on the table or shoes on your feet." She began to refasten her own shoes. "But if such as that didn't matter, well . . ." She grinned. "I'd want a big house with sunshine in every room. Water would come right out of the spigot, and I'd have a cook to make my meals." Standing, she looked Serepta up and down. "I'd still cook now and again—when I felt like it. It's just I wouldn't have to do it." She turned to leave, then looked back before moving on toward the others. "That's the thing about want. It's got nothin' to do with *have to*."

Serepta nodded and stared into the flow of water rushing down the mountain. Lena had just described what Serepta had—what she had worked so very hard to attain. And yet it did not satisfy. She wasn't sure she'd ever truly believed it would.

She shook her head. "Have to" was something she'd been running from all her life.

Colman sat up slow and easy. Here he was again, sick and alone in the dark. He felt like he had when he'd tumbled out of the cavern at Ivy's feet all those months ago. It was as though the strength he'd rebuilt had been stolen by the pressing darkness, leaving him a hollowed-out shell of the man he'd thought himself to be. He began to pray. It wasn't a very good prayer, and it took a few jumbled thoughts and words before he began to make sense, even to himself. He spoke aloud to the stones and the mountain around him.

"I have done what you asked. I preached to the McLeans. I even told Serepta about you as best I could. And now all I want is to find Ivy and go home. I'll set up my own little church there and tell everyone who comes all about you. And Ivy . . . maybe she'll come with me." He took a deep breath and felt a little calmer. "Just show me where she is, and I'll fetch her and the child out. Then I can be done with this place. Can be done with what you asked of me."

He sat, letting the weight of darkness wrap him in its cocoon. It wasn't quite peace that he felt, but his hopelessness subsided. Then he heard a whisper of a voice. Had the others returned?

Do you suppose I love Ivy more than the rest?

He looked around, his blood running cold. "Hello?"

While he didn't hear an audible voice, words poured into his mind.

"For the Lord seeth not as man seeth; for man looketh on the outward appearance, but the Lord looketh on the heart."

His head cleared, and he started to feel as though he were on the edge of figuring out something really important.

And then the silence began to sing.

chapter
thirty-five

Serepta settled the sleeping Emmaline in the back seat of her automobile. She was tempted to leave the group waiting for Colman and Ivy, but something about the way Lena had sought her out made her want to stay. She walked toward the people gathered near the cave entrance. She'd sat at the stream turning her sins over and over like rocks tumbled by the water. Not that she'd let anyone else call them sins, but she knew that was what they were. Sins of commission and omission. She supposed she'd known them to be sins all along. It's just that she'd always thought she was justified— excused because of the sins that had been visited upon her first.

Maybe not.

Maybe there was a price to pay.

One of the two Harpe men who'd come from the train station sat under a tree, carving on a stick—Johnny, she thought. She stood near him and watched.

"That was a good thing you done, taking in that orphan child," he said at last.

"Was it? That's not why I did it."

He looked at her as though seeing her for the first time. "Well that's honest. Still, people credit it to you as good—not knowing your purpose."

"Does that work the other way, I wonder?" She saw him look a question at her. "Do people credit an action as bad because they don't know the reason behind it?"

Johnny set his stick down. "Well now, that's one to ponder. Although I reckon some things are bad even if you've got a good reason for 'em."

Serepta nodded. "I expect you're right."

Johnny leaned back and gazed into the leafy canopy above. "Wish you'd tell Elam. He don't think I'm ever right."

She felt a smile quirk her lips but resisted. She took a step closer to Johnny. "Do you think Jake will come back?"

"I wouldn't were I him. Not much left for him here." He tilted his head and looked at her. "Maybe he'll have an easier time of it if he don't have you to live up to."

"Well that's honest," she said.

Johnny perked up. "Maybe that's my gift. Maybe I'm honest."

Serepta did smile this time, although it felt stiff, like it was a smile she hadn't used in a very long time.

Johnny sat up straighter. "Looks like something's happening," he said, nodding toward the cave. He climbed to his feet, and the pair of them—a Harpe and a McLean—walked to the entrance together.

Colman rubbed his head and found a tender spot where he'd bashed his skull into solid rock. He wondered if the blow was causing him to hear things. But no. He could hear someone singing. Come to think of it, it wasn't just someone, it was Ivy. But this time she wasn't singing a hymn, but rather a song he'd heard on the radio—"All of Me." He listened to her sweet voice and began moving toward her.

Soon he could see a light, and then there she was, sitting like an apparition in the glow of a lantern. She smiled but finished her song.

"You took the part that once was my heart,
So why not take all of me?"

"There you are," she said. "I followed the marks as far as they went and then trusted you would hear me."

Colman eased down beside her. "Are you alright? Did Webb hurt you?"

She shook her head, her uncovered hair almost sparkling in the dim light. He guessed she didn't need her hat or gloves here in the cave. In a way, she looked more at home here than she did outside in the daylight.

"He manhandled us a bit, but we're both fine. Serepta found us, and when we realized you hadn't come out of the cave, I came back in after you."

"Why would you come back in here?" Colman felt as though he'd slept through something important and was now having to sort the pieces in his mind.

"Because I care for you," she replied, ducking her head. "I thought about marrying Mack simply because he was the only one I thought would ever ask." Tears welled in her eyes. "But he wasn't being honest, and now he's gone." She took a stuttering breath. "And I realized that not only did I not care for him, but I cared for someone else."

Colman felt light-headed and hoped it wasn't from the hit he'd taken. "For me?"

She nodded, and her eyes glowed with something Colman hadn't seen since his mother died.

"I care for you, too," he whispered. "It just never seemed like the time to tell you so, and this probably isn't the time, either."

She laughed, light and musical. "I guess sometimes we have to get lost all over again if we want to find the path we've been searching for all along."

Colman reached out and laid his ruddy, callused hand against her pale cheek. "I think I see the path I'd like to take," he said, and leaned in to kiss her.

⁓

They all gathered on the wide porch at Walnutta. Hallie kept bringing around pitchers of tea and lemonade and setting out plates of pound cake like it was a party. Of course, Serepta had never had a party at Walnutta, so she wouldn't know. Ivy had tended to everyone's cuts and bruises, including her own, and in spite of the ordeal no one seemed too much the worse for wear. Especially not Emmaline, who whirled from person to person like a honeybee afraid she might miss a flower.

Of course, everyone else was subdued. Jake had Mack's body carried to the house, where some of the women were tending to him, washing away the blood and dressing him in his best suit. Serepta left it to them, although she supposed she would need to call someone to handle the funeral before Mack was buried in the family cemetery out beyond the barn. Charlie would see to . . . no, Charlie wouldn't.

Ivy stepped out the front door and spotted Serepta at the far end of the porch. She walked over and settled into a swing and patted the slats beside her. Serepta realized she'd never actually sat there before. She considered not doing so now, but then sighed and rested her slight bulk beside Ivy—dark and light in so many ways.

"I'm sorry about Mack," Ivy said, setting the swing in motion with the push of her foot.

"Are you? It seems to me he treated you poorly."

"Not really. I suppose his motives weren't the best, but he was kinder to me than some others have been."

Serepta pushed the swing again as it slowed. "Jake left word that he would not be returning to these parts." She let silence swell. "As I assumed."

"I'm sorry about that, too," Ivy said.

"It's ironic. I longed for a daughter instead of foolish sons, and now—" she cleared her throat—"that's precisely what I am left with."

Ivy held her pale hand up in front of them, turning it as though admiring the blue veins visible beneath the ivory flesh. "When I was ten or so, I tried every remedy I could dream up to give my flesh color." She smiled, but it didn't warm her eyes. "Walnut dye, tea leaves, and coffee grounds. I even washed in stump water gathered by the light of a full moon every day for a month. It's part of the reason I became so interested in the healing properties of plants. I thought if I could find just the right combination, I could . . ." She stopped and took a deep breath. "I could look like everyone else."

"The foolishness of a child," Serepta said. "People will discover what is different about you no matter what."

This time Ivy's smile did reach her eyes. "You're right. I guess my point is that sometimes we want what we can't have. And sometimes, when we get what we thought we wanted, it doesn't suit us at all." She nodded toward Emmaline, who seemed to have had enough rest to fuel her for the remainder of the day. "Regardless of what else you have done or why you did it, taking in that child is a gift. I suspect you'll have the pleasure of unwrapping it for a long time to come."

Serepta found she had nothing to say to that. She'd lost so much these past weeks. Things she hadn't even realized could be taken from her. She'd thought she had safeguarded herself from such painful losses by hardening her heart, but somehow sorrow had broken through the shell.

Colman came around from the back of the house and stopped when he saw the two women sitting side by side. Approaching them, he said, "We've got some men digging the grave. Not sure who you want for a preacher, but I'll fetch whoever it is."

"You may perform the service," Serepta said. It was almost worth it to see the shock wash over Colman's face.

"But I'm a Harpe and you're—"

"Yes. Mack was a McLean, as well. But it looks to me that you've found favor with my family, and since I generally have no use for men of God, it might as well be you."

Colman appeared like he might be sick on her shoes. "Will you . . . are you . . . what about Webb?"

"What about him? He left, didn't he?"

"But he shot Mack. Aren't you going after him, or sending someone after him?"

Serepta looked around as if assessing those gathered at her home. "Whom would I send? Lena? I suppose I could find someone who would accept payment for hunting down your uncle and putting a bullet in him, but I'm tired of this fruitless back-and-forth." She stood and brushed at some dirt smudged on the front of her slacks. "If Webb wants to continue this feud, he will have to do it without me. I have a daughter to raise." She nodded to Ivy and went inside. Let the rest of them find their own ways home.

chapter
thirty-six

Colman felt like he'd just swallowed his own tongue. Preach a funeral for a McLean? Wasn't that a step too far? He looked at Ivy for help, but she wore a bemused expression that let him know she wasn't going to save him.

"How am I supposed to preach Mack McLean's funeral?"

Ivy motioned for him to take the seat Serepta had vacated. He plopped down and tried to think as she set the swing in motion again. The easy back-and-forth combined with a breeze that stirred the muggy air and soothed him.

She patted his arm, and her touch almost made up for what Serepta had just asked of him. "It seems to me you've been asked a riddle. And it's a tough one." She smiled and stood. "But I think you're smart enough to figure it out. Now I'm going to go wrangle Emmaline and Grandpa so we can go home."

"I'll take you—"

She held up a hand. "No need. Lena and Nell are taking folks in their wagon, and they'll drop us off."

Colman watched her go, feeling five or six emotions at the same time. Talk about a riddle—what he was going to do about his feelings for Ivy was going to take almost as much sorting out as what he was going to say at a funeral for a man who'd caused him and his family a wagonload of trouble. Apparently, God wasn't finished testing him quite yet.

He almost expected Jake to be in the cabin when he finally arrived, footsore and weary. Yet there was no sign of the enemy who had begun to feel like a friend. Colman shook his head and sat down to take off his boots. The evening was quickly fading into night as he sat on the tilted porch, his back against the wall of the cabin. He stared across the meadow, trying to think what would be right for Mack's funeral. Shoot, he didn't even know if the man had been a believer. Serepta sure didn't act like one. He'd never preached a funeral before, much less one for someone he was supposed to hate.

He went inside and found his pack with his mother's Bible. It was one of the few things he'd bothered to carry back from Thurmond. He held the worn leather and feathered the fragile pages. It was too dark to read, and he didn't want to light a fire. He held the book to his ear and fanned the pages as though he could hear them whisper.

An owl hooted nearby, and Colman felt a chill. He'd always heard that an owl hooting at dusk was a sign that someone would soon die. He supposed someone already had and hoped that would be the end of the dying for now. Caleb was gone, and now Mack was too. Did that make things fair? Did it even out like the Old Testament's "eye for an eye"? He'd heard fire-and-brimstone preachers suggest such things, but he'd never preached anything like that and sure didn't want to now.

Colman set the Bible down and laid his hand on it as if he

could absorb information through the cover. He wondered if a preacher had ever been shot down in the pulpit by a rival clan. Riddle indeed. Ivy didn't realize the half of it.

⁓

It was time to dress for her son's funeral. Serepta sat at her dressing table in her undergarments. Emmaline sat on the floor nearby, playing with a paper doll Hallie had made for her. The child was already dressed in a navy blue, sailor-style dress. Serepta slid the right-hand drawer open to extract her pearls. There, beneath the necklace, she saw Charlie's last letter. She withdrew the paper and smoothed it on the dresser in front of her.

Revelation 3:17–21. She never had looked those verses up. She fetched Charlie's Bible from her bedside table. She kept it there not to read but to have some part of a trustworthy man close by. The leather felt good in her hands.

Even she knew Revelation was the last book of the Bible. She feathered the pages until she came to chapter three. The verses were from a letter to a church. She read the entire letter—it was short enough. But it was verse seventeen that struck her to the core.

"*Because thou sayest, 'I am rich, and increased with goods, and have need of nothing, and knowest not that thou art wretched, and miserable, and poor, and blind, and naked.*"

A sob caught in her throat, and she clamped a hand over her mouth before Emmaline could hear. She continued to read the verses Charlie had noted.

"*As many as I love, I rebuke and chasten: be zealous therefore, and repent. Behold, I stand at the door, and knock: if any man hear my voice, and open the door, I will come in to him . . .*"

Oh, she had been rebuked and chastened, but only coming from Charlie did such words feel like love. Maybe if she let him open the door for her . . .

She had overcome so much. Had worked so hard for everything she had. And today she knew she would give it all away if she could simply live in peace with Charlie and Emmaline. Hot tears scalded her cheeks. Charlie believed in God, but more important, he believed in her. Even now that he was beyond her reach, she knew he believed.

"Momma?" Emmaline curled her hands around Serepta's arm and wormed herself close. "Are you going to wear a dress?"

Serepta wiped her face and glanced at her usual slacks and blouse laid out on the bed. When had she last worn a dress? It must have been the black crepe she'd worn when Eli died. After his funeral and the interminable family gathering that followed, she'd gone to her room, removed the dress, and had not worn it—or any other dress—since.

"Perhaps I will," she said.

"My momma died."

Serepta turned so that she could more easily look into Emmaline's eyes, cradle her face. "Do you know what that means—to die?"

"It means you go away to heaven." Emmaline furrowed her brow. "I don't want to go away."

Serepta bit her lip. She wasn't sure she believed there was such a thing as heaven, although hell was something she knew existed. "There's no reason for you to go away."

"Did Mack go to heaven?"

"I don't know," Serepta said. And she didn't. But for the first time in her life she could see how it would be comforting to think so.

"I hope he did," Emmaline said.

"So do I," she whispered.

Serepta rose and tugged the black crepe from the back of her wardrobe. She was sure it was horribly out of style. Still, it would look well with her pearls. She dressed quickly and fastened the necklace.

"Come, Emmaline. This will not be a pleasant day, but it is one we must get through. Will you be on your best behavior?"

The child sighed and tugged her own skirt straight. "Yes, Momma. When it's over, may I have a cookie?"

Serepta nodded. "You may have two, and perhaps I will join you."

***

Colman thought he might lose his paltry breakfast. He felt like he had those first days at the brush arbor meetings—sick, weak, and unworthy. While he'd filled a real pulpit inside a church twice before, stepping into Elizabeth Chapel on Hoke's Mill Road in Hinton was a completely new feeling. Lena had persuaded the pastor to let them use the church for Mack's funeral. They'd certainly never had a Harpe in their pulpit before.

And he'd never preached a funeral before.

He hadn't slept, trying to think what to say today. The church was filled with McLeans, Serepta first among them. But there were Harpes present, as well. Johnny, Elam, and his father sat in the back pew and nodded solemnly when he entered. Seeing his father gave him a jolt. He couldn't remember the last time he saw Dad anywhere other than his own house. He realized he was grateful to see him now.

Mack had been dressed in a suit and laid out in a fancy coffin in front of the pulpit. Colman remembered how folks had tucked items into Caleb's casket. No one dared this time. It was just Mack, looking unexpectedly peaceful. Colman swallowed hard and stepped up behind the pulpit.

"Let us pray," he began. The congregation bowed their heads with a stir and a rustle like leaves in a gentle breeze. Colman spoke a simple prayer and then opened his eyes.

"I've been wanting to call myself a preacher for a long time now, but being asked to speak today . . . well, it's made me realize I'm no such thing." He glanced at Serepta, whose attention appeared to be focused on the light fixture above his head. "I'll just tell you, I'm not sure what I ought to say." He cleared his throat and rested a hand on the massive pulpit Bible lying open there. "In the front of this Bible, there are pages listing births, marriages, and deaths. Mack McLean's name was written here for the final time today." He looked at the people who seemed to be hanging on his every word. They didn't know what he should say, either.

"But the rest of us, we're not done yet. We've still got some time before our names are chiseled in stone." Serepta still wasn't looking at him, but he had the sense she was listening. "I didn't know Mack very well. And our families didn't exactly get along." There was a murmur of laughter that hushed as quickly as it started. "But Mack's mother asked me to preach here today." This time Serepta did look at him, narrowing those brilliant blue eyes of hers. "And I agreed. But like I said, I've realized I'm no preacher. I'm a storyteller. So I guess I'll tell you a story."

He let his gaze drift up above the heads of those in the pews. "A stranger was passing through some pretty country one day and decided to stop and rest in a field full of daisies and black-eyed Susans. He was dipping some water from the creek when he saw a big old gold nugget. He got to looking closer and realized the creek was full of gold. So he hurried home, sold his house and his automobile, and bought that piece of land. Soon he became richer than before." Colman refocused on the people. "God's kingdom is like that field—valuable enough to give up everything you've got for it."

Serepta was staring a hole in him now. He couldn't read her expression, though. Of course, no one could. Emmaline was tucked in close to her side, smiling as though delighted with his story.

"Here's another one," he said. "A woman came walking into a big-city jeweler's store one day. She had a perfect pearl, flawless and big as an orange. Well, the jeweler knew a good thing when he saw it, so he sold everything else in the store and bought the pearl." Serepta's hand drifted to the necklace at her throat. "God's kingdom is like that pearl—perfect and worth everything else you have."

He breathed in deeply and looked down at the dead man. "I don't know what Mack held most dear. I guess in some ways he was trying to figure life out just like the rest of us." He looked from face to face in the chapel. "I hope he knew what I'm telling you, that nothing beats being part of God's kingdom. No matter what earthly thing you're chasing after—money, property, position, or power—none of it will matter once your name is written in this book for the last time."

Serepta felt as though the pearls at her throat were choking her. She had worn them every day since she purchased them. They were nearly a part of her now. She looked from Mack to Emmaline wiggling beside her. She had failed her son. She wasn't sure how exactly, but the truth of the matter washed over her and left her feeling empty. Webb had murdered Mack, but she'd lost him a long time ago. Maybe when she ignored his advice about natural gas. Maybe when she sent him away to school. Maybe when she focused on Jake as heir of all she'd built, leaving Mack to find his own way. Or maybe it was before any of that.

She laid a hand on Emmaline's curly head, and the child stilled under her caress. Had she ever stroked her son's hair? If she had, she couldn't remember it.

As Colman finished the service, she looked around the chapel. She'd never set foot in here before and didn't suppose she would again, unless it was for her own funeral. Who would speak words over her? Most likely someone who knew her as little as Colman knew Mack.

She noticed the few members of the Harpe clan seated in the back. Who would have thought? Maybe she really could let the feud die. Perhaps if she scaled back on the bootleg business and focused more on coal . . . without Charlie or her sons to help run things, that would make the most sense. Then Webb would be free to start taking over the territory she released. She could loosen her grip and let him move in without saying a word. She could just let it happen.

She felt a tug on her sleeve. "Momma, are you sad about Mack?" Emmaline asked, her dark eyes holding more compassion than seemed possible in one so young.

Serepta considered the question. "Yes. I am sad. I wish . . ." She left the thought unfinished.

"What do you wish?"

Serepta stood and tugged Emmaline to her feet. "Wishes are for weak people who are too busy looking backwards to make plans for what lies ahead." Emmaline frowned. "So my plan is for the future. I plan to do better by you than I did by Mack."

She stepped up to the coffin, reached forward, then pulled her hand back.

"Are you allowed to touch him?" asked Emmaline.

"Yes." And with that, Serepta reached in to touch her son's soft hair. Then she unclasped her pearls and let them fall against the satin lining of the coffin.

chapter
thirty-seven

With the funeral behind him and Ivy beside him, Colman finally gave in to the community's desire for a baptizing. After Webb and Serepta's confrontation and the ensuing rescue, folks seemed more than happy to let the feud begin a gradual slide into the past. Colman hoped that a joint baptizing would reinforce whatever goodwill had risen to the surface. He planned to dunk folks in the New River near Alderson, which was more McLean territory than Harpe but close enough to neutral ground.

When he'd been preaching Mack's funeral, those stories had just come to him. And when they did, he'd realized they were for him as much as anyone. He'd finally done what God had asked by preaching to the McLeans, but he'd been doing it like it was some foul-tasting medicine he had to get down. And then he'd heard the truth coming from his own mouth—the kingdom of heaven was worth any sacrifice. Even forgiving his enemies and maybe, just maybe, learning to love them. When Jake made him realize he'd lost his taste for revenge, he came to see that he couldn't wish hell on anyone. He guessed God loved them all—even Serepta McLean.

And so he would baptize anyone who wanted it. Not because he had the power to save them, but because God did, and he'd invited Colman to work alongside Him. Shoot, he'd almost refused to accept that pearl of great price.

Lena and the other ladies rounded up quite a crowd. And Johnny and Elam brought a contingent from Thurmond. Nell was there, making eyes at Walter Harpe, Colman's third cousin and a strapping fellow of twenty-two. Maybe Lena would see her daughter wed to a Harpe yet.

Some of the older fellows, including Hoyt, sat on a fallen log at the back of the crowd. Ivy greeted them before coming to stand beside Colman. "When you told us you'd come to preach to the McLeans, I wasn't sure what to think." She looked up at him from under the brim of her hat. "I'm sorry I didn't have more faith in you."

Colman shrugged. "If you'd had faith in me, it would have been misplaced. I've dragged my heels every step of the way. Guess I'm harder headed than I realized."

She laughed, and her face lit like sunshine through frosted glass. "It's good, what's happening here today. Harpes and McLeans coming together in faith. How many do you expect to baptize?"

"I'm not sure," Colman said. "Of course, the main person I was supposed to draw to God isn't even here."

Ivy looked over his shoulder. "If it's who I think it is, she's coming now."

Colman turned and saw Serepta step out of her car, followed by Emmaline, who bounced past her and ran to throw her arms around Ivy. "I'm getting nap-tized today."

Colman tried to hide his shock. "You are? Does Serepta know that?" He felt Ivy dig an elbow into his side as the woman herself approached.

"Momma said I could."

Colman glanced at Serepta before crouching down to the child's level. "Do you know what it means, being baptized?"

Emmaline took a deep breath. "It means when I die I'll get to be with Jesus."

"And who is Jesus?" Colman asked.

"He's the only good man ever. If I love Him, He'll watch over me."

Colman guessed he'd seen folks baptized who understood it less. He looked at Serepta, who raised her chin a notch as though daring him to refuse this child.

"And you?" he said, feeling hope leap in his chest. Had he actually accomplished the task God set for him?

"Perhaps another time," she said with a twist of her lips. "I haven't quite made my mind up to trust any man—even a perfect one."

Ivy linked her arm through Serepta's. "One day," she said. "Your heart is getting softer."

Serepta snorted and reached for the neckline of her blouse, then let her hand fall away. "You assume I have a heart."

Ivy caressed Emmaline's cheek. "Oh, but you do. Here it is."

⁓

Serepta wasn't sure she could stand this. Wasn't it enough that she'd brought the child? Wasn't it enough that she was mingling with all these common people here on the bank of the river? How much more would they ask of her?

She had little hope that her own life could be set to rights, but she would do everything in her power to ensure Emmaline had every opportunity to be loved—to be safe. Serepta believed in God, sure enough. She just wasn't convinced God could ever have any use for her—He certainly hadn't up to this point. She looked at Emmaline, cheeks pink and eyes bright. At least He hadn't before the day this child came into her life.

Thankfully, Colman and Ivy started down toward the river to organize the baptizing, taking Emmaline with them. Colman held his hands in the air, spoke a few words to the people, and began praying. Serepta couldn't hear him, but she didn't suppose it mattered. One set of ears more or less made no difference. She cast her gaze across the crowd, noting people she knew and those she didn't. That was when she saw a woman walking from the road down to the river. She was carrying an infant. Ivy saw them and rushed over to gather the child in her arms. They circled the crowd and came to stand near Serepta. As she listened to their chatter, she realized the woman was Maggie, the one whose child Ivy had delivered.

Focusing on the people stepping into the river so Colman could dunk them one by one, she turned an ear to the women's conversation.

"Webb's come 'round. He set me and the baby up in a little house at the far end of the tracks. It ain't fancy, but it's better than working in Ballyhack. Says he'll help me get a job when William's older." Maggie looked tired but pleased. "It's more than I'd hoped for."

Ivy kissed the babe's downy head. "I was hoping William would be a consolation for Webb. You can't replace your own child, but having a grandchild may soften the blow a little."

Maggie elbowed her. "When you gonna have a young'un of your own?"

Serepta saw Ivy turn and focus on Colman, who even now was tenderly dipping Emmaline beneath the surface of the water. "Maybe one day," Ivy said. She looked hopeful, and Serepta wondered if the preacher and the healer might find the kind of match that had eluded her. She realized with surprise that she hoped so.

Emmaline, hair and clothes sopping wet, came tearing up the riverbank to where they stood. "Momma, Momma, I did it! I belong to Jesus now."

Serepta opened her mouth to correct her, to say, *No, Emmaline, you belong to me*, but then checked herself. Instead, she managed a smile and moved to wrap a towel around the girl.

Ivy crouched down to show baby William to Emmaline. The two gazed at each other—Webb's grandchild and Serepta's new daughter. Emmaline touched the baby's cheek. "He's so little."

"No smaller than you were when you were born," Ivy said.

Emmaline looked up at Serepta. "Is that true, Momma? Was I this small?"

Serepta felt the honest answer would be to say she didn't know, she hadn't been there, but she decided she could do better than that. She knelt down and drew the wet child to her.

~~~~~

Colman scanned the riverbank to see if there was anyone else in want of baptizing. He felt humbled and maybe even shamed. He had tried so hard to avoid this calling. Nearly died inside that endless cave because he ran away. And now God was using him to reap a harvest of peace and salvation. He'd nearly missed this.

No one else approached, and some folks had already headed home, where dry clothes and warm food awaited. He hoped Ivy and Hoyt were still here. They might take him home with them and feed him, too. He had something in particular he wanted to discuss with Hoyt.

He saw Ivy's grandfather talking to Elam and let his gaze continue until he spotted the small cluster of women in the distance. Ivy held Maggie's baby while Serepta knelt in the grass, speaking to Emmaline. Of course, if he aimed his ears in that direction, he could pick up what she was saying.

"I was not there when you were born, but you almost certainly were as small as William." Serepta—the woman he'd thought of as his enemy for so long—paused as she cupped the child's face. "I may not have been with you when you were born, but I am with you now. And I will be with you for as long as I live. I promise."

Emmaline threw her arms around Serepta's neck, and the woman he'd always seen as cold and hard returned the hug, folding her own compact frame around the child's as though to protect her from anything that might come.

And Colman heard a voice—not in his ears or even his mind, but in his heart: *Go ye therefore, and teach all nations, baptizing them in the name of the Father, and of the Son, and of the Holy Ghost: Teaching them to observe all things whatsoever I have commanded you: and, lo, I am with you always, even unto the end of the world.*

He nodded his head and slogged to the bank, a smile playing at the corners of his mouth. He'd thought his work here was done. He'd thought he was free to go home to Thurmond and make his own plans. But now he knew God still had work for him to do.

He took off his shoes and poured water from them onto the thirsty ground. He felt strong. Powerful. Not because of anything he had done, but because he finally realized God would use him wherever he went. He slipped his shoes back on and made his way toward the women and the children, facing his future head-on—whatever it might be.

Author's Note

Up until now, I've set my stories in imaginary towns that look a whole lot like the places where I grew up. I steered clear of real places so that no one could accuse me of getting them wrong.

Not this time.

Thurmond is real. As are Hinton, White Sulphur Springs, the Big Bend Tunnel, and other places named in this story. Of course, while Thurmond was a thriving railroad town at the turn of the twentieth century, today it boasts seven residents. They take turns serving as mayor. So, if I get some things wrong, there are fewer folks to take umbrage.

I will confess here and now to taking some liberties in placing facts along my timeline. The burning of the Dunglen Hotel in 1930 is pivotal to the story, so everything unfolds that spring into fall. But I "borrowed" some tidbits from the town's earlier, wilder years. For example, Alden Butterfield was the first manager of the Dunglen Hotel when it opened in 1901 but was long gone by 1930. I just couldn't resist that name! And while Harrison Ash was a notorious police chief for Thurmond, he died in 1924, well before my story begins. However, his physical description (down to the Stetson hat) and the fact that his wife was tried for murder when she shot another man while aiming for her husband are accurate.

There were also some wild stories I couldn't quite squeeze into the novel. Like when a man jumped from the railroad bridge to his death in the river below. After his body was recovered downstream, the mayor fined him the contents of his pockets for the crime of committing suicide within the town limits.

I had the pleasure of visiting Thurmond, which is now largely owned by the National Park Service, in the company of Dave Fuerst. A park ranger, historian, curator, and all-around gracious gentleman, Dave led me on a guided tour "behind the scenes" of what is essentially a ghost town. I'm so very grateful for how he made it possible for me to walk around inside my story. It's definitely given me a taste for setting stories in *real* places!

If you'd like to learn more about Thurmond or, better yet, visit, go to www.ThurmondWV.org. You can also visit the National Park Service site for the New River Gorge for information about a walking tour.

Sarah Loudin Thomas is a fund-raiser for a children's ministry who has time to write because she doesn't have children of her own. She holds a bachelor's degree in English from Coastal Carolina University and is the author of the acclaimed novels *The Sound of Rain* and *Miracle in a Dry Season*—winner of the 2015 INSPY Award. Sarah has also been a finalist for the ACFW Carol Award and the Christian Book of the Year Award. She and her husband live near Asheville, North Carolina. Learn more at www.sarahloudin thomas.com.

Sign Up for Sarah's Newsletter!

Keep up to date with Sarah's latest news on book releases and events by signing up for her email list at sarahloudinthomas.com

---

More from Sarah Loudin Thomas!

After a terrible mine accident in 1954, Judd Markley abandons his poor Appalachian town for Myrtle Beach. There he meets the beautiful and privileged Larkin Heyward, who dreams of helping people like those he left behind. Drawn together amid a hurricane, they wonder what tomorrow will bring—and realize that it may take a miracle for them to be together.

The Sound of Rain

You May Also Like . . .

Famous author Josephine Bourdillon is in a coma, her memories surfacing as her body fights to survive. But those around her are facing their own battles: Henry Hughes, who agreed to kill her for hire out of desperation, is uncertain how to finish the job now, and her teenage daughter, Paige, is overwhelmed by fear. Can grace bring them all into the light?

When I Close My Eyes by Elizabeth Musser
elizabethmusser.com

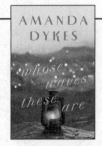

In the wake of WWII, a grieving fisherman submits a poem to a local newspaper asking readers to send rocks in honor of loved ones to create something life-giving—but the building halts when tragedy strikes. Decades later, Annie returns to the coastal Maine town where stone ruins spark her curiosity, and her search for answers faces a battle against time.

Whose Waves These Are by Amanda Dykes
amandadykes.com

In spring 1918, British Lieutenant Colin Mabry receives an urgent message from a woman he once loved but thought dead. Feeling the need to redeem himself, he travels to France—only to find the woman's half sister, Johanna, who believes her sister is alive and the prisoner of a German spy. As they seek answers across Europe, danger lies at every turn.

Far Side of the Sea by Kate Breslin
katebreslin.com

◊ BETHANYHOUSE